Pearl Necklace

Stephen N. Burton

Pearl Necklace

by

Stephen N. Burton

NEW MILLENNIUM
292 Kennington Road, London SE11 4LD

Copyright © 1997 Stephen N. Burton

All rights reserved. No part of this publication may be reproduced in any form, except for the purposes of review, without prior written permission from the copyright owner.

British Library Cataloguing in Publication Data.
A catalogue record for this book is available from the British Library.

Printed and bound by Arm Crown Ltd. Uxbridge Road, Middx.
Issued by New Millennium*
ISBN 1 85845 166 3
*An imprint of The Professional Authors' & Publishers' Association

This book is dedicated to my three sons, Chris, Robert and Michael, and my lovely wife Jeanette, without whose constant encouragement and support, it would not have been possible to finish. S.N.B.

Prologue

Dock cranes pointed to the sky, to show the sun had peeked, through the clouds, the ground was dry, the heavens no longer leaked, as he watched a seagull fishing, just wishing he was one, Monday in Southampton.

He passed God's house, then Westgate too, and turned down Cuckoo Lane, stopped and thought for a moment or two, before carrying on again, as he watched a seagull flying, just dying to be one. Monday in Southampton.

Pulling on his coat, with collar high, he turned down Bugle Street, gazing into the cloudy sky, the feeling still so sweet, as he watched a seagull turning, just yearning to be one. Monday in Southampton.

Chapter 1

A sexless marriage, with a loveless wife,
was surely no way, to live one's life.

It was 8.45, and raining as usual for early March, when Dave Price slammed his front door and walked to his car for work. Another Monday morning, and as always he felt low. His life had certainly changed in the past few years. He'd met, and after a lightning romance, only lasting a couple of months, had married Janice Davaris, moving into her three bed-roomed semi-detached house in Hedge End, a suburb just outside Southampton. She had been married before and had a sixteen year old daughter named Sarah, who lived with them. Janice's first husband had been tragically killed in a freak works accident, some 11 years earlier. Dave wasn't totally sure why he had married Janice, but realised that at 39 years old, he might not get too many other offers, and had jumped in with both feet. He had few real friends, and no family to speak of, and it just seemed the right thing to do at the time.

As Dave opened the car door, little drops of rain fell into the side pocket of his Company Ford Fiesta, soaking his cassettes, and causing him to curse loudly.

"Bloody English weather," he shouted to the sky as he climbed into the driver's seat and fumbled for his seat belt. Turning the ignition key, the car sprung into life, and the digital clock on the dashboard read 8.48.

"Shit, late again," he thought as he struggled with the clip on his belt. However, he was not unduly worried because his boss, at Calvin Marine, was an even worse timekeeper than he was. Twelve years at the company, and all he had to show was the illustrious title of Export Manager, and the company car. In reality he was no more than a glorified clerk.

To get from his home in the east of Southampton to his office, he had to cross the river Itchen, which was never easy. There were two main routes to follow, one was to cut to Bittern, and travel over the Northern Bridge, which, due to fourteen sets of traffic lights, usually meant a travelling time of about an hour. The other, and slightly quicker route, was to drive southward towards Woolston, and cross at the Itchen toll bridge. The traffic across the toll bridge, the peage, and on its approach road, was, as always, horrendous, and he spent twenty minutes bumper to bumper, before finally turning into Canute Road, where his office was situated.

The Company specialised in marine equipment and maps, selling to the trade as well as direct to the public.

"Good, Calvin's not here yet," he noted as he slammed the car door, and ran across the road, carefully avoiding the puddles that had formed on the pavement outside the office doorway.

At reception sat the gorgeous Joanne, nineteen years old, long brown hair, hazel eyes and a figure that would drive most men crazy.

"Good morning beautiful," Dave said as he entered the shop front, in his best macho voice.

"Morning Dave," she answered, whilst thinking "Wanker."

"It's persistently raining out there," he joked, causing her to smile embarrassingly at a line she'd heard a thousand times before.

The office was cluttered with lights, buoys, bells, and all things nautical, with two aisles of racks running the whole length of the building, literally covered in everything a mariner could want, or need. Marine charts, books, leaflets, instruments, clocks, barometers, VHF radios, yachting equipment and chandlery goods were all on show.

Joanne's job was telephonist, receptionist and general dog's body, basically serving anyone who came in off the street, wanting to buy nautical equipment.

Dave's desk was at the back of the room, with easy access to the small map room which fed off to the right. Arriving at his desk, Dave hung up his coat on the hook by the toilet door, and sat down to peruse the morning's post.

His whole life was a total and utter bore, he had a strange, loveless type of marriage, crass job, and a sense of humour, which, at best could be described as antiquated, and sadly pathetic. This last fact was the main reason he had no friends. It wasn't his life that was a bore, it was him.

People shunned him and had always done so, making him retreat into his own little fantasy world.

On his desk were two letters from a ship owner requesting maps for his vessels, which were moored in foreign ports, three purchase invoices from the courier company DHL, and a Customs notice explaining the new regulations regarding VAT on ECC imports. He reached into his pocket and took out his 'Raffles' cigarettes, just as Joanne brought him his morning coffee.

"Thanks lover," he said in a deep voice, and Joanne once again thought "wanker."

Dave looked at his mail again. He needed a map of the waterways and harbours around Malta, and a notice to mariners for the Port of Hamburg.

He quickly estimated that to get the two items from the chart room, arrange their dispatch, and pass the three DHL invoices would take no more than fifteen minutes.

"God, work's so bad at the moment, I'll be lucky to keep my job much longer," he thought as he set about inspecting the H.M. Custom's directives.

Boredom is always a problem in a small office and Dave had become an expert at moving various pieces of paper around his desk, giving the impression that he was busy. With notices, directives and a Customs tariff in front of him, Dave's mind started to wander to licentious matters.

"Sex, that's the problem, when I first started seeing Janice, she was like a cat on heat, couldn't get enough, in the car, in the park, even in the office on that Sunday I had to work, but now, since we've been married, it's so different, I'm lucky if we do it once a week, and as for oral, well ..."

This problem is one which most people generally encounter, to a lesser degree, but for Dave it was unbearable. Only a few days earlier, after finishing work, he'd driven to Derby Road, the red light district of Southampton. However the fear of being arrested by the police for kerb crawling, and the ever present risk of catching Aids, meant he did not stop. However, just the sight of the prostitutes promenading gave him a very pleasant tingle in his groin. He'd already decided to do it again, and maybe stop. Suddenly, his daydream was shattered.

"Dave, could you come into my office please?"

He looked up to see his boss, Mr John Calvin.

"Certainly John, I'll just finish this ..."

"Now Dave, if you don't mind," Calvin demanded in a tone which suggested he was in a foul mood, which was usual for a Monday. Getting up from his desk, Dave crossed the room, and followed Calvin into the boss's own little office.

John Calvin was in his late fifties, and had obviously spent a lot of his life on yachts and outdoors, as his brown, weathered face could testify. But for all that, he had kept himself in very good shape physically, and could be described quite accurately as a handsome man.

"Dave, I think it's only fair to warn you, that due to this damned recession, it's tough for all of us, and in order to keep our heads above water, I've needed to review your position with the company."

"Oh fuck, it's the big 'E', I knew it." Dave's mind was racing.

"I've been thinking about this for some time and feel that if you were able to take a cut in salary, it would at least go some way to securing your employment with us." Before Dave could answer, Calvin continued:

"However, if you feel you can better yourself, then I will not stand in your way, and understand completely, your need to move on."

Dave stood mortified, and shocked.

"You fucking bastard," he thought, trying to think of an answer, which would correctly sum up his views.

"Well, sir," he stumbled over his words, "Um ..." He knew what he wanted to say, "Poke it where the sun don't shine, you scumbag," seemed perfect, however, he was sensible enough to realise that in the current economic climate, finding another position would not be easy.

"Well sir" he repeated. "what new salary did you have in mind?" His tone incredulously humble.

"Let me see," Calvin said as he opened a large brown file,

"Your current salary is £16,000 a year, perhaps £14,000 would be nearer the figure we could afford, obviously if business picked up again, your salary would increase accordingly."

"Um ..., can I have a little time to think about it please?"

"Of course, give me your answer tomorrow. OK?"

Calvin closed the file, and placed it back in his drawer, Dave slowly turned and walked from the office.

"What a bastard, what an absolute bastard, I'll show him, I'll ring 'Masons', they've always said there was a job for me, just pick up the phone, that's all I have to do."

After another three hours of paper shuffling, it was finally lunchtime.

"Fancy going for a drink Joanne?" Dave shouted as he put his coat on. He should have spent the lunch hour in pursuit of a job, but going for a drink with Joanne was just the tonic he needed. Unfortunately, Joanne would rather make love to the Elephant Man than go to lunch with Dave, and she politely refused his offer.

"Suit yourself," he mumbled as he stepped out of the office into the rain, and scurried the sixty yards or so up the road into the 'Smelly Slug and Flaming Toad', a traditional real ale pub with its own mini brewery.

Although Dave Price was not a particularly bad guy, he had a way of making people dislike him. Nobody hated him, but nobody liked him either.

"A pint of Slug Pellet please," he requested from the barmaid, "Oh, and a cheese and onion toastie."

"That'll be three pounds exactly please," she said politely, after she'd poured him his pint.

Dave paid her the money and sat down at a chair near the window. The pub was empty. Dave lit a cigarette and surveyed his surroundings.

The Slug and Toad, as it was usually called, was a typical Camra Ale house, bare floorboards covered in sawdust, rickety old tables and chairs, and four real ales, two of which were brewed on the premises. The walls were covered with old adverts for breweries that no longer existed, and the beer had a strange 'home made' taste, which was not to everyone's liking, but it was handy for a lunchtime drink, and Dave used it two or three times a week. Looking out of the window into the damp March afternoon, Dave could see his own reflection in the glass. Brown receding hair with white/grey flecks, red blotchy face, with more broken veins than a man twice his age, and three chins. His nose was red and bulbous, like an old scrumpy cider drinker, you might see in Somerset or Avon. "What a bloody sight" he thought to himself.

Some men look distinguished as they age and get grey hair, Dave just looked grubby, weary and old.

After struggling to drink half of his beer, the cheese and onion toastie arrived and was placed on the table in front of him.

"Thanks darling," he said, stubbing out his cigarette, and smiling. The barmaid was totally unimpressed, and didn't answer, although she too thought "Wanker." Biting into the blackened toastie, the piping hot filling burnt his mouth, causing him to almost choke. He made strange little noises and blew into his hands, as if this would in some way cool down his burning tongue. He decided to leave the food to cool, and as he lit up another cigarette, his mind went back over the events of the morning.

"God, what a life, what do I do now? If I accept the old bastard's offer, he'll be free to walk over me whenever he sees fit, but if I don't ..." He had a large sip of beer and a drag on his cigarette, "Call his bluff, that's what I'll do, if he thinks he can reduce my salary without a fight, he's very much mistaken, I'll have another pint and go back and tell Mr High and Mighty John Calvin that this worm has turned."

He finished his lunch which was now stone cold and tasted like rubber, and took his beer glass to the bar for a refill, drinking the last dregs, en route.

"What's the strongest beer you have?" he enquired.

"Toadstool Porter, original gravity 1061," replied the barmaid.

"Great, I'll have a pint please."

Walking back to his table, he placed the ale down. Two large drayman's bogies (yeast particles) floated on the top, and it looked like it had been strained through the brewer's undies, (which indeed it had). To the real ale drinker, this was just about par for the course, but still nectar of the Gods. After another two cigarettes, he finally managed to finish his drink. Carefully leaving a quarter of an inch of ale in the bottom of the glass, he decided to return to the office, and face the dreaded Calvin.

By now, it was indeed 'pissing down', and Dave ran along the pavement, trying desperately to avoid the huge puddles which had formed, in the short time he'd been in the pub. He bolted into the office and stopped by Joanne's desk.

"Nice weather for ducks eh?"

This time Joanne could not smile, she just looked at him with pity and muttered, "Yes Dave" in such a condescending manner, that even he noticed the implication meant in her tone.

"Is Calvin in?"

"No, he's out with a prospective client" Joanne replied.

"Prospective client my ass, he's out on the piss with the petty cash," he joked, as he walked into the back of the office to his desk.

Hanging up his coat, he decided to get the maps that had been requested in the morning's post, and dispatch them to their foreign destinations.

At 3.35pm, when John Calvin returned, he smiled briefly at Joanne, and went straight into his office.

"Excuse me Mr. Calvin, can I have a word?"

"Of course Dave, my door is always open to you."

Dave entered the little office and waited while Calvin hung up his coat.

"Well sir, it's like this ..."

Calvin flopped into his large, leather, executive chair as Dave continued.

"I've been here for twelve years, and in that time showed you my complete loyalty, and although I've got a company car, I really don't think I'm exactly overpaid," he paused briefly, for breath, but Calvin interrupted.

"Look Dave," he said, lowering his eyes attempting to look very sincere, "Don't you think I've taken all of this into account, I should really make you redundant." He stopped, his voice sounding like a politician explaining why his policies had not worked. "But instead, I've taken a chance that the recession is nearly over and offered you a decrease in salary, in order to keep your job secure." Calvin rubbed his hand across his brow and continued, "However if you can't live with that, then I'm sorry you'll have to leave this employment."

"I appreciate that Mr. Calvin," Dave said, trying to find words from thin air, but there seemed nothing more he could say. Here he was thanking Calvin for a pay cut, if only he had more bottle, more aggression, but he didn't, and that was that. He turned and walked slowly from the room. What would he tell his wife? There was no way she'd understand any of this. At 5.30 he packed the few remaining papers on his desk into a pile, put his coat on and walked out of the office to his car.

"Goodnight Dave" shouted Joanne, as the door shut.

"Yeah, goodnight Joanne."

Back over the Itchen Toll bridge, bumper to bumper, Dave thought of ways of telling his wife Janice, without causing a row. He pressed the cassette into the player, a 'Simply Red' song played back to him, "Money's too tight to mention". "Oh God not that song" he rejected the cassette and continued the rest of his journey in silence. Pulling into Lambeth Crescent, then Lambeth Gardens, he stopped in the driveway of his house.

"Well, here goes nothing." he sighed.

Jumping out of the car and running to the front door, Dave opened it, and walked into the hall. The air was full of the smells of home cooking. If nothing else his wife was a great cook, and always had a meal prepared for him when he came home and tonight, if he was not mistaken, it was lasagne.

"Evening love," he shouted, "I'm home."

"Hi ya," Janice replied as she came to meet him in the hall.

"How did your day go?" she asked politely.

"Don't ask," came his reply as he hung his coat up and walked into the lounge. Flopping down on the settee and picking up the local paper, he opened it at the TV page.

"Dinner will be about fifteen minutes," shouted Janice from the kitchen doorway, "it's lasagne."

Just then, Dave heard heavy footsteps on the stairs and his stepdaughter, Sarah, wandered into the lounge.

"Evening darling," said Dave.

"Oh, hello Dave," Sarah replied without looking at him.

She was an attractive girl, almost sixteen, with long dark hair, beautiful brown eyes, and slim but busty. Sarah went over to the stereo and put on a CD. 'The Shamen' with 'Ebenezer Goode' came blasting out from the speakers, it was deafening. Dave looked over and noticed she was wearing a tight black mini skirt and a white open-necked silk blouse.

"I see we're dressed to kill," Dave shouted "going out are we?"

"What?" she answered screwing up her eyes.

"I said, 'Are you going out tonight?' Oh forget it."

Sarah seemed to go out most nights and although Dave had often said that she should spend more time at home, her mother always reminded him that he was not her father and there would be plenty of time for her to settle down when she was older.

Sarah ignored him and stepped into the hall.

"How long before dinner Mum?" Sarah asked.

"About ten minutes" came the reply, and Sarah went back upstairs, leaving Dave sat in the lounge with 'The Shamen'.

"God this is shite," Dave thought, "there's no melody and the lyrics! What the hell does it mean?"

"Got any Veras?" shouted the singer.

"Any of Vera's what?" Dave asked himself, he could stand it no longer. "Do I have to have this racket on?" he shouted as he ejected the CD. Silence, but only for a second because both Janice and Sarah came back into the room.

"What did you do that for?" Sarah inquired angrily.

"If you must listen to that rubbish, then do it in your own room," snapped Dave.

"Oh come on Dave, don't be so miserable, Sarah's going out at seven, surely she can have her music on until then."

Dave sighed and walked back to the settee, just as the music started again.

"Naughty, naughty" came blasting from the speakers, and Dave picked up the paper again and headed for the toilet.

"At least I'll have some peace in there," he mumbled.

This had become something of a daily ritual, trousers down, paper on the lap and silence. He rarely read the paper or even had a shit for that matter, he just sat and let his mind wander to his favourite subject – sex. His daydream always took the same course. Big, black women, two or three of them, all naked, all waiting for their stud (himself) to satisfy their every need. He got an erection just thinking about it.

"I'm just about to serve" Janice shouted through the door, shattering his dream, "You going to be long?"

"No, just coming," he replied wishing he was 'just coming' when in fact he was nowhere near ejaculation. Reluctantly Dave folded up his paper, pulled up his trousers and came out of the toilet. Entering the lounge, he saw that his wife and stepdaughter had both started their meals.

"Want a drink?" he asked as he walked over to their cocktail cabinet.

"No thanks, no time," mumbled Sarah between mouthfuls of lasagna.

"Yes please, I'll have a gin," said Janice.

Dave opened the cabinet, poured two large gins, and topped them up with a dash of tonic.

"May I have some ice please?" Janice asked politely.

Dave frowned and tutted and took both drinks into the kitchen where he added the ice cubes, before returning to the dinner table, just as Sarah was finishing her meal.

"Thanks Mum, must fly," she said, as she leapt from her chair, and darted from the room.

"Couldn't she at least eat her meal with us?" Dave muttered, almost under his breath, but loud enough to be heard.

"Don't go on Dave, she's got a date."

"It's just that we never see her, she's always out, what's she up to, that's what I'd like to know."

"I don't know why you keep on about it, she's nearly sixteen for Christ's sake."

"Oh forget it," said Dave, resigning himself to the fact that he could never win the argument. He picked up his cutlery and started his meal.

They finished the meal in total silence and Dave had already decided to keep quiet about his pay cut. Of course, it wasn't really totally quiet because 'The Shamen' were still blasting away out of the stereo system.

"Can I switch this row off now?" he asked.

"If you want," Janice answered indifferently, as she collected the plates and went into the kitchen.

Dave turned off the stereo and switched the TV on. He returned to his spot on the settee and started thinking about the board he'd seen on the way home. It had read: 'EVERY WEDNESDAY NIGHT AT 7.30 – LIVE STRIPPERS AT THE COACH & HORSES – NO ENTRANCE FEE'. The Coach & Horses was a run-down pub at the back of his office mainly used by dock workers because it stayed open all day. Obviously, it had a reasonable trade due to its position near the docks between midday and early evening, but since the demise of Southampton Docks, it did very little business at night-time, and this was an attempt to rectify that shortfall.

Dave rubbed his face and tried desperately to think of a reason to go out on a Wednesday, when suddenly he had the answer. Janice finished stacking the dishwasher and had wandered back into the lounge. She sat the opposite end of the settee and started to read the paper. Dave waited awhile then said: "A couple of the lads who work next door have started going to snooker on a Wednesday night, I quite fancy giving it a bash sometime."

Janice looked up from the paper somewhat surprised. "You don't play snooker do you?" she questioned.

"I used to, before I met you, if it's a problem I won't bother," he said, almost indignantly.

"No I don't mind, where do they play?"

"Dave thought, "Why all the questions?" "Um. There's a club in Southampton called 'Pot Black' where I believe they play." This was pure luck, because there was a club called that and he'd made the name up on the spur of the moment.

"That's fine by me, are you playing this week?"

"Well, I thought I'd give it a go, but only if it's OK with you."

"No problem," she replied, and returned to reading her paper. Dave quietly sighed, and had an inner smile, feeling very pleased with himself.

* * *

As Dave removed the white lace bra of the black girl he was lying with, her huge forty-inch bust fell into his hands. Her breasts were dark sepia-brown, covered in oil and shiny, with enormous black nipples, pointing to the sky and ripe for sucking. He moved into a position on her waist, his legs astride her and pressed his erect penis between the mounds of flesh. It was almost completely hidden as he wrapped the slippery orbs over it, rubbing them up and down his shaft.

"How would you like a pearl necklace?" he breathed lustily.

"Fuck away white boy." she answered.

"Good morning, it's just approaching five past seven, and the weather word is cold, but bright, with only a twenty percent change of rain. You're listening to Radio Itchen on 93.2 in stereo and here's the new hit from Cliff ..."

The alarm radio had burst into life and shattered Dave's dream. As he woke from his slumber he cursed the fact that once again his sexual fantasy was interrupted. Turning slowly towards his wife, he kissed her back and rubbed his still erect penis into the cheeks of her bottom. Janice wriggled, and for a moment Dave felt he might be able to carry on where he'd left off in his fantasy.

"Not now Dave, I've got to get Sarah up and ready for school, there's not enough time in the mornings for hanky-panky."

"There's never enough fucking time," he though, as Janice

leapt from the bed, put on her dressing gown, and disappeared downstairs.

Dave rolled onto his back and took his member in his hand, he closed his eyes and tried to get back into his dream, but it was no good. He considered a wank, but in a small house like theirs, privacy was something you didn't have.

"Fucking bitch, I'm desperate, we haven't had it for weeks, and all she can say is 'there's no time for hanky-panky', I'll give her hanky-panky." He rolled back onto his side. "Perhaps I'll score at the strip show, yeah, I'll take her back to the office and fuck her over Calvin's desk. Brilliant, come all over Calvin's nice executive desk."

Just then Janice walked back into the room with a cup of coffee.

"Do you want some toast?" she asked rubbing her eyes.

"Yes please, with fanny on it," Dave thought, but mumbled "Please, just one slice."

"Sarah," Janice shouted, "it's twenty past seven, come on."

"Where was I? Oh yeah, take the stripper back to the office, maybe a big black chick with 44DD tits and lips to match." He took hold of his member again, and descended once more into his fantasy world.

"Come on Dave," Janice had silently returned and was combing her hair at the dressing table, "you'll be late, if you don't shake a leg."

"OK." He climbed out of bed slowly, walked towards her, hoping she'd notice his erection and change her mind. She did notice, but it didn't tempt her in any way.

"Don't be disgusting, cover yourself up before Sarah sees that thing."

Dave put on his dressing gown and headed for the bathroom. He was too late, Sarah had taken up residence, and would be at least 30 minutes. He wandered downstairs to eat his toast, and heard Sarah come out of the bathroom. He dashed upstairs, and noticed the floor was soaked, making the bath-mat squelch under his feet. Opening the shower cubicle door, he turned on the water and climbed inside.

Getting a lather around his pubic hairs he thought of the fun he was going to have at the strip show. He finished showering, got out, had a shave, combed his hair and returned to the bedroom to get dressed. Passing Sarah's room he noticed the door was slightly ajar. He could see her sitting on the bed with only her bra and panties on.

"God she's gorgeous" he thought. "If only I was twenty years younger." He moved back into the bedroom as he heard his wife coming back on to the landing.

After he had finished dressing, he went back downstairs, and grabbed another coffee. It was 8.35, "Better go," he sighed, and grabbing his coat, shouted upstairs, "I'm off now, see you tonight."

"Have a good day, see you the usual time." Janice called back.

Dave started the car and drove off, ready to face the horrendous peak hour traffic. Fortunately, it was light, and he arrived fairly quickly at the office. He bounced through the front door, grinning, and quipped:

"Good morning Joanne, another day, another dollar. What?"

Joanne groaned, "One day he'll say something original," she thought as she nodded at him grimacingly.

"Mr Calvin rang, he'll be in about tenish."

"What's new?" said Dave as he went over to his desk and surveyed the morning's post. Six DHL invoices and other bumph, which would take about ten minutes to finalise. The job hardly warranted a part-time person, another few mornings like this and he would be out of a job.

Joanne arrived with his coffee.

"Thanks. Hey, you look nice today, going out lunchtime?"

"Yes my boyfriend's taking me out," she replied excitedly.

"Lucky old boyfriend, I'd say." Dave joked.

"Thank you," she said coyly, and returned to her desk.

John Calvin arrived just before 10.30 and went straight into his office. Dave noticed that his boss looked a little ragged, worse for wear. He was desperately trying to look busy whilst slyly glancing at his watch, willing it to be lunchtime. Just before one, Calvin emerged from his office, he still looked dreadful and was in obvious need of the 'hair of the dog'.

"I've got a lunch appointment with the Bank Manager and two other appointments this afternoon, so I won't be back in the office today, can you please lock up before you leave?"

"Sure," said Dave, as he watched his boss leave the premises.

"The old sod's still drunk." Dave shouted to Joanne.

"Don't be so horrible, he's got a lot on his mind, neither of us would have a job if it wasn't for him. You've got to remember if the Company went bust, he'd also be without a job and would probably lose everything as well."

"Big bloody deal" Dave replied, "Who gives a shit?" He got up and put on his coat, adding sardonically, "I'm going for lunch, see you later."

Joanne was also due to go for lunch, she'd set up the ansaphone and went to the toilet to retouch her make-up. As Dave got to the door a handsome young man was about to open it, Dave stopped and bowing like a doorman, gestured him in.

"Hi, is Joanne about?" the young man said politely. Dave looked him up and down and replied gruffly: "Yeah, she's just gone into the loo, to tart herself up, you can wait here for her, if you like."

"Thanks mate."

Dave snarled, "What does she see in him, she'd be much better off with an older man; someone with experience. I'd treat her like a princess, spoil her rotten ..." his mind was running away with him, he had more chance of being elected King than dating Joanne, but unfortunately didn't realise it. He walked out of the office down Canute Road towards The Coach And Horses. "Let's see where these strippers are going to perform." The pub was a typical male drinking house, it didn't cater for the namby pamby real ale drinkers who sit and sup one pint an hour, it was a place to get drunk in. At one time, it would've been quite a decent pub, but now the paint was peeling and flaking on the frames and hung like flecks of skin on a leper's face. On a blackboard just outside the lounge bar door, it advertised the Wednesday night strip-show. Dave struggled to push the handle down and it soon became transparently apparent that a shoulder barge was the only way to gain entrance. Dave stepped back a few paces and body charged the door, it flew open with enormous speed, and he almost fell flat on his face in the doorway.

"Afternoon mate, do come in, why don't you?" snarled the

barman, putting down his newspaper. Dave walked cagily over to the bar.

"What'll it be?" snapped the barman, more as an order than a request.

"Pint of bitter, please," Dave said quietly, feeling slightly uneasy.

Selecting a jug from under the bar, the barman pulled down the ceramic hand-pump and the ale crashed into the glass with an amazing glugging sound.

"That'll be £1.40 mate."

Dave duly paid him, and looked around the bar for a seat. To say that the decor was sparse was an understatement. Six round tables, surrounded by assorted chairs, which were scattered in no particular order, and three bar stools, was the sum total of furniture. Bare floorboards, covered in spilt beer and cigarette burns (most with the butts still attached) and a little raised stage in one corner, completed the picture. Three of the tables were occupied, so Dave sat down in the far corner of the bar, near a door marked 'Toolshed.' Lighting a cigarette, Dave surveyed his surroundings. "What a shithole," he thought, "this makes the Slug & Toad look like a bloody palace."

The six or seven other drinkers in the bar had by now gone back to talking amongst themselves, and Dave heard various references to 'Fucking John Major' and 'Fucking Tories ruining the fucking country' as he looked around the room, making sure he did not make eye contact. Along the side of the bar, against the wall, he noticed a jukebox and decided that some music might, in some way, lighten the atmosphere. He got up and walked over to the machine, but after nearly five minutes of scrutiny, realised there was nothing he wanted to hear. This seemed to prompt the locals into wanting some music, and a man with a skinhead haircut, 'Doc Martin' boots and torn jeans, walked over, slotted in some money and started pressing buttons. After three selections, he shouted across the bar to one of his friends: "Do ya wanna choose anythin' Mike?"

"Fuck off! Just get the fucking beers in" came the reply. The skinhead shrugged his shoulders, finished making his selections and walked back to the bar. Within moments, a truly crass Country and Western song about a trucker and his teddy bear came blasting out from the speakers, and Dave realised why he knew none of the records on the juke box: they were all Country and Western, which was the one type of music he hated. Gulping down the remainder of his beer, Dave quickly got to his feet, once again being careful not to look at anyone, and hastily left the pub.

Outside on the pavement, Dave felt he was lucky to leave alive and started to wonder if Wednesday night might be a mistake. "Oh, what the hell, in for a penny, in for a pound, at least it's sleazy."

Shrugging his shoulders, he walked back towards his office. Knowing that Calvin would not be coming back that afternoon, he'd decided to go to the Slug & Toad, and have a few more beers. Stepping straight into the pub, he ordered a pint.

"What time d'you close love?" he asked the barmaid.

"Last orders are at three, then drinking up time."

"Good," he muttered as he walked across the bar, "plenty of time to get pissed."

After four pints, the barmaid declared in a heavy Northern accent, shouting at the top of her voice: "Last orders at the bar, if you please."

Dave jumped, and felt it was time to return to work. As he entered the office he noticed Joanne was unusually red-faced, with a very cute twinkle in her eye.

"Had a few drinks have we?" he slurred.

"Yes, only two glasses of red wine, but it goes straight to my head at lunchtime," she replied.

"Well, I've had a couple too," Dave said, as he sat on the edge of her desk.

Even though she'd been drinking, she could still smell the stale odour of beer and cigarettes on his breath, and felt like opening a window to let some fresh air in. Dave removed himself from her desk, nearly fell over her wastepaper bin and dragged himself, very unsteadily, to the toilet, where he urinated over the seat, floor, wall and cistern before finally hitting the pan. He leant against the wall to support himself, and shook his penis sending the remaining few drops splashing onto the floor tiles. He stood quite still thinking of Joanne, and an idea started to formulate. Leaving the lavatory, he hung up his coat and sat down at his desk.

"Any chance of a coffee darling?" he mumbled, and Joanne got up without speaking and duly made him a cup. She didn't like Dave when he was sober, but when he was drunk he was obnoxious. As she walked over with his coffee, he noticed again just how nice she looked. White blouse, unbuttoned to reveal a little cleavage, tight mini-skirt, hinting at suspenders and dark shiny nylons.

"I must say you look fabulous," he leered as she put the coffee down on his desk. She felt a little nauseous as Dave stood up and tried, rather obviously, to look down her cleavage. "Calvin's not here this afternoon, why don't you bring your chair back here and we'll have a little chat?" he suggested, like a dirty old man letching after a schoolgirl.

"Better not," she said with a little smile, brought on by the lunchtime drink, and not Dave's incredibly pathetic chat up line. "You never know with Mr Calvin, he might return." She continued as she quickly nipped back to her desk.

"I was right," thought Dave, "I know the signs, I saw that little prick teaser smile, she's begging for it, that woofter of a boyfriend of hers couldn't fuck a whore on heat." Dave followed her to the front of the office, and put his hand on her shoulder. She wanted to throw up as she pushed it off.

"Ever fancied having a fling with an older man?" he asked.

"Get off," she shouted, as she jumped from her chair, and turned abruptly to face him. "What the hell do you think you're doing?"

The drink was now controlling Dave, and he completely misread the situation, thinking it was some form of foreplay, lunging forward, he grabbed her arm and tried to pull her into an embrace.

"Fuck off you old pervert, I'll tell Mr Calvin if you touch me again!" she screamed as Dave suddenly came back to reality. He slipped and tripped over her chair, and in an effort to keep his balance, reached out for her shoulders for support, but accidentally grabbed her left boob instead.

She jumped backwards, and he fell onto the floor in an untidy heap.

She stood shaking, as she looked down at the moronic idiot on the floor, almost under her desk. She took one step backwards so that he could not look up her skirt. Tears of anger filled her eyes.

"I'm so sorry Joanne, please, I beg you, let's forget it ever happened. I'm so embarrassed, I don't know what came over me." he pleaded, as he clambered to his feet.

"How could you?" she said shaking her head "you're a mental case, you ought to be locked up."

"Look, I've said I'm sorry, it won't happen again, I promise."

"I'll tell you this Dave 'fucking' Price, if you ever, and I mean, ever, touch me again, I'll not only tell Mr Calvin I'll tell the bloody police as well, I swear it."

She shook her head, readjusted her mini-skirt, and hurried into the Ladies' toilet. Dave went back to his desk, and sat down with his head in his hands. After ten minutes the toilet door opened, and Joanne walked back into the office.

Without looking up, Dave said humbly, "Why don't you go home now and have an early night, I'll cover the phones."

"That's exactly what I intend to do," she stormed and picking up her coat and handbag ran from the office, leaving Dave alone with his thoughts.

"What a mess, what a bloody mess!"

Dave Price had always had a problem with women and sex, and it was possibly due to two traumatic experiences he had had when he was young. Born in the fifties into a working class family, he was an only child and lived with his parents in a council flat in Millbrook, just on the outskirts of Southampton. As soon as he had started at infants school, his mother got a job, which meant that both of his parents were at work most of the time. One of his neighbours would look after him when he came home from school, and he was a bit of a loner as a child. When he was about eleven years old, he came back to the flat, after playing in the park, to find that both his parents were out. As this was a Sunday lunchtime, this was not all that unusual, they quite often went out for a drink at the weekends, leaving young Dave to fend for himself. Like a lot of children at that particular age, he spent hours playing around the house with 'Mickey' his imaginary friend, and this Sunday was no different. He had gone into his parents' bedroom and was bouncing on their double bed, when he heard Clifford and Doris, his parents, returning from the pub. Opening the front door, his mother called out his name, but as he was not allowed in their room, he quickly hid in the large wardrobe, crouching down amongst the clothes and peering through the gap in the doors. He could hear them in the other room, laughing and joking.

"Come on Doris, Dave's out" he heard his father say.

"Stop it Cliff, he could come back any time." giggled his mother.

"That's OK, I've dropped the latch on the door, if he does come back, he'll have to knock won't he?"

The giggling continued, and to Dave's horror they came into the bedroom.

He wanted to shout, to let them know he was there, but fear of the consequences made him stay silent. His father had obviously had a 'skinful', as he pulled at Doris' blouse.

"Careful, you'll rip it," she said as she undid all the buttons and slowly let it slip to the floor.

Clifford showed no such restraint, and quickly threw off his shirt, vest and trousers, and stepping out of his underpants, stood naked at the end of the bed.

Dave gasped at the huge thing he saw between his father's legs, he wanted to look away, and imagine he was somewhere else, but he couldn't.

By this time Doris was also naked, she knelt before her husband and gently kissed his erect member, holding the shaft and licking its large purple head.

Clifford pushed Doris onto the bed, and turning her onto her stomach, entered her from behind. She screamed in ecstasy as he pumped back and forth, and quickly reached a climax.

Dave wanted to scream "Don't hurt my mummy," but the words wouldn't come, so he closed his eyes and prayed it would stop.

Clifford finished with a grunt, withdrew, and Doris flopped face down onto the bed.

From that day on, whenever Dave heard strange noises coming from his parents' bedroom, he knew exactly what they were doing, and the sight of his father's erection would haunt his dreams for many years to come.

When Dave was fifteen, in his last year at school, he had the chance to go on a summer camp vacation with his class to a tiny seaside resort in Hampshire called Hill Head. He'd been billeted with a lad from his year called Bernie Newman, who was much more mature and street-wise than Dave was. After a few days at the camp, the pair of them sneaked out after 'lights out' and with Bernie leading the way, went down to the seashore. Although a stony beach, the back of the shore was divided into lots of little 'nooks and crannies' separated by thick gorse and brambles. Bernie assured Dave that this was where all the night's action would be, and that they only had to wait quietly at this little spot before they'd witness something 'special'. Bernie had often joked about wanking, and Dave had always made it seem as if he too indulged in this male pastime. In fact he'd never ejaculated. He'd had erections many times, but nothing else.

The two lads arrived at a spot between two gorse bushes, overlooking a little clearing. This was grassed over, but covered in rubbish, old cigarette packets, crisp bags, and assorted litter, almost making a carpet. It was a lovely summer evening and, although nearly ten o'clock, it was still light enough, thanks to a full moon, to see quite clearly. Bernie sat quietly bragging about his conquests, including a time when he and five mates had taken turns to shag a girl on the common with Bernie, taking the last go, because he was the biggest, and it made sense to save the best until last

"When I finished with her, her fanny was like a bucket of porridge," he sniggered. Dave sat wide-eyed and totally mesmerised.

"And then there was this time when me and my mate was in London for the weekend, and ..." Bernie rambled on and on, but Dave was easily impressed. Bernie had such great phrases for everything he did, for masturbation, he used 'pushing Percy with me palm' or 'giving Gordon some glove.' He also described his penis in a number of colourful ways: 'one-eyed trouser snake', 'blue veined piccolo' and 'purple pussy puncher' were three that young Dave liked.

Bernie was just finishing his story about London when they heard the sound of shingle being trodden underfoot.

"Shhh." Bernie whispered, "I finks the fun's about to begin."

A young couple in their late teens came walking across the beach and sat down in the glade next to Dave and Bernie. Peering through the gorse, the two lads watched as the couple started their foreplay. Dave's mind flashed back five years, and things started to fall into place, the love-making was taking a similar course to what he had witnessed in his parents' room.

Suddenly, and without any sign of embarrassment, Bernie pulled his member out of his trousers, and started frantically rubbing it. Dave had one eye on the couple, and one on Bernie. He too had a stirring in his loins. Bernie stopped for a moment, then nodded to Dave, encouraging him to follow suit. Dave was unsure, but slowly undid his flies, and took out his half erect penis. They were both kneeling, alongside each other, peering through the foliage. Then it happened, Bernie moved a little closer to Dave, let go of his own penis, and took hold of Dave's. Dave froze on the spot.

"Come on, it's only a wank," Bernie whispered.

Dave closed his eyes, took a deep breath, and grabbed hold of Bernie's manhood, pumping it up and down like a madman.

"Ouch," squealed Bernie "not so rough, for Christ's sake."

Suddenly, and almost without warning, Dave started to ejaculate. "Ahh ..." he sobbed as the first burst of white sticky fluid came shooting into the air.

The couple they had been watching, stopped in mid flow, "What the fuck's that?" shouted the man, standing up and trying to make out where the noise had come from.

Dave and Bernie jumped to their feet, and ran off into the undergrowth, willies dangling between their legs like little white tails.

"You fucking prat," shouted Bernie, "I didn't even come."

"I'm sorry," replied Dave, trying to put his still erect member back into his trousers.

They got back to the camp in double quick time and managed to get into their dorm without detection.

From that moment on, Dave kept away from Bernie, never quite sure whether he was gay or not. He continued to masturbate most nights through his teens, but always in private and as he went into manhood, had an almost unnatural hatred of all things homosexual.

At five-forty, Dave put on his coat, switched on the 'ansaphone', set the alarm, and after locking the office door, walked rather shakily across the road to his car. He was worried about Joanne, and wondered if she might say something to Calvin.

"I ought to get to work early tomorrow, see if I can square it with her," he mused to himself, as he turned on the car ignition, pulled out into the road, and headed across the Itchen Bridge for home. Tuesday nights were generally quiet, and he'd resigned himself to a night in watching the TV, which might give him the opportunity to mention to his wife about his impending pay cut. Arriving home, he opened the front door, and shouted: "Evening love."

"Hi ya," came the reply.

"What's cooking? good looking," he quipped, as he walked down the hall, and peered into the lounge.

"Nothing actually, there's a new wine bar opened in the village, and all week they've got half price meals, fancy giving it a try?"

Normally, Dave would have gladly gone out for a few more drinks, but as he'd already consumed four or five pints, was less than enthusiastic about it.

"Um ... well, if you really want to."

"Don't force yourself."

"No, no, if you want to, then we'll go," he conceded, with a sigh, "Where is it?"

"In the arcade, next door to the Chinese, it's called 'Bluffers' I think."

"OK, I'll have a quick wash, and we'll go out early. Eh?"
He left the room and climbed the stairs to the bathroom. Stopping at the upstairs landing he called back, "Where's Sarah?"

"She's stayed for tea at one of her school friends, should be back about eleven," came a muffled reply.

"Really, does that mean we've got the house to ourselves then?" he yelled, hoping she'd notice the sexual overtone.

She did and was unimpressed. "You'll have to wait until later, I've just done my hair," she shouted back.

"Bloody typical," he mumbled, as he went into the bathroom to start his ablutions. He quickly washed and changed, and they left for the wine bar, finding a parking space right outside the main entrance. It was finished and panelled in light pine, with solid dark pine tables and chairs placed carefully around the room. Because the windows were painted black, it was very dark inside, with little curtained partitions and alcoves.

"A perfect place to bring the mistress, but a ghastly place to bring the wife," Dave thought as he made straight for the bar.

"Good evening Sir. What's your pleasure?" said a very smart, but somewhat effeminate young man.

"Tit fucking! You shirt-lifter, what's yours?" Dave thought as he turned to his wife.

"I'll have a gin and tonic, please."

"Make that two, and we'll share a tonic."

After paying, they walked across the bar, and sat down at a cosy corner table.

"Christ, it's bloody pricey in here," Dave moaned as they simultaneously took a sip from their glasses. Dave decided that now was the perfect time to mention his pay cut. Taking another, but larger swig from his glass he started: "Bloody old Calvin called me into his office today and gave me an ultimatum."

"Oh no! What's happened? You've lost your job, haven't you?"

"No, it's not that bad, I've got to take a £2,000 pay cut, no discussions, just a pay cut or out. The bastard ..."

Janice had been working for the past few years in a convenience store. Three afternoons a week, just for a little extra spending money.

"Well, it's not the end of the world, my boss is always saying I could work extra afternoons if I wanted, so if I did another two, maybe three, that would almost cover it, wouldn't it?" she said sympathetically, trying to make him feel better.

"Yeah, I suppose so," Dave sighed. "It's not the money, it's the way it was done, that's all."

Dave was genuinely surprised at how well Janice had taken it, and finished his drink, asking if she would like another.

"No thanks, I'm OK."

Dave shrugged his shoulders, and went back to the bar.

"Same again Sir?" enquired the barman with a smile, straight from a toothpaste advert.

"Just one gin, but make it a double." Dave snapped.

"Another tonic?"

"Obviously," snarled Dave, who didn't like the barman at all. In fact, he didn't like the wine bar either.

Dave wandered back to his wife, put his drink down, mumbled something about going for a slash, and promptly marched to a door marked 'Guys'.

After a few minutes, Dave came out, and Janice watched him walk awkwardly across the room.

"Have you been drinking today?" she asked, as he reached their table.

"Yes, I had a few lunchtime. Why?"

"You seem unsteady on your feet, and you're slurring your words."

"Look!" Dave said angrily, "I told you I had a couple lunchtime, I'm under a lot of pressure at the moment, surely that's OK isn't it?"

"Alright. Keep your shirt on, I just don't want you drinking a lot at lunchtimes, just because Calvin's upset you. Getting drunk won't help."

"He hasn't upset me, for fuck's sake, get off my back."

"God, you're in a mood, I wouldn't have suggested coming out tonight if I'd have known," she paused, searching for the words, then added, "and don't use that gutter language with me, I think we should go home."

"Suits me fine." he stormed, and downed his drink in one.

Turning around, he looked across the room, and noticed there was now a barmaid behind the bar along with the barman who had served him. She had long straight brown hair, bottle base glasses, and a large unattractive nose. However, even from a distance, Dave could quite clearly see that what she lacked in looks, she made up for with an incredibly large breast. She was probably 18 or 19 and Dave stood transfixed, his eyes almost on stalks staring at her heaving bosom.

"Fucking hell." he said under his breath "what a pair of top bollocks. Absolutely perfect for a pearl necklace."

Several years before, when he was living on his own, Dave had read about a 'pearl necklace' in a soft porn magazine. This was a sexual act, whereby a man ejaculated between a woman's boobs, and onto her neck, and had spent nearly every day since fantasising about it. Although it was not essential for the woman to have large breasts, it was obviously preferable from the man's point of view. Like many men, Dave also assumed that if a girl was plain, or even downright ugly, she would jump into bed with basically anyone. It was a mistake he had often made, and over the next few weeks would cost him dearly.

"Look, I'm sorry darling," he said as he turned round to face his wife, smiling sweetly. "I'm just a little uptight at the moment, let's forget it and have another drink. Eh?"

His wife frowned, but didn't want to spend the whole night rowing. "Oh, OK, same again then please, but do try to cheer up."

Dave almost ran to the bar, positioning himself right in front of the girl. He spoke in a strange and put-on voice.

"Two gin and tonics please."

"If they're not 44DD then I'm a Dutchman," he thought to himself.

The girl smiled politely, and turned to the optics to get his order. From the rear view she certainly was a big girl, and had 44DD buttocks as well as breasts. Turning back to the bar she asked, with a smile, "Will there be anything else please Sir?"

Dave took a deep intake of breath, he knew what he'd like to say: "Let me put my dick between your chesticles," but refrained. "No, that's all thanks. I must say this is a very nice bar. How long has it been open?"

"Only since last weekend, that's why the food and drink are on half-price offer."

"Yes very nice," he letched, "I'll certainly come back. Do you work here every night?"

He wasn't looking at her face as he spoke, but down into her cleavage; she noticed this, and re-adjusted her blouse, folding her arms across her chest.

"I only work Tuesday, Thursday and Sunday evenings," she replied, feeling a little embarrassed and strangely awkward. "That'll be two pounds exactly please," she continued, as she held out her chubby little hand.

"How about one yourself?"

"No thank you Sir, it's a long night."

"Yeah, and I've got a long prick just waiting to send you to heaven," he thought as he fumbled for his money.

She could obviously tell what he was thinking, because she blushed slightly and bowed her head to the floor. It was painfully apparent that many men had had similar thoughts, and she was not quite sure how to handle the situation she found herself in. Dave gave her a five pound note and watched her walk to the till. He wanted to sit at the bar and chat until closing time, but with Janice there, it was impossible. Taking his change, he gave her a sly sickly smile, and returned to his wife with the drinks.

"There you are, one G and T." he said chirpily.

"Christ, you took your time," Janice snapped.

"Sorry, just inquiring how long the bar had been open."

"Staring at the barmaid's tits more like."

"What?" he questioned, and trying to make it look as if he hadn't noticed, glanced back at the bar. "Are they?" he asked.

Janice could see through Dave as easily as looking through her glass of gin and tonic. He was that transparent.

"She's much too young for you," she laughed as she picked up her drink.

"Suppose so, as I said I hadn't really noticed, I'm a one woman man, you know that."

"Huh," she muttered, but decided to drop the matter.

Janice had always known that Dave was a big boob man, and often wondered why he'd wanted to marry her, because she was slim with breasts that could best be described as 'bee-stings'.

They had another drink, and scampi and chips in the basket, which allowed Dave two more trips to the bar. He discovered the young barmaid's name was Helen; she was twenty-two years old and lived at home with her parents, only a short distance from the wine bar.

During the meal, Dave sat supposedly listening to his wife, when in fact, he was hatching a plan on how to 'accidentally' meet the barmaid. First, he'd need to find out where she worked, then ask her out for a drink at lunchtime, and go on from there. It was a great plan.

"Come on then," Janice said, interrupting his thoughts, "drink up, it's time to make tracks. And I think I'd better drive."

"Fair enough."

Dave finished his drink, and they left. Getting home, Dave offered to make a nightcap, but Janice declined, and they both had a coffee, before retiring. Dave, as usual, wanted to make love, and figuring that, as his wife had had a few, would obviously oblige. Once in bed, he rolled over and kissed her gently on the back of her neck.

"Mmmm," she sighed, as Dave tried to push her onto her back and climb on top. "Careful, I'm so full up. I feel a bit sick," she moaned.

"Brilliant, don't you ever fancy it?"

"Of course I do, but you always seem to pick the wrong moment."

He tried again to mount her.

"Dave, stop it, I'm really bloated. You'll see that scampi again."

"All I want is fishy fingers," he crudely thought. "Aw, come on, I'll do all the work, you get on top."

He was starting to get a little rough, and Janice had never liked sexual foreplay which involved the more violent aspects of love-making. She was a great romantic, who had to be one hundred percent in the mood, a 'Mills and Boon' type who liked her men strong, but gentle. Dave was not.

"Dave, please, I'm ..." she pleaded, but he interrupted her, mid-sentence.

"Come on, let me pop in 'Peter'. I'm desperate."

She hated this kind of smutty talk, but laid still, and let him continue, certain in the knowledge that, she'd get no peace until he'd done the deed.

Dave pushed his hands between her legs, and groped madly. She tried to relax and thought back to her first marriage, and how different it had all been.

* * *

Janice had had a completely opposite upbringing to Dave's. Born in the lovely mediaeval Hampshire city of Winchester, to middle-class parents, she had two sisters, and being the youngest was always her daddy's favourite. Her childhood was a very happy one, with fond memories of holidays and birthdays, and wonderful times together. She'd done reasonably well at school, and finished up with a creditable six 'O' levels, enabling her to gain employment as a clerk with a local firm of solicitors. They were gorgeous, halcyon days, full of laughter, music, and great expectations for the future. She was fairly pretty, without being stunning, but had no shortage of admirers. She'd met Nikos Katsaros at a party, when she was eighteen, and they immediately became an 'item'. He was the son of Anglo-Cypriot parents and had inherited his mother's dark Greek looks, with olive skin and jet-black hair. From the day they met, Janice loved him dearly, and they duly married in 1976, with a typical Greek styled family wedding. She could honestly say it was the happiest day of her life. They danced and sang into the night and went for their honeymoon to his spiritual homeland of Cyprus. Two weeks in Paphos with his mother's family, just crowned the whole affair.

Nick's parents owned a big restaurant and were reasonably well-off and gave the couple a large sum of money as a wedding present, which was used as a deposit to buy the house in Hedge End.

When Sarah was born in 1977, Janice thought she'd cracked it. She had everything she ever wanted. A great family, wonderful home, a caring, considerate husband and a healthy, gorgeous dark-eyed daughter. Life for her was one happy merry-go-round which she never wanted to get off.

Nick worked as a highly paid maintenance man for the British Transport Dock Board and his duties included shift work in the docks, ensuring that the cranes and straddle-carriers, used for off-loading the ships in Southampton's new freight terminal, could run trouble-free throughout the day and night.

On a cold and extremely windy February night in 1982, Nick was required to climb the port's floating crane, (aptly named 'Goliath') to effect a simple repair to the jib mechanism. Half way up its old and frozen steel ladder, he lost his footing, and fell head-first onto the quay of the dry dock and was killed outright.

Janice could still remember vividly the knock on the door that fateful night, when the dock manager gave her the tragic news. She was devastated, all their dreams and plans disappeared like smoke through an 'Expelaire' fan, and even after ten years, she would still cry unashamedly, whenever she thought of that dreadful night. She had been a devout Catholic during her marriage, but gave up Catholicism almost immediately, and even several visits by the local priest, and encouragement from Nick's family, could not make her take the vows again.

As is so often the case, financially she was set for life, with the mortgage paid off and a reasonable inflation-linked pension to cushion the blow, she at least had no money worries. But no manner of material wealth could ever make up for, or ease the great sense of loss, and guilt that she felt.

When she met Dave Price in 1991, she was strangely attracted to him, feeling that it might be the time to try to start her life again. He was the complete opposite of her first husband, and all her friends tried desperately to talk her out of making it permanent. But, being single minded, the more they discouraged her, the more she was determined to make it work. He wasn't that bad, she told herself, and she wasn't getting any younger. If she was to remarry, then Dave

Price was the man for her. Within two years of marriage, she'd resigned herself to the fact that she was wrong and all her family and friends had been absolutely right.

* * *

She was brought back to the real world as Dave roughly entered her. He leant over slightly to one side, took her nipple into his mouth and started to pull on it, as if, in some way, trying to make her breast larger.

"Dave," she pleaded, "You're hurting me, not so hard."

He ignored her and continued to pull and suck, until she could stand it no longer.

"For Christ's sake, stop it," she screamed, "What's the matter with you?"

Unfortunately, he could not hear her plea, he was in a trance-like state, his sexual fantasy world seemed real. He flicked and tweaked her papilla in a frenzy, biting the end, whilst twisting his head from side to side.

Pushing at his face, she tried to prise him off, without success. The harder she pushed him, the deeper he sank his teeth.

"You bastard!" she shouted, as she managed to get his vice-like grip released. He stared at her with wild eyes, he had just reached the 'vinegar-stroke' and ejaculated over her thighs.

"You disgusting git!" she yelled, as she pushed him off, sending him crashing onto the floor.

"What'd I do? You crazy bitch, you could have killed me."

She quickly got out of his side of the bed and stood shaking with anger, looking down at the pathetic sight on the bedroom floor.

"I'll bloody well kill you, if you ever do that to me again, you're nothing short of an animal. No, not even an animal would bite someone like that."

He got to his feet and stuttered: "What you on about? Just a bit of foreplay, that's all."

"Foreplay?" she yelled. She was so angry she couldn't find the words to describe her feelings. Sighing loudly, she stormed out of the bedroom and into the bathroom, slamming the door behind her. Looking at her reflection in the large mirror, she wiped a tiny tear from the corner of her eye. Her left nipple, crimson red, had a trace of blood on the tip of the teat, and the lower part of her body was splattered with minute drops of semen. She made a conscious decision, there and then, that this could not continue.

Dave rubbed his eyes and sat up, his penis still semi-erect. He couldn't figure out what was wrong with Janice, but put it down to the wrong time of the month. He snuggled back under the duvet, and somehow convinced himself that his wife had, in fact, enjoyed it.

"Not quite a Pearl Necklace, more a Pearl belt."

The heady mix of alcohol and sexual fantasy was starting to affect his judgement.

Chapter 2

*As the prostitute said,
whilst giving him head,
"A meal without meat in,
is hardly worth eatin'."*

Janice had spent the rest of the night in the spare room, and when Dave awoke, he was slightly surprised to find her missing from their bed. Rolling onto his side, he assumed his wife had gone downstairs to make coffee, and felt quite satisfied with himself.

He'd met a young barmaid, with massive tits, had a good session with his wife, and it was Wednesday, and stripper show night. On the minus side, he realised he had a dreadful headache, sore stingy eyes and a taste in his mouth, best compared to the flavour of the inside of a Sumo wrestler's jock-strap.

"Ahhh ..." he moaned, "must have a coffee."

He sat up quickly, which was the wrong thing to do, and moaned again, placing his head between his hands, praying that the banging would subside.

He could just about hear Janice in the kitchen, and from the smell that was wafting upstairs, she was obviously making toast. Normally the aroma of butter melting on freshly made toast, would make Dave's mouth water, but at the moment, it was making him nauseous.

Janice was stood in the kitchen, nibbling her toast, and mulling over the events of the previous evening. She could not decide how far she wanted to take the matter. It was her house, she could ask him to leave whenever she wanted, but did she want him out of her life permanently? Her nipple was still very sore, and she didn't know if she could ever sleep with him again. She gently caressed the damaged papilla through her nightgown.

"Don's be daft," she whispered to herself, "he's got to go, no way round it, but when? Timing will be crucial."

She sipped her coffee and finished her toast, whilst trying to formulate a plan.

Dave slowly rolled out of bed like a slug on heat, his body was willing, but the brain non-functioning. He took his dressing-gown off the hook on the back of the bedroom door, tentatively putting it on as he crawled downstairs to the kitchen.

"Hello love, do us a coffee, will ya? I've got a blinder of an headache." He mumbled, as he rubbed his brow, searching for sympathy.

"Are you kidding? I think we need to talk, you really hurt me last night, and I don't like you when you're in that sort of mood."

"Yeah, point taken. I know I drank a little bit too much, but it's all these problems at work, I'm under considerable pressure you know."

"Rubbish. Under pressure or not, it's not the drinking I object to, it's this sadistic streak of yours, I've not noticed it before, and I'm sure as hell not going to put up with it."

"Look, I'm sorry, I really am. I didn't mean to hurt you, I just got a bit carried away, that's all."

"You bit my nipple so hard, you made it bleed. It's still painful this morning."

"Did I? I don't remember. I thought you were enjoying it, honest I did."

"Enjoying it? Are you completely mad? I was screaming for you to stop, and all the time you thought I was enjoying it. What do you think I am, a bloody masochist?"

"Oh come on," he said, trying to change the mood of the conversation, "you're exaggerating, surely it was only a bit of harmless foreplay?"

"Harmless? You call this harmless?" She moved the shoulder strap of her nightie and exposed her breast. The nipple was deep scarlet and obviously swollen, and even Dave was a little shocked.

"If this is your idea of foreplay, then count me out. I'd rather sleep with a gorilla, I'd obviously be safer."

Dave stared at his wife's enlarged and bright crimson papilla, and bowed his head.

"I'm sorry," he whimpered. "I honestly didn't realise that I'd bitten you so hard, I don't know what to say ..."

There was a pause, and Janice re-adjusted her negligee. "It won't happen again. Honest."

Janice could see right through him, and was having none of it. "You're damned right it won't." she snapped.

Dave leant towards her, trying to look passionate, but she moved away. His head was pounding, it felt like someone was playing bongos on the insides of his eyes.

"Got any aspirins?"

"Drawer," stormed Janice, pointing at the kitchen cupboard. He found the jar, opened it, and swallowed three.

"I don't feel a hundred percent, perhaps we can discuss this later," he mumbled, almost choking on the tablets.

"I'll just say this, and I'll only say it once. If it ever happens again, you're out. Understand OUT! and I mean it."

"OK, no need to shout, I get the message." The bongos in his head had been replaced by kettle-drums, and he now also felt nauseous. "Any chance of that coffee please?"

"I'm not a piece of meat that you can just play with, make your own sodding coffee."

She turned and stormed from the kitchen, leaving Dave slouched over, and leaning against the kitchen work-top.

"Charming, I must say. Kick me out would she? Well, that might just suit me fine." He muttered, as he switched on the electric kettle, and fumbled for a coffee-mug from the cupboard.

Taking his coffee into the lounge, he lit up a cigarette, and flopped out on the sofa. The first drag sent him into a coughing fit, and the nicotine-filled smoke made his head spin. "Fuck-(cough)-king hell." he spluttered, as he stubbed the cigarette out, "I think I'd be better off with toast."

He walked back into the kitchen, still coughing and wheezing, and taking some bread from the bread-bin, rammed it into the toaster, crumbling one of the slices, as it slid down.

He could hear Janice walking about upstairs, she was obviously going to keep out of his way, until he'd gone to work, which was probably for the best. When the toast popped up, the broken slice jammed, and he burnt his fingers trying to get it out. "Ah, fuck it." he yelled, and left the damaged slice jammed in the toaster. Finishing his coffee, and finally managing that first fag of the day he went upstairs, straight into the bathroom, where he washed, shaved and brushed his teeth. He had hoped this might make him feel a little better, but unfortunately it didn't. Leaving the bathroom, he cagily entered the bedroom. Janice had obviously gone back downstairs, and with some relief, he got dressed and ready for work. Janice was in the lounge watching breakfast television, and he stopped in the doorway.

"See you later then, won't be ..."

"Yes. Bye," she snapped, and Dave walked to the front door, put on his coat, and left the house.

Driving to work, he tried to figure out exactly what was going on in his life. Was he in some sort of mid-life crisis, or on the verge of a nervous breakdown? Was he raving mad, and everyone else sane or was he the only sane person left?

As he joined the Portsmouth Road, a red Renault Five cut him up, and its two occupants laughed.

"Watch out you spunk-bubble," Dave yelled, receiving the 'two-fingered' salute from the driver, and the 'Nescafe' coffee advert's 'wanker' gesture from the car's passenger.

"Yeah, and up yours ya bastard!" Dave screamed back. How he hated driving to work. The pressure and aggression always put him in a bad mood, even before he arrived at the office.

Stopping at some traffic lights, outside the large comprehensive school, Dave watched as several schoolgirls crossed the road in front of him. "Look at the tits on that one," he thought out-loud, "Fuck me, she can only be fourteen."

The lights had changed to green, but Dave was still watching the girls stroll into the playground. "What I couldn't do with ..."

The car behind beeped its horn several times.

"Yeah, yeah, keep your fucking hair on."

Dave hammered the car into gear, and screeched off across the lights. As he arrived at the Itchen toll bridge pay booth, it started to pour with rain. He opened his window, held out his money. His entire arm got soaked.

"Just terrific," he yelled as he pulled away, desperately cranking the window up, "thanks a lot."

After the usual bumper to bumper crawl across the bridge, he finally turned into Canute Road, and arrived at his office. Turning off the engine, he sat pensively for a few moments, hoping the rain might ease off a little. When there seemed to be a break in the downpour, he quickly leapt from the car, and ran across the road, charging straight into the office.

"Good morning Joanne, and how are you today?" he said with a sickly grin, the words almost sticking to his lips.

"Fine thanks," replied the girl, with a slightly puzzled look, "And I wonder, what gem will it be today?" she thought to herself, waiting for some witticism from the master of corn.

"Nice weather for ducks eh?" he said in a funny voice, followed by two little "quack-quacks".

The word 'wanker' again sprung into her mind.

He flapped his arms, shaking off the rain, and continued in a more sombre tone. "Look, about yesterday, it was too much booze, and ..." he stumbled over the words, "well, I'm sorry."

Joanne sighed, and looked at him, stood in the doorway like a drowned rat. "Forget it," she said, then added in a serious voice, "but if it ever happens again, I swear I'll go straight to Calvin, and then you'll be in trouble."

"OK, OK, 'nuff said, it won't ever happen again. How about I make you a lovely cup of coffee? Eh, how's that?"

"Don't worry, I'll put the kettle on."

She got up, gave him a snarl, and disappeared into the little kitchenette.

Dave walked over to his desk, hung up his coat, and flopped into his chair. As usual, the morning post was on his desk, duly opened and date stamped. He quickly flipped through the documents, and realised that, once again, there was not much new work there. Joanne came back into the office, placed a steaming cup of coffee on a coaster, and started back towards her own desk.

"Ah, nectar of the gods." he enthused, in such a smarmy voice, that she wanted to throw up.

"Just once, that's all, just one original quote." she thought as she sat down, and continued with some typing. The phone rang.

"Good morning, Calvin and Company. How can I help you?" she said in her brightest telephonist tone. "I'm very sorry Sir, but Mr Calvin is not in at the moment, can Mr Price help you?"

The person on the phone, obviously said no, and inquired when Calvin was expected in.

"One moment please," she politely replied, and placed her hand over the phone receiver. "Dave, do you know when Mr Calvin's due in please?"

"Well, he said he wouldn't be late, so I suppose about lunchtime." he said sarcastically, shrugging his shoulders.

Joanne screwed up her nose, and returned to the caller. "About nine-thirty, can I get him to call you?" She listened for a while, frantically writing on her note pad, and continued, "Yes, I've got that Mr Jackson. I'll get him to call you when he arrives. Bye."

Dave was gazing blankly at the paperwork on his desk; he still had a slight headache, but at least the banging had stopped. He scratched his nose, and drifted into a daydream. He thought of the young barmaid he'd met, her massive boobs covered in baby oil, and the pleasure he would have, moulding them in his hands, and tweaking the nipples with his lips. Oh! the pleasure. Suddenly the phone rang again, making him jump. This time the call was for him, and he snatched at the receiver.

"Hello, Dave Price, how can I help you?"

The person on the phone asked if the company had any maps of the Scilly Isles.

"One moment please, I'll check in the map room," Dave replied, and placing the call on 'hold', he walked into the map section. After a few moments he found what he was looking for. "Yes I've got the Scilly maps," he quipped, tickled by the pun he'd made. "Fucking Scilly maps, if you ask me," he thought, as the caller asked for the price, accepted it, and said they would collect them from the shop at three.

"That's fine Sir, and your name? Right, I'll leave them at reception with the invoice. You're welcome."

He replaced the receiver, took a large manila from his desk drawer, placed the maps inside, sealed it, and wrote: MR SINCLAIR – T.B.C.F. in block capitals on the front.

"Cor, this is busy, I don't know if I can cope," he joked, looking down the office to see if Joanne found his quip amusing. She didn't. At that moment, John Calvin came into the office.

"Morning Joanne, morning Dave, any calls?"

"Yes Mr Calvin, could you call Mr Jackson immediately on this number please?" said Joanne, as she handed her boss a post-it sticker.

"Excellent, just the call I've been expecting, I'll do it right away. Oh, could I have a coffee please," he added, as he went into his office, closing the door.

Dave watched Calvin through the glass partition, separating the offices. "Fucking turd-bottle." he thought, as he continued to look at his post. Amongst the mail, was a request for a small marine compass from a company yacht moored in Oslo, Norway. This was urgently required, and needed dispatching by air. The Customs' requirements for duty free entry into Norway meant that Dave would have to complete a customs declaration 'EUR1' form, which then had to be duly certified by HM Customs and Excise at the Customs House. Lifting an old manual 'Olympia' typewriter from a side cabinet onto his desk, Dave typed (with two fingers) the document, followed by an export sales invoice and a 'DHL' dispatch note. When he had finished, he signed various copies and pinned them all together with a large paperclip. Standing up, he shouted across to Joanne, "Right, I've got to go to Customs House with these papers, and get them certified, shouldn't be too long, but you know what Customs are like." He put on his still-damp coat, and added, "Oh, you couldn't ring DHL for us, and say there's a small package for Oslo, ready for collection this afternoon, could you?"

"OK." said Joanne, without looking up.

"Fine, see you in a while then."

Dave opened the office door, pleased to see that it had stopped raining, and walked across the road to his car. Struggling in, he decided to play some music on the car stereo. Removing the cassette tape that was in the player, he noted that it was his favourite, 'simply Red'. He ummed and ahhed for a moment, and took several other tapes from the door pocket. "Let's see, Abba's greatest hits, Sounds of the Seventies, or ...yeah, this will do nicely." He duly placed his new selection in the player, started the car, and drove along Canute Road towards the Customs House.

Whitney Houston's shrill and colourless voice cracked the air, filling the car with an ear-achingly high pitched whine. Dave tapped his fingers on the steering wheel, and hummed along with the murdered melody. Within a couple of minutes, he arrived at the Customs House, and encountered the same problem that had plagued many before him. Where to park? Her Majesty's Customs and Excise had cleverly built the ghastly looking sixties style building, (a twelve storey glass and concrete sky-scraper) so that it was completely surrounded by double yellow lines. Dave drove around for a few minutes, turning off Orchard Place and into Queensway. "Bloody place," he muttered, desperately searching for a parking space. Eventually, and fairly luckily, he found a meter, and it had some time on it. He walked back down Queensway, through the front door, passed the security officer in the little foyer, up one flight of stairs and into the 'Long Room'. Fortunately, the place was empty, and his 'EUR1' was certified almost straight away. The female Customs Officer handed back his documents and mumbled something through the 'Hygen-screen' glass window. Dave nodded, and returned to his car. Although his headache had now subsided, the dehydration effect of the previous day's drinking had given him a terrible thirst. Needing some cigarettes, it made sense to grab a coffee, when he stopped for his fags. Driving into the main shopping area of Southampton, he encountered the same problem, he'd had at the Customs House and could find nowhere to park. He knew of a little cafe next to Kingsland Market in St Mary's Street, and made a quick detour.

Many years previously, St Mary's Street had been quite an affluent area but was now very run down and in serious need of re-development. It ran in a curve, from Central Hall, just off East Street to the red light district of Derby Road. Nearly all the shops in the lower part were boarded up and covered in bills and posters, advertising obscure groups and underground acts. Any windows that weren't boarded, were smashed, and every wall had graffiti scrawled upon it. Dave drove past the derelict shops until he arrived at Kingsland Market, almost half way along the street, and stopped on a parking meter. Locking his car, he bought some cigarettes from a little newsagents' shop on the corner of the market, and crossed the road, entering a double shop-front hostelry aptly named the 'Market Cafe'.

Sitting down at one of the many empty tables, Dave glanced around. The walls were covered in 'day-glo' yellow, orange and red cards, each one offering a different special of the day. The choice seemed endless, everything from cottage pie to spaghetti and chips was apparently available, and all at prices between two and three pounds.

A large middle aged woman, possibly of Greek extraction, with oily skin, weathered face and substantial facial hair, walked over.

"What you like please?" she asked, in strange almost joke-like accent, her moustache quivering on every word.

"Aaa, just a coffee please," said Dave, trying desperately not to look at her hirsute lip.

"You no-a like some breakfast maybe, I do-a nice Inglish food."

"Um, no, just a coffee will do fine."

She disappeared around the side of the little wooden counter and Dave lit up a cigarette. His headache was now just a dull sensation but he had a pain between his shoulder blades, and stretched his neck, trying to alleviate it.

The woman returned with his coffee and placed it on the table, together with a slip of paper (obscurely numbered 71) with the sum of 50p scrawled on it. The coffee was piping hot and disgusting, and obviously made with a very cheap type of coffee powder. Dave stubbed out his cigarette and immediately lit another. Glancing through the grubby, off-white net curtains, he looked across St Mary's Street. Directly opposite was the 'Intimate Book Exchange', a grubby little sex shop, complete with black boarded up windows, and a huge sign declaring that only persons over eighteen would be admitted, due to the nature of the material sold. He had never been into a sex shop before, but had often thought about doing so. Dare he go in? Why not? He was an adult, and he liked sex. Surely it was his type of shop, and besides, who was about to see him? He almost finished his coffee, walked to the counter and handed the woman a fifty pence piece.

"Many thanks, see you again," he lied, as he left the cafe, walking straight across the road, and stopping outside the sex shop. He hesitated, looking up and down the street, and praying that he was not seen by anyone he knew. The street was all but deserted. His stomach knotted, and his palms became sticky, as he tried to get up the courage to go in.

"Right," he said to himself, sucking in a large intake of air, and after one more glance up and down the street, he darted in. If the outside was grubby, then the inside was positively and disgracefully tacky. No sooner had he entered the shop, peering into the gloomy half-light, when a voice boomed:

"Good morning."

Dave jumped, and looked up to see a young man, possibly early twenties, with a very short skinhead haircut, sat at a small trestle-table with posters draped on the outside to make a type of counter. The place had a repulsive damp smell to it, the walls were painted black and a single dim light bulb, unshaded, hung from the centre of the shop.

The youth had gone back to reading his newspaper and had a cigarette in the corner of his mouth, the ash, hanging precariously, awaiting a single movement to send it floating to the floor. Dave's first reaction was one of blind panic, he wanted to turn and run, and felt strangely guilty, as if he had no right to be there. He bit on his lip and looked down at the floor. As his eyes slowly adjusted to the light, he moved into the middle of the room and glanced around. Along the walls, on rickety wooden shelves, each about three foot from the ground, were cardboard boxes, their fronts roughly ripped, to reveal a cornucopia of magazines. Each box was carefully marked in black felt tip. Spanking, Leather, Bondage, Lesbian, Gay, Big Boobs, She Male and Hard Porno. The list seemed to encompass most, if not all types of perversion. Dave took a deep intake of the stale, damp air, and walked over to the box marked 'Big Boobs'. Condensation seeped and dribbled down the shiny gloss black walls, like sweat on a fat man's forehead, making the atmosphere almost taste sticky.

"Looking for anything special mate?" said the skinhead, as he glanced up from his paper, causing Dave to jump once more.

"Um ..., no thanks, just looking."

"OK, need any help let me know."

"Sure," gulped Dave, almost out of breath.

Without looking up, Dave moved slowly about the room staring at the merchandise, but somehow afraid to make contact. Several times he reached his hand out, tempted to flip over a magazine, but he didn't.

In the corner, opposite the counter, sat an inflated rubber woman, her mouth forming an 'O' shape, and her grotesque, malformed body draped over an upturned case. Her ugly face stared sightlessly back at Dave, and made his skin creep. "How the fuck could anyone sleep with that?" he asked himself, as he once more moved over in front of the Big Boob's box.

Slowly, with his hands shaking, he reached forward and flipped through the first two or three magazines, stopping at a mag called 'USA Brabusters'. He carefully lifted it out, with his forefinger and thumb, almost as if he were frightened of it. On the cover was a beautiful blonde woman, with breasts so large that they looked like skin coloured footballs stuck to her chest. He sucked in, and nearly yelled "Fuck me!" as he dropped the book back into its box. It was not possible to look inside the magazines because they were completely sealed in cellophane pouches. Obviously, if you wanted to see more, you had to purchase them.

The particular mag Dave had pulled out had a sticker in the corner with the sum of £5 written on it, and this seemed to be the going rate for most of the books in the section he was looking at. He placed 'Brabusters' back, and continued to flip through the rest of the stack. They all had titles which suggested large women, Amazons,

Knockers & Nipples, Busen, Big Jugs and Peaches were just a few to catch his eye. He had never seen anything like it, and the nervousness he'd felt when he'd entered the shop had now almost completely vanished, and was replaced by a quirky excitement.

"If you're looking for something a bit stronger," said the skinhead, "I've got some hard core porno mags out the back."

"No, um ...it's OK," mumbled Dave, stumbling on his words, his breath heavy, pulse still racing, making speech difficult.

When he reached the end of the stack, he paused for a moment, scratching his forehead, undecided as to which books he should choose. However, one thing he had noticed, was that all the girls featured in the big boobs section were white, no black girls figured at all. Turning his head to the counter, but keeping his eyes low, he asked:

"Excuse me, have you any with black chicks?"

"Yeah, there's a few, but there don't seem to be much call for black meat these days, but I fink you may find a couple in that box," replied the man, pointing at the section marked 'Scandinavian Porn'.

Dave felt uneasy, and decidedly embarrassed, like a dirty old man letching over a schoolgirl. He moved once again across the dingy room. The section contained magazines featuring straight sex, and all the covers had well endowed young men, in various lewd positions of fornication, but were priced from £10 upwards.

"Tell you what I'll do mate, if you want any mags from there, you can have two for fifteen quid, how's that?"

"Fine," muttered Dave, as he started to look through the section. He stopped at, and pulled out a copy of a magazine called 'Private' which had two large black women with an incredibly well endowed white man, on the cover.

"This is more like it," thought Dave, as he gazed, almost glassy eyed at the photograph, "this is what I want."

Unfortunately, the shop door opened, and Dave's dream was suddenly and abruptly shattered. A scruffy looking man entered and walked straight across the shop and up to the counter.

"How's business, Luke?" he asked in a strong Hampshire accent.

"Yeah, not bad, how you been?"

"Had a fucking great night Friday, with that young bit from the supermarket. Got any new videos worth seeing?"

"As it so happens, I got a couple of new ones in this morning, hang on, and I'll get 'em."

The skinhead disappeared through a door at the back of the counter. Dave froze, he couldn't look. What if he knew the man, someone who came into his office, or worse still, someone who knew his wife? He waited a few short moments, carefully placing the book he was holding, back into its place, and marched briskly to the door, and out into the street.

"Fuck me, that was close," he moaned, gasping for air and sighing. Without looking, he ran straight across St Mary's Street, jumped into his car, started the engine, and pulled out into the road. A green Audi 80 was unfortunately also negotiating the same stretch, and screeched to a halt, blasting its horn.

"You bloody wanker," mouthed its irate driver, but Dave was already some thirty yards up the road, oblivious to the carnage he'd almost caused. Driving back to the office, Dave started to calm down a little. He couldn't figure out why he'd been so embarrassed. He reasoned that plenty of men bought magazines, and assured himself that it was natural. He'd certainly got a kick out of going into the sex shop, and one thing was definite, another visit was going to be imminent.

He arrived back at his office, parked, and went straight in. He sat at his desk, paper-shuffling.

"Fancy a coffee Joanne?" he asked,

"No thanks, I'm fine," she replied, "but I think Mr Calvin will."

He tapped on the door to Calvin's office, and entered.

"I'm making coffee, do you want one?" he inquired.

"Yes please Dave, I'm gasping," said Calvin without looking up, but placing his head in his hands, "Oh, by the way, how's business?"

"Well ..." struggled Dave, he seemed to spend half his life looking for the right words to say. "Um, it's still a little quiet, but

I've sent some goods to Norway, and sold a few maps, it's definitely looking better."

"I see, and you feel there is an upward trend, do you?"

"Oh yes, absolutely. I can almost see the green shoots of recovery from here," Dave joked.

Calvin was not amused. "That's good, because as from next week, I want you to keep a weekly sales record, so that we can all see these green shoots of yours."

"OK, I'll make sure it's done John," said Dave as he left the room, heading for the kitchenette. He filled the kettle, plugged it in, and leant against the work-top, fuming.

"Fucking weekly sales report indeed, miserable old bastard. Never done a full day's work in his life. I'll show him, I'll give him figures so good, he'll give me a rise."

He'd never really liked Calvin, he'd worked for him, laughed at his silly jokes, but deep down, he hated him.

The kettle boiled, and Dave made two cups of coffee.

"I'd like to wank in yours, you prick," he muttered under his breath. "See how you like real cream."

Dave was angry, he knew that if the situation was monitored, his job would certainly be in jeopardy. He opened the fridge, and poured some milk into each cup, stirring each one frantically.

"Dave," Joanne shouted from the office, "there's a customer for you."

He tutted loudly and walked into the main office, to find a woman of about forty-five standing by the reception.

"Sorry," he said in his most creepy voice, "how can I help you?"

"I'm looking for some maps, and guidance," she said in a snobby voice. "My husband and I are travelling around the old Aegean this summer and wondered if you could help."

She was dressed strangely for the time of year, with a windcheater, unbuttoned to the waist, revealing a flimsy low-cut t-shirt. Her cleavage leapt at Dave, like a caged animal. She wasn't particularly busty, but had a wonder bra, pushing her up in all the right places.

"Certainly madam, if you'd follow me to the map room, we'll

see what we can find."

Dave pointed to the map section, and cut across the office. The woman followed, and, behind the partitions, he pulled out several maps for the area she'd requested. As she leant forward, Dave could see right down the front of her t-shirt, and stood on tippy-toes to get a better view. She could see what he was doing, and seemed to like it.

"These older wealthy bitches love it," he thought to himself, as his penis started to enlarge. "We've got some more," he mumbled, "in the room there, if you'd like ..."

"But of course," she replied, and Dave led her into a little side room, not much bigger than a cupboard.

He didn't know what came over him, but he suddenly blurted: "You've got a fabulous pair of knockers, I must say,"

She went strangely coy. "You think so," she answered, knowing full well he was right.

"Do I get a discount if I let you see them?"

"Discount? You can have the whole fucking shop," Dave thought, as she slipped off her coat, and pulled down her t-shirt.

When Dave saw her mountainous moulds, beautifully restrained by her cream brassiere, he almost came in his underpants.

"Oh God," he sighed.

"Come on then, I haven't got all day, I've got to meet my husband in half an hour."

Dave was mortified, and stood unsure of what to do next.

She was obviously more used to these type of situations, and pulled her bra down, exposing her huge brown nipples.

"I've shown you mine, let's see yours." She laughed, as she expertly undid his trouser flies. "It's big, I'll give you that."

Dave grabbed hold of her right boob, and forced it roughly into his mouth, the nipple was so large, it almost choked him.

He was very near ejaculation.

She pushed his head away, and knelt in front of his penis.

Carefully, pulling at the foreskin, she gently massaged him, rubbing the throbbing purple head between her breasts.

"How's that?" she purred, but Dave could not answer, the pleasure was almost too much.

Taking a nipple in one hand, she rubbed it around his penis head, and pulled the foreskin over it, several times, so that almost the entire nipple was under, and almost inside his penis.

"No, no," he moaned, as she rubbed his 'jap-eye', firmly but with a skill, Dave had not experienced before.

"Lick it, suck it, put it in your mouth, for fuck's sake."

"What?" came a voice from the doorway, and Dave glanced around to find he was still in the kitchen, rubbing himself against the cupboard door knob, tweaking it like an udder. It was Joanne, standing in the doorway. Fortunately, he had his back to the door, and she could not see exactly what he was doing. She left, shaking her head, and Dave gathered his senses, readjusted his trousers, and picked up the coffees.

After returning to his desk, still shaking, Dave passed a couple of purchase invoices, and then placed them into the accounts tray on Joanne's desk. With only twenty minutes to go before lunch, Dave wasn't going to begin anything new, and started thinking of the night that lay ahead, and the strip show at the Coach & Horses. His mind painted a picture of gorgeous women, in fabulous costumes, erotically dancing as they stripped.

At five minutes past one, Dave went to lunch. He walked straight to the Slug & Toad, had a couple of pints and an excruciatingly hot cheese toastie, before returning to the office at twenty minutes after two.

The afternoon dragged, and because Calvin had not gone out, Dave spent nearly all his time looking for something to do. At last it was five-thirty and he got up, collected his coat from the hook by the toilet, shouted "Goodnight" to the door of Calvin's office, said the same to Joanne only with "Darling" added, and headed for home. Surprisingly, the traffic across the toll-bridge was extremely light for a Wednesday, and Dave arrived home in almost record time. Slowly opening the front door, he called out, "Evening Love, how's things?"

Silence. Where was everyone? All the lights were on but nothing stirred. He walked into the kitchen, there was no sign of cooking. "Strange," he thought as he checked the kettle for water, and then switched it on. He stroked his face, pulling down hard on his chin. "Most peculiar," he thought, although this time aloud, "where is everyone?"

He returned to the hall, hung up his coat, and called up the stairs.

"Hi, anyone in?" His voice echoed slightly, but still no reply was forthcoming.

"Oh well," he sighed and returned to the kitchen, selecting a mug from the mug-tree, he waited for the kettle to boil. After making the coffee, he walked into the lounge, turned on the television and lit up a cigarette. Before he had finished it, he heard the front door open.

"That you, Love?" he shouted over his shoulder in the general direction of the hallway.

"No, it's me" came the reply, from a voice, he knew to be Sarah's.

"Where's your mum?" he questioned, as his step-daughter came into the room.

"She's next door, talking to Vicky, I shouldn't think she'll be long."

"Oh, I see, any idea what's for dinner?" he asked in a funny squeaky voice.

"Yeah, she's going out to get a Chinese takeaway. Did you two have some sort of a row last night, only she's very angry about something, and I don't think it's anything I've done?"

Sarah left the room and went upstairs.

Dave sat pensively for a moment, picking his nose, and desperately trying to get a fingernail under a bogey that had been annoying him all day. He had hoped that the row would have blown over by now, but obviously it hadn't. Just then, as if on cue, the front door opened.

"Hello Darling, in the lounge," Dave shouted, as he jumped to his feet and charged into the hallway.

If looks could kill, then Dave would have died there and then in the hall. He came face to face with his wife, and she snarled, baring her teeth, like a wild cat.

"Hello Love," he squeaked again, "Can I get you anything?"

"No thanks," snapped Janice, "I only came back for my purse. I'm going for a Chinese, 'cause I can't be bothered to cook," she added, pushing past him, and making her way into the lounge.

"Oh, come on Love, be fair, give a guy a break."

"Give a guy a break," she repeated, "where the hell d'ya pick that one up from? A fifties gangster movie."

"Well, at least let me order it, and go and get it for you," he whimpered.

"Oh for Christ's sake, stop grovelling, the only break you deserve, is a break in your neck."

They stood looking at each other in the lounge. Janice still couldn't see what she'd ever seen in the man.

"Oh, OK, I'll have sweet and sour chicken, beef Cantonese style, and a portion of egg fried rice."

"Right I'll phone for it straight away."

"Don't forget Sarah," she commanded, in a voice full of venom.

"No, of course not."

Dave walked to the bottom of the stairs. "Sarah, I'm going to the Chinese, do you want anything?"

"No thanks, I'm going out for a pizza with some mates tonight," boomed the reply, "I'm OK, really."

Dave turned round and walked the few paces to the phone, and placed the order.

"Ready in five minutes. OK that's great, the name's Price. See you in a while, thanks," he shouted to the foreign voice on the phone. Glancing into the lounge, which by now was empty, he wandered out into the kitchen.

"You haven't forgotten that I'm going out to snooker tonight have you?" he said to Janice rather timidly.

"Do what you like," was her reply, "you usually do."

She was placing plates into the cupboard.

"Look," he said, trying to sound macho, "I've said I'm sorry about last night. I didn't mean to hurt you, it was too much booze, that's all."

"I don't know why you married me, or why I married you, come to think of it. It's just not working, and I am not prepared to carry on with something that's obviously so wrong, and ..."

Oh, come on," he interrupted.

"No, let me finish. It seems you've changed in the past few months, I don't know, it may be me, but what you want, and what I want, well, it's not the same any more."

"What? That's just not true, I had a few sherbets last night, and suddenly I'm this evil demon. Surely one night doesn't ruin a marriage?"

"It's not just last night. Nothing seems right for you, you're always moaning about Sarah, you're not satisfied with me sexually. Oh, and lots of other things, I can't explain."

"Look, if you'd rather I didn't go out tonight, I'll stay in and we'll try to work it out, how's that?"

She took a large intake of breath, looked up at the ceiling and continued, only in a much more sympathetic vein.

"No. I don't want to stop you. Perhaps a night out with the lads will give you a little space?"

"OK, if you're sure you don't mind, I'll go and get the Chinese, we'll have our meal together, then I'll go out, and be home just after the pubs chuck out. How's that?"

"Fine, but I'm warning you Dave, if you ever come home really pissed again, and start on me, it's finished, there and then, no ifs, buts or maybes, you're on your way. Understand?"

"Perfectly."

Dave sucked on his lips, went to say something else, decided against it and left the room. Walking to the front door, he put on his coat, and shouted. "See you in a bit."

He was not answered.

Driving to the Chinese take-away, he was tempted to pop into the Wine Bar to see Helen, but remembered that she only worked on Tuesdays, Thursdays and Sundays. The take-away was empty, and his order was ready within a few minutes. He duly paid the old Chinese lady behind the counter, and drove straight home.

Walking into the hallway, he was met halfway by his wife, who snatched the take-away bag from him.

"I've laid the table already, if you go into the lounge and sit down, I'll serve up in the kitchen, so that we save on the washing-up," she said snappily.

"OK," he answered and walked into the lounge.

Almost immediately, she placed a plate of steaming food in front of him, and he commenced eating straight away.

After what can only be described as a plate of greasy noodles in a thick gravy sauce, with carrots as the only recognisable ingredient, he retired to the bedroom to get ready for his night out. He shaved, washed, put on some deodorant, and changed into a sweatshirt and jeans. He splashed a dollop of his favourite aftershave, 'Corduroy Vert' into his palms and rubbed it into his face. "Right Tiger, let's go get 'em," he said to himself into the mirror, and went downstairs to find his wife sitting on the sofa watching the television.

"Is there anything I can get you before I go?" he asked almost sheepishly.

"No thanks," Janice answered, "I'm fine."

"OK then, I'm off, see you about twelve."

Janice only nodded and continued to watch the TV.

Stopping only to put on his bomber jacket, Dave left the house, got into his car and headed into Southampton, and the Coach & Horses. On the way, he had his favourite tape blasting out hits from the Seventies, and felt like a naughty schoolboy.

As he turned the car down Canute Road, he decided to park outside his office, so that anyone noticing his motor, would not know where he was. He felt strangely nervous, but at the same time positively excited. Parking the car, he made the short walk around the back of his office, and stopped outside the public house door. The name was lit by a neon sign, with two of the letters not working, and read ".oach & Ho.ses" which Dave thought was a better name anyway.

Taking a sharp intake of air, and glancing behind, he barged the door and entered.

The layout had been changed slightly, with all the tables and chairs in a semi-circle around the tiny stage. One free standing spotlight lit the stage area, with a microphone and stand placed centre-stage. Going to the bar, Dave ordered a pint of bitter, and looked around. About 20 or 30 people were standing by the Jukebox and side of the bar, seemingly waiting for something to happen. A few of the tables were full, but Dave found a seat at the edge of the stage at an empty table. Reaching in his pocket he took out a cigarette, lit it, and for the first time since he'd left home started to relax a little. The clientele were all male and judging from most of their dress, mainly dock and manual workers.

Over the stage a large hand-written banner proclaimed that the strip show would start at 08.30, and Dave casually glanced at his watch, "Just right," he thought.

Fidgeting in his chair, he had another dig around in his nostril, and finally managed to pull something from it. Rolling it into a little ball, he carefully placed it into the ashtray, and covered it with the ash from his cigarette.

Some men at the bar were laughing, but Dave didn't look round. He stared straight ahead at the stage, and picked up his pint. It didn't touch the sides, as he finished it with almost one gulp. "Time for another," he said to himself, and getting up, he returned to the bar.

"What will it be?" asked a skinhead barman.

"I'll have another bitter please," Dave replied, noticing that by now most of the men were seating themselves at tables. He returned to the still empty table, put out his cigarette, and immediately lit another one.

After approximately 10 minutes, there was a loud murmur within the room and a very overweight man in a silver lame suit walked from the back of the bar and stepped into the spotlight, and onto the stage.

"Good evening lads, how the fuck are ya?" he shouted into the mike, "Welcome to the Oach and Hoses." He had obviously noticed the broken sign too.

This was greeted with various calls of "Get off," "Fuck off," and "Bring on the girls" which he seemed to ignore, as he had heard it all before. For the next fifteen minutes or so, the M.C. told his audience a selection from his repertoire of the bluest jokes he knew, most of which were old gags, spiced up with expletives. The crowd were starting to get decidedly nasty, and being an old pro, he knew exactly when to stop.

"Well, you ain't come to see me, let's bring on the girls."

"'bout fucking time," shouted one wag in the audience.

"OK, so let's give a nice round of applause to the lovely 'Crystal Balls,' he stood to the side of the stage with his arm outstretched, and "Beat It" by Michael Jackson came blasting from the P.A. From the door behind the bar appeared Crystal, an extremely skinny girl, about 20 years old, with long blonde hair, dressed as a cowgirl. To the calls of "Get 'em off," she wriggled and danced her way across the bar-room floor and climbed onto the little stage, into the solitary spotlight.

As she moved about the stage in a fairly suggestive manner, she began to undress, starting with her gloves, which she removed by pulling at the fingers. She stood still for a moment, and then started to rub them between her legs. Using them in a sawlike manner, she pulled them backwards and forwards in time with the pulsating music. Holding them above her head, she smelt them, and one after another, threw them into the crowd. There was a bit of a scramble, as people fought to grab them. Dave sat quietly, desperately wanting her to take more clothes off. Most of the men in the room were, by this time, on their feet, screaming and shouting like wild animals, making various gestures at and to their private parts. It was not a place for the faint-hearted. It was strange to Dave, because in this room, full of chanting men, he didn't feel aroused, it was almost as if they were intruding into his space, into his fantasy world. For the past few days, he'd thought of nothing else, but now was somehow disappointed, somehow restricted, as though his innermost thoughts were being shared.

The girl on the stage took off her little tartan waistcoat, to reveal a peephole bra, and then removed her skirt, revealing a pair of black panties, suspenders and stockings.

Grabbing hold of the microphone stand, she sat astride it and gyrated up and down. The music reached its coda, and she stepped from the stage. Straight away another song started, and she walked to a man sitting two tables away from Dave, and after sitting on his lap, rubbed her breasts into his face.

"Lucky bastard," thought Dave, "why didn't I sit at that table?"

The man grabbed the girl around the waist, and started licking and sucking at her nipples, his face bright red, as he was cheered on by all around him. As if on cue, she pulled herself away, and climbed back onto the stage. Quickly taking off her bra and pants, she rubbed them in the crease of her behind, smelt them, and ran from the stage, just as the music finished.

The audience cheered, shouted more obscenities, and stamped their feet, as the M.C. returned to the microphone.

"How the fuck was that?" he screamed, "there's plenty more where that came from."

He then went into another routine of blue jokes, causing the vast majority of punters to make a mass exodus to the bar. Dave had also finished his beer, so he joined the throng of people, waiting to be served.

Noticing the queue at the bar the M.C. said, "You know what they say, don't you? First come first served, but here it's more like first served, first come."

The gags were coming thick and fast, but Dave was not really listening, he got his pint, took one sip, and went back to his table, where he lit up another cigarette.

The M.C. had just finished a joke about a donkey and an Irishman, "And now for your wanking delight, we have the biggest mamma on the circuit, and I mean biggest. If she don't give you a fucking hard on, you're fucking dead. Let's hear it for Joycie Juggs, the biggest fucking slag in Britain."

He once again stepped to one side of the stage, and everyone in the room turned their head to the back of the bar. The door opened, and out she came. He had not been lying, when he'd used the word biggest. The woman was at least 18 stone in weight, with measurements in the region of 58, 58, 58, and, as they say, that's one hell of a region. She wore a ridiculously long blonde wig, with a large red flower over one ear, and had enough make up on to keep Estee Lauder in profit for a year. The music she'd chosen to strip to was very apt – 'Blockbuster' by the 'Sweet'. As she waddled across the floor, she had some difficulty climbing onto the stage, before flopping in front of the mike stand. From where Dave was sitting, he could see she was at least 50 years old, but this somehow fascinated him sexually. He stared at her heaving chest, which was covered by a flimsy black blouse.

Underneath she had the statutory red Basque, with black stockings and suspenders, although most of her stomach poked through the straps. Dave was in awe, although most of the audience were less impressed, and started to shout the usual comments about fat people. Dave looked around the bar, and wanted to tell them to be quiet, but thought better of it.

Suddenly, and like some grotesque string puppet, she removed her blouse, and started strutting up and down the stage. She resembled some huge blancmange, wobbling about, and as she reached Dave's side of the stage, he could control himself no longer. He leaped to his feet, and yelled, "Yeah. More!"

Joycie stopped right in front of him, leant over as far as she could (which was not far), licked her lips, and pushed her breasts into the air, supporting the weight with her hands. Dave was hooked. His eyes peered into the spotlight, and he felt a tingle in his groin. Moving back centre-stage, she struggled with the back of her Basque, until it finally sprang off, as if in relief, and fell to the floor, revealing two huge white orbs, each with a tiny pink nipple, almost exactly in the centre.

Dave's heart was in his mouth, he gulped like a fish, trying to breathe. Suddenly she clambered from the stage, and walked straight over to him. She noticed he was enjoying her act and made a bee-line for him. Pushing Dave back onto his seat, she flopped onto his lap.

"Bloody hell, she's heavy," he thought as she crushed his now erect penis. She grabbed the back of his head, and thrust it into her bosom, rubbing it first one way, and then the other, the smell of sweat and cheap perfume, almost intoxicating.

"Like this, do ya?" she said, although through all the noise in the room, Dave couldn't hear a thing. He just smiled, and tried to lick her nipples. She could feel his erection, and wriggled on his lap. She then jumped up and climbed back onto the stage. Dave followed, but she pushed him away, wagging a finger at him, as if he were a naughty boy, and she was his school mistress. The music finished, she collected her clothing from the stage and left the bar.

The room was in an uproar, most people were shouting, "Put 'em on." and other similar quips, but for Dave it had been the most sexually exciting five minutes he had ever had.

The M.C. leapt back to the mike. "Fucking hell, you don't get many of those to the ton, do you?" he shouted, "when I said big, was I joking or what?"

"If you were, then it's the only joke you've cracked all night," replied one less than happy customer.

"Well, that's the end of the first set. We'll be back in half an hour, with some more."

The spotlight was turned off, and the normal houselights came back on, and the rush for the bar started again.

Dave sat for a while, quietly thinking to himself.

"That's more like it, if I go round to the back of the pub when it's finished, I wonder if there's a chance I could see her again."

The plan was formulating in his mind, when he suddenly realised where he was, and coming back to earth, he finished his beer, and went to the bar.

"Fuckin' state of that," said one punter to his mate, "I wouldn't touch her with yours," he joked.

"Christ, you'd need a prick like an elephant's truck to satisfy her, wouldn't you?" his friend replied.

Dave heard what they said, but ignored it. He was quite simply infatuated.

"At last a woman made for a pearl necklace," he chuckled to himself.

"Oi, you want a drink or just finkin' about it?" the skinhead barman shouted, and Dave jumped.

"What? Oh, sorry. Yeah, I'll have a pint of bitter please," he replied, his mind still on higher things, or bigger things to be precise.

The sheer size of Joycie's bust, the feel and taste of it, just would not leave his brain, and he ran the image through his mind again and again. Walking back to his seat, he lit up a cigarette, and sat down with his dreams, completely oblivious to anything or anyone around him. "Why is it that a woman with such large tits has such small nipples, not that there's anything wrong with it, just looks a little weird, weird, that's all." Dave's mind debated.

A few men standing by the jukebox had decided to enliven the proceedings with a few classic C & W tracks, and duly selected their favourites. "Because you're mine, I walk the line," came booming from the speakers, only slightly quieter than the music used for the strippers. Dave tapped his fingers in time with the music, when a middle aged man sat down at the table beside him. After rolling a cigarette, he turned to Dave.

"What a load of shit," he said loudly. "I've seen sexier girls on Songs of fucking Praise."

Dave was in no mood for talking to this person, and just nodded politely, whilst thinking "Fuck off!"

"It's always the same, ain't it. I mean, these so called free strip evenings, always the same, second rate comedian, fat old slag strippers, fucking crap, that's all, fucking crap."

Dave looked at the stranger, but said nothing.

"Please fuck off," he thought again.

"When I was on the ships, ..."

"Oh no, not a fucking sailor, reminiscing about his time on board some merchant tug."

"When I was on the ships, I saw some cracking sex shows. You know the proper thing, not this jumped-up soft porn for poofters, the real thing. Cairo, Lisbon, Port Said. Christ, you'd pay to see a show there and it was a real show, not this fucking crap."

"Why don't you go there then?" Dave thought, but added, "Really?"

"Yeah. I remember once in Cairo, this girl, pretty little Egyptian piece, got on stage with a donkey. Know what I mean? A fucking donkey ..."

"Yes, I know what a donkey is," Dave said rather irritably. "They got this donkey to get a hard on, and it shagged the girl, never seen nothin' like it."

"Really, well excuse me, I must go for a piss."

"Not only that, she gave it a blow job. Bloody hell, that's what you call a sex show; not this crap."

Dave was on his feet, but the man just continued to talk.

"Yeah. Then a man leapt onto the stage and took her from behind, while she was gobbling the donkey. Never seen nothin' like it."

"Yeah, right. I must go."

Dave rushed across the room and ran into the loo.

As he stood having a slash, he frantically thought of ways of changing tables. "Nah, no need, if he thinks it's that bad, hopefully he'll piss off home." Doing up his flies, he returned to the bar. The man was patiently sitting at the table, and watched him return from the bog.

"There was also this time, in Lisbon I think, yeah Lisbon, in the Texas Bars. This little cracker did a strip and you'll never guess, it wasn't a woman at all, fucking bloke with tits, nice, mind you, but with a knob. Christ, if I hadn't known, would of fancied her meself."

"Transvestite," Dave said.

"Yeah, that's right, fuckin' trans-whotsit."

Dave finished his beer quickly and stood up before the man had a chance to say anything else. He walked slowly back to the bar.

"All I wanted was a quiet night out and some bloody asshole has to ruin it."

"Could I have a pint of Directors please?" he asked the barman. He'd decided to start drinking the pub's strong ale, in an attempt to get drunk quicker. "Is this going to be a weekly thing?" he inquired.

"As far as I know, it's been booked for at least the next three weeks. That's one pound sixty please."

Dave paid with the exact money, and stood for a while at the bar, not wanting to return to his seat. He drank the beer down in one, and ordered another. He finally returned to his seat, and the man started again.

"You know what I was saying, well, I've just thought about another. Brazil, it was, Christ they know how to put on a show, they got this ..."

His sentence was cut off by the light being dimmed and the M.C. returning to the spotlight. Dave was never so grateful to anyone before, and sat back in his chair, ready to enjoy the rest of the show. The M.C. continued where he'd left off, old jokes rehashed into blue ones. Dave started to count how many times the M.C. used the word fuck, after ten minutes he counted 26 and decided to stop doing it.

"And now you fucking perverts, it's party time again, please welcome back, that little prick teaser ... Crystal Balls."

By now, most people in the bar were so drunk that Barbara Cartland would have got a standing ovation, and Crystal was met with wild cheering. She'd changed into a schoolgirl's uniform, complete with false plaits. "Pity it wasn't false tits," thought Dave as she danced her way across the floor. This was met with the usual abuse, together with wolf whistles and cat calls. She threw herself into it, and tried to make it look as if she was enjoying it. Unfortunately, nothing could be further from the truth. She was an unmarried mother, whose only way of subsidising her low state handout was to strip. She'd tried prostitution, but was never any good at it. So here she was taking her clothes off, three nights a week, for a load of drunken bums, but at least it gave her some sense of independence.

Dave watched her, but was thinking of Joycie.

After ten minutes of tit rubbing and pelvis thrusting, she finally stripped naked, turned her back to the audience, and touching her toes, was gone from the stage, and back into the relative safety of the room behind the bar.

Dave took the opportunity to rush to the bar, get a refill, and nip quickly into the toilet. "Christ, once you start going, it seems you have to go every two minutes," he muttered to himself in the loo.

Walking back into the bar, the M.C. was back on stage.

"Hello mate," he shouted over the microphone to Dave as he left the toilet. "Been having a wank, have we? There's always one, isn't there? He can't leave his pecker alone for more than a minute."

This caused great amusement around the bar as Dave collected his pint and walked back to his seat. He was to learn that one should never leave one's seat and go to the loo when there's a blue comedian on the stage. He sat down and the comedian carried on. Finally, the M.C. shouted "OK, enough of this you wankers. She's big, she's fat, she's more than one man can handle, the one and only Joycie."

This time she entered the bar much slower, almost knocking over a table as she lolloped her way to the stage. It was obvious she'd been drinking in the interval.

"Christ, don't fall on me gal," shouted a young man on the table she'd bumped into, "I'm too young to die."

Dave watched as she struggled to climb on to the stage.

"For God's sake, someone give her a hand," a voice shouted.

"What, and fuckin' lose it," came a reply.

"Anyone got a crane or lifting tackle?"

"Nothin' big enough to handle that."

And so it went on, the only person in the entire room who seemed to be enjoying her act was Dave.

She was dressed the same as in her first show, but could not get her Basque off, so like the true old pro she was, she pulled her massive boobs out of their cups, and swung them around for a while. She was too inebriated to completely finish her act, and didn't bother to leave the stage to give one of the punters a faceful. As soon as the music stopped, she picked up her blouse, gave a 'V' sign to the room, and sloped off.

Dave was extremely upset, but still had thoughts of seeing her afterwards. The M.C. came back, finished with a couple of gags, to fairly muted applause, and the house lights came back on.

Dave looked at his watch, the digital dial said 10.40pm. The man sitting next to him, whose name was Pat, said: "That's my name, not an invitation!" He continued to bore Dave with antidotes from around the world.

"God, will it never end?" Dave thought.

His glass was again empty, so he stood up, and rather rudely went to the bar without saying a word. The area around the bar was two or three deep, and Dave waited his turn. It was now very close to closing time.

"Pint of Directors and a large gin and tonic please," he ordered, when he finally got served, and stood at the bar to finish them.

He had no sooner put the glass to his lips, when Pat arrived, ordered a pint for himself, and carried on where he'd left off.

"Malaysia, now that's another good place, get anything you

want there, girls, boys, two in a bed, anything. I remember the time ..."

Dave stood, leaning against the bar, trying to finish his drinks, as fast as he could. He felt decidedly wobbly, and went to the loo again.

"Way past time lads, your glasses please," shouted one of the bar staff.

Pat drank up, and wished Dave "Goodnight. See ya again," before leaving.

"Thank Christ he's gone," Dave sighed loudly.

"Pardon?" said a man collecting glasses.

"Nothing" replied Dave, "just talking to myself."

"You want to watch that mate, it's the first signs of madness."

By now there was only a few people left, and the barman demanded the remaining glasses, so Dave duly obliged, and walked out into the street.

Going around to the side of the pub, he realised he was too late the entourage of entertainers had long since left.

"Aw, fuck it," Dave mumbled, as he staggered back to the front of the public house, and headed for his car.

The cold evening air went straight to his head, and he felt dizzy and sick. His legs became impossible to control, and he wandered back and forth across the pavement. As he had drunk his last few drinks very quickly, he had a strange gurgling sensation in his stomach, it was obvious that something inside, was about to re-appear. He'd only walked a few hundred yards, and was standing alongside the overnight lorry park, which was situated just behind his office. He leant against the wire fence, peering into the darkness, he hadn't felt this bad since his stag night.

"Oh ..." he moaned "I'm going to ..."

With that, he started to vomit, sending a spray through the chain-fence, some of which came back at him, covering his shoes and the lower part of his jeans.

"Ahhh ..." he gulped as he retched and retched, bringing up foul smelling liquid. It burnt the back of his throat, and went up his nasal passage, making him feel as if he had been snorting sulphuric acid, through his nose. "Aaaa ..." he groaned, finally bringing up the Chinese take-away he'd eaten some hours before.

When he had finished, the ground was covered in a goocy mess, the only thing recognisable being the carrots.

"Fucking carrots," he said, as he spat out the last pieces of food that had stuck in his teeth and behind his tongue. "Must get a coffee," he heard himself saying, as he staggered on a few paces more. He felt he was in a sort of time warp, he knew what was occurring, he felt it, but simultaneously, it seemed to be happening out of sync. with real time. The whole thing was in slow motion, like some kind of surrealist dream by Dali. He stopped and spat into the gutter, his stomach turned over again and again. He finally reached his office, and after a struggle, opened the door. The alarm buzzer started, and in a desperate bid to get to the control box, he kicked Joanne's waste-paper bin across the floor, scattering litter into the darkness. "Bastard!" he yelled, as he eventually turned off the alarm, and giving a loud sigh, put the office lights on.

"What a mess," he moaned. "Aw well, the cleaner can fix it." He made straight for the toilet, urinated on the floor and wall, and made a cup of strong coffee in the kitchenette.

Back at his desk, he sipped at the coffee, and found himself dozing off. Bib boobs he saw, not like the ones Joycie had, big black boobs, ripe for sucking.

Chapter 3

You might try fantasy,
in an attempt to escape,
but what possible evil,
could make a man commit rape.

At about 11.35, Gladys Umbala, crossed over St Mary's Street just minutes away from the Coach & Horses, on her way home from the Royal South Hants hospital. She'd been working on the late shift as a nurse, and was exhausted. She'd come to England, from her native Uganda, when all the trouble started with Idi Amin, and had studied hard for her qualifications as a State Registered Nurse. She loved living in Southampton, but like most people, hated the weather. The wind was icy, and she buttoned up her overcoat, trying to keep out the chill-night air, causing her breath to show like smoke, as she hurried on her way.

She quickened her pace, as she walked down St Mary's Street, an area she never liked being in. She walked past countless drunken men, all weaving their way home from a night in the boozer. Some stopped as she went by, and shouted abuse at her, but she didn't look up, just marched by, single-minded in her task to get home safely.

She turned into St Mary's Churchyard to take the short cut to her home in lower Chapel, a district of Southampton near the old docks. The path zig-zagged through the churchyard, bending slightly as it rounded the church. The daffodils were starting to show their blooms, and during daytime, it was a very pleasant and popular spot. It had lampposts every twenty yards or so, but vandals had smashed nearly all of them, so it was barely lit at all.

He stood at the far end, hiding behind a tree, watching her make her way towards him.

She was a very large buxom woman, of 28 years old, with a face that seemed to have a perpetual smile upon it.

He watched in silence, held his breath, and waited. It wouldn't be too long.

As soon as she walked around the Church and alongside the tree, he pounced, suddenly, but very quietly, grabbing her from behind and dragging her off the path and onto the grass. It was 11.48 exactly. Screaming, she tried to fight him off, but he was too strong. He held her around the waist, just below her bust, with his left arm, and with his other arm, squeezed her tightly around the throat. Throwing her facedown onto the ground, he jumped on her, grabbing roughly at her face, and pulling at the skin around her right eye. His fingernails drew blood, as they probed for her eyeball.

"Scream you fucking bitch, and I'll rip your eyes out!" he shouted, and she froze.

Moving from her slightly, he thrust his free hand underneath her coat and uniform, until he reached her crutch. Ripping frantically at her tights, he managed to tear a hole in them, and get his finger inside her panties and between her legs. Like a man possessed he insanely probed her private parts, making her squeal and squirm under him, until she could stand the excruciating pain no more.

"Heeelp ..." she screamed, which stopped him for a moment.

"Shut up you black bitch, you know you want it," he yelled, into the side of her face, and she could smell the all too familiar smell of alcohol.

He got onto his knees by the side of her, still pinning her down with his right hand, and fumbled to undo his flies.

She seized the moment, and scrambled to her feet, knocking him over. "Help me, please dear God, someone help me," she screamed as she ran across the graveyard.

He was up in a moment, and chasing after her, he grabbed hold of her hair, and threw her to the ground once more.

"You want rough, I like rough, understand bitch, I like fucking rough. Rough is good."

Suddenly he stopped, and looked around. There was someone coming. Voices in the churchyard. She looked around to try to see him clearly, but it was too dark. She started to get up again, but he grabbed her hair, and punched her in the side of the face.

"You do like rough, yeah?"

She fell flat into the wet muddy grass, sobbing, and he was

gone. Running across the graveyard, he leapt over the small wall, and landing in the street below, disappeared into the darkness of the dank March night.

"You OK?" said a kind voice. "We'll call the police, come on, let me help you up."

She got to her feet, and noticed the daffodils, growing up through the grass. She rubbed her bleeding eye, and saw the young couple, who'd probably saved her lie.

* * *

" ... that was an oldie by Bucks Fizz, 'My camera never lies' and the time is just six minutes past seven. You're listening to fabulous Radio Itchen, coming to you on 93.2FM in glorious stereo ..."

Dave opened his eyes, and stretched out an arm, frantically trying to turn the radio off.

"Aw ... I feel dreadful," he mumbled, trying to adjust his eyes to the light. Through half-opened eyes, he looked across the room, his wife was sitting at the dressing-table brushing her hair.

"Hi ya, any chance of a coffee?" he said, in a frog-like croak.

"You joking?" she stormed. "What sort of state did you come home in last night?"

"What? I wasn't that late was I?"

"The time's not relevant, I bet you can't even remember getting home, can you?"

"'Course I can, it was about twelve, right?"

"Wrong. It was nearly one, you were so pissed you slammed the front door so loud, you woke up everyone in the street, stamped up the stairs and fell into bed, without taking off your clothes."

Dave looked down his body he was naked, except for his underpants.

"But how ..."

"I undressed you, you were covered in vomit, stunk of booze and fags, and mumbling about some black girl."

"Did I wake you?"

"Of course you woke me, you prat. You woke the whole estate, I thought I told you not to come home in that state."

"Sorry love, got any paracetamols?"

"In the bathroom cabinet, you can bloody well get them yourself."

Was it cold in the room, or was it the atmosphere?

"I see you drove home, that was clever, doesn't the law apply to you then?" she shouted.

"Alright, alright," he said back, rolling out of bed, and falling onto the floor, "point taken."

He staggered into the bathroom, rummaged around for some headache tablets, and after finding them, took three. He looked at himself in the mirror.

"What a bloody mess."

He left the bathroom, collected his dressing-gown from the back of the bedroom door, and walked downstairs. He noticed that the bed in the spare room had been slept in, and guessed his wife had spent the night there. He made himself a cup of coffee, and returned to the bedroom.

"What the hell are we going to do?" she asked quietly. "I asked you not to come home drunk, and you completely ignored me. I can't see that we have any future together at all."

"I'm sorry love, I had a great night out, and it just got out of hand, that's all. I promise no more booze until the weekend, then I'll take you out for a nice meal, how's that?"

"Look Dave, I don't mind you drinking, I realise you're under a lot of stress, what with your job and everything, but surely even you can see that getting pissed out of your brain isn't going to solve anything."

"You're right, I'm wrong. I'll make it up to you, I promise."

"Your promises are not worth a light, I ..."

"OK," he interrupted, starting to get a little irritated, "I'm a bloody fool, I should have phoned you, I should have taken a taxi, I just didn't think."

"You never think, you're selfish, just do what you want to do, and sod everyone else."

"Oh, come on, that's not fair, I've said it won't happen again, what more do you want?"

"To be honest, I think I want you out. That's what I want."

"Well fuck your luck missus, I ain't going until I want to go, and that's an end to it."

He picked up his coffee, and walked into the landing. "Me to go? I'll go when I'm ready, not before," he mumbled as he walked downstairs and into the lounge.

By this time, Sarah had got up, and Dave could hear her having a shower. "Fuck, I'm gonna be late again."

After another cup of coffee, he heard Sarah come out of the bathroom, and headed upstairs for his turn. He stopped outside Sarah's bedroom, she'd once again left the door slightly ajar, peeking through the crack he could see her sitting on her bed, wearing just bra and pants.

"Morning Sarah," he said in a sickly voice. "Sorry if I woke you last night. Went out for a few drinks with the lads."

She got up and walked to the doorway. "Who cares? It doesn't worry me what you do, it's mum I feel sorry for."

"Very true, and I've tried to apologise."

Even when he was hung over, he could still appreciate beauty, and Sarah was turning into a gorgeous young woman. He looked at her like an old lecher peering through a keyhole, and when she realised what he was doing, she slammed the door in his face. "If I was ten years younger," he thought, "Christ, don't even think about it."

He entered the bathroom, and urinated for what seemed an hour, took off his dressing-gown, broke wind, and climbed into the shower cubicle. Still thinking of Sarah, he turned on the water.

"Shit, that's cold," he yelled as he tried to stand out of the streaming water. Gradually, it became warm, and he started his ablutions. "Better out than in," he joked as he broke wind again. If he had not had the problems he did at work, he would have phoned in sick, and stayed in bed for a few more hours, but as it was, he was compelled to make the effort.

After his shower, he felt somewhere near human, got dressed

and after one more coffee, left the house.

"See you tonight," he shouted as he closed the door, but there was no reply.

Walking to the car, he was pleasantly surprised to find it was a beautiful spring morning.

Maybe this was the start of a change in his luck.

* * *

Detective Inspector Tony Quinn was sitting at his desk in the Southampton Civic Centre Police Station, studying a brown file that had been put into his 'IN' tray.

"Mike, you seen this?" he said to his young colleague, Sgt Michael Crouch.

"What's that, Sir?" the Sergeant replied politely.

"There was an attempted rape in St Mary's Churchyard last night, and some black nurse was grabbed from behind, punched around a bit, before a young couple arrived and basically saved her. The bastard ran off, dick in hand apparently."

"Yeah, I heard the report on the radio on my way in."

"Can't see we've much to go on though, the description she's given us could fit almost anyone."

"Really? Wanna cup of tea?"

"Love one please," said Quinn, still perusing the file, with a pensive look on his face.

Mike Crouch went over to the tea-table, placed two tea-bags into a couple of dirty mugs, and switched on the kettle.

"How we gonna play it sir?" he asked, while waiting for the kettle to boil.

"Let's let the local press run the story, see if anyone saw anything, and see where we go from there. Someone must have seen something."

"Isn't that near the pub that's started doing the strip shows?" Crouch asked, looking for Brownie points.

"Yeah, that's a point, could be one of those pervies, up to their old tricks. Check it out, will you?"

"Sure, I'll go and see the landlord at lunchtime, find out if he knows anything."

Born and raised in the Gorton area of Manchester in 1946, Anthony James Quinn, as he was christened, had soon obtained the nickname of Zorba the Greek, after the film starring his namesake, and this had prompted him to change his name to Tony Quinn, thus avoiding the unfortunate pseudonym, following his every move in his rise up the higher hierarchy of the Police Force. Fortunately for him, however, the nickname was soon dropped, as most of the younger policemen had neither heard of nor seen the film.

He served his early years in the Chinatown district of Manchester, and had been promoted very quickly for his work with the drugs squad. Although only 5'9" in height, he was quite chunky (but not fat) and had a strange way about him, which made most people, particularly criminals, feel very uneasy. His no nonsense style was tolerated, more than encouraged, and because of this he did not endear himself to his superiors and found that he had to move more often than perhaps he would have liked, in order to get the promotions he felt he deserved. He had light brown hair, which he kept cropped very short, and a large dark mole on his cheek.

After he married in 1972 to Carol (a very proud Mancunian girl) he moved South to take up a promotion in the Basingstoke Constabulary in North Hampshire. Unfortunately, due to an accident involving a car-thief with a crowbar, (Quinn struggled to take the weapon from the man, culminating in the villain receiving hospital treatment for a compound fracture of his right arm and three broken ribs) Quinn was strongly advised, (ordered), by his superiors that another move would suit all concerned, and he ended up in Southampton, buying a house on the western outskirts of the city in a little hamlet called Marchwood. The Quinn's life-style had been very good in the South of England, and after nearly 20 years, they both decided that when he retired, they would stay in the warmer climes of Hampshire. They had retained all of their Northern humour and hospitality, but really enjoyed living on the edge of the New Forest. They'd returned home a few times to Manchester, but after his parents had died, they very rarely bothered to go back. Quinn sat with the mug of tea in his hand, looking at the file in front of him.

* * *

Dave arrived at the office at just after nine, and the previous night's drinking had by now caught up with him.

"My God, what did you get up to last night?" Joanne said as Dave entered the office.

"Just had a few beers," he replied, looking down the office, at the day's work, neatly arranged on his desk by Joanne.

"I'll get you a coffee, looks like you could do with one."

Dave crawled to his desk, and looking through glazed, bloodshot eyes, he muttered loudly to himself. "Oh God, the usual old crap, wonder if old Calvin will let me have the afternoon off, I've still got some holiday left, I think."

Joanne placed a steaming cup of coffee in front of him, stopped and remarked: "Why don't you take the day off? It's really quiet, and I'm sure Mr Calvin won't mind."

"Funny that, I was just thinking the same thing. I'll just sort out a few bits and pieces, and perhaps go home this afternoon."

Fumbling in his pockets, he found his cigarettes and lighter, lit one up, and took a long hard drag. As he inhaled the smoke, it made his head swim, and he coughed.

"What a fucking life, problems at home, problems at work, bloody problems everywhere. Who needs it? Who fucking needs it? All I want is a quiet life, and there's always some cuntface ready to sod it up." He was feeling bitter, and very sorry for himself. He had a headache, his stomach was churning, and he was in two minds whether to just get up and leave. He looked at the papers on his desk for about ten minutes, when Calvin arrived.

"Morning Joanne, morning Dave, lovely day, what?" said Calvin, full of the joys of spring.

"Good day to hang yourself," Dave thought morosely. "Excuse me John, could I have a quick word please?"

"Sure Dave, come into my office. God, you look dreadful, everything alright?"

"Well, that's what I need to talk to you about," mumbled Dave, as he followed his boss into the office.

Calvin sat down at his huge executive desk.

"OK Dave, let's have it," he said, smiling with those nice white teeth, and nice brown face all glowing and healthy, which made Dave feel even worse.

"I think I've got some sort of virus, can't seem to shake it and wondered if I could take the afternoon off, I'll take it as holiday, obviously."

"Of course you can Dave, I'm not an ogre you know, if you don't feel too well, have a few days off, it's no problem, no problem at all."

"You supercilious bastard, love it don't you? You love to see me crawling, you'd replace me tomorrow and think nothing of it. You BASTARD!" Dave thought angrily, but meekly said, "Oh thanks, John, that won't be necessary, just a few hours that's all, then I'm sure I'll be OK."

"Whatever you say Dave, no pressure, just get better."

Dave returned to his desk, a few minutes with his boss was enough to make him want to throw up.

"I'll have my day, you'll see," he muttered. "One day Mr high and mighty Calvin, with your white teeth and ..."

Strangely enough, as is so often the case, the morning post had brought an enormous amount of work. All week, barely a job, and today there was mountains of the stuff. Six firm orders for maps, three sizeable quotes for assorted marine equipment and supplies etc., and a query from the Customs & Excise about an earlier shipment of transceivers, which had apparently not been exported correctly.

Dave found it very difficult to motivate himself, he started paper-shuffling, something he was good at, and thought back over the past few years. He always fancied a change of direction, and before he'd married, had toyed with the idea of bumming across Europe for a few years. He had no real ties, he was an only child, both his parents were dead, nothing really to keep him in England, nothing that was until he'd met Janice, and now even she didn't care if he stayed or not. But, like everything else in his life, he had put it off, until it was too late, and now at nearly forty, he was far too old to go off hitching and living rough.

He looked at the pile of documents on his desk again, and decided to complete and dispatch all the firm orders, and leave the quotations until later, (hopefully Joanne might do them in his absence.) Opening six files, he moved workmanlike around the shop and map-store, until all the orders were ready for dispatch. As two of them were to be shipped to E.F.T.A. countries, he'd need to complete the necessary Custom's forms (EUR1's) to effect their export, and this would necessitate certification at the Customs House.

He carefully lifted his manual typewriter onto the desk, and proceeded to complete the documents. Each tap on his old Olympia typewriter jarred, and sounded like a sledgehammer hitting an empty dustbin, sending shock-waves through his whole body. He stopped every few moments and held his forehead, "Bloody hell, the sooner I get a beer down me, the better. Hair of the dog, that's what's called for, hair of the dog."

It was almost 10.30 when he finally finished, and when the tip-tapping stopped, the relief he felt was immense.

"Right, that's it," he said to Joanne, "I'm off to the Customs House, should be about 25 minutes."

"OK Dave, sure you don't want me to go?" she said kindly.

"Nah, I'll be fine, a little fresh air might do me good."

Crossing the road and getting to his car, he felt shaky, and his legs refused to do what his brain instructed. He felt in his pocket for his keys, and found they were tangled up with the lining. He struggled to get them out, and finally achieved it by ripping half the pocket out as well. Opening the door, he flopped into the driver's seat, and sat thinking for a moment. A definite plan was evolving. After the Customs House, he'd go to the sex shop, buy a few boob magazines, have a beer or two, then go home to read them. Perfect.

After the usual trials and tribulations at the Customs, where they seem to think it's clever to keep members of the public waiting, hoping that they'll go away, (before any work is involved), Dave drove to St Mary's Street, and parked just a few parking meters away from the Intimate Book Shop.

He went through the ritual of walking past the shop, making sure that there was nobody about who might know him, and pretending he was going somewhere else. Just as he seemed to be walking past the shop for the second time, he made a quick side-step into the doorway, and entered, pushing so hard on the door, that it sprang open and hit the inside wall of the shop with a bang.

"Hello mate, do come in," joked the shop assistant, seemingly recognising Dave from his previous visit.

Dave said nothing, and made straight for the box marked "Big Boobs" frantically flipping through the glossy mags. They were all wrapped in cellophane, and made a strange thacking noise as he thumbed them.

"Looking for anything stronger?" said a voice from behind, "I've got some real hard core out the back."

"No, these are fine," said Dave in a deep macho voice.

He quickly pulled out 'USA Brabusters' then '50+' and a third mag, 'Private – Big Jugs Special', and took them to the counter. He could hardly speak, and gulped as he handed them to the scruffy individual, who patiently, and almost lovingly took them from him, and placed them into a brown paper bag, which he sealed with sellotape.

"Anythin' else mate, I've got some real hard core videos."

"No, that's all thanks," choked Dave embarrassingly.

"Right oh, that'll be fifteen quid please."

Dave fumbled in his pockets, first in the one with no lining, then his inside one, making sure he made no eye contact. Fortunately he had the exact money, and placing it on the counter, picked up his package, and almost ran from the shop.

The sheer exhilaration of going into the shop, had made him go weak at the knees, and this, coupled with his present hung-over state, meant he could barely walk to the car. He breathed a huge sigh, as he climbed into the motor, quickly glancing around to make sure he had not been seen by anyone he knew.

He sat still for a moment, and contemplated his life.

It seemed very strange that someone of nearly forty years old, particularly someone like Dave, a big boob man, had never been in a sex shop before, but he'd never really felt the need, always assuming that only dirty old men used such places. Was he now "that" kind of person? Over the years, he had bought soft porn magazines from the top shelves of newsagents, and also seen a few porno movies, but to actually purchase stronger material, seemed somehow dirty, and strangely alien to him.

After a few minutes, he regained some sort of composure, started the car, and headed back to the office, to finish off his work. Driving past the boarded up shops, a thought occurred to him, where was he going to keep his newly purchased books? His wife already thought he was some kind of pervert, and if she found them, he was in deep trouble. The office was also a no-go, he didn't have a drawer with a lock on it, and Joanne and Calvin were always rummaging around in his desk, when he was not there.

"Where? Must be somewhere," he thought. Then it came to him in a flash. A stroke of inspiration.

"The car, of course, it's the only place no-one else ever has access to."

It couldn't be the glove compartment, Janice sometimes kept things in there, it had to be a place that could be reached fairly easily, and yet completely secret.

"The boot, yeah, under the mat in the boot, on top of the spare wheel, that's the perfect place, no-one ever has cause to look in there, Janice rarely drives the car, at least not without me, and it gives me almost instant access."

He felt good now, and as he pulled up to the office, he carefully placed the brown bag in the glove compartment, and after turning off the engine, locked it.

Back in his office, he quickly finished the paperwork, and gave Joanne full instructions on their dispatch.

"Do you want another coffee?" Joanne asked.

"No thanks Love, it's nearly quarter to twelve, I'll just make one call to the courier company, arrange the collection, and then get going."

"OK, hope you feel better tomorrow," Joanne said, as he finally finished, and walked across the office towards the door.

"Thanks, I'm sure I will, perhaps get my head down this afternoon, and have a kip," he said as he left the office.

His mind was on one thing only, and that was opening up his parcel and ogling his mags. He'd already decided to go straight home, and have a drink later on in the day. Fortunately, most pubs were open all day, so getting a drink would not be a problem.

He arrived home, unlocked the glove compartment, and hurried into the house, running straight upstairs into the bedroom. Ripping frantically at the paper bag, he ceremoniously unwrapped each magazine from their cellophane covers, and rolled all the odd bits of paper into a large ball. He carefully placed each magazine on the bed, then went back downstairs, out into the back garden, and threw all the debris into the dustbin. He felt like a child on Christmas day morning, as he returned to the bedroom, took off his coat, and sat on the edge of the bed. He laid the three magazines out, and wondered which one to look at first. 'USA Brabusters' got the verdict, and he opened the book, the first model was called Chestie Moore, and she certainly was 'more chesty' than any woman Dave had seen before. Her breasts were so large and symmetrical, they looked man-made (which thanks to the silicon implant, they were) and Dave slowly turned page by page, studying each pose and position, whilst thinking he was actually with the woman. The ecstasy he felt made his groin tingle with lusty delight, and his penis grew so large, he actually believed it was about to burst out of his trousers. He put the book down on the bed, knelt on the floor, and undid his flies, letting his large member thrust out. With one hand he turned the pages, whilst gently rubbing the other up and down his shaft. He moaned gently as he reached his climax, he was very close to ejaculation.

"Not in here," he whispered, and getting up rather awkwardly, took the magazine with him, and walked hastily into the bathroom. He placed the book on the top of the cistern, and opened it on a page, with a girl with a 52" bust licking her own nipples.

"Oh, let me help you with those, Christie," he murmured. "Perhaps a nice pearl necklace would suit?"

It was too late, he started ejaculating, sending his sperm all over the back of the toilet seat and onto the cistern.

It seemed never ending, he squirmed in pleasure, and moaned in delight, as he pulled back and forth, shooting semen into the air.

When he'd finished, he stood still for a moment, staring down at "Olive Orbs" wishing the thrill had gone on forever.

Taking some toilet roll, he cleaned the seat, cistern and edge of the toilet bowl, before throwing it down the pan, and flushing it away. He washed his hands, still shaking with pleasure. He wanted to look at all the books, perhaps start again with a different magazine, but decided instead, it was time for a beer.

Taking the books downstairs into the lounge, he took a large manila envelope from the sideboard, and placed all three magazines inside it. "Let's go get pissed," he said loudly, feeling very pleased with himself, and picking up the envelope went out to his car. Opening the hatchback, he removed the back shelf, and lifted up the mat, which covered the spare wheel. The envelope fitted snugly into the recess, and he replaced the mat and the shelf.

"What a hiding place," he chuckled to himself. "Now for a beer." He suddenly realised he left his coat in the bedroom, with his keys in it. "Oh fucking hell, what a prat," he said as he saw that the front door was pulled shut. He walked through the side gate, and into the back garden, the kitchen window was half open.

"Thank fuck for that," he thought as he placed his arm into the kitchen and opened the window up fully. He was always telling his wife not to leave windows open, but she liked fresh air and did not pay any attention to his request, which in the circumstances was very fortunate indeed.

He soon got into the house, collected his coat and was on his way. He wondered if Bluffers wine bar was open at lunchtimes, but remembered that the barmaid had told him she only worked evenings, so he decided to head for the 'Baytree' in Locks Heath, as he knew that was open all day. He felt so good, he'd completely got over his hangover, and driving to the pub thought of all those lovely breasts he'd just seen. "Wanks for the mammaries" he sang loudly, laughing to himself about his clever play on words.

* * *

It was 1.15, when Sgt Crouch arrived at the Coach & Horses, and after parking outside on double yellow lines, walked into the pub.

"Good afternoon sir," he said to the barman as he got to the bar.

Immediately the barman knew he was a policeman.

"I'm Sergeant Crouch of the Southampton Constabulary, and I'm making enquiries about an incident that took place at St. Mary's Church last night. Can I ask you a few questions please?" He flashed his warrant card and continued. "A serious assault took place between 11.30 and midnight, and I wondered if you had any knowledge of it."

The young man behind the bar gave the policeman a look that said "Fuck off." He'd obviously had dealings with the police and hated them. "What fucking assault?" he snapped. "I was here until well after one, got loads of witnesses to prove it."

"No-one's accusing you of anything, I only asked a civil question, and a civil answer is all I required."

"Well, fuck your luck then, as I've said, don't know nothin' about no assault."

"I see, and can I ask your name please?"

"Phil Smith," came a very angry and poisonous reply.

Crouch took out a note pad, and started to write in it.

"OK, Mr Smith, let's just start with another question, could you tell me if any of the people in the bar now were also present last night"

"Look, I've already told you, I was here until one, what am I, their fucking keeper."

"Well, surely you know who was here, and who wasn't?"

"Can't remember. I only keep the bar, nothin' else."

"Alright, do you mind if I ask them myself?"

"Who cares what you do."

"Thank you for your help, sir," Crouch said sarcastically, and turned around to look at the motley assortment in the bar. Walking from table to table he asked the same question, and got the same set of answers.

"Don't know nothing about it."

"Wasn't here."

"Went home early."

As his boss had told him before he left the Police Station, he'd be lucky to get any help in a public house like this one. Replacing his note pad in his pocket, he walked to the door, turned and said with his best community smile: "Thank you gentlemen, you've been very ..." and left.

The pub had gone very quiet, but as the door closed, various shouts of "Pig" "Filth" and "Fuzz" burst forth.

"What's that all about, Phil?" asked a customer of the barman.

"I heard on the radio that some black chick was raped last night at the old churchyard, and obviously because we had a few strippers here, we're prime suspects. Fucking fuzz, got nothing better to do than harass pubs like this one. Who gives a shit if some stupid black bit got raped, typical police thinking, they ought to be out chasing real villains, but that's too fuckin' easy, ain't it?"

The customer completely agreed with his host, and the rest of the day was spent slagging off the police force.

Crouch grabbed a burger from 'Macdonalds' on his way back to the station, and ate it in the car

Sergeant Michael Crouch was a very likeable man. Born and raised in Southampton, he'd recently been promoted to Sergeant, got married, and bought his first house, not far from Dave Price's on the east side of the City. He looked up to and admired Quinn, but sometimes thought his methods of crime busting left a little to be desired. However he got results, and in these times of soaring crime, perhaps the end justified the means. If Crouch had one fault at all it was gluttony, he was hungry all the time, and ate continually throughout the day, much to the disgust of Quinn, who being a Northerner, believed in a right time and place for everything, and food was for eating at mealtimes.

Arriving back at the Civic Centre Police Station, Crouch informed his boss of the negative response he'd received from the Coach & Horses.

"Well Mike, I did warn you, it was always going to be a problem, and if the Phil Smith in the pub is the one I think he is, you'll never get any co-operation from a toenail like him."

"Oh, you know Phil Smith then?"

"Let's just say we've crossed swords before, and leave it at that, shall we?"

"Right-ho Guv, whatever you say."

"Mike, what have I told you before. I don't like being called guv, this ain't a TV police series, you know. If there's one thing gets right up my nose, it's calling all your superiors 'guv': got it?"

"Yes sir, sorry."

"Alright, no problem, let's drop it, and go back to our rape case, it's bloody impossible, no description, no witnesses. I reckon we'll have to put it on ice for a while, and hope the bastard strikes again. Don't like doing it, but we have no choice, he's bound to make a mistake, and when he does, we'll be there to nab him."

"OK," said Crouch, looking disappointed. "If you think it's the only way, it's just ..."

"I know, Mike, I know, but what other alternative do we really have?"

"True."

"Just put the file in pending. We've got to go to Winchester this afternoon, and interview that witness in the hit and run case, I'm sure he knows more than he's letting on."

"Do you want to go straight away sir," said Crouch, hoping there might just be time to get to the canteen for a sandwich.

"Yeah, suppose so," sighed Quinn as he put on his coat, "we'd just as well get it over with."

Crouch picked up a folder, and followed his boss out of the back of the Police Station and into the car park. Crouch unlocked the car and they both got in.

"Bloody hell, what you been eating in here?" screamed Quinn.

"Burgers sir, sorry!"

* * *

Before entering the 'Baytree', Dave had bought a local paper from the newsagent, and took it into the public house with him. Walking up to the bar he ordered.

"Pint of bitter please,"

"Certainly sir, which one?" said the chirpy young barman.

Dave looked up and down the hand-pumps and was pleasantly surprised at the number of real ales on sale.

"Mmm, let's see ..."

"Well, let me run through them. We've got Boddingtons, Bass, Ringwood, Strong Country, Directors and Whitbread Best."

It was obvious the young barman enjoyed his work, and Dave was reassured by his seemly good knowledge.

"Make it a Bass please, and I'll have a packet of dry roasted peanuts as well."

Taking his wares to an empty table by the window, Dave sat down and lit up a cigarette. "Nice little boozer, must use it more often," he thought to himself as he looked at his newspaper.

"GIRL RAPED IN ST MARY'S CHURCHYARD" read the headline,

"Shit, I was near there last night," Dave muttered somewhat perturbed. He read the whole article and was feeling slightly apprehensive, not with any sadness for the girl, but thinking himself lucky, that with all the police there must have been in the area, he'd driven home while completely paralytic.

"Christ, if I'd have been caught last night, they'd have locked me up and thrown away the key," he said under his breath. "Next week, I'll definitely book a taxi."

Taking a few swigs of beer, he then turned to the sports pages at the back of the paper, and read about the latest developments in the Southampton Football Stadium saga. Finishing his pint, he returned to the bar and ordered another.

"Same again?" asked 'Chirpy'.

"Yeah, that's fine, nice drop of beer," he replied.

Returning to his table, he opened his peanuts, and his mind again went back to his magazines. He decided there might just be time to get home before his wife, and have another session with Olive Orbs or Chestie Moore.

The bar was almost empty, and the young barman was going around the tables, emptying the ashtrays, and cleaning the tops.

"You like the old real ale?" he asked Dave.

"What? Sorry, I was miles away."

"I said, do you like the real ales, only we're having a small beer festival here next weekend, if you're interested."

"Oh, really, might try to get here then."

The barman smiled, and carried on walking around the bar, cleaning and wiping.

Another cigarette, a quick glance at the TV page, and Dave was ready to leave.

As he arrived at the house, he noticed the downstairs window was open. Someone was home. Getting out of the car, and opening the front door he shouted "Hi, anyone home?"

Sarah came out of the lounge, and faced him in the hall.

"What you doing home?" she asked, whilst screwing up her nose.

"I was about to ask you the same thing. I didn't think you finished school until 3.15," he replied.

"No, I don't usually, but my last two periods were revision, so I've brought it home to do."

"Oh, I see."

"How come you're home early then?"

"I didn't feel too good, so I took the afternoon off."

"I'm not surprised after the amount you obviously drank last night," she snapped, and returned to the lounge.

Dave followed her. "Oh, come on, be fair, I get enough stick from your mother, without having you rub it in, as well."

"Sorry for breathing," she moaned, returning to a pile of books on the dining room table.

"Want a cup of coffee?" he meekly asked.

"No thanks, I've just had one."

She looked up at him, shook her head, and immersed herself in her revision.

Dave hung up his coat, he didn't want to get too close, in case she smelt the beer on his breath.

"Think I'll have a shower, might make me feel a bit better," he said and disappeared upstairs, thankful that she hadn't come home earlier.

The next few days were fairly uneventful, although Janice had taken to sleeping in the spare room, and only spoke to Dave when it was absolutely necessary.

The books stayed in the boot of the car, but he had not stopped thinking about them, praying for a chance to have another look.

On Saturday, Janice had told Dave she needed time to decide what was best for all concerned, but agreed that they should show a united front for the present, and not make any rash decisions.

On Sunday afternoon, Sarah was out, as usual and Janice had announced she was going to see her parents.

"Wanna come with me?" she asked, not sounding as if she really wanted him to.

"No thanks love, think I'll watch the football on the telly, but perhaps we could go out for a drink tonight."

"Maybe, see how I feel," she said as she pulled on a thick jumper, and left.

Dave knew she'd be gone for a couple of hours. She always was when she visited her mother.

He stood by the front window, and watched her walk off, round the end of the road, and out of sight. Waiting 10 minutes, he went to his car, opened the boot, and took out the envelope. As he turned, he noticed his next door neighbour, Peter Mellor, working in the garden.

"Hello Dave, haven't seen you lately, what's occurring?" he inquired, leaning on his spade, glad of a reason to stop.

"Oh, hi ya, Peter, you gave me a start, how's things with you?"

"Usual, you know, bit of this, bit of that. Thought it was about time I tried to do something with the flowerbeds."

"Yeah, I think I need to look at mine, just don't seem to have the time to get round to it."

He could see Peter was curious about the envelope he was holding.

"Some work that needs finishing, hate to bring it home, but you know how it is," he said pointing to the package.

Dave felt embarrassed, and could feel the colour coming to his cheeks. "Still, must go, catch you later, give my love to Louise."

"Will do, perhaps now the summer's coming, you and Janice could come round for a barbecue or something?"

"Yeah, love to, we'll arrange it."

Dave slammed the hatchback door closed, and walked back into the house. He sighed, wiped his brow and muttered, "Nosey bloody Parker, just like his wife," as he ran upstairs.

Carefully he opened the package and took out his three books, almost straight away his breathing had become heavy, and he felt that lovely feeling in his groin, causing an almost instant erection. He hadn't even looked at the mags, but in anticipation, was aroused.

He opened the magazine called '50+' and was certainly not disappointed. One girl, sitting by a pool, had boobs so large that he couldn't imagine a brassiere large enough to accommodate them. He unzipped his flies, and held his member in his hand. He didn't need to stroke it, such was the eroticism of the pictures that he felt ejaculation was very close. He didn't want to get up, in fact he didn't want to come yet, he just wanted to keep that moment with him for a while longer. Unfortunately, his penis did not share his wish, and it started shooting white liquid over the magazine.

"Oh no, fuck it," he yelled as he ran from the bedroom, just in time to deposit the last few drops into the toilet pan.

"Why's it always so quick?" he questioned. "I must be sex starved," he answered himself, as he returned to the bedroom, with a piece of toilet tissue, for the purpose of cleaning up the mess. Most of the semen was on the opened page of the book, with only a few splats on the bed quilt cover. He wiped the magazine clean, and flushed the tissue away in the lavatory.

He sat on the bed, quietly looking through all the mags, stopping at certain pages which he found particularly erotic.

"Where do you find women like these?" he asked himself reflectively. "Me as Joe Public, where could I find tits like this? This is all well and good, but I must have the real thing. Wanking's great, but I need a woman, and I need one soon."

He thought of writing to the magazine, asking for addresses, he'd pay, he didn't mind, surely these girls were on the game anyway.

Surely they did it for a living. His mind ran over great plans. "Pretend you're a photographer," an inner voice was saying. Suddenly his thoughts turned to the young barmaid he'd met in Bluffers, the busty young girl who worked evenings. Tonight, that's where to go, play it right, find out where she lives, where she works, it was easy, just chat her up, she was pretty unattractive, surely she'd like to go out with him. The plan was evolving, when he thought he heard a noise at the front door.

"Oh fuck, not Janice. Please dear God, not her."

He quickly replaced all the magazines in the envelope, and hid it in the bottom of his wardrobe. Cagily walking to the top of the stairs, he sighed, no one there, just the wind rattling the lock.

He hurried back to the wardrobe, collected the envelope, and took it straight downstairs, and hid it in his car.

He went back inside the house, into the lounge, turned on the TV, and flopped out on the sofa. That was too close for comfort, caught wanking in the bedroom would definitely earn him a red card. He settled back, and watched the football, awaiting the return of his wife.

When Janice returned at 5.30, Dave was asleep on the settee. She stopped, and looked down at the man she had married. Receding hairline, red blotchy face, unshaven and about 2 stone overweight. What a sorry sight, what did she ever see in him, he smoked like a trooper, drank like a fish, and farted like an incontinent old man on a diet of syrup of figs, and prune juice. He made her feel quite sick.

Dave stirred and opened first one eye, then the other.

"Oh, hello Love, how's your folks?" he croaked, just before having a coughing fit. When he finished, he cleared his throat of phlegm, and swallowed it.

"Finished have we?" she asked.

"Yeah, sorry. I think I smoke too much," he said, wiping the sleeve of his shirt across his nose.

"THINK? I know you smoke and drink too much."

"I'll try to cut down."

"Yeah, and I'm going to be a super-model." she snapped.

"Anyway, how's your mum and dad?" he asked again.

"They're fine. They've just booked a holiday and have let me have some brochures."

"That's nice, where do you fancy going this year?"

"I fancy going to Majorca," she said, emphasising the 'I'.

He swung his legs around, and placed them onto the floor.

"What? You thinking of taking a holiday without me?"

"I'm not thinking of it, that's exactly what I intend to do."

"Come on, Janice, aren't you taking this all a bit too far, I mean, OK, we've had our differences, but surely by July or August, things would have sorted themselves out?"

"I sometimes think you live in another world, your own little fantasy world, you haven't heard a word I've been saying in the past few weeks, have you?"

"'Course I have, but I thought we'd try again."

"And what, may I ask, Mr Einstein, gave you that impression?"

"Oh, forget it, you're obviously in one of your moods, wrong time of the month, is it?"

"You stupid bastard, it has nothing to do with that. Surely you realise we're going nowhere fast, and that something has to change, surely even you're not that thick?"

"Let me get this straight," he said, lighting up a cigarette, "You're saying that it's completely over between us, no way back?"

She moved across the room and sat next to him on the settee, placing a hand on his knee.

"Dave, when we got married, I dunno, I sorta thought things would be different, you know, better, we had a great time courting, then we got married, and it seemed ..."

"There's someone else, isn't there?" he interrupted. "You've got another bloke."

"Now you are in the realms of fantasy. Of course I haven't got another bloke, bloody hell, sometimes you're so daft, it's unbelievable. Me? With another bloke? That's a laugh."

Dave was so stunned by the whole conversation, he couldn't think straight. He turned to Janice, with tears welling up in his eyes.

"Janice, I love you, you know that. I don't know what I'd do if you ever left me," he sobbed. "Please let's talk it through, surely I deserve that at least?"

"Of course you do, isn't that what we're doing? Talking it through, I think I need some space, that's all."

Dave got up, rubbed his eyes, and continued softly. "I don't understand what you want from me."

She was starting to feel sorry for him, perhaps she had been a little harsh, perhaps she should give it another shot. She looked at him, and moved closer, and he put his head on her shoulder.

"Anything you want, anyway you want to play it, that's fine, I'll do anything you want, only let's give it one more try," he whispered into her ear, as he put his arms around her, and hugged her tightly. She was hooked.

"OK, you're right, let's try and sort this out like adults, and see how it goes."

"You won't regret it, I promise, you'll see I was right."

"OK, but please let go, you're choking me. Want a coffee?"

"Yes please, shall I make it?"

"No it's OK, I'll do it," she went to the doorway and stopped, "No Sarah yet?" she asked.

"No, she hasn't come home or phoned."

"Oh well, never mind."

Janice went into the kitchen, and Dave could hear her making the coffee.

"Christ, that was close. When I go, it will be on my terms and not hers," he thought to himself, and although he really was upset about the whole matter, he felt he had to put on a brave face.

Janice returned with the coffees, and they spent the rest of the afternoon discussing holidays. They agreed on Majorca, and set a date in June.

"What time do you want to go out tonight?" Dave asked.

"Early, I think, we've got work in the morning, and I don't want a late night."

"Great, what shall we do about food?"

"I'll do us some sandwiches and a few chips, if you like, and we'll go out about sevenish. Yeah?"

"OK. Want me to do anything?"

"No, I'll do them in a minute, you sit here," she said, and returned to the kitchen.

Dave sat staring at the television screen, but not watching it, his mind drifted to the barmaid. Whether it was the amount of alcohol he'd consumed lately, or his age, was uncertain, but he couldn't keep his mind on any one thing for long, and seemed to have the memory retention of an amoeba. Things just floated in and out of his mind, and he couldn't seem to concentrate at all. Tuna sandwiches and chips were served up by Janice, and after their consumption, they both went to the bedroom and changed. Dave carefully surveyed the area around the bed where he'd earlier ejaculated, and was relieved to notice that there were no visible stains.

They left the house, just after seven, and went straight to Bluffers, parking right outside the entrance.

Inside, Janice sat down in an alcove, and Dave went to the bar. They were the only two people in the place.

"Good evening, sir, what's your pleasure?" asked the polite, and smartly dressed young barman.

"Not you again," Dave thought. "Bloody little shirt lifter."

"Two gin and tonics please," he said.

The barman made up the drinks. "Would you like ice and a slice?" he politely asked.

"Obviously," Dave rudely snapped, then calmed a little.

"Tell me," he said quietly. "Where's Helen tonight?"

"She doesn't start until seven thirty on Sundays, I'm sure she'll be in soon. Anything else I can get you?"

"No, that's all thanks."

"That'll be three pounds forty please."

Dave handed over a five pound note, waited for his change, then took the drinks back to his wife.

"I didn't think you liked this place," she said as he sat down.

"It doesn't do a decent pint, but it's alright for a quiet drink, and it's handy for us, isn't it?" he replied, his eyes firmly fixed on the bar area.

They didn't speak for the next ten minutes, until Janice, finally looked up and said, "Dave, is everything all right with you, you seemed to have changed so much in the past few weeks."

"Well, I think it's the job that's getting me down, it's so boring, and with the amount of time I spend at work, it starts to get to you after a while."

"Perhaps I'm to blame as well, we don't talk enough, I never know what's going on in that mind of yours, you keep it locked up."

"Look, I made you a promise that things will get better, and I'm sure they will, just give it a little time ...please."

"It's just that after the other night, you were so rough, that's not like you, you're not going through some sort of mid-life crisis, are you?" she joked.

Dave was starting to get annoyed, why wouldn't she let it go, always asking stupid questions, why didn't she just shut the fuck up? He took out his cigarettes and lit one up. Just then the door opened, and Helen walked in, went over to the coat-pegs, hung up her coat, and went behind the bar. She really was a plain girl, and did nothing to make her appearance even marginally better. How she ever got the bar job in the first place was a mystery, as wine bars generally only employ attractive staff.

All of her life had been a misery, because of the size of her bust and bottom. She'd been ridiculed at school, and although quite intelligent, had become withdrawn and shy, and only took the barmaid's job at the insistence of her mother, who felt that it might in some way bring her out of herself. It did not do this, and she became more and more conscious of her size and weight, as time went on.

Dave was transfixed by her presence, his eyes almost on stalks, like some character from a cartoon. He immediately finished his drink. "Want another?" he asked Janice, who had looked around to see what he was staring at.

"God, you're really incredible, you're old enough to be her father," she said with a mocking laugh.

"What?" he snapped, "give me some credit, please."

"Look, when you come out with me, at least pretend you're enjoying yourself."

"I am enjoying myself. Christ I only asked if you wanted another drink, let's not row again."

"I'm not rowing, can't you take a joke?"

"Yeah, well, alright then." Dave said like a spoilt child.

"God, you're so touchy, truth hurts, does it?"

Dave stood up with his glass, and waited for Janice to finish. Taking both glasses, he strolled to the bar.

"Hello Helen, how are you?" Dave asked in a silly voice.

"I'm fine thanks," she answered, trying to remember where she'd met this man before, and how he knew her name. "What can I get you?"

Dave noticed the puzzled and surprised look on her face, and tried to remind her. "I'm Dave Price, I came in on the opening night, you obviously don't remember me."

She didn't remember him at all, but she knew the look alright. She'd seen it many times on dirty old men, and didn't like it. He was talking to her, but looking at her boobs. She walked to the bar's edge, covering her breasts by folding her arms and said, trying to smile, "Oh yeah, I know, sorry it's just a little dark in here, and my eyesight's not so good. What can I get you?"

"A nice long suck on your nipples, please," was what he wanted to say.

She asked again.

"Oh ... umm, two gin and tonics please," he finally blurted.

"Certainly sir, with ice and lemon?"

"Yes please."

She took two clean glasses from under the bar, and duly filled them from the optics.

"Where do you work in the day?" Dave politely asked.

"In Southampton, near the Civic Centre. Why?"

"Just curious, that's all. What do you do?"

"I'm an audio typist for an insurance company," she replied cagily, she could feel her cheeks turning red.

"Oh, that's interesting. I work in Southampton as well, near the docks, for a chandlery company."

"Really," she said. "That'll be three pounds forty please."

It would have been obvious to anyone with even half a brain that she was not in the least bit interested, but not to Dave. He held the money out to her in his hand, and as she took it from him, he tried to keep hold, squeezing her hand tightly. She pulled away, with a look of disdain and disgust, and walked to the till.

Dave stayed at the bar, wanting to continue their conversation, but after ringing the amount on the till, she went to the end of the bar, and started to talk to her young colleague.

Dave reluctantly picked up the drinks, and returned to his wife.

"How is she?" Janice asked sarcastically, grinning sweetly, putting her head between her hands, "Well, I trust?"

"I was only being polite, nothing wrong with that, surely?"

"Of course not Darling, just not like you, that's all."

"What is this? Have a go at Dave week? I was only passing the time of day with her, nothing else."

"Forget it," Janice said as she poured the tonic into her gin and took a large swig. "I think we ought to go after this one, don't want a late night, do we?" she added, rhetorically.

"OK, that's fine by me, I think I'll have a soak in the bath when we get in, there's not much on telly anyway."

They spent the next few minutes in silence, as Dave tried desperately to stop staring at the bar, but the draw of those huge breasts was irresistible.

Janice finished her drink, and patiently waited for Dave to do the same. "You nearly ready?" she asked.

"Yeah, just pop to the loo first," he replied, and leapt from his seat, as if he had been dying to go for hours.

Helen saw him get up, and assumed he was coming to get another drink.

"Do me a favour, Ben," she said to her young assistant, "serve him, will you?"

"Sure, is there a problem, I thought he knew you?"

"He knows my name, that's all."

Dave made a beeline for the bar, then stopped.

"Where's the toilet?" he asked, smiling a sickly grin in Helen's direction, whilst winking.

"Down the side of the bar," replied the barman, and Dave walked slowly along the bar, and into a door marked 'Guys'.

"False alarm," laughed Ben as he walked back to Helen.

"He gives me the creeps, such horrible piggy eyes," she said with a shudder, "he's just a dirty old man."

Ben laughed again, it was the most Helen had said to him since she'd started working there.

Dave came out of the toilet, dawdled a bit by the bar, and returned to his wife, in the alcove.

"Sure you don't want one for the road?" he asked, "Perhaps a quickie, or something?"

"No thanks, we've got plenty of booze at home, if you're desperate, and anyway, I thought you were going to cut down?"

Dave's face dropped. "Miserable old cow," he thought as he finished his drink, got up, and walked with his wife to the exit. "Goodnight, thanks a lot," he shouted as he held the door open for Janice.

"Thank you sir, please come again," said Ben, as Helen looked away, pretending to be busy with bar cleaning.

"I'd come again, and again, if I had her tits in my mouth, you little poofter," was the reply that ran through his mind.

"Yeah, see you."

When they got in the car, Dave pushed in a cassette, and turned the music up loud. " ... The Dancing Queen ..." by Abba was the selection that came bursting from the cheap in-door speakers.

"Christ Dave, haven't you got anything more modern?" shouted Janice, over the noise.

Dave was oblivious. Abba's music, and his dirty thoughts, what a delicious combination.

When they arrived home, all the lights were on.

"Oh good, Sarah's home," said Janice as she climbed out of the car.

"Yeah, brilliant," Dave mumbled as he followed his wife to their front door.

Opening it, Janice called out to her daughter. "Coowee ...we're home," she yelled. A voice from upstairs shouted back, "In my room, doing some revision."

"OK Love."

Dave went straight into the lounge, and immediately opened

the cocktail cabinet.

"Want one?" he asked, as he poured himself a very large gin.

Janice entered the room and tutted.

"Only a small one, and the same for you."

"Yeah, Yeah. I know, I'll make this one last all night."

He turned on the television, and walked to the kitchen with the two glasses, filling them with ice from the freezer, and tonic he took from a bottle in the fridge. He flopped on the sofa, and lit up a cigarette.

Janice was not too happy with him, if this was cutting down on drinking and smoking, "Oh what the hell, no time for another round of arguments, it just wasn't worth it."

Dave finished his drink and announced he was going to have a bath. He ran the bath, and climbed into the bubbles. He loved to let his willy float on the top of the water, and lather it with soap. His mind was wandering.

"Wonder if Helen's got little pink nipples like that stripper, or great big dark red ones. Big ones, it must be, huge great papillas, set on a dark red aureola, something to get your teeth round."

For the second time that day, he was getting an erection.

"Better not wank in the bath, I've forgotten to lock the door, and young Sarah might come in. Well? So what? It's my fucking house, and I'll do what I like."

The thought then dawned on him that it was not his house, and if Janice came in, and saw him unloading his stash, he'd be in big trouble. The very thought made his penis go soft, like a little pickled gherkin. "Jerking me gherkin, that's it," he laughed, and started to sing a silly little song: "Jerking me gherkin, and pulling me pud, makes me feel happy, makes me feel good."

"You alright?" Janice shouted from the bottom of the stairs. He froze, he'd completely forgotten where he was.

"Yeah, sorry, I'm fine."

Janice stood and listened for a while, shook her head, and returned to the lounge. "You're not all there, David Price, not all there at all."

Dave quickly finished his ablutions, climbed from the bath, and dried himself off. He put on his dressing-gown, and slowly went down to the lounge. Janice was watching TV, and glanced at him as he sat down next to her.

"Any good?" he said nodding at the television.

"Don't know, it's only just started," she replied.

"Perhaps we should have an early night, you can watch the rest of this in bed."

"Yeah, OK, but I must have a shower first though."

Dave felt pleased, if Janice was going to watch the TV in bed, it meant she would be sleeping with him tonight, as the spare room did not have a television in it.

Janice got up, and announced she was going to have her shower, and left the room. Dave lit up a cigarette, his mind still on Helen. Ten minutes later, he heard Janice come out of the bathroom, and shout from the upstairs landing, "I'm finished now, you coming up?"

"Yeah, OK. I'll just lock up."

He turned off the TV, switched off the lounge lights, and bolted the front door, before retiring to the bedroom.

Janice was sitting at the dressing table, brushing her hair, she was still an attractive woman, and Dave watched her as he disrobed. After brushing his teeth, he got into bed.

"Nearly ready?" he asked, implying more than he'd said.

"Just getting all the knots out," she replied. Once finished, she climbed into bed, and turned over facing away from him. "I don't think we'll bother with the telly," she sighed, "I'm totally knackered."

Dave rolled over, and put his arm around her, gently kissing her shoulders. Janice shuddered, it was not going to be easy, her feelings ran deep.

"Turn off the light, Dave, and let's have that early night we promised ourselves."

Dave just mumbled something, leant across his bedside cabinet, and switched off the light.

"Give us a cuddle," he said, when he really meant "How about a bonk? My bishop's ready and willing."

Janice did not reply, pretending to be asleep.

"Sod you then," Dave thought and started to doze himself.

The massive boob brigade were out in force, Olive Orbs,

Chestie Moore *et al*, each one, oiled up and ready for pleasure. It was going to be a long hard night.

* * *

Monday morning found the two police officers talking about the 'Umbala' case.

"I'm sure there's a connection between the attempted rape and the Coach & Horses, sir," said Sgt Crouch to his less than interested boss.

"Could be Mike, but with no real witnesses, and no positive I.D. it's a tough one. I think we should talk to the woman again and see if we missed anything."

"Agreed, but in her statement, Miss Umbala stated that our suspect stunk of beer and he was quite possibly in a pub beforehand, and as the Coach & Horses is just round the road from the churchyard, it's ..."

"Yes, yes I know all that," Quinn interrupted, "and I take your point, but we've got a hundred and one other cases to crack, and if I know our man, I'm sure he's going to strike again."

"But surely sir, we should be doing preventative police work and not just hoping he's going to rape again."

Quinn laughed, "Oh Mike, you've got so much to learn."

* * *

As a girl was pressing her breast into Dave's face, the ever faithful alarm burst into life, with the disgustingly friendly D.J. trying his best to sound happy. Dave rolled over, and realised that Janice had obviously already got up.

"Strange," he thought, as he sat up, rubbed his eyes and let them become acclimatised to the beams of light that were shining through the curtains. He glanced at his surroundings, subconsciously fingering his erect penis with one hand, whilst picking his nose with the other. Janice entered the room with a cup of coffee and Dave stopped, putting both arms in front of him on the bed quilt.

"Morning," he said, coughing, "You're up early."

"Yeah, it's great, having an early night was just what I needed."

"Bollocks, I've got what you need, right here under the quilt. It's big, it's hard and it's beautiful. How about kissing the bishop?" he mused. Dave, like most men, always got an erection in the morning, and no matter how many times it happened, it never ceased to amaze and please him.

"There we are," Janice said as she put his coffee down on the bedside cabinet. "What you thinking about?"

"Thanks," he smiled, "fancy a little cuddle now?"

"No, I can't, I've got to get Sarah up and ready for school."

Dave sighed, and picked up his coffee.

After a couple of slices of toast, and another coffee, Dave finished dressing and was ready for work. It was only just eight thirty, and Janice had barely spoken two more words to him.

"Right, I'm off to work then," he shouted from the downstairs hall, to Janice, who was somewhere upstairs.

"OK. Have a good day, and see you tonight."

"Sure thing, should be home normal time. Bye love."

"Bye."

Getting into the car, he began his search for a tape to play on his trek into the office. 'Simply Red' was the choice of the day and Dave loved them. On his way to work, he sang his heart out, causing all the other road users who noticed him to point and nod. "I'd love to be a pop star, all those women after you, Christ, most of them are fucking ugly, but they can pull all sorts of pretty girls." The weather had improved immeasurably, and at last it seemed as if the harsh bite of winter had vanished.

At the office he noticed a marked upturn in the volume of work he was handling.

The lovely Joanne had made him his coffee, he'd just lit up his first cigarette of the day, and he was sitting at his desk wading through the morning's mail. He had already decided to go into the city centre at lunchtime, and see if he could accidentally bump into barmaid Helen. There were three large insurance offices in Southampton, and Dave had reasoned that she must work for one of them.

Calvin arrived just before ten, and after a few minutes in his own office, came out to Dave and said: "You remember our conversation of last week, when I asked you to compile a list of transactions, so that we could monitor the situation?"

"Aaa, yes ..." said Dave hesitatingly.

"Well? Have you got it?"

"Oh I'm sorry John, but the work's got so much busier recently, that I completely forgot."

"It's good that the business is picking up, but for your own sake, as much as mine, I still need a report."

"OK. No problem. I'll definitely do it today."

"Fine" said Calvin, and returned to his office.

"Bloody lazy bastard, wouldn't hurt you to get off your backside for once, and see how the other half lives."

Dave opened up some new files, and turned to his daybook to enumerate them with reference numbers. "If it's a list the bastard wants, then so be it. Surely I've got enough other crap to do around here, without him creating even more."

His mind was in hyperdrive, as the anger swelled up inside him. He thumbed back through the previous weeks work, and unfortunately, it was a very short list of jobs. Dave thought of ways of lengthening it, perhaps put some of today's work into the end of last week? Much too risky. If Calvin caught him doing it, there would be trouble. It was no good. No matter how he juggled the figures, he could not even cover his salary.

"What the fuck" he pushed the pad to one side and went about his current work. The old adage that time flies by when you're busy was certainly true. He glanced at his watch, and was pleasantly surprised to find it was almost midday.

"I think I'll have an early lunch," he said to Joanne, "although I've got to go to the Customs again, so I might be a little late getting back."

"OK," she replied, without looking up from her typewriter, although, in truth, she didn't care if he never came back.

Dave drove straight to the centre of Southampton, and parked in the multi-storey car park. Quickly getting a ticket, he hurried to the Civic Centre, getting there just before twelve. He decided to wait in a convenient spot, overlooking the three large insurance buildings, in the hope that he would see Helen going to lunch. He realised that it was a long shot, because there were hundreds of smaller insurance companies, and she might not work for one of the big three. Also, she might take a later lunch, in which case he would return at one o'clock and check again. He stood in a shop doorway and waited.

At ten past twelve, all three office entrances were busy. People were rushing into the street and disappearing in every direction. After another ten minutes, the throng had become a trickle, and Dave assumed Helen was having a later lunch. He'd come back at one. He cut through the 'Marlands' shopping mall, and made his way down the High Street to the 'Judges Lodge' public house. This was a smart town pub which would be described by most CAMRA* members as a 'Right royal plastic fizz palace'.

Dave walked in, and up to the bar. The place was full of 'Grey Suits', all with their half of bitter and roast beef sandwiches, busily talking of the deals they had made that day.

"A pint of bitter please," Dave said to a rather scruffily dressed woman behind the bar.

The beer arrived, and Dave took a sip as he handed over some money. It was awful. A typical 'Eurofizz' with an OG just above water. If this brew had ever seen a hop, it was certainly not the plant, Humulus lupulus, (which gives beer its bitter flavour) but more likely the frog variety. Dave quickly lit up a cigarette to disguise the taste, and walked over to a stool by the window. He sat gazing through the net curtains, down the little alleyway, which ran from the High Street to the public house.

He started to daydream, when he saw 'his' Helen walking alone down the alley towards the main road. He could hardly believe his eyes, (or his luck), and quickly extinguishing his cigarette, he ran from the pub and into the cutway.

"Helen, hey Helen, wait up a minute," he shouted.

Helen stopped and looked over her shoulder. She was smartly dressed in a two-piece suit, which looked about two sizes too small.

Dave realised then that it was not only her breasts that were enormous, she was bordering on fat, and her legs thrust upwards into her skirt, like two massive tree trunks.

He caught up to her. "Fancy meeting you here," he said cheerfully.

"Hello" she replied, with a puzzled look, quickly trying to put a name to the face. Then she realised, it was 'old piggy eyes' himself. "Where the hell had he sprung from?" she thought to herself.

"Remember me? Dave Price, I was in the wine bar last night."
"Oh yes," she said, her face dropping.

"How about a drink or something? I've just got one in," he continued, pointing back to the pub.

"Er ...no thanks," she stumbled on the words, trying to think of a good reason why she couldn't have a drink, "I only get half an hour for my lunch, and I promised to get some tights for my mum from British Home Stores.

"Oh, that's a pity. Perhaps another time then? Maybe I could call you?"

"No!" she snapped abruptly, "I'm not allowed personal calls at the office."

She carried on walking, but he followed, moving in front.

"Well, how about if we arrange a meeting now, I'm free most lunchtimes, you know."

"No thanks, I'd rather not." She increased her pace, and started to walk across the High Street precinct, by now almost running.

Dave wouldn't give up, and gave chase. "Well, how about a little drink one night after work, I could pick you up and give you a lift home, how's that?"

"Look, I'm sorry, but I don't want a drink with you. I work at the wine bar several evenings a week, and when I'm not, I have to do my college revision."

"Surely, you could miss your revision one night, Christ it's only a drink," he said, grabbing hold of her arm, as she was about to go into BHS.

"Please let go, you're hurting me," she pleaded, as she looked around for someone to help her.

"I'm sorry," Dave mumbled as she disappeared into the shop, leaving him slightly bemused on the pavement, amidst the bustle of the lunchtime rush. "I'm sorry," he shouted again, but she didn't hear him. He turned, shaking his head, "Bloody little tart," he said, but deep inside felt a strange loneliness, as if he was the first male ever to be rejected by a female, as if it had some deeper significance. Was he going over the edge? Or had he already started on a slow downward spiral to insanity? He slowly plodded up the High Street and back to his car, he couldn't pull a stripper, he couldn't pull a stupid young fat girl, his wife refused to have sex with him. Was it him?

"Was it fuck, pull yourself together, there's plenty more fish in the sea, it'll work itself out, you'll see, it'll all be fine."

As he arrived at his car, he suddenly remembered he still had to go to the Customs House, he glanced at his watch, 12.42.

At Customs, his documents were certified in a couple of minutes, (obviously the Customs Officer wanted to get to lunch) and he decided a few more beers were definitely in order. He couldn't go to the Slug and Toad, in case Old Calvin saw his car, so he made straight for the Coach & Horses.

Inside the pub were the usual crowd, most of them already three parts intoxicated, and just getting into their stride. He drank two pints of bitter in rapid succession, and returned to the office.

"Any messages, gorgeous?" he said to Joanne as he came through the door.

"None," she replied with her usual 'wanker' look, "but I'm glad you're back, I want to pop up town, so you can cover the phones for a while."

"Oh, alright, where's Calvin?"

"Gone to lunch with a client," she said as she put on her coat, "See you later."

Dave sat at his desk, and realised he'd done most of his work in the morning. He sighed, and went into the kitchen area and made himself a cup of coffee.

"Should of brought my mags in, could of had a wank in the sink," he surmised.

The afternoon dragged, and he spent most of his time watching the clock. Calvin returned just after three, and again asked for the list, and Dave promised to let him have it on Tuesday morning. The problem still existed, how to make the last week's work look better than it was. He decided to back date that morning's work, into the previous week, and hope that he might salvage some decent figures from the exercise.

Finally, it was time to leave, and Dave drove straight home. Janice was still cool with him, but at least they were talking, although she made it quite clear that sex was still out of the question. When they went to bed, he rolled over onto his side, and went back to his 'girls'.

At about eleven on Tuesday morning, Dave had finally finished his list. He'd doctored it so much, in fact, it actually looked quite reasonable. He marched into Calvin's office with a certain cockiness. Calvin put on his reading glasses, moved his head slowly from side to side, and sternly said:

"As I suspected, this makes pretty grim reading, doesn't it Dave?"

Dave was clearly shaken. "Um ..., well I, I didn't think they were too bad, when you consider the economic climate," he stuttered.

"Perhaps not, maybe I'm being a little harsh."

"I think so, I've already done a lot of work this week, and I know the figures will get better."

"OK, fair comment, let's wait and see how it goes this week, and I'll look forward to the next list."

Dave left the office, cursing under his breath. "You fucking spunkbubble, how you ever started your own company, I'll never know."

He sat at his desk, he would have to remove Monday's work from last week, and reinstate it into this. But even he was not stupid enough to think that he could keep on doing this week in, and week out. Fortunately, the work load did seem to be increasing, so it should all even itself out in the end.

The rest of the day was uneventful. He didn't even bother to have a drink at lunchtime, and left the office exactly at five o'clock.

At home, nothing had changed, he had a meal, watched a little television, had a wash, and then went to bed.

Something strange was going on, he couldn't put his finger on it, but there was an atmosphere at home that he did not like. Sarah waltzed in, had a bite to eat, and went out, stating she would not he home again that evening, because she was staying at a friend's house. Janice hardly spoke two words to him, and he felt like a stranger in his own home. Every time he tried to broach the subject of sex, Janice just stated that she needed a little mote time.

"No matter," he thought, "tomorrow's stripper night," then gently fell asleep, to dream his lovely dreams.

He woke up on Wednesday morning, just before the alarm, unsure whether it was due to the contents of his dream, or just to the early morning 'rise', that he had an enormous erection. Rolling over to his wife, he gently kissed her on her back. She turned over to face him, this was nice, it was gentle, and Janice liked it. He put his hand between her legs, and gently caressed her soft hairy mound. She wanted to stop him, but felt honour bound in a marital way, to let him continue. If they were to have any chance at all of making a go of their marriage, she realised she could not keep him at arm's length forever.

He'd soon entered her and they made love, in an almost touching, loving way, which to Janice seemed very civilised.

"Mmm." she murmured, "That was nice."

"Yes, I told you it would be OK," he lied, pretending that he'd enjoyed it as much as she had. However, nothing was further from the truth. He'd been so bored that the only way he'd managed it at all was to keep thinking of his dream, and a certain black girl, with huge 'organ-stop' nipples, and shiny ebony skin.

He pulled out slowly, and rolled back onto his side of the bed.

"Dave, I know it's not been exactly great for you lately, but gently, gently to start with, and we'll see where we go from there. OK?"

"Sure, it's fine by me, I want the marriage to work, as much as anyone," he answered.

"I'll make you a nice breakfast, fancy a fry-up?"

"Yeah, OK, but how about some coffee first, eh?"

"'Course, I'll have a quick wash and get you one right away."

She jumped from the bed and disappeared, going straight into the bathroom.

Dave lay on his back, trying to make faces out of the artex patterns in the ceiling.

Hopefully life would get back to some sort of normality, and he laid there, thinking of the night ahead. Stripper night at the Coach & Horses.

Chapter 4

It could be easily said,
that the life he had led,
was one where he'd stayed on the shelf,
but it could also be stated,
and some might say fated,
that he had no one to blame but himself.

When Dave arrived home on Wednesday evening, he was in a great mood. The work load had continued to increase, and his figures for the week were now starting to look quite encouraging. He'd had a few beers at lunchtime in the Slug, but had made a special effort to remain reasonably sober for his evening out. Walking into the hallway, he took off his coat and shouted:

"Evening Love, what's for tea?"

"Steak and chips," came the reply from the kitchen, "ready in five minutes."

"Magic, I'm starving."

He walked into the kitchen, and kissed Janice on the back of her head.

"Good day?" she asked.

"Yeah, not bad, work's picking up."

"I'm pleased, go into the lounge, and I'll be in shortly."

"OK. How's your day been?" he said as he left the kitchen.

"Quiet, you know, same as usual."

The television was on, and he sat down and started watching the early evening news. Janice entered the room, and stood between him and the television. "You haven't mentioned it, but I assume you're going to snooker tonight," she said in a slightly offhand manner.

"Yes, if that's alright with you."

"No, I don't mind at all, but don't come home drunk, will you? Remember your promise."

"Of course I will, I'll have a few, and no more."

"Good. If you lost your licence, you'd be in real trouble."

"OK, point taken. If, and I mean if, I have over the limit, I'll get a taxi home, and take the train to work tomorrow."

"Why don't you get a lift home from the mates you're playing snooker with?"

"Not possible, they both live the other side of Southampton."

"Really? Where?"

"In Totton, why?"

"No reason, it's just that you've never mentioned who you play with, that's all."

"Just a couple of lads from the paint company next door, why the sudden interest?"

"I wasn't aware you were friendly with ..."

"Hang on," he interrupted, "what is this one hundred and one questions? I know a couple of drivers from the office next door to mine. I met them in the pub, their names are Jack and Ron, and they invited me to a game of snooker, that's all, there is no more."

"Alright, keep your shirt on, I was only interested."

"Well, if you're that worried, I won't go, how's that?"

"No, no, I wouldn't dream of depriving you of your night out, but don't get drunk."

"Yeah, you've said that already, have I got time to change?"

"Suppose so, d'you want a drink?"

"Yes please, whatever you're having."

Dave went upstairs, and Janice started to prepare two very weak gin and tonics. She had a funny, uneasy feeling about it all, as if something didn't quite fit. "What the hell," she mumbled, after putting the drinks on the coffee table, and returning to the kitchen, she turned over the steaks. They were just about ready.

Dave quickly washed and changed, but had decided to shave after he had eaten. When the food was placed in front of him, he started to eat very quickly, with an almost shovelling motion.

"It's not a race you know," said Janice angrily.

"Yeah, awlwight," he mumbled, his mouth full of food.

Janice raised her eyebrows, dropped her jaw, and thought how disgusting he was. She said nothing.

The food finished, Dave excused himself and ran upstairs,

and into the bathroom. He shaved, and then splashed on his favourite aftershave, the latest fragrance called 'Corduroy Vert' a highly scented preparation, and guaranteed to be irresistible to women. In fact, a cross between 'Brut' and 'Hai Karate' and most females found it completely overpowering. However, the extensive advertisement campaign used by the marketing company had ensured that it was the number one best selling aftershave lotion (or *Apres Rasage pour Homme*, as it was called on the label) in the UK.

"You haven't a care, wearing Corduroy Vert," was the catchy slogan, and Dave loved it.

"God, you've overdone the aftershave a bit," said Janice as he entered the lounge.

"Not at all, it's just very strong when you first put it on," he replied, looking around the room for his car keys.

He found them on the coffee table, and glanced at his watch, 7.10, it's digital dial informed him. He decided to get to the pub early this week, to ensure he got a good seat.

"Right, if there's nothing else, I'm off."

"OK, but remember, don't get ..."

"I know, drunk!"

Janice shook her head, and returned to watching the television.

"Don't worry Love, I'll only have a few."

"OK, see you later."

Dave bent down and kissed her on the cheek, then went into the hall, collected some money from his jacket, which was hanging by the door and left. Janice heard the front door slam, got up, and cleared the table, taking the plates into the kitchen. Dave hadn't even finished his drink. "I'd love to know where he's really going," she thought to herself, "to know what he's really up to." She shrugged her shoulders, in a couldn't care less gesture, and carried on with her housework.

As the traffic at that time of night was very light, Dave made excellent time, and reached the pub just after seven thirty. It was already beginning to fill up, and Dave was starting to recognise some of the faces. He ordered his usual pint of bitter, and sat down at a table in the middle row, right in front of the stage.

He was the first person to sit down, as everyone else in the pub, was standing at the bar. Looking around, he felt a little anxious, as if he was the only person there, actually interested in the strippers. He was undecided whether to get up and move back to the bar, or stay put, and hog the best seat in the house.

The door banged open, and Sgt Mike Crouch walked in. The bar immediately went quiet, except for the jukebox, which was manfully struggling with a Johnny Cash record. Every single person in that room knew he was a policeman, every one that is, except Dave.

"Half a pint of lager please," Crouch politely asked, when he reached the bar.

"Didn't think you were allowed to drink on duty," said the skinhead barman.

"Well, for your information, I'm not on duty, just out for a quiet drink, any problems with that?"

"No fucking problem at all, just thought you bastards were always on duty," said the barman, as he turned to get a glass. He went through half a dozen glasses, and selected the dirtiest one, which also had a chip in it. "Any preference on lager, SIR?" he said venomously, holding the 'R' in sir for an extra few seconds.

"What's your problem?" Crouch snapped back.

"Nothing Sir, just don't want any trouble, that's all."

"And, why should my presence cause any trouble?"

"Look, do you want a fucking drink or not?"

Crouch was starting to lose his patience. "Listen you punk," he'd been watching too many American detective movies, "I just want to see what sort of vermin come crawling out of the woodwork in a pisshole like this, that's all, now I'll have a Stella please."

The barman banged the full glass onto the bar, spilling some of its contents onto a cloth beer-mat. "That'll be a quid sir," he demanded.

Crouch gave him a pound coin, and looked around the room. Dave was sitting oblivious to it all, having a cigarette, and looking at the empty stage. He stuck out like a wart on a witch's nose, and

Crouch picked up his glass and walked over to him.

"Evening," said Crouch, "mind if I joint you?"

Dave looked up, glanced around the bar, and wondered why, with every other table empty, this guy was asking to join him. "Not another bloody bore, who'd seen it all, done it all, or even worse, a raving poofter." Dave struggled to find an answer. "Umm ...well I suppose so," he said, when he really wanted to shout, "Fuck off you wanking shirt-lifter."

Crouch sat down, and leant over to him. "I'm an off-duty policeman, and just making a few off the record enquiries."

"Oh," said Dave as he frowned, "this is all I fucking need in a place like this."

"I just wondered if you were here last Wednesday?"

"Last Wednesday, um, yes I might have been, why?"

Crouch wanted to arrest the little pervert, or slap his stupid blotchy face, but kept his cool, and continued. "If you were here, how late did you stay?"

"Hang on a minute, I'm over 18, and there's no law against a man having a drink, is there?"

"Of course not, I'd just like to know what time you left."

"'bout elevenish."

"And when you left here, which way did you go home?"

"What?"

"Sorry, too difficult for you is it?"

"Look, I've done nothing wrong, and don't see why I should answer your questions."

"But if you've done nothing wrong, what have you to hide?"

"Who says I've got something to hide, I'm just out having a quiet drink."

"OK, if you won't co-operate, that's fine, perhaps we can do this at the station."

"Listen, I thought you said you were off-duty."

"Didn't you know, we fuzz are never off-duty."

"Alright, I left here just after closing time and went straight home."

"And did you go via St Mary's Street?"

"'Course not, I live in Hedge End, and went home over the Itchen Bridge, which is in the opposite direction."

"And what time did you get home?"

"How the bloody hell can I remember, I'd had a few."

"So you were drunk then?"

"No, I didn't say that."

"I see, and how did you get home?"

"Dave froze, he'd walked right into it, "Mmm ..."

"Well, surely you know how you got home, don't you?"

"Yeah, of course, I got a cab, that's it, I taxied home."

Dave was digging a hole for himself.

"Which cab company?"

"How the hell do I know?"

"I see, and where did you get the cab from?"

"I dunno, I was walking along Canute Road, and flagged one down."

"Gosh, that was lucky, a cab just happened to be driving along the road, at eleven o'clock, and you stopped it."

"Yeah, that's what happened, d'you mind telling me what this is all about?"

"Just enquiries, that's all ..." Crouch stood up, then added as an afterthought, "and your name is?"

"Dave Price."

"Well, thank you Mr Price, you've been very helpful, we might be in touch."

Crouch downed his lager in one, and walked back to the bar. There was a decidedly violent atmosphere in the pub, and he had no wish to see some old strippers, and getting beaten up outside a grubby public house in the Chapel area of Southampton would serve no useful purpose at all. He surveyed the motley assortment around the bar, he'd get nothing out of them.

"OK, thank you very much for your public spirited helpfulness, I wish you all a good night," he said with a smile as he walked across the bar, and into the chill night air.

"Bloody bastard," said the barman. "They never give up, do they?" The conversation around the room continued in a similar vein, with everyone telling his own story of how the police had at some time 'wronged' them.

Dave sat quietly, he'd never had any dealings with the police before, and felt guilty about lying. He picked up his beer and drank it in one. "What if they check with all the taxi companies in Southampton, and realise I was lying, they could easily find out my address, and come round and interview me. Shit, Janice will kill me if she finds out where I've really been." His mind tried to think of solutions to the problem, but there were none. "Another beer, that's the answer."

He went to the bar, and ordered another pint.

"What did that fucking pig want to ask you?" said Phil the barman.

"Oh, nothing, just questions about last week, that's all."

"Bloody knew it, still trying to tie us in with the rape that happened last week."

"Rape?" said Dave, who'd forgotten the newspaper story.

"Yeah, some stupid black bird was raped over the back by St Mary's, and they seem to fink we had somethin' to do with it."

"Bloody typical," shouted a Scotsman, standing next to Dave at the bar, "they're filth, nothing more, nothing less, just filth," he continued in a broad Glasgow accent, which Dave could barely understand.

"Quite agree," said Dave, as he turned and went back to his table, lit up a cigarette, and pondered the implications of this latest turn of events. He'd had nothing to do with the rape, had he? He couldn't remember exactly what he'd one that evening, he was too inebriated, but he was damn sure he'd not gone anywhere near St Mary's.

By 8.15 the bar was packed, and Dave had just started his third pint. A long-haired youth had just set up a microphone and spotlight on the stage, and it was getting close to start time.

A couple of middle-aged men had sat down at Dave's table, and from their conversation it was apparent they were stevedores at the Car Freight Terminal in Southampton's new dock. He moved uneasily in his seat, he didn't want to get involved with them, and so decided to go to the toilet, prior to the start of the show.

Returning to his seat, he finished his beer, and just got to the bar when the house lights dimmed. A slim man in his early twenties, dressed in sweatshirt and jeans, stepped onto the stage.

"Evening wankers," he shouted. "The management have asked me to tell you that wanking in the ladies' toilet is forbidden, if you must punish Percy, please do so in the gent's urinal."

This was to set the tone for the evening, with the next ten jokes or so, about a man with a six inch foreskin. Dave wasn't really listening, but laughed in all the right places.

"OK enough of this, you're going to love our first act, she's fifteen going on fifty, and with an IQ less than her bra size, let's here it for Lulu Lovelips."

"New York, New York," by Frank Sinatra prompted the start of the act. A woman appeared from behind the bar, and danced her way across the floor. She was in fact only 35 years old, but looked much older, medium build, and dressed in a long satin evening gown, with matching gloves. As the comedian left the stage, taking the microphone and stand with him, she stepped into the spotlight.

"Not bad," thought Dave, "not bad at all."

"Old dog," was what most of the other patrons thought.

"Get 'em off," shouted one of the men on Dave's table, which prompted the usual chorus of abuse, from just about everyone else in the room. She slowly removed her gloves, rubbing each one between her crotch, and then smelling them. The dress was next off, and this she dropped to the floor, next to the gloves, kicking the lot to one side. She stood in black bra, pants, suspenders and stockings, and continued to move in time with the music. The record finished and another of Frank Sinatra's hits was the cue for her to remove her bra, and step out of her panties.

Dave's eyes were on stalks, as was his penis, for although she had reasonably small breasts, they were completely covered by the aureola, and because she was very pale skinned, the effect was both unique and, to Dave, very erotic.

"Fucking hell, saucer nipples," someone shouted from the back, "all fucking nipple, and no tit."

She ignored this, and carried on with her act. She'd heard it all before, and had even been to see a specialist, to find out if they were abnormal. They weren't, and the only way to get rid of such large aureola, was to have a complete plastic surgery job done on them. She decided that it was not worth the great expense, and remained as she was. She didn't know then that she would become a stripper, and it may well have changed her decision if she had.

Stepping from the stage, she sat down on the lap of a bespectacled man on the table next to Dave. She removed his glasses and rubbed them around her breasts, and in between her cleavage. The crowd seemed to like this, and shouted their approval, and although she was not in the spotlight, Dave could see her every move.

Putting the glasses down onto the table, she wriggled on the man's lap, and then thrust her boobs into his face.

"Let him put his prick between 'em" shouted the man on Dave's table.

"Let me put my prick between them," Dave thought.

She stood up and got back onto the stage, just as the music finished. She stood motionless for a few moments, then collected her clothes from the stage floor, and skipped across the room and out through the back door.

The comedian leapt onto the state, with the mike in his hand, "Fucking hell, what an amazing pair of top-bollocks, there ain't many like those around, are there?" he shouted. "Wouldn't know whether to suck 'em or milk 'em."

Dave's glass was empty, so he went to the bar for a refill.

The comedian carried on with a relentless barrage of sexist jokes, this time on the subject of sex with animals.

Dave didn't really have a sense of humour, and hated stand-up comics. More stripping and less quipping would have suited him better. Returning to his seat, he lit up another cigarette, and started to daydream.

"Take a girl with the face of the blonde bit from 'Abba', the tits of Olive Orbs, the legs of Angela Rippon, and the nipples of that last stripper, and what have you got? Fucking perfection."

He came back to the world with a jolt, the comedian was just finishing his routine, and introducing the second stripper of the night. "Here she is, all the way from Croydon, the Delicious Dolly Donuts."

Dave was not impressed with Dolly at all. She was at least six feet tall, but could not have weighed more than eight stone. She was so skinny, her ribs stuck out further than her breasts and with short red hair, and anaemic white skin, she was a fairly unpleasant sight.

"More like Dolly No-nuts," shouted a wag from the back of the bar.

"Ladies night," by K.C. and the Sunshine Band, had signalled her entrance, and she gyrated across the room, dressed only in a see-through body stocking, which cut between her legs with a single sash, that ran between her cheeks.

To overcome her obvious lack of traditional assets, she was far raunchier and more risque than any of the other strippers. In her hand she held a large ripe banana, which she licked, and sucked as she climbed onto the stage.

She stood centre-stage, directly in the spotlight, and rammed the banana into her vagina, with one confident movement, then turning around, she bent over, to show that only the little brown tip was not inside her.

The vast majority of the audience seemed to love the act, and the usual derision had turned to an almost quiet admiration, with some people even pleasantly shocked. Several men jumped to their feet, cheering her on. The place was very close to pandemonium. Dave sat, and watched, still unimpressed. One drunken patron leapt onto the stage, and undoing his flies, pulled out his member, and shouted: "Use this instead darlin'."

At least that's what Dave thought he said, it was the Scotsman he'd talked to earlier, and the broad Glaswegian accent had gone up nearly two octaves, making it almost inaudible.

She removed the banana, handed it to him, and he started to sniff and lick it.

"Go on Jock, give her one."

Kneeling in front of him, she took hold of his penis, and gently toyed with it. She thought she knew what she was doing, thought she had the situation in control. Unfortunately, although his member was semi-soft, he ejaculated almost immediately, showering her face with semen.

"You fucking dirty old creep," she screamed.

The audience went wild, there was a surge to the front of the stage, with everyone stamping their feet and screaming. "Jock, Jock, Jock, Giver her your cock, cock, cock."

The stripper ran from the stage, out across the bar room floor, pushing wildly at anyone in her way, and was gone. Jock stood in the spotlight, penis in hand, his bald head reflecting the light, like a mirrored dome, he continued to dance to the music, resembling a demented puppet.

The comedian was obviously used to handling randy mobs, and appeared with the microphone: "Come on lands, let's have some decorum, or in plain English, go back to your fucking seats."

"Woo ya cullin' Anglish, ya bastar'!" screamed Jock, as he tried to push the M.C. back off the stage.

Dave sat bemused, the sight of an old drunk coming on the face of an ugly stripper was not his idea of a turn on.

Two very large men seemed to arrive from nowhere, and started to drag Jock from the stage.

He took great exception to this, and even though his penis was still poking from his trousers, he threw a wild punch at the largest of the men. This brought swift retaliation, and he was laid out with one punch to the face. As he was dragged across the floor, several of his friends jumped onto the two bouncers, and tables and chairs were scattered in the ensuing melee.

Dave wanted none of this, and quickly made for the toilet. Inside, he went straight into the singular crapper, locked himself inside the cubicle, and sat on the toilet. From the noise, it was quite clear that World War III had erupted in the bar.

Terrified, Dave lit up a cigarette, and waited. After about fifteen minutes, it went ominously quiet, and Dave left his hiding place. Opening the door, he cagily looked into the bar.

Tables were upended, chairs were smashed, glass was everywhere, and about six or seven of the locals were propped around the bar, holding various parts of their anatomy.

"Christ, so much for a quiet drink," Dave thought to himself.

Phil the barman was arguing with the comedian, Dave listened in.

"Look, you've been paid for a full evening's entertainment, and if you think you're pissing off now, I want a fucking refund."

"You must be fucking joking," replied the comedian, "the girls ain't going back on, and that's final."

"You're asking for a smack in the mouth, if I don't get a refund mate, and that's a fucking promise."

The two bouncers, who'd obviously arrived with the acts, moved in between the two arguing men.

"Calm down," continued the comedian, "we can't go back on, the place is a shitheap. I can't ask the girls to come out in this mess, not after what happened."

"Oh, yeah, and what did happen, eh? nothing, fuck all, just some old boy having a good time, and then your gorillas give him a hiding."

"They didn't give him a hiding, he threw the first punch."
"Wow, big deal, he must be over sixty."

"OK, you start getting the place tidied up, and I'll go back and see what the girls want to do. Fair enough?"

"Well, if you don't go back on, I want a refund."

"I'll see what I can do."

The comedian and the two bouncers left the bar area, and entered the little back room, which doubled as a changing room.

"Quick girls, grab all your gear, we're off, the bloody landlord's madder than the punters."

Collecting their costumes, the five of them left by the back exit, climbed into their transit van, and were gone.

Phil and several of the regulars, were busy picking up chairs and tables, as Dave returned to the bar. Surprisingly, very few punters had gone home, most of them stood along the side of the bar, next to the jukebox. Although from his hide-out in the toilet, the fight had sounded particularly violent, no-one seemed seriously injured, and most casualties seemed fine, after a quick visit to the loo.

"Come on lads, let's all calm down, clear up the mess, and try to salvage something from the evening. We don't want the police involved, or they'll revoke me fucking licence," said Phil, sounding more human than normal. "There's a free drink for everyone, once we've sorted out the mess."

This seemed to go down well with everyone, and after a while, with the broken tables and chairs removed, and several other ones brought in from outside, the place looked probably better than it did at the start of the evening.

Dave eventually got his free beer, and returned to the table he had been sitting at. The chair had been slightly damaged in the fracas, and wobbled when he sat down on it. He felt disappointed with the evening, neither of the strippers was exactly his cup of tea, although the first one, with her massive nipple-caps, was certainly different.

Phil went into the back room to find the entourage had gone. "Bastards!" he shouted in an angry tone, as he returned to the bar, and raising his hand continued, "Can I have your attention please...," the bar went quiet, "I'm afraid that's it for the night, the strippers have fucked off."

This went down as well as a condom at a Roman Catholic convention. For a few moments, it seemed as if another fight would start, as several of the punters blamed the landlord for the loss of their cabaret.

"Look, it's not my fucking fault," Phil told some irate customers at the bar. "Blame that prat Jock, it's his fault, stupid old bastard."

Dave was very upset, and sat, silently staring at his half full beer-glass.

"Bloody typical," he thought, "my only night out and it's ruined by some stupid old Scottish git."

"OK, OK, another free beer, but that's your lot. There'll be more strippers next week."

This offer caused a stampede to the bar.

Dave did not stir, he hadn't come to the pub for booze, just the strippers, however, a free beer was better than nothing. He quickly finished his pint, and joined the throng of less than happy punters at the bar.

"Pint of Directors please," he said when finally served, and lit up another cigarette. His packet was empty, "and some change for the fag machine," he mumbled, duly purchasing another pack from the machine by the toilet door.

The jukebox had been turned on, and the usual selections of Country and Western music came droning from the speakers. "Not this dirge again," Dave thought as he returned to his seat. "Can't stay here all night, and I'm not going home, that's for sure."

A thought hatched in his mind: what about the little wine bar in Oxford Street? He'd heard that sometimes unattached women used the place, and as it was only five minutes drive away, he decided to go there. Finishing his beer, he left the pub, and drove straight to 'Victor's' Wine Bar.

Oxford Street had been a very run down area, only a few years previously, but with the help of large council grants, the whole street had been transformed into a very pleasant district, possibly even trendy. With its sweeping Georgian Terrace, and graceful shop fronts, it now boasted three public houses, one wine bar, and several very good restaurants. It was quite a popular gathering place for a lot of Southampton yuppie types, and was well favoured by the yachting fraternity.

Dave parked on a meter just outside Victors and went in. It was deserted. Obviously, with the economic climate still hitting a lot of pockets, most people only used the place at weekends.

A fat lady with dyed jet black hair greeted him. "Evening love, what'll it be?"

"Have you any real ales?" he quietly asked.

"Oh yes, we've Ringwood best, Tenderfoot and Fuller's London Pride."

"Um, a pint of Fuller's please."

"Straight glass or jug?"

"No matter, as it comes," Dave replied as he fumbled for his cigarettes.

"One pound seventy please," she said, and he paid her with the exact money.

"God, it's quiet tonight, isn't it?" he remarked, looking around the empty bar.

"It always is on Wednesdays, I don't know why I bother to open, but sometimes there's a little passing trade," she said with a shrug of her huge shoulders.

He had no intention of sitting at the bar, making polite conversation with her all night, and took his beer to a table by the window, lit up a fag and looked out into the street. His mind wandered, "It's quarter past nine, far too early to go home, but what else was there to do?"

He suddenly realised he was fairly drunk, which was hardly surprising, considering the amount of alcohol he'd consumed during the day and evening. Where to go? What to do? "Could go back to the office, I've got the porno mag in the car, get a few bottles to go, mm ..." He stubbed out his cigarette, and took a swig of the frothing brew.

Unfortunately, the booze had taken over his mind, he was in a sort of limbo region, between being paralytic and just merry, and once this point was reached, it was very difficult to stop drinking.

Across the road from the wine bar, was the Grosvenor Arms, a smart new pub, which had retained much of its character from the days when it was a Victorian drinking house. He decided to give it a try. Finishing his beer with one gulp, he got up, and left.

"Thanks a lot, see you again," shouted the barmaid, as Dave walked through the door and into the street.

He crossed the road, and went into the Grosvenor, noticing with some relief that at least half a dozen other people were drinking there.

"Good evening sir," said a very effeminate barman in a funny voice, "what would you like?"

"Not you ya poofter," Dave thought as he looked around the bar, realising that all the patrons were male. "Just my luck to stumble into a poof's parlour," he thought.

"A pint of Boddingtons," he demanded in his most macho voice.

"Certainly sir," squeaked the barman, as he took a glass from the shelf, wiped it clean with a tea towel and filled it with two pulls from a hand pump.

"Anything else?"

"No, that's fine."

Dave paid and went to a small table in the corner of the room. Placing his glass down, he looked around for the toilet, and fortunately noticed the sign, just thankful that he did not have to ask the barman where it was.

He stumbled over the two steps leading to the loo, and felt almost giddy.

Inside the toilet were the obligatory photos of young men, and a condom machine.

"Extra thick, specially designed for woofters," Dave remarked, as he did up his flies, and returned to the bar.

By this time he was drunk, walking was an effort, and he almost tipped up the chair as he sat down. He signed and wasn't sure if he could finish his beer or not, a cigarette would help, he surmised, and lit one up. At no time during the evening had he considered his promise to his wife, in fact he'd not considered his wife at all. He struggled through his beer, and finally gave up, with about a quarter of a pint still left.

He got up, stumbled to the door, and left without a word. Walking back to his car, the cool night air went straight to his head, and he had problems finding his car keys, let alone unlocking the door.

He eventually worked out how to get the key into the ignition, and started the engine.

"Back to the office for coffee," was all he could think.

* * *

It was 11.20, as Diane Michells left the Oxford Arms public house, she had been working since seven, and felt dead on her feet.

The Oxford Arms was a very neglected pub, mainly used by the Asian community, those whose religion let them drink, at the top end of St Mary's Road, some two minutes walk from St Mary's Street. She hated the work, but like so many other young unmarried mothers in Britain today, just could not survive on the social services payments she was entitled to. Her life had always been an uphill struggle. Pregnant at twenty four, she had refused to marry the father of her child, and had moved out from her parents' home into a council flat, to avoid the continual arguments with her mother. She was determined to make it on her own, but life had dealt its usual cruel hand. She was not qualified in any profession, and the only jobs she could get, paid less than the cost of a child minder. She was caught in a poverty trap, and when an Asian friend suggested working at the Oxford Arms, on a cash in hand basis, she was only too pleased with the work.

Her flat was in an estate just off St Mary's Street and at least it cost her nothing to get to and from her job. She had a lovely daughter, now ten years old, and although times were still tough, and money very scarce, she felt a great sense of pride in her independence. Although, at this moment in time, there was no man in her life, which was how she liked it, she still had plenty of offers, and had kept herself in fairly good shape. With long brown hair, trim figure, and nice legs, she still could turn the odd head or two.

She cut across the open air municipal car park, and headed for the subway, which leads from the six dials area of St Mary's Road into St Mary's Street.

He waited for her in the darkness, at the end of the subway, listening to the fast approaching footsteps. He had been there for a while, but knew from the sound of her stilettos, she was what he sought. He wobbled slightly from the excesses of booze but still had his mind focused on the job in hand.

The subway had been vandalised, and had no lighting, and she always hated walking through it. It was full of broken bottles, cans and assorted litter and stunk of vomit and urine. Most of the City's winos and homeless used the place when the weather turned inclement.

He stepped back into the shadows, out of view, and as she got closer, held his breath, and waited.

"Come on you bitch, come on," he thought, mind and pulse racing, "this won't take long, just long enough ..."

She strained her eyes, and slowed down as she reached about halfway inside the subway, she knew someone was there, probably a drunk or deadbeat, lying in his own excrement. She couldn't see anyone, but felt a presence. She stopped, and listened, there was nothing, only silence. A strange echoey quietness, a silence of fear.

She slowly started to walk again, still anxious, still cautious, she wanted to call out, but didn't. Perhaps it was best if she went back, and crossed the road outside, there were very few cars about, it would be easy.

"Now you're just being silly," she said to herself, and continued along the passageway.

As she reached the end of the subway, he pounced. Grabbing her by her hair, he threw her to the ground, and she banged her knee on a broken paving slab, and hit her head on the tiled subway wall. She struggled to get to her feet, but he punched her in the back of her neck, sending her sprawling into a pile of garbage. She screamed at the top of her voice, and it echoed down the dark passageway, as he grabbed her coat, trying to rip it off. Her screams were amplified in the confined space, so he tried to put his hand around her mouth, prompting her to bite him very hard. Getting strength from her inner fear, she somehow managed to push him off, and got onto her feet.

He slapped her across the side of the face, shouting foul obscenities, "Fuck you, you bitch, your time will come, just wait, I'll be back, and next time, you won't get away so easily."

As he ran down the subway, she caught the smell of alcohol, and something sweet. She couldn't place the fragrance, but knew she'd smelt it before, it was some cheap aftershave, but its name escaped her.

She crawled out of the subway in a daze, her leg was badly grazed and bleeding, while her head already had a large bruise showing, from her collision with the tiled wall.

A group of young men were just leaving a Chinese take-away, a few yards from the exit of the subway, and started running across the road, to where all the commotion was coming from.

"You alright love?" said one of them, as she came into view.

"No, some bastard's tried to rape me," she sobbed, shaking with fear.

They helped her across the road, and took her into the take-away, where the owner immediately telephoned the police.

* * *

Dave half opened his eyes, it was almost two o'clock, and he had fallen asleep at his desk. The porno mags were still in their envelope, with a cup of cold coffee next to them.

"Oh ..." he moaned, he felt dreadful, and burped loudly. Holding his head in his hands, he tried to recall the events of the evening, besides the fight in the Coach & Horses, he could remember nothing. He seemed to have a boxer in his head, trying to punch his way out, and his tongue felt like it had a fur coat on it.

"Must have a piss," he said, as he realised his bladder was at bursting point, and desperately needed emptying. He struggled into the toilet, and urinated, mainly on the wall, directly behind the cistern.

"What a waste of an evening," he thought, "what the fuck will I tell Janice? Where the hell have I been? My trousers are filthy."

He initially toyed with the idea of a taxi, but decided that he was OK to drive home, it was very late, and the traffic would be extremely light. He sat back down at his desk, and looked at the urine stains on his trousers, they were still wet, but there were other marks too.

Picking up the magazines, he walked out of the office, and across to his car. He'd forgotten to lock the door, or even reset the alarm system, he just wanted to get home.

He arrived at his house, without any problem, although he had hit the kerb on three occasions.

The house was in total darkness, Janice had obviously gone to bed.

"Thank God for small mercies," he said to himself as he carefully unlocked the front door. For a drunken person, to be quiet it is impossible. The more attention one pays to being silent, the more chances there are of making a row. Dave had opened the door brilliantly, but dropped his keys into the darkness, and as he bent over to find them, knocked the door shut with his behind.

"Shh ..." he whispered to himself, as he found his keys, and crept up the stairs, with all the finesse of an elephant break-dancing on china plates.

Janice opened one eye and looked at the alarm clock. 2.25. She lay still and listened to him go into the bathroom. First, he turned on the tap too much, and it sent water spraying over his shirt, and onto the floor. Then, he dropped the soap into the bath, and finally tripped over the bathroom mat, banging into the shower cubicle door, which slammed shut.

"Fuck it," he murmured, as he picked up his clothes. His head was swimming.

He eventually made it into the bedroom, and threw his clothes onto the floor of his wardrobe, the belt buckle in his trousers thwacking against the wooden bottom.

"What bloody time d'you call this?" Janice suddenly snarled, making an entrance like a vampire jumping from its coffin.

"Oh shit, you scared the life out of me."

"Where the hell have you been? It's nearly half past two."

"Sorry love, went back to Barry's for a nightcap, and forgot the time."

"Who's Barry?"

Dave struggled to remember the names he'd invented.

"Ah, Ron's mate."

She sat up and turned on the bedside light.

"Look at the state of you, you're pissed again, aren't you?"

"No-I-not..," he said angrily, slurring his words, so that they ran into each other.

"You can hardly talk, don't think you're getting into this bed in that state. You can sleep in the spare room, we'll TALK about this tomorrow."

He scratched his chin, and mumbled something about it not being fair, but she would have none of it.

"Go on, I mean it, I've told you before, if you ever came home drunk, there'd be trouble, but what do you care, just self, self, self, you've probably woke up Sarah, you're a disgrace, look at you ..."

He didn't wait for her to finish, and just stumbled out of the room, and straight into the tiny spare-room. He flopped on the bed, which was a big mistake. The booze was about to come back to greet him, whether he wanted it to, or not. About a gallon of bear, steak, chips and miscellaneous other items, were pushing their way from his stomach, up his gullet and into his mouth, via his nasal passage.

"Aahh ..." he yelled, as he ran from the bed and into the bathroom, just making it to the toilet pan. Unfortunately, the seat and lid were down, and before he had a chance to lift them, he exploded.

Most of the foul smelling liquid did go into the sink, but not all of it.

He retched several times, his throat burning with the acidity of the bile. He turned on the tap, and frantically tried to send all the little orange bits down the plughole.

"Oh, that's bloody charming," shouted Janice from her bed. "If you think I'm cleaning it up, you can think again."

Dave was in agony, but with all the noise he was making, didn't hear her.

Eventually it stopped, and Dave sat on the toilet seat, head in hands, surveying his surroundings. He leant over, and rested his head in the sink, spitting a few remaining drops of vomit into it. He turned on the tap, and after a moment, took a drink of water with cupped hands, the horrible taste in his mouth, and strange burning in his nostrils, made him feel possibly worse than before he'd started to vomit. He slowly got up, left the bathroom, and went back to the spare-room.

"Disgusting bastard," Janice murmured, as she turned off the light, and snuggled under the duvet. "Tomorrow you're out, no ifs, buts, or whyfors, just out."

* * *

Thursday morning in the Civic Centre police station, found D.I. Quinn looking at the papers on the new assault case.

"We've got to get this bastard, Mike," he said to his young partner, who was munching his way through a bacon buttie.

"He's obviously the type of shit who likes to hurt women, and I'm afraid that next time, he could end up really doing some damage. We could even have a murder case on our hands."

"Who's the latest victim, Guv. I mean Sir?" said Mike, his mouth full of food.

"Do you have to eat all the time?"

"Sorry Sir."

Quinn looked back at his file, and ran his finger along the text. "A single parent called Diane Michells, lives on the council estate, just over the back of St Mary's Street."

"You sure it's the same man, and not a copycat crime?"

"Must be, Mike. It all fits, Wednesday night, just after the pubs have chucked out, woman grabbed by her hair from behind, and punched. Yeah, it's the same man alright, on that I'd stake my pension."

Crouch opened his notebook. "I went into the Coach & Horses early last night and there were a few likely candidates in there, I can tell you. One bloke," he flipped through some pages, "name of Price, seemed very shifty indeed."

"Really, anything on him in records?"

"Dunno, haven't looked yet, perhaps I'll do it now, anything new to go on?"

"Well, the uniformed lads got a statement, it seems our man is about five foot eight tall, average to well built, mid to late thirties, brownish hair, white, and stunk of booze."

"Great, that narrows it down to about fifty thousand men in the Southampton area."

"Yeah, I know. I think we'll go and see her ourselves, could be that something's been overlooked."

"All of that fits my 'Mr Price', but then it could fit almost anyone."

"Oh, she did notice he was wearing a very strong type of aftershave, you know that new one, Corduroy Vert, it's so horribly pungent, she's sure it was the one."

"Right, let me see if I've got this right. We're looking for a man of average height, average build, who's middle-aged, has brown hair, drinks a lot, and wears the UK's number one selling aftershave. Well, shouldn't take too long to find him then?"

Mike Crouch smiled, and left the office to go to records. Quinn sat with the file on his lap, tapping it with his fingers, contemplating his next move. When Sgt Crouch returned, he entered the room shaking his head.

"Nothing on Dave Price, I don't even think he's had a parking ticket."

"Well, that doesn't make him innocent, does it Mike?"

"True. I just ..."

"Don't just stand there," Quinn interrupted, "make us a cup of tea."

"Sure."

"I've been thinking, Mike, perhaps you're right about this connection with the Coach & Horses, they have the strip show on a Wednesday, and it seems our man might just go for that kind of thing. I think we'd better pop down there at lunchtime, and have a little look-see."

"Right," Crouch said enthusiastically, pouring the boiling water into the cups, "I'd better warn you, they're a pretty rough lot, seem to hate coppers."

"So what's new? If we get any trouble from them, I'll personally revoke the licence."

"Fair enough," said Crouch. He loved it when Quinn played the hardman, hoping that some day he might be the same sort of policeman.

* * *

Dave woke up with the mother of all hangovers, his eyes were bloodshot, stung, and could not focus on anything more than a couple of feet away. His tongue had fur on it, and felt like he'd licked out the bottom of a gerbil's cage, while his head ached with such intensity, the slightest movement seemed to jar his brain, which was somehow moving independently of his skull.

He could hear Janice downstairs, she hadn't bothered to wake him, and even through all his pain, he knew why. He reached for his watch.

"Aw, fuck, twenty past eight," he ranted, and jumped up from the bed. "Aahh ..." he stopped, feeling decidedly shaky on his legs, "must have a slash," he mumbled as he walked cagily to the bathroom.

On the tiles, behind the sink, just above the ceramic splashback, was a carefully hand-written 'post-it' note, "CLEAN THIS SHIT UP OR ELSE," was all it read. He looked around the room. Shit was indeed the operative word. In the sink, the plughole was completely bunged up, with something he didn't like the look of. Down the side of the bath panels, on the sink pedestal, and all across the back of the toilet cistern, the dried-on remains of vomit were fully visible. The little ornate soap dish was full to overflowing with what can best be described as the result of putting a lasagna in a food blender. The set of bathroom scales, which Janice used every day, had been pebble-dashed with mucus, and the quaint pink bath mat was covered in footprints, which judging by their colour, had to be some kind of animal (possibly dog) excrement.

Even Dave was amazed at the extent of the carnage. The smell was also disgusting, and Dave almost retched again, as he stood trying to decide what to do first. He was only wearing his underpants, and so he went to the master bedroom and removed them. They too were in a pretty wretched state and he carefully threw them into the pink plastic laundry basket. Putting on his dressing-gown, he went downstairs for a coffee. In the kitchen, Janice was obviously making sandwiches, buttering bread at quite an amazing speed. He walked over to the kettle, and switched it on. She ignored him totally.

"Look, about last night," he timidly said, after a few moments. "I'm really sorry, but I can explain."

"Don't come near me, you smell like a brewery," she snapped, as she turned her head away from him in disgust and held her nose.

"OK. I'll just have a coffee, then shower."

"You'd better clean that toilet up before you go," she continued, placing the sandwiches in little poly-bags with multicoloured tie-ups, "'cause I ain't doing it."

"Yeah, alright, keep ya hair on. I'll have a coffee and sort out the loo before I go."

He made a coffee, and went back to the bedroom. He sat on

the edge of the bed, his arms resting on the tops of his legs, head bowed, and tried to gather his thoughts. What if Janice told him to go, which seemed fairly likely? Where could he go? "Aw, fuck it," he took a sip of coffee and headed for the bathroom for a much needed wash. Tippy-toeing through the mess, he climbed into the shower cubicle and wallowed in the luxury of a hot shower, and for those few brief moments, felt almost human. Unfortunately, he still had the small matter of cleaning the bathroom. Going back to the bedroom, he phoned his office, and told Joanne he was running late, but would hopefully be in by ten.

"Right," he said to himself, as he put on some old clothes, "let's see about clearing up the crap."

As anyone knows, cleaning up the mess of a room full of vomit and dog shit is certainly not a pleasure, but Dave stuck bravely to the task, and finished it as best he could in about an hour. He went back to the kitchen, made himself another coffee, and eventually got changed and ready for work.

Janice was sitting in the lounge, and he leant through the doorway: "Right, I'm off to work. I've cleaned the bathroom and ..." she interrupted him mid-sentence.

"Don't think that this is the last you're going to hear about last night. We need to talk, and I mean TALK," she sternly, but calmly said.

"Yes, I realise that, I'll be home early, we'll talk then."

He walked to the door, grabbed his jacket, and quickly left.

Driving to work, Dave again tried to piece together the missing hours of the previous evening. He remembered going to the wine bar, but after that, everything was hazy. Even though he was much later than usual, the traffic across the toll bridge was, as always, bumper to bumper. "That's one thing that never changes," he thought to himself, sitting in silence, his headache so bad, he couldn't even bring himself to turn on the car stereo.

Arriving at the office, Joanne commented on his disgusting appearance. "Jesus Christ, what happened to you?" she said.

"Don't even ask," Dave replied, as he walked straight into the kitchenette and filled the kettle. "Got any aspirin?" he shouted.

"Yeah, they're in the first-aid kit in the cupboard," came the reply from Joanne, straining to hear what he was up to. He fumbled in the box and finally managed to find the jar. "These fucking child-proof lids are impossible," he grumbled, as he desperately struggled with the bottle, eventually opening it, and sending most of the contents across the room and onto the floor.

As he tried to collect them up, he trod six or seven into the floor, but managed to get three tablets into his mouth. He went to his desk, coffee in hand, and flipped through the morning post. The workload had levelled off a little, but it was still up on previous weeks. Fortunately he could do most of his work with his eyes closed, (which they basically were) and the morning, what was left of it, passed fairly quickly. Calvin was still not in, and Dave was informed by the lovely Joanne:

"He's got an early morning meeting."

She always covered for Calvin, and it really pissed Dave off. At lunchtime, Dave had decided to go for a stroll into the town centre, and have a quiet pint. Just one, he knew he'd have to be on his best behaviour for the forthcoming evening's inquisition, but needed something, just to stop the shakes he'd acquired from his over indulgence the previous night. After a somewhat tiresome walk to the bottom end of the High Street, he entered 'The Hart' a beautiful Tudor public house which had unfortunately become very scruffy. He really struggled to drink his pint of 'Flower's Original' and left nearly a half of it, before making his way painfully back to the office.

"Crumbs, you're back early, is the pub closed?" Joanne asked, as he entered the office.

"Oh, very funny, I don't drink every lunchtime, you know."

"You could of fooled me," she laughed.

"Well, if you must know, I don't feel a hundred percent. I think I've eaten something that hasn't agreed with me," he lied, hoping for some sympathy.

"Well, ask Mr Calvin for the afternoon off, you've still got loads of holiday left, and he's just come in."

"Well, it seems I'm always taking time off," he mumbled, as

he sat at his desk and tried to focus on the documents he still had to process. The beer he'd had seemed to help a little, he felt a little more perky, and his head was starting to clear slightly.

"I'll finish these couple of map orders, then push off home." Joanne heard him, but did not answer, she preferred it when he was out of the office anyway.

* * *

The door flew open at the Coach & Horses and D.I. Quinn and Sgt Crouch entered.

"Well, well, well, if it isn't Phillip Smith," Quinn said jokingly to the skinhead barman. "And what pray tell are you doing here, you little toe-rag? Up to something dishonest, no doubt?"

"I'm the landlord, Mr Quinn," said Phil, baring his teeth, "I see you've brought your monkey with you."

"Listen lad, I know you've got no time for the police, but I could shut you down, just like that," Quinn snarled as he snapped his fingers, making Phil back off.

"Look, I've been going straight for a few years now, and run this pub kosher."

"Kosher, my ass, you couldn't run a synagogue kosher."

"I want no trouble from you, I'm straight now, so what do you want?"

"What I want, Phillip," Quinn said with a poisonous tone, "is a few answers, that's all, just a few answers."

"OK, what do you want to know."

"There was another attempted rape last night, just at the top end of St Mary's, and it seems strange that every time you have a stripper's night, I have a rape."

"You can't hold me responsible for every person who drinks in here, it might just be a coincidence."

"That's very true, Phillip my lad, but just a few names, that's all I ask."

"Fucking hell, I don't know the name of everyone who drinks in here."

"Alright, let's try and make it a bit easier. The man we're looking for is about 40 years old, maybe younger, five foot sevenish, and with brown hair, anyone like that?"

"Yeah, nearly all of them."

"Anyone of that description who only drinks here on Wednesday nights?"

"Yeah, a few maybe, in fact your mate was talking to one last night."

Quinn turned to Crouch, who was eyeing up a cheese and tomato sandwich at the bar.

"The guy Price I told you about, only chap sat down," Crouch said.

"And this person only drinks on Wednesday nights?" Quinn continued.

"Well, actually, he's been in a few times at lunchtime, I think he works around here, probably in an office."

"I see, and what leads you to this wonderful deduction?"

"Well, he wears a suit, doesn't he?"

"And he's the only one you can think of. Eh?"

"Yeah, most of the others are regulars, been coming in here for years."

"I see, well I'm sure you won't mind if we ask a few questions around the bar."

"Suit yourself."

The two policemen went around the room, questioning and probing, but they got the same tired answers, "went straight home", "wasn't here", "don't know nowt" from the assembled clientele. It was hopeless.

Going back to the bar, Quinn stopped and looked straight into Phil Smith's face. "OK, we've finished here for the time being, but if this guy comes in again, try and find out anything you can about him, anything that might help us. It'll earn you Brownie points, and at this moment, you need all the help you can get."

The two policemen left the pub and everyone looked around to Phil.

"That Quinn's a fucking bastard, he never forgets a face, he nicked me years ago, but still brings it up every time I see him. He's one evil motherfucking pig."

"He didn't look that hard to me," said one of the men, sitting on a bar-stool, leaning over, with both his elbows on the bar.

"Well, don't let looks deceive you, he'd bite off your dick, and stuff it up your ass lengthwise, if he thought it would get a conviction."

The whole bar laughed and carried on drinking.

Outside, the two officers walked to their car, "Well, Mike, it certainly looks as if your hunch could be right."

"Thank you sir," said Mike, feeling chuffed at receiving some recognition. "Also, while I was in there, I remembered something else. I think Price may have been wearing that aftershave, you know, 'Corduroy whatsit'.

"OK, he said he taxied home. Try a few cab companies, see if any of them took our friend home to Hedge End, and issue another full statement to the local rag, see if that throws up anything more."

"If it is the Dave Price I checked on this morning, I'll get his address from the electoral role, and perhaps we could pay him a visit."

"Get his address, but hold back for a while, let's see if we can get a little more on him, before we flush him out. I don't want him to know we're on to him."

They got into their police car, and drove back towards the station.

"Fancy a burger sir?" said Crouch as they passed the 'Burger King' restaurant in the High Street.

"No I don't Mike, and I'd rather you didn't eat one in the car."

"OK Gu... Sir."

* * *

Dave had got on and finished his work, and was staring down the office, his tongue felt like a squirrel's tail. "It's no good, I've got to have some hair of the dog," he thought, and going into Calvin's office, he explained he didn't feel too well and would it be alright to have the rest of the day off?

"You seem to be making a habit of this, Dave," Calvin said as he looked at him over his reading-glasses, "you've got no problems at home I trust?"

"No, of course not John, I'm just a little run down, that's all, I was telling Joanne, it was something I've eaten."

"Well, OK, if you've done all your work," Calvin replied looking at his watch, and adding: "So it's still not that busy then?"

"You bastard, you fucking bastard, even when I'm on death's door, you've got to mention work."

"Um, I wouldn't say that. I hurried through this morning's work, and my figures are up again," said Dave with a frown on his face, not looking entirely convincing.

"Really," mumbled Calvin, as he picked up his phone, and started to dial a number, "OK, off you go."

"Thanks, see you tomorrow then."

Calvin did not reply, but started talking to the person he had just telephoned.

"Miserable prick," Dave thought as he left the office. He tidied up his desk a little, put on his coat, and informed Joanne that he was going home. She shrugged her shoulders nonchalantly, but managed to say "Goodbye," as he left.

"Oh, hang on a minute Dave," she shouted after him.

"Yeah?" he said as he stepped back inside the door.

"I meant to ask you earlier, did you come into the office last night?"

"No, why?"

"Only the door was unlocked, and the alarm was not on. If it wasn't you, I'd better speak to Mr Calvin about it."

"Last night, you say," Dave muttered, awkwardly fumbling on the words, "Um ... come to think of it, I did. Yes, of course I did, after going to the pictures, I popped in to get my jacket."

Joanne screwed up her nose, and shook her head. "But you wore your jacket home, why would you? ..."

"No, sorry, not my jacket, my cigarettes. I thought I put them in my pocket, but left them in my desk. Sorry about the alarm, but I'd rather you didn't tell Calvin, I'm in enough trouble as it is and ..."

He spoke in short sharp phrases, each one disjointed, almost as if they were prompted by someone else.

"Well, I should really say something."

"Please," he begged, "don't ..."

"Alright, but it's the last time I cover for you, if anything ever happens, I'm not taking the can."

"Oh, thanks pet, you're a treasure," he said sickeningly.

It made Joanne feel ill, she disliked him enough when he was normal, but when he called her 'pet' and 'treasure' it made her stomach turn.

"You'd better go, if you're not well."

"Yeah, you're right," he said, winking at her. "Thanks for your concern. You really are lovely."

This made her feel even more nauseous, and she put her hand over her mouth, and gulped.

Dave drove straight to the 'Bay Tree' public house in Hedge End, stopping only to buy a newspaper on the way. Remembering they sold Boddingtons he ordered a pint. The place was empty, except for a scruffy individual, in a 'Guns 'n' Roses' T-shirt, playing the fruit machine, whilst humming to himself a very strange tune indeed.

Dave sat down at a table near the window, lit up a cigarette, and took a swig of his beer.

"Aaa, nectar," he declared as he looked at the front page of his paper.

"RAPIST STRIKES AGAIN IN ST MARY'S" ran the headline.

"Oh Christ, not again, I suppose PC Plod will be asking more questions," he quietly murmured. "Better not say I took a taxi, better to say I was sober, and drove home."

He read the story in full, nothing much was revealed, only a plea for the public to come forward with any possible leads. He neatly folded the paper, placed it on the table and finished his beer.

"One more for the road, and then home. If Janice smells booze on me, I'm right in the shit."

Returning to the bar, Dave duly ordered another pint, took it back to his table, and opened his paper again, this time at the TV page. He was definitely feeling a lot better.

* * *

Sarah was having a torrid time at school, she hated it, and used any excuse to bunk off. Since she'd met her new boyfriend, her life had changed. He was older than her, and had the money to take her to restaurants, clubs, movies, and really show her a good time. Her lovely long dark hair, and sultry looks (from her father's side) had made her just about the most popular girl in school, and although she was only sixteen, she'd already had several lovers. One as old as thirty. Her latest one was a financial whizz-kid, called Malcolm, and with his own sports car, penthouse flat near the yachting marina, she considered him a bit of a catch, although in reality, he was the one who had made a 'catch'.

Whenever she told her mother she was out with school friends, she was usually round his flat making love. She already had a 36B bust, (probably due to the fact that she'd been on the pill since she was fourteen) with a fairly small, slim frame, which made her look very voluptuous. She had long since stopped playing netball for the school, because of the comments she got, particularly from the male teachers.

She'd arrived home from school, just after lunchtime, and was in her room reading the latest Jackie Collins' novel. She was imagining herself in the role of the heroine, and getting quite turned on. Knowing her mother wouldn't be home for several hours, she'd decided to take a shower, and have some fun with her body, she felt quite horny, and had had many such afternoons.

In the shower cubicle, she started to massage her breasts with some shower gel, lathering around her nipples. She'd once done the same with Malcolm and found it very pleasurable. Leaning back against the cold tiles, she placed her hands between her legs, and started to finger herself. She'd often masturbated in bed, but in the shower it was sheer luxury.

* * *

Dave had finished his second pint, and had started for home. He'd decided to take his porno mags in with him, and took them from the boot of his car as soon as he arrived back at the house.

Opening the front door, with the envelope under his arm, he froze. "Bloody hell, there's someone in," he whispered, as he heard the noise coming from the shower-room.

Turning around, Dave ran back to the car, and put the books back in their hiding place in the boot.

"Who could be in?" he asked himself, as he returned to the hallway entrance and listened again.

Creeping along the hall and up the stairs, he peered around the bathroom door. Through the frosted glass of the shower cubicle, he could see the outline of his stepdaughter as she writhed in the steamy water. Squealing and moaning, he could hear her making strange little sounds.

At first, he was amazed, but soon realised what she was doing, and became breathless. A bulge appeared in his trousers.

"Mmm, that's it, mmm, harder, harder," she murmured.

He reached down to his crotch and squeezed himself gently.

Sarah opened her eyes for a moment, and noticed the shadowy figure in the bathroom doorway. She stopped, frozen on the spot.

"Who's that?" she shouted, as she stood bolt upright.

Dave quickly moved forward and threw open the cubicle door, his face bright red, but not with embarrassment, only with lust.

"What are you doing?" he asked.

"How long have you been there?" she replied, trying to cover up all her exposed parts.

"Long enough, my girl," he leered at her lovely brown breasts, covered in soap suds, it was like a picture from one of his magazines.

She stepped from the shower, and pushing past him, grabbed a towel from the rail by the sink.

"You bloody pervert, got nothing better to do?" she said angrily.

"Don't come the high and mighty with me. I ought to put you over my knee," he stammered, his breath irregular.

"Yeah, you'd like to do that, I'm sure."

"Don't talk to me like that, you little tramp, I ..." he grabbed at her, causing the towel to drop to the floor.

"Get off me!" she screamed. "Lay one finger on me and I'll tell mum."

"Oh really, and what if I tell your precious mother what you were doing, eh?"

She bent down to pick up the towel, and Dave saw right down between her cleavage, all the way to her hairy mound.

"I'll give you something you really want."

He moved towards her, but as she tried to avoid him, she fell onto the bathroom floor. He quickly sat down on top of her stomach, pinning her arms with his knees. His member was so large it was hurting, pushing against his trousers, trying to escape.

"How about a nice pearl necklace, bet you've never had one of those before," he slobbered.

"Get off you bastard!" she screamed, "or I'll tell Janice and she'll kick you out."

"Fuck Janice," he sneered, as he moved one hand to his flies, and unzipped them.

She turned her head away, wriggling, and trying to hit him with her knees. As his penis sprang out, he grabbed her head. "This won't hurt, I promise."

His huge pussy puncher stood proud, as he tried to manoeuvre it into position, between her two young upright breasts.

"Put that thing near me, and I'll bite it off," she said defiantly, twisting and turning under him, but he was too heavy, and was starting to hurt her. Her mood changed. "Please don't Dave," she sobbed, "not like this."

"I heard you in the shower, playing with yourself, you must want it, or you wouldn't be doing that, would you?"

His breathing was so heavy, she could hardly understand him, but she knew the 'moment' was close. She'd had enough dealings with men to know when they'd passed the point of no return, and Dave certainly had. In the position he was in, he was sitting a little too high up her body, and his penis stuck out over her boobs, by her neck. He fell forward, grabbing her wrists with his hands, and moved his torso down her body. Just as it slid through her cleavage, he started to ejaculate. The white liquid spewed forth, showering her shoulders and chin.

"Aaa ...you dirty git," she yelled, as she made one last effort to move him. He was sent sprawling across the floor, and she jumped to her feet.

"You fucking pervert!" she screamed, as she turned on the tap and washed her neck and face.

"I'm sorry, you led me on."

"Led you on, you fucking raped me, that's what."

"Don't say that, I'm sorry, I've got these urges."

"Fuck your urges, you're in dead trouble now."

She was screaming and Dave's vision blurred. Suddenly he was back in the doorway, with his prick in his hand, with Sarah still in the shower. He frowned. What had happened. Had he given her a Pearl Necklace, or imagined it? He shook his head, and rubbed his eyes. Sarah was indeed shouting at him, but she was still in the cubicle.

"Is that how you get your kicks?" she said, "jerking off in bathroom doorways?"

He didn't understand. One minute he was on top of her, the next ...

He turned and went into the bedroom, Sarah had wrapped a towel around herself and followed him.

"You're mental, you need help."

"Please don't say that, look I'll give you money, every week, surely we can come to an arrangement."

"The only arrangement we can come to is for you to leave, pack your bags, and leave me and mum alone."

"What are you saying?"

"What I'm saying you pervy is that mum wants you out, I want you out, is that clear enough?"

"Don't say anything to your mother, it wouldn't help."

"You're pathetic. I'm going to my room and I suggest you start packing."

She sat in her room, thinking about what had happened, it was weird. He was standing in the doorway, like a man possessed, mumbling about some sort of necklace. The thought of him wanking while watching her made her feel dirty. She decided to have another shower. At last she had a way of getting rid of him, and nothing could give her greater pleasure. In the shower, she scrubbed herself clean, but couldn't forget the sight of his horrible, blue veined penis, ejaculating in the doorway.

Dave returned to the bathroom.

"Do you want a coffee?" he said in a wimpy voice.

"You must be joking," she replied from the cubicle, "do you mind, I'd like a little privacy."

Dave slowly went downstairs, and started making a coffee, he knew he was in trouble now, and he could see no way out of it. He heard Sarah come out of the shower, and walk across the upstairs landing, into her room. He finished making his coffee, and walked back up the stairs to her room. Standing in her doorway, he said:

"Look, Sarah, there's no harm been done, if you keep quiet about it, I'll cover for you, whenever you want to go out, and I'll also give you some money, extra pocket money each week, surely that's a good deal?"

"Get out of my room, I've said all I'm going to, just keep away from me, that's all."

"But if you tell Janice, it'll achieve nothing, what can you possibly gain from it, it'll only upset your mother, and you don't want that, do you?"

"I can't believe this, you wanked in the bathroom doorway, while I was having a shower, and you want me to forget it, you're mad."

"But what good will telling Janice do? All I'm asking, is for you to keep stum."

"Alright, you pack your bags and leave, and I'll say nothing, and that's my final word on the matter."

"But ..."

"Do you mind, I want to get dressed, or do you want another wank, while I'm doing that?"

Dave's head fell, and he sloped from the room. She had him,

now he'd have to leave, no other course of action was open to him. But where to go, a bedsit for a few nights, just 'til he sorted himself out, maybe Sarah would have a change of heart? Maybe he could come back after a week or so?

"What a mess."

As he stood on the landing, he heard the front door open, "Hello," shouted Janice.

Dave walked down stairs to greet her in the hallway,

"Hi ya, work's a bit quiet, so I took the afternoon off."

"Oh, is Sarah in?"

"Yes, she's upstairs in her room."

"Sarah," Janice shouted from the foot of the stairs, "I'm home love, is there anything I can get you?"

"No thanks mum, Dave's been looking after me," came the reply. Dave gulped, and started to move awkwardly, he felt sick, and could feel himself sweating.

"Make us a coffee?" Janice demanded as she disappeared into the lounge.

"What? Oh a coffee, yeah, sure."

Janice leant back through the lounge doorway,

"You alright, you look like you've seen a ghost," she said.

"No, I don't feel too good."

"Well, that's hardly surprising after the state you came home in last night, is it? I think we need to talk."

"Do we?"

"You're damned right we do, make me a coffee, and we'll do it now."

Dave made the coffee, and joined his wife in the lounge.

"I know that everything you've said is true, I don't have any excuses, and maybe you're right. I think a trial separation is what we both need," he said as he handed her a coffee.

Janice was slightly taken aback, it was true that she could not take any more of his drinking, but she hadn't expected him to be quite so bold. She looked at the man she had married, and felt a little sorry for him, but perhaps that was what he wanted.

"Well," she said, "I must admit the last few weeks have been a nightmare, and maybe a little space could help us both to sort things out."

"I thought I might move out for a while, perhaps stay in a bedsit, and we could meet up again in a week or so, and see if anything has changed."

Janice looked sad, she had really hoped the marriage would work, but she had to make a stand.

"OK, let's leave it like that then, you have a few days away, and we'll see how it goes, but I'm not promising anything, I've got to sort myself out, and make sure it would work, before I'll have you back."

"I understand," he said, with tears welling up in his eyes, "I'll pack enough shirts and undies to last about a week, and" he gulped, "see you when I see you."

Dave left the room, and she heard him climb the stairs, she wanted to cry too, but bit hard on her lip to hold back the tears.

He packed a bag, and poked his head into Sarah's room.

"Look, I've told your mother I'm going for a while, I don't think you should say anything, it won't help."

Sarah looked up at the pathetic figure in the doorway, she didn't feel sorry for him, she just felt anger.

"Good, I think it's for the best," she said, "Don't let me keep you."

Head down, Dave walked out of her room.

"And look," she added, "if I keep quiet, it's only to spare mum any further pain, I'll do nothing for you."

He stopped at the lounge door.

"I'll say goodbye then," he mumbled, very close to tears.

Janice looked up, "OK, take care." she said, then quickly looked away.

"Bye, and I'm sorry."

She heard him slam the front door, and then started to cry. Although she had stopped loving him, in a strange way, she still cared. She wanted him out of her life, but didn't want anything bad to happen to him. It was a weird feeling. As soon as she heard the car pull away, Sarah came downstairs to see her mother.

"You alright mum?" she said sympathetically, "you want anything?"

Janice put her arms up, and the two women hugged each other.

"You'll be much better off without him, you'll see," said Sarah after a short time, "he's bad news."

"You're probably right, but it still hurts. I thought it would be so different, I knew he could never replace your dad, nobody could, but I dunno ..."

"Come on, let's get you a drink, you'll feel a lot better in a while."

"Alright, make me a G and T will you? And I'll make you something to eat."

"Don't worry about food, I'll get us a take way, what do you fancy?"

Janice sat with her thoughts, as her daughter made her a drink. Her life would never be the same again.

Chapter 5

There was nothing really kind or nice,
that he could say about her,
but could he handle life alone,
could he get by without her?

In the Civic Centre Police Station, Quinn and Crouch sat discussing the St Mary's assault case.
"Did you get the description etc. into the local rag Mike?" Quinn asked his young colleague.
"Yes, I think it was too late for the first edition, but they assured me it would be in the City final."
"Good, did you manage to ask any cab companies if our friend did, in fact, taxi home?"
"Yeah, I spoke to all the major ones, but no one took a fare that night to Hedge End. I reckon he drove home pissed."
"Mmm, possibly, and what about an address?"
"Well, there are four Prices listed in that area, but only one with the Christian name David, it's got to be our man."
"OK, tomorrow I want to interview Diane Michells, and probably the first victim, I know the uniformed lads got a fair amount from them, but it may just be ..."
The 'phone interrupted him.
"Yes, Detective Inspector Quinn," he snapped. "I see, yes, OK, well can she come in to make a statement, yes it would be better, yes, no, I understand you don't want to get involved, but it would really help us, yes we can keep your daughter's name out of the papers. OK, yes, lunchtime tomorrow, fine, and your name is ...OK, I've got all that, can we reach you by 'phone? 0489 ...right, thank you."
Quinn finished writing some numbers on a pad.
"Anything interesting sir?" Crouch asked.
"Could be, some woman, would you believe from Hedge End, reckons her daughter was accosted by a man in the High Street,

wants to give a statement, after reading about it in the paper."

"Hedge End again? It all seems to point to out friend Price."

"Yes, but perhaps too much."

"Who is this girl?"

"Helen Wright, she'll drop by tomorrow at lunchtime for a little chat."

"Great. Want anything from the canteen? I'm just goin' to nip there for a sarnie."

"No thanks, Mike," said Quinn, shaking his head.

* * *

Dave had driven to the Shirley district of Southampton, an area on the western side, where almost every other building is a guest house, B&B, or private hotel. He drove down Languard Road, undecided where to stop, as the choice was so great, and every one had 'vacancies'. He finally pulled up outside the 'Kimberley Guest House'. He'd once known a girl called Kimberley, and although this had no relevance at all, he'd always liked the name.

Walking up to the door, Dave was about to ring the ornate brass bell push, when he noticed a small hand-written sign, "Please enter." Opening the solid wooden door, he stepped inside, and the door slammed shut behind him.

"Hello," said a female voice, "please do come in."

It was fairly dark inside the room, and it took a few moments for his eyes to adjust. Straight in front of him was a large Victorian staircase, bowing out of view at the first landing, with a small counter to the left hand side. On the counter was a card that read 'Reception' and a little button bell. An elderly lady, not much taller than the counter, stood behind and greeted him with a gummy smile.

"Looking for a room?" she asked, with a toothless grin. Dave wanted to run, it was like a scene from the 'Adams Family' movie.

"Um, yes."

"With or without TV?"

"With."

"Ten pounds fifty a night, in advance," she continued still grinning, "and that includes full English breakfast."

He stared at her, and tried to think of a reason to leg it.

"It's only for one night."

"That's OK, we get lots of travelling salesmen here, I think you'll find the rooms are very nice."

She'd spoken about four sentences, but still had the same grin on her face, it looked like it was a permanent fixture.

"Well, alright, will you take a cheque?"

"Of course dearie, if you've got a cheque card."

Dave gulped. "Christ, I hope the room's got a good lock on it," he thought, "I'll just go to the car and get my things, be back in a minute."

"Don't you want to see the room first?"

"What? Oh, sorry, yes please."

He followed her up the buckled staircase, to the first floor, and she unlocked room number 1.

"Um, am I your only guest?" he asked timidly.

"Well, it's very quiet this time of year, but it should fill up a little tomorrow, it's always busier at the weekends."

Dave glanced into the little box-room, "Oh, what the hell. Yes it'll do fine, I'll get my things."

"Oh, the bathroom and toilet are just up the landing on the left," she added.

"OK."

Walking back to the car, he wondered if he hadn't been a little hasty, but it was cheap, and he could always find better accommodation tomorrow.

Back at reception, Irene Marshall had put her teeth in, which at least stopped her grinning, but unfortunately, she had now acquired a whistle.

"Would you like to pay now sssir?" she asked.

Dave placed his case down, and took out his cheque book. "Who shall I make the cheque payable to?"

"Kimberley Guessst Houssse," she replied, spraying Dave with saliva. He wiped the front of his clothes, wrote out the cheque and handed it too her, with his cheque card. "Thanksss," she whistled, almost hitting a top 'C' as she handed him a key, and his cheque card.

Dave went up to room number 1, unlocked the door, and looked around the room. It was so small that when the door opened fully, it hit the bottom of the bed. A 14-inch television set was perched on top of a brown chest of drawers, next to a half size white wardrobe. Nothing in the room matched. The bed was covered with a brown quilt, the carpet was navy blue, and the curtains were green. It looked as if it had been furnished by a colour blind person from a car boot sale. Next to the wardrobe was the smallest vanity unit and sink he'd ever seen.

Dave sighed and placed his case on the bed, and started to unpack. As he'd only packed the bare essentials, this did not take too long. He pushed the empty case under the bed, and turned on the TV. It was early evening, and a regional news programme was on. He sat on the bed and wondered if Sarah had told Janice about what had happened.

"Nah," he decided, "I've left, and she'd have no reason to say anything."

He was still unsure whether he'd actually done anything to the girl, or if it was all in his mind. "Great pair of tits though."

A knock on the door made him jump.

"Who is it?" he asked.

"Sssorry to bother you, but before you go out, could you sssign a regissstration card?" said a voice through the door.

"Yeah, OK, I'll be down in a few minutes."

"Thanksss."

"God, must remember not to ask for sssausssagesss for breakfast," he joked, before splashing on his favourite after-shave, and following the old lady down the stairs. The little reception area was empty, so he rang the bell. A serving hatch behind him squeaked open, and the woman's head poked through it.

"Oh, I didn't expect you ssso sssoon, hang on, I'll be right round."

"Thought I'd go for an early evening stroll," Dave replied as he waited for her to appear. Coming through a side door, she handed him a pink card.

"Are you in Sssouthampton on busssinesss?" she hissed, almost losing her teeth on the last word.

"Yes, that's right."

"Where you from?"

"London."

"Really, I used to live in London. Which part?"

"Oh shit, you bloody well would, wouldn't you?", he thought. "Well, not actually in London, just outside you know, one of the suburbs."

"I see," she said, realising he didn't want to be any more specific, "if you fill in the card then."

Dave had never before realised how many times the letter 's' was used in the English language. He picked up a pen from the counter and started to write. Name: David Price, Address: London, Nationality: English, Length of Stay: 1 night, "Look is all this necessary?" he questioned.

"Certainly. I have to keep recordsss," Dave stepped back to avoid being soaked, "the police are very ssstrict on it."

"Bloody waste of time, if you ask me."

"OK, let'sss sssee what you've written," she said, taking the card from him and putting on her glasses.

"Haven't you got a better address than thisss?"

Dave tutted and took the card back from her. At the back of the counter he noticed a packet of Walker's crisps. He scribbled an address in the appropriate box: 16 Walker Avenue, Staines, London.

"Anything else?" he asked sarcastically, as he handed back the card.

She scrutinised it. "No, that's fine."

"OK, see you later," he mumbled, as he left and walked out into the cool evening air. Standing in the front garden of the guest house, he was undecided what to do.

"A little stroll up Shirley High Road, see if I can find a bank, and get some money out, then back for a wank," he mumbled to himself, as he turned left out of the gate, and headed for Shirley. The evening was fine, but some fairly strong March winds made it feel chilly.

After obtaining some cash from his bank's 'hole in the wall' he went back to the guest house, collected the magazines from the boot of his car, and returned to his room. He'd inadvertently left the television on in his room, and an Aussie soap opera was showing.

"Fucking crap," he said, as he turned off the set.

There was no room for a chair, so he sat on the edge of the bed, and opened up the envelope.

"Hello girls," he quipped as he glanced through the mags, when there was a loud knock on the door. "Now what?" he muttered, as he quickly threw the items under the quilt.

"Mr Price," said a voice through the door.

"What's the old dragon want now?"

"Mr Price. Sorry to bother you, but as you're the only resident staying tonight, I wondered what time you would like breakfast."

"Oh God," he said as he opened the door.

"I said, 'as you are the only ...'" she repeated.

"Yes, yes," he angrily interrupted. "I heard what you said, about eight o'clock please."

"Thank you," said the old lady, "sorry to have disturbed you." Dave sighed, tapping his fingers on the opened door, "Fine," he added and slammed the door, listening to her go back down the rickety old stairs, muttering something about manners to herself.

He collected his books from under the quilt, but was not in the mood. He put them back in their envelope, and hid them under some clothes in the chest of drawers.

He lay on the bed, and felt himself drifting into sleep.

* * *

Janice had stopped crying, and was sitting drinking coffee with her daughter.

"Men," she said wiping her eyes and smiling, "they're all bastards."

"Don't worry mum," said Sarah softly, "we've all made mistakes."

"You never liked Dave, did you?"

"Well, to be honest, I always thought you could have done a lot better, you still look great."

"Don't be silly," said Janice slightly embarrassed, adding coyly, "you really think so?"

"Of course, you'll see, there will be plenty of men banging on the door."

"I don't know if I want lots of men banging on the door, perhaps just a few, eh?"

The two women cuddled. Sarah wondered whether she should tell her mother of the happenings that afternoon. Would it help? They embraced on the sofa and Janice started to sob again.

"I've made a right mess of it, first your dad dying, now this, and all while you're trying to take your exams."

"Now stop it, dad's death was not your fault, just forget this Dave character, and get on with your life."

"Such an old head on young shoulders."

"You know I'm right, in fact, I think the manager at the shop you work at fancies you, and he's a bit of alright."

"What?" Janice got up, "you don't even know my manager, that's a very strange thing to say."

They chatted like old school friends, talking about men, and joking about life, but all the time Sarah wanted to tell her mother about the shower incident. But when?

* * *

Under a massive pair of black breasts, Dave was laid. He was licking and sucking, when suddenly he jumped, finding himself alone, in a very dark and strange room.

"What?" he croaked, opening his eyes, and glancing at the surroundings of his cheap and tacky room. Slowly it all came back to him.

The argument with Janice, the scene with Sarah, and he felt gutted. Getting up slowly from the bed, he turned on the light, and fumbled for his cigarettes. After a couple of puffs, he looked around for an ashtray. "Oh, sod it," he said as he flicked his ash on the floor and rubbed it into the carpet with his shoe. He'd decided to go out for a few beers, and as it was Thursday, thought about going to a new wine bar called 'The Jumping Jive' which was locally known as a 'grab a granny' venue on Thursday nights. He crept down the stairs, praying that Mrs Marshall and her amazing dentures would not hear him.

He opened the front door and felt he'd escaped from Colditz.

"Goodnight Mr Priccce," came a whistle from behind him, and he ran for the car.

Driving straight to the wine bar, he parked a short distance away, and walked in.

The bar had a low timbered ceiling and was completely panelled in dark antique oak. The place was about half full, with a high percentage of women clientele, mostly sitting in pairs. He walked to the bar.

"Pint of bitter, please" he politely ordered.

"Sorry mate, only serve halves," came the reply from an effeminate sounding barman in his late fifties.

"OK, half a pint then," he muttered angrily.

"That'll be one pound exactly."

"Christ, that's expensive," he said under his breath, as he handed over a pound coin, and walked over to an empty table, almost in the centre of the room.

On the table next to him sat two young women, in their early twenties.

"Mmm, not bad," Dave thought as he lit up a cigarette, in a very nonchalant manner. One of the girls noticed he was staring, and moved her chair round, so that she had her back towards him.

The half pint disappeared in seconds, it always seems much easier to drink two halves than one pint. Glancing around the room, Dave soon realised that the females present were all much too young for him, not so much 'grab a granny' as 'yank a youth' or 'take a teeny'.

"Fuck it, I'm not sitting here all night paying these prices," he thought, and got up and left.

He drove across town and arrived at 'Victors' guessing that it would be much busier on a Thursday than it had been the night before. And so it was. There were 5 young 'student' types sitting on stools around the bar, whilst the rest of the room was empty. He ordered a pint, and settled for 'Fullers'. It was the same dark-haired woman who served him and he suddenly started to piece together his movements from the previous evening.

"Anything else?" asked the barmaid, interrupting his thoughts.

"Sorry, no that's all, thank you."

He paid, and sat at a table near the bar. He started to realise why he'd married Janice. Boredom. It was so difficult for a single man, especially someone like Dave, to meet new friends. Southampton is not known for its friendliness or hospitality, being a typical Southern Town, where everyone tends to keep themselves to themselves. The few friends he had were all married, and he'd lost touch with every one of them. He noticed a pay-phone on the wall, and thought he ought to ring Janice, and let her know where he was, just in case she needed to get hold of him. He fumbled in his pockets for some change, and walked over to the 'phone.

The telephone ringing tone sounded four times and was answered by the familiar voice of his wife.

"Oh, hello," Dave stammered, "it's me, I thought I'd better let you know where I am staying, in case you need to contact me, you know, in an emergency or something."

The 'phone line was ominously quiet.

"Hello, Janice, is that you?" he said, his voice shaking.

"Sorry, I didn't expect to hear from you so soon," she snapped. "Give me your address, why don't you?"

"I'm at the Kimberley Guest House in Shirley. I'm not sure of the address, but I think it's Languard Road."

"OK, I've got that, everything all right?"

"Yeah, it's fine, lovely room," he lied. "I'm sure it will be perfect until I can find something more permanent.

"Oh good, look I've got to go, the dinner's on the table, and I don't want to let it get cold."

"No, of course not, well, I'll be in touch then."

"Sure," was all he heard, and the 'phone line went dead.

"Supercilious old cow," Dave moaned as he walked back to his table.

He heard someone at the bar mention that they'd have one more beer before going for something to eat. With all that had happened that day, Dave had completely forgotten about eating. "What a good idea, I'll finish this and go get some grub," he thought.

Dave had never been that keen on very spicy food, and although he'd eat some pasta, and enjoyed the occasional Chinese, the one food he hated was Indian. Several years earlier, there'd been a scandal in Southampton, where an Indian restaurant owner was prosecuted, for making his chicken massala sauce creamier by masturbating into the mixture. Dave had never really liked Indian food anyway, but when he heard this he'd made a conscious decision never to eat Asian food again. Even the thought of a curry made him feel queasy.

He had one more cigarette, finished his beer and left the bar. He drove to the 'Aberdeen Angus Steak House' just off Southampton High Street, and ordered a well-done sirloin steak with chips and a bottle of Liebfraumilch.

After his meal, which had arrived in minutes, he finished his wine and ordered a large gin and tonic.

"Would you like a coffee sir?" asked the polite waiter.

"No thanks, just the gin and tonic, and the bill."

He duly paid, stepped from the restaurant and glanced at his digital watch. 10.15. Knowing the pubs close at eleven, he reasoned he had time for a couple of jars, and headed back to his guest house. Parking right outside the 'Kimberley' he walked up Languard Road and turned into Shirley Road. During the day, it was quite a busy main street, but at night it took on a very different facade. Most of the public houses that were evenly spread up and down the road, were in the main, shabby. The first one Dave came to was the 'Duke of Cornwall' an old Victorian building, with arched frosted windows, each proclaiming a different bar: 'Public Bar', 'Lounge Bar', and 'Snug'. Opening the centre door, Dave was hit by a pungent smokey/beery atmosphere, and he was possibly the only person to have walked through that door within the last few hours. As his eyes adjusted to the smog, he noticed that although the windows had different names on them, there was in fact only one large bar. It was a 'Marston's' house, which should guarantee a good pint of real ale. In one corner, four young black men were playing pool, each with a cigarette gripped between their teeth. They stopped, and looked momentarily at Dave as he entered, before continuing with their game. Dave walked up to the bar, and surveyed the real ales on show.

"Yes please," snapped a very fat man in a 'Metallica' T-shirt. He had a roll-up wedged in the corner of his mouth, with his long grey hair tied back in a pony tail. Beads of sweat were visible on his temples, as well as under his arms.

"I'll have a pint of Pedigree please."

The fat man wheezed, causing the ash on his cigarette to fall onto his beer-gut. He rubbed it in and collected a glass from under the bar. Dave stood praying that the remainder of the ash would not drop into the beer and fortunately, and rather remarkably, it didn't.

"One pound fifty five please."

Dave paid, and made his way over to a table by the CD jukebox, placed his glass down, and looked at the selections while reaching for his cigarettes. He selected three 'Simply Red' tracks, and flopped into a chair. At the table next to him sat a woman. Dave glanced in her general direction. She was dressed in a tight leopard skin blouse, with matching pants. Her hair was obviously dyed jet black, and the style of her eye make-up and the brass gypsy earrings, made Dave figure her to be fifty-something. Oddly enough, she was not unattractive, and was probably something of a peach in her youth. She thrust out her chest and ran her fingers through her hair.

"Oh, I like these," she uttered in a strange girly voice as the music began to play.

"God!" Dave thought, then replied, "Yes, they're my favourites. I've got most of their records."

"Really?"

"I'm down from London on business, do you live around here?"

"Yeah, just up the road, wanna buy us a drink then?"

Dave was surprised and slightly taken aback by her boldness, "Sure, what is it?"

"Just a large vodka and orange," she answered.

Dave went to the bar, bought her the drink and returned to find her sitting at his table.

"There you go," he said as he sat down. "I'm Dave Price, a price by name, but a prince by nature," he quipped. "And you?"

"Margaret, but everyone calls me Maggie."

"Yeah, Shaggy Maggie," quipped one of the young black guys, as if prompted.

"Hi Maggie, nice to meet you," Dave said, ignoring the remark. As he looked at her again, in a better light he reckoned she was nearer sixty, with her face make-up plastered on so thick, it resembled Polyfilla. Still it was better than nothing.

"So, you're from London, don't have much of a London accent, what part you from?"

"Actually, I was born in Southampton, but have just moved up to Staines."

"What business you in?" she said, seemingly interested.

"Chandlery, and you?"

"None, I don't work, ain't fucking worth it. I gets enough on the dole to keep me in fags and booze, so what's the point. Eh?"

"Fair enough," said Dave, raising his eyebrows slightly.

"I used to be a model, but I 'spect you could tell that."
"Oh yes," Dave replied politely, the booze finally getting to him. He took out his cigarettes, and before he had even opened the packet, she leaned forward.

"Don't mind if I do," she said.

They carried on their small talk, and Dave discovered that she'd been widowed for several years, but now lived on social handouts in a council flat. Dave finished his beer and got up.

"Same again for me Luvey," she demanded.

This was turning out to be an expensive evening, but he'd never fucked a sixty year old, and felt sure that was about to change. Obviously, the law of the land did not apply in this little part of Shirley, and they carried on drinking for another hour.

By this time, Dave was near paralytic, but she seemed to have hollow legs. His words were slurring, and he was rocking gently to and fro in his seat. When they finally left, they stopped on the pavement in the cool evening air, right outside the pub.

"Want me to walk you home?" he mumbled.

"Why? Fancy a shag?" she replied, grinning strangely.

"Well, put like that, why not?"

"Cost ya twenty quid, and I don't do blow jobs, and you have to use a Johnny."

"Twenty quid, you joking? You ought to be paying me," he stormed. "I ain't got twenty quid, I nearly spent that on you in the boozer."

"Oh well, suit yourself, see you around sometime," she said as she threw back her head, and walked off, fairly briskly.

Dave stood mortified. "Fuckin' old whore," he shouted.

She stopped, turned around, and sticking one finger upright replied, "Up yours, Ugly," and was gone.

Dave struggled down the road, his legs were playing up.

"I can't believe it, twenty quid. Twenty bloody quid, I can't even pull an old bag like that," he mumbled.

Turning into Languard Road, he was dying for a piss and so climbed over a garden wall to relieve himself in the house next door to the Kimberley. Unfortunately, he did not notice the gnome and ornamental fish pond and fell backwards over the little fellow's fishing rod and landed bum down in the shallow water.

"Aw ... fuck it!" he yelled, and urinated where he sat.

*　*　*

Friday morning was a turning point for the police. Since the story had appeared in the local paper, they'd had several calls, albeit anonymous, of which one was most interesting.

A lady caller had stated she'd been walking her dog in the St Mary's Street area, on the night in question, and had noticed a blue Ford car speeding away. The only thing she remembered about the car was that it had a lot of stickers in the back window, all of them advertising various marine products, mainly outboard motors and the like, and although she didn't get a perfect view of the driver, he certainly seemed to fit the description, as given in the newspaper.

"Right, Mike," said Quinn, "'phone the number you've got for this Price fella, and let's have a word with him. Will you?"

"OK sir, shall I do it now?"

"Yes, it's just eight-thirty, and he might not have left for work yet."

Mike Crouch took out his note pad, found the page with the Hedge End telephone number on it, and dialled.

"Good morning madam, is it possible to speak to Mr D Price please?" he said in his best police voice. "I see," he continued. "Yes, it's Southampton Police. Sgt Crouch speaking ... No, just inquiries, can you give me his work number? ... Yes, I've got that, and the name of the company? ... Mmm ... right Calvin Marine, and they're in Southampton are they? ... Yes, I've got that ... no it's nothing to worry about, but we may be back in touch. Thank you."

Crouch replaced the receiver and turned to his boss.

"Well that's interesting, he works for a marine company," continued Crouch, getting excited, "and he's not home at the moment."

"Well, what are you waiting for, ring his works number and let's have a word with him."

Crouch dialled the number given to him by Mrs Price. It rang twice.

"Good morning, Calvin Marine, Joanne speaking. How can I help you?" came the prompt reply.

"Could I speak to Mr Price please?"

"I'm sorry sir, but Mr Price has just 'phoned in sick, he will not be in today. Perhaps Mr Calvin could help you? Who should I say is calling?"

"'Phoned in sick?" questioned Crouch, "that's strange."

"Who's calling please?"

"Oh yes, I'm sorry. This is Southampton Civic Centre Police Station, do you have a number I can reach Mr Price on?"

"I'm sorry sir, but I cannot give you that information over the 'phone, its ..."

"Yes, of course you're right, perhaps you could confirm your address, and I'll pop down to see you in person ... yes, I know it Canute Road, yeah, I've got that ...Oh, and just one other thing, could you confirm what car Price drives ... yes, and the colour ... thank you. You've been most helpful ...no, there's no problem, just routine ... Bye."

"Problem Mike?" said Quinn

"Yes, it's very strange, I was told by his wife he was at work, but he's just 'phoned in sick, so where do you think he could be?"

"Maybe he's got a lover," said Quinn in a patronising voice.

"And also, he drives a blue Ford motor, now surely that's too much of a coincidence?"

"Could be right. Make us a cup of tea, then pop down to check it out, will you?"

"OK, Gu-sir."

"Careful Mike," smiled Quinn, "you know my feelings on the G-word."

"Sorry."

* * *

A short time earlier, Dave Price had been woken by several heavy bangs on his door.

"Mr Price, Mr Price, it's Mrs Marshall, it's your morning call, do you want to come down for breakfast? It's about eight."

Dave rolled over. "What the fuck?" he murmured, trying to get his thoughts together. He rubbed his eyes and let them acclimatise to the weak light, straining through the drawn curtains. He was still fully clothed and smelt of urine.

"Go away," he screamed, then had a coughing fit.

"OK dear, see you in a minute."

"Deaf old bag," Dave muttered, when he'd finally finished coughing. He swung his legs off the bed and felt between his crutch. It was soaking wet. "Aw shit, well there's no way I'm going to work today."

After visiting the bathroom, he got changed into a pair of clean jeans, put on a sweatshirt, and very carefully crawled downstairs.

When he reached the bottom of the stairs, he cagily looked around for the dreaded Mrs Marshall.

"Good morning sssir," she whisstled, "ready for your breakfassst?"

"Oh God, she's put her teeth in," Dave thought. "No breakfast thank you, just a coffee, and have you a 'phone I can use?"

"Of courssse, itsss by the door in the dining-room," she sprayed, causing Dave to jump back awkwardly.

He telephoned the office, made his excuses, and sat down in the dining room to drink the coffee Mrs Marshall had left for him. He noticed strange little globules floating on the top.

"Please God, tell me she wasn't singing when she made this."

* * *

Mike Crouch walked out of the Civic Centre, and to the Police car. Although it was only 09.15, he knew a little transport cafe which sold the finest bacon butties in the world. He'd already decided to get one on the way to Calvin Marine.

"This is the life," he said to himself, as he devoured the greasy item in four bites, leaving tomato ketchup all around his lips. Finding an old piece of tissue paper in his trouser pocket, he wiped his face, and finally headed for Canute Road. He entered the office, with his official walk, and produced his warrant card immediately.

"Good morning, I'm Sgt Crouch, I think I spoke to you earlier," he said, smiling at the lovely Joanne.

"Yes," she replied, "how can I help you?"

He meticulously took out his note pad and pen, and continued, "As I said on the 'phone, this is only an enquiry, but I wonder if you could confirm where Mr Price is today."

"Well, as I told you, he 'phoned in at about twenty five past eight, saying that he was still unwell, and would not be in."

"I see, and when you say still unwell, has he been poorly recently?"

"Yes, he hasn't looked right for a few weeks, between you and me, I think he might have problems at home, what with all his drinking and that."

"Oh, he drinks a lot, does he?"

"Yeah, I can smell it on him most days."

"Well, we need to speak to him, and I wondered if you knew where we could contact him?"

"What do you mean? His home address?"

"Well, that would do for a start."

"I'll go and get Mr Calvin, he keeps all the records. Would you like a drink, or something?" she asked with a very seductive smile.

Crouch knew he'd rather have the something, but settled for a drink. "Love a tea, please."

"OK, I'll just get Mr Calvin for you."

Crouch watched Joanne walk up the office and tap on a door at the end of the room. An older man appeared, and gestured for Crouch to approach. He held out his hand, as the young policeman reached him.

"Good morning. I'm John Calvin. How can I help you officer?"

"Good morning sir, as I was explaining to the young lady, I would very much like to get in touch with your Mr Price, and wondered if you could oblige with his home address."

"Of course, anything to help the police, just step into my office and I'll see what I can do. Dave's not in any trouble, is he?"

"Oh no sir, just routine, that's all."

"Now let me see," said Calvin, flicking through his filing cabinet, "Ah yes, here it is."

He handed Crouch a brown manila folder with the name PRICE written in block capitals on it. The officer made a note of the information.

"Thank you very much sir, you've been a great help,"

"Least I can do."

"Right, if you'll excuse me, your charming secretary has very kindly made me a cup of tea, and with your leave, I'll quickly drink it and be on my way."

Crouch shook Calvin's hand again, and left his office. Joanne had just arrived with the beverage, and Crouch thanked her for it as he took the steaming cup from her. They walked back down the office, and Joanne said, "This is nothing to do with those rapes, is it?"

Crouch was a little shocked. "Now, why would you think that?" he asked.

"Oh, no reason, just forget I said it."

Crouch was not going to let it go that easy. "No, come on, let's hear it, you want to tell me something, don't you?"

"Well, I don't like to say anything really, but he's pretty weird you know, particularly when he's had a few."

"Really, when you say weird, how weird?"

"I wish I hadn't of mentioned it ..."

"Come on, you started so you must finish," he joked in a Magnus Magnusson type voice.

Joanne sighed, and gulped a large intake of breath.

"Well, the other day, just after lunch, he'd been drinking and when he got back to the office, he grabbed me, it was nothing really, but it frightened me, you know?"

"Yes, I know, when you say 'grabbed' what exactly do you mean?"

"He tried to hug me, and give me a kiss, that's all, perhaps I over-reacted, perhaps I shouldn't of ..."

"Of course you should, did you tell your boss?"

"No, but I threatened Dave, and said if he ever tried it on again, he'd be in trouble. Look, I don't want to ..."

"No, OK, I understand, let's leave it there, but perhaps, if I need to, we could talk again. OK?"

"I don't want to get him into any trouble."

"No, of course not, don't worry, we can be very discreet when we need to be, just leave it to me."

He finished his tea, and left the office, the only question on his mind being whether to have another sandwich or not, prior to going back to the station.

"Oh, why not?"

While Crouch had been seeing the Calvin operation, Quinn had received a disturbing call from the hospital. It appeared that Diane Michells had contracted Hepatitis A, probably from the gash on her knee, which had come into contact with faeces in the subway. The doctors were particularly worried about the speed with which the virus had spread, and feared it could be a very dangerous, if not fatal, strain. He'd arranged to go to the hospital later that day to speak to the doctor handling her case, and also to have a chat with Diane herself.

Crouch had arrived back, via the cafe, and was feeling fairly happy with himself. He strolled through the front door of the police station, head in air, pressed the security code on the door lock mechanism, which led straight to the general office, via a small connecting corridor, and went directly to his desk. His boss was apparently out, so Crouch turned to one of his colleagues and enquired: "Where's the guv?"

"I think he's down the loo, Mike, but don't let him catch you calling him that."

"Sure, I know. Oh! by the way, Jeff, how's the missus these days? We haven't seen you two in ages."

"No, I was just saying to ..."

"Mike," Quinn interrupted as he entered the room. "We've got to do this bastard quick, what news from his works?"

"You OK sir?"

"Yeah, I'm OK, but there's been a development, and we need to close this one a.s.a.p."

"Really, why's that?" Crouch asked.

Quinn told his sergeant the news from the hospital, and Crouch relayed the information he'd obtained from Calvin Marine.

"Right, let's go round to the Price's house and see if Mrs Price knows where her husband is."

"Shall I ring first?"

"No, don't bother, I can do with some air and we also need to call at the hospital sometime this morning, so we can do it all on the way back."

They left the station and got into their car. Quinn flared his nostrils, looking around for evidence of food. Crouch started the car and said nothing. They drove across Southampton and through the plethora of traffic lights, in and around the city centre, out onto the

M27 motorway, arriving in Hedge End at 10.20. They found the house easily, parked the car outside, and both walked up the driveway to the front door. Quinn rang the door bell. There was no reply. A woman appeared from the house next door and stopped when she noticed the two men.

"I don't think they're in," she said. "They both work you know."

"Oh, I see," said Quinn. "Have you any idea when either of them will be back?"

"Well, Janice, Mrs Price that is, only works part time, and I think she usually gets home sometime in the early afternoon."

"OK, thank you madam, we'll call back later."

They returned to their car.

"Next stop the General, let's go and see how Miss Michells is doing."

* * *

After Dave had finished his coffee, he decided to spend the day trying to find some suitable accommodation, and had wondered if his old flat was still available. It had only cost £280 a month and would be ideal. Returning to his room, he threw his dirty clothes into the wardrobe and went into Southampton City centre, and the 'Homefinders' property agency.

"Well, Mr Price, I'm afraid your old flat is no longer on our books," said a smartly dressed woman at the agency. "However, we have three or four others in that area that might suit."

"OK, I have the day off, so perhaps you could arrange some viewings this afternoon."

"I'll see what I can do. Here's my card, give me a call at about two-thirty and I'll try to sort out something for you."

"Great, see you later then. Oh, will I need new references?"
"No, I don't think so, the ones we have on file seem fine, but you will need to pay a month's rent in advance and sign a lease for at least three months, maybe even six."

"No problem," said Dave as he got up and left the shop.

He stood outside and pondered. "Perhaps I should give Janice a ring before I take on a flat, just in case she's had a change of heart. No point wasting money."

Just a few hundred yards from Homefinders was a public house called The Duchess and Dave fed two more twenty pence coins into the parking meter and made for the pub. It had just opened and after ordering a pint he walked across the empty bar to the pay 'phone, and dialled the number of Janice's place of employment. It was answered by a very strange sounding young girl with a lisp, and Dave asked to speak to his wife.

"Hello, Janice? It's me, Dave."

"Oh, hello. Where are you?"

"I've taken the day off work to sort out my accommodation. I can't stay at the guest house for ever and just wondered how things were with you."

"I'm fine thanks, but it's a bit awkward at the moment. The shop's full of customers."

"I see, well I wondered if you had had a change of heart? You sure we're doing the right thing? I mean, we've ..."

Janice interrupted him in a rather rude and off-hand manner. "Look, Dave, I'm sorry, I really am, but the more I think about it, the more I'm convinced this is right for us, I really need some space to sort myself out."

"Yes, I know, perhaps I need some space as well, can I come over sometime at the weekend and collect a few more things once I've sorted out a flat?"

"Of course you can, but I'm having the locks changed, so you'll need to ring me first."

"Christ, you don't hang around, do you? I've only been gone a few hours and you're changing the locks!"

"Dave, I don't want to argue about it, I've made up my mind, and that's that."

"OK, OK, so who's arguing? I'll ring you later."

Dave slammed down the 'phone receiver and stood red faced. He realised there was no way back now, but at least it seemed as if Sarah had kept quiet about his little misdemeanour. He walked back to the bar, had a swig of his beer, and took out his cigarettes. There was only one left in the packet. He sighed and tutted, almost at the same time.

"'Scuse me mate," he said to the barman, "Where's your fag machine?"

"Round on the right, just outside the gent's loo."

"Thanks."

He went to the machine and fumbled in his pockets. "Bloody hell, the old cash situation's bad," he murmured, as he found his last two pound coins, and realised that it was the only money he had left.

Dave left the pub after finishing his beer, and went to a bank in the High Street. He checked his account balance. He was somewhat surprised to find he had under £230 left, and that did not allow for the cheque he'd given to the Kimberley. It was the 12th of March and his payday was not until the 28th, so he'd have to try to be a little more careful over the next few weeks. But that might be difficult. He drew out some cash, bought a roast beef sandwich from BHS and drove to Mayflower Park, which overlooks Southampton Water. He stopped the car and unwrapped his food. A large Japanese container ship was being carefully towed up the Solent to its berth. Seagulls were dipping and diving around its bow, searching for scraps of food, and squawking frantically.

Dave sat in silence feeling sorry for himself. He'd have to pull himself out of this depression, but how?

"What I need is a nice bit of pussy, that would do the trick."

* * *

Quinn and Crouch had arrived at Southampton General Hospital and ascertained the room Diane Michells was in. She had been transferred from the main ward and had her own private room on level D. The two police officers took the elevator, and walked along the corridor, neither had spoken, and this was one of the jobs Quinn hated. He had no trouble handling villains, but victims he found embarrassingly awkward to deal with. They arrived at the door and tapped once before entering. A uniformed WPC was sitting on a chair by the bed.

"Good morning sir," she said, as she jumped to her feet, unsure whether to salute or not.

"Good morning Harris," snapped Quinn. "We're here to speak to Diane."

"Certainly, sir," she replied, and moved away from the bed to stand in a recess near the window.

Diane Michells looked up from the book she was reading and smiled. Her face said it all, this was something she'd probably never get over and Quinn felt his blood pressure rising with anger and rage.

"Good morning, Diane. I'm Detective Inspector Quinn and this is Sergeant Crouch. Is it OK to ask you a few questions, it won't take long?"

"Of course," said Diane, her eyes welling with tears. She coughed very quietly and wiped her moist eyes. "I'm sorry, but it was so horrible."

"I know, I know, this won't take long, I promise, but it needs to be done now if we are to catch the man who did this to you."

"I'm alright, honestly."

"Good," Quinn sat down in the chair vacated by the WPC and continued in a very soft voice. "I know you've said it all before, but can we just go over a few of the facts, just to make sure we've got them right? Did you get a look at the man; can you give us a little more on what he looked like?"

Diane gulped back the lump in her throat. "All I know is that he was wearing some sort of car coat or anorak, seemed to be about five foot eight tall and had brown hair, and not much of it either."

"Could you identify him, say, from a mug shot?"

"No, I'm sorry, it all happened so quickly."

The very thought of the incident was making her tearful again and she rubbed her eyes with the backs of her hands. Quinn looked down at her bruised face. If he got hold of the bastard ... He continued: "You mentioned an odour, something you recognised?"

"Oh yes, I don't think I can ever smell it again without reliving the whole nightmare."

"An aftershave?"

"Yeah, you know the one. It's always being advertised on telly with the stupid tune 'Corduroy Vert'."

"Oh yes, I know the one. Unfortunately nearly everyone and his granny wears it."

She laughed, "I can't imagine my granny wearing it."

"No, nor mine." It had broken the ice and any tension in the room seemed to lift.

Quinn carried on gently questioning the girl but, in the end, didn't have anything more to go on.

"Well, thanks very much, you've been a great help," he lied. "We'll leave you in peace and hope that you feel better soon.

Diane reached over to Quinn's coat sleeve. "You will get him, won't you?" she murmured.

"Oh, don't worry, we'll get him and I promise you this, when we do, he'll get exactly what he deserves."

Crouch was quite impressed with the way Quinn had handled the delicate situation and was somewhat surprised how the 'hardman' of the police force could be so gentle when he needed to be. They left the room and walked back down the corridor.

"Let's have a word with this Doctor fellow, shall we? Now what did the nurse say his name was?"

"Doctor Leonard Henderson, I believe," interjected Crouch.

"Yeah, that's it. And where can we find him?"

"In the office in the middle of this floor, I think."

"Good. Just making sure you're paying attention," smiled Quinn, as they walked into the middle section of the level. Stopping at one of the rooms, which had its door ajar, Quinn peered around the edge and gently pushed the door open with his foot.

"Yes?" said a very loud and booming voice. "Can I help you?"

"Police! Madam, we're looking for Doctor Henderson."

The door flew open and a very large nurse in a matron's uniform filled the entire space of the door frame.

"Well, you won't find him here, will you? This is matron's room."

"Ah, right. And which is the doctor's room?"

"Third on the left, but he's not there, he's on his morning rounds."

"Fine, and when will he be back?"

"If I know Doctor Henderson, in about fifteen minutes. There's a canteen just across the hall, you could wait there."

"Is he the doctor dealing with the Diane Michells' case?"

"Yes, he is now. The doctor who admitted her has since gone off duty."

"Thank you madam," Quinn hesitated. He so much wanted to call her sir, but resisted the temptation. "Could you tell the doctor we want to see him and will be back in about fifteen minutes. If for any reason he needs to leave, could you ask him to make himself known to us in the canteen before he leaves?"

"Yes," she stormed, and shut the door in their faces.

"If you ever have to come into here for a vasectomy, Mike, just pray she's not the one who does it."

They both laughed and walked across the hallway, down a side corridor and into the visitor's canteen. Quinn just had a cup of tea but Mike had something a little more substantial.

Dr Leonard Henderson had returned from his morning round and, as with most doctors within the National Health Service, had already done a full day's work. He was in a fairly tetchy mood. Matron had informed him of the policemen's presence and he just tutted and retired to his room. He'd never been a very good doctor, adequate some might say, but at 52 years old was just working his way to retirement. He had his own practice, albeit a small one, and did his obligatory few days in the hospital for the NHS. Like many doctors, his hair had become very thin on the top of his head, but this was more than compensated for by a hirsute nasal passage. Hair positively thrived up his nose and was so long, it almost looked like a handlebar moustache. He sat in his office, reading through some notes, when he heard a knock on the door.

"Enter," he yelled and the two police officers strolled in.

"Good morning sir. I'm Detective Inspector Quinn and this is Sergean..."

"Yes, yes, I know who you are. How can I help you? I've got lots of other work to attend to as I'm sure you have."

"Yes, of course," Quinn replied. He did not like this man one bit. Perhaps a punch in the mouth, followed by a kick in the groin might just help his attitude problem. "I wonder if you could tell us about Miss Michells please? She's the young lady brought in last ..."

"Yes, yes I know who she is, it's very simple, she obviously grazed her knee in a fall and contracted the infectious hepatitis or Hepatitis A virus through contact with faeces, possibly human, possibly vermin."

"Well, I've heard of hepatitis, but what exactly does it mean?"

"What it means, my friend, is," the doctor paused, stood up and walked across his little room, as if giving a lecture. "What it means, in laymen's terms, is that an accumulation of bile is present in her blood stream and causing jaundice. Now, we cannot actually give her any medications because the liver is inflamed and sensitive to most drugs, but complete bed rest should help, and hopefully stop the virus from becoming full blown cirrhosis."

"I see. And in this case, you think she'll be OK?"

"My dear friend, I'm just a small town doctor. We'll keep her under observation and do our best. However, if it becomes a fulminant case, this can lead to total liver failure and then, well ..."

"OK, thank you Doctor, we'll be in touch. But should there be any developments, can you please let me know immediately?"

"But of course."

Quinn and Crouch left the doctor's office and headed back down the main corridor to the lift.

"What a bloody prat. Did you see his nose hairs," Quinn said, shaking his head, "Christ, if I was a doctor, I'd get them seen to, even if it meant having me nose sewn up!"

Crouch nodded in agreement as they got into the lift and went back to their car.

"Right, back to the civic, we've got a lunchtime appointment which I think is going to be very interesting."

* * *

Dave sat in his car, contemplating what he should do for the next hour or so, when he was startled by a gentle tap on the window.

Glancing around, he was pleasantly surprised to see a young blonde-haired girl. He frowned slightly and wound down his window.

"Excuse me to bother you, but do you lives in Southampton please?" said the girl in a possibly Scandinavian accent.

"I'm sorry?" stuttered Dave.

"Are you coming from Southampton?" she replied.

"Yes. What can I do for you?"

"I looking for the railway station, do you know it, please?"

"Yes, of course, it's straight along that road, about a mile away," said Dave sitting upright in his seat and peering over the door, trying to look at the girl's body.

"It's kind, many thanks you," she said and started to walk off.

Dave leapt from the car and took a proper look. She was on the short side but certainly had a nice behind. Dave called after her. "Look, if you want, I'm going that way. I'll give you a lift."

The girl stopped and turned, facing Dave. He gasped. Her lovely tanned face was perfectly framed by long ash-blonde hair and even though she had a raincoat on, Dave could see she was very well endowed.

"I'm sorry?"

"I said, I'll give you a lift to the station, it's no trouble. Come on, I'll take you there straight away."

The girl smiled and Dave nearly fainted. He wiped his forehead and gulped for air, covering his mouth as he did so and she walked back towards him.

"My name's Dave," he said in a suave manner as he held out his hand.

"Oh," she giggled. "I am known as Katrina."

"Right Katrina, the station it is."

Thy got in the car and Dave helped her with her seat belt. She smiled at him and her coat opened a little, showing black tights under a very short mini-skirt. Dave's hand shook as he tried to place the key in the ignition. Eventually he managed it, the car burst into life and they were on their way.

"Why do you have to get to the station?" Dave asked, before they had travelled two hundred yards.

"I have to go to my pen friend, that is where I stay, and I only come to Southampton to see the shopping."

"I see. And where does your pen friend live?" continued Dave, frantically trying to keep his eyes on the road. He desperately wanted to touch her leg, grab at her thigh, but he didn't dare.

"My friend she lives in Salisbury. You know it, yes?"

"Salisbury, yes I know it, it's not far, about 20 miles I suppose."

"Yes, I think so."

"Look, I've got the day off and, if you want, I'll give you a lift, um, but only if you want."

"That is very nice, but I couldn't and anyway I have a train ticket."

"Oh, you know British Rail, they never run on time. You could be sat in the station for hours. Come on, I don't mind, honestly."

"Well, it is very kind, if you are sure it's no ..."

"Of course it's no trouble, it'll only take half an hour."

"Thanks you," she said and sat back in her seat. Dave reached over to the temperature control on the dashboard and turned the dial to maximum. It was an old trick but it just might work. After ten minutes, they were out of Southampton, and a sign stated 'Salisbury 16 miles'. Dave kept glancing at her, she was gorgeous, and she seemed very much at ease, almost snuggling down into the car seat.

"Excuse me, but I very warm, can you turn down the heat please?"

"Yeah, um, it's a problem, always playing up, major fault with all Fords, let's see ..." He twiddled with the control, but left it on full.

"Perhaps I could take my coat off, yes?"

"Sure, hang on, I'll pull over."

Dave glanced in his rear view mirror, indicated, and pulled off the road into a little lay-by. She undid her seat belt and struggled to take off her coat.

"D'you need a hand?" Dave said, finding it difficult to breath, let alone speak.

"Yes, just ..." she sat forward and Dave pulled at the coat from the back as she lifted her behind.

"There we are, that's better, isn't it?"

"Yes. Thanks you."

Dave looked at her, beads of sweat were appearing on his forehead, dare he make a move?

"You're very kind. I like Engleesh. They all very nice to me."

"Well, I'm not surprised. You really are a beautiful woman."

She looked strangely surprised. "You think so?"

"Gorgeous, no doubt about it."

She wriggled in her seat and Dave noticed a slight coloration in her cheeks. She was embarrassed. "In my country, I am just ordinary."

"Well, here you're a cracker."

She laughed, "A cracker? What is this?"

"It means very attractive." Dave seized the opportunity and leant over, kissing her on the cheek. She sat up, grabbed him behind the back of his head and pulled his face onto hers. They French kissed for a while and she put her hand between his legs, gently caressing his now enlarged penis. He pulled away. "Hang on, not here, let's pull off the main road."

"No, this is daring, this is how I like it."

"But we're on the main Southampton to Salisbury truck road, how can we ..."

He stopped as she unzipped his flies and released his throbbing member. It stood proud and red and even Dave was surprised at the size of it.

"Mmm, what a big one," she said as she bent down and gently kissed its crimson helmet.

"Oh ..." Dave cried, taking her head in his hands, and making her move up and down very slowly.

"Yeah, that's it. That's what he likes."

It was so utterly earth-shattering that in seconds Dave was close to ejaculation.

"Oh, I'm going to come," he squealed. She stopped and turned up to look at him.

"I don't mind, it always tastes great, and no calories."

He pushed her head back down and sat back in delight. Suddenly, there was a bang on the window.

"What are you doing?" shouted a menacingly masculine voice. Dave sat bolt upright and looked out of the window. He glanced back at his lap, his penis was in his hand and he was still in Mayflower Park. He was totally disorientated. "What the fuck?" he screamed as the man outside the car tried to open the door. Dave quickly pressed the lock, turned on the ignition, threw the car into gear and sped from the parking space. His penis still standing out of his trousers. He grabbed the tissue his sandwich had been in and laid it on his lap, covering the offending item.

"What the hell happened?" he mumbled to himself. "One minute I was in Salisbury with a foreign piece, the next ..."

He drove around the Southampton ring road and finally managed to get his penis back into his trousers. He rubbed his hand over his face, it was sticky. "Christ, if that had been a copper, fuck knows what would have happened."

He was now in Portswood, a suburb on the north east side of Southampton, and satisfied that he had not been followed, he stopped outside a public house called the Albert, switched off his engine and, after a few moments, went inside.

* * *

Quinn and Crouch had arrived back at the Civic police station and Quinn was talking to the desk sergeant.

"Look Paul, we're expecting a young lady in about half an hour, Helen Wright, and I think she's going to be nervous, so can you try to be a little tactful when she arrives. She may prove valuable in our rapist case."

"Me? Tactful? It's my middle name."

"Your middle name is sarcastic bastard and I don't want her scared off."

"OK, OK, keep your hair on."

Mike tapped in the security number on the door lock and they went into the main office.

"Make us a cup of tea Mike," Quinn ordered and his sergeant duty walked over to the kettle and turned it on.

"If I may say so sir I was very impressed how you handled the Michells girl, it was really quite touching."

"What you mean is the old bastard's going soft."

"No, no I don't, I think you were ..."

"Alright Mike, point taken, let's try and be nice to young Miss Wright when she gets here."

Mike made one cup of tea and suggested a visit to the canteen. "Would you like anything sir?" he asked.

"No thanks, but don't be too long, I need you to take notes."

Mike Crouch disappeared and Quinn sat at his desk, reading the file on the St Mary's Street rapist. His mind was wandering when the 'phone on his desk rang.

"Yes? Quinn."

It was the desk sergeant informing him that a Miss Wright had arrived.

"I see. Could you see her into interview room three? I think it's empty, I'll be there straight away."

Mike had just arrived back from the canteen with a large ham and salad bap.

"Put that down and follow me," Quinn snapped.

Mike placed the food on his desk, picked up his note pad and followed his boss. They left the main office by the back door and, turning down a small scruffy corridor, cluttered with old files, arrived at the interview room at the same time as the desk sergeant and Miss Wright.

Quinn looked at the fat young girl in front of him. She was obviously nervous and held her chubby little hands in front of her large body.

"Hello," said Quinn cheerily. "I'm Detective Inspector Quinn and this is Sergeant Crouch. Please come in. Would you like a cup of tea or anything?"

"No thank you," squeaked the young girl, so quietly that Quinn could hardly make out the words.

"OK, don't be nervous, this won't take long."

She smiled but looked close to tears.

"You sit down here. I'll sit opposite you and Sergeant Crouch will sit at the end of the table and take some notes. OK?"

"Yes thank you," she mumbled, her arms and body trembling.

"Now, I believe your mother said something about a man. Would you like to tell us what happened?"

She glanced around the room, looking for an escape route.

"In your own time, just tell us what happened." Crouch was ready with his pen poised over the note pad, like some journalist getting a front page news story.

"I told my mum about this man who's been pestering me and, when she saw the story in the paper, she said it might be the same one who'd committed the rapes. I hope I don't get anyone into trouble."

"Now you won't get anyone into trouble, but you might help us catch the bas... um villain we're looking for. Please carry on."

"Well, I work at a wine bar in the evenings, and a couple of times this man ..."

Quinn interrupted. "Do you know his name?"

"Yes, sorry, I think it was Dave. Dave Price or Prince or something like that. He told me his name and asked me where I worked."

"Go on."

"Well, a couple of days ago, I was in town, when he came running out of a pub ..."

"Sorry to be a pain, but what pub?"

"I'm not sure what it's called, but it's the one in town, just off the High Street at the back of the shopping precinct."

"Right, I know the one."

"Um, he came out of the pub and ran after me, calling my name. I told him to go away, but he grabbed my arm and asked me to have a drink."

"And did you have a drink?"

"No, of course not." She looked indignant and scratched the side of her face. "I'm not like that. I told him I only had half an hour for lunch, but he wouldn't let me go."

"And where was this?"

"Just in the High Street, outside the British Home Stores."

"And then what?"

"Well, I had to push him off. He stunk of beer and shouted

after me, saying we could have a drink one night, if I wanted, but I ran into BHS and he walked off."

"Mmm ...well, thank you for coming in and telling us. You've been most helpful. If we need anything further from you, we'll be in touch. Can you give Sergeant Crouch your full name and address, and a number we can reach you on?"

"Is that it?" she questioned, looking slightly more relaxed. "Yep, that's all. Do you want that tea now?"

"No thank you, I've got to get back to work."

"Well, thanks again, you've been very brave coming here and telling us," Quinn said in a very patronising tone and wished he'd phrased it differently.

After she'd left, Crouch turned to Quinn: "What d'you think?"

"It's hardly a criminal offence to ask a girl to have a drink with you, but then again it does prove this guy's on the prowl, and ..."

"Yes, and he did grab hold of her, which was the same phrase that the girl from Calvin Marine used."

"True, but just because he's a pervert mentally, doesn't mean he's actually done anything physically, does it?"

* * *

Dave had sunk a couple of beers and had also 'phoned the agency arranging a meeting for 2.20 at a flat in the Shirley district. He glanced at his watch. "Time for one more and another fag," he decided and ordered a pint of Marton's Pedigree. He hadn't really noticed much about the pub, his mind still frantically trying to sort out the reality from the fantasy. It had been so real, so brilliant, why did it have to be a dream. It was a dream, wasn't it?

"Do you do the gee-gees, mate?" said a gruff voice.

"What?" Dave came back to earth and looked across the bar in the direction of the noise. It was the barman and for the first time, Dave noticed what a scruffy looking individual he was. Possibly fifty-five years old, unshaven, grey unruly hair, almost standing on end, two black moles on the same side of his red bulbous nose, each sprouting four or five hairs, nicotine coloured lips and the worse blood-shot eyes Dave had seen.

"I said," said the man, sniffing and wiping his nose at the same time. "Do you do the horses? You know, the nags?"

"Oh, I see. Sorry, no. I don't gamble."

"That's a pity, a great pity, and I'll tell you why," he continued, pointing a finger in Dave's general direction. "I've got a tip, sure fire winner, running today in the free-firty, can't lose, can't fucking lose."

"Really? Who gave you the tip?"

"Now, that would be telling wouldn't it?" He tapped his finger on the side of his nose before continuing. "Let's just say someone from the stables, shall we?"

Dave wasn't really interested but for the sake of shutting him up, inquired: "What's it called?"

"Homer's Boy."

"Homo's Boy?" Dave questioned.

"Not Homo's Boy, ya cunt, Homer's Boy, fucking Homer, you know the Greek bastard," he tutted and pushed his finger deep inside his left nostril, up to the knuckle.

"OK, take it easy, Homer's Boy you say, well I might put some money on it then, if it's a dead cert."

"Dead cert, the fucking horse couldn't lose, if it started ten minutes after all the others."

"Well, thanks very much." Dave decided it was time to leave and stubbed out his cigarette, downed his beer in one, and got off the bar-stool.

"See you again," he said as he got to the door, "and thanks for the tip."

"Homo's Boy," said the man, shaking his head and chewing the bogie he just prised out of his nose. "What a fucking prat."

Dave slowly drove back across Southampton heading for Shirley and his appointment with the woman from the agency. The car was getting a little low on fuel so he stopped and put some petrol in and arrived at 22B Purcell Road just before 2.15. The woman from Homefinders was already there and walked across the street to greet him.

"Good afternoon, Mr Price. Shall we go straight in? It's the flat round the side of the house."

They entered the front garden of the large bay-windowed brick-built semi-detached des. res., walked along the side path, which was broken and uneven and stopped at a bright red door with the number 22 on it. The 'B' had obviously fallen off.

"Here we are," breezed the woman in a very estate agent sounding voice, as she selected a key from her fob and opened the door. Inside, there was no hall to speak of, and a staircase lay straight ahead. They climbed the stairs to a little landing which had four white Georgian style doors off of it, all closed. Opening the first one on the right, she started her sales pitch: "Right now, this is the lounge-diner, not a bad size really, it could ..."

"Yes, it's fine," interrupted Dave, completely uninterested. Back on the landing, she opened the second door. "And this is the kitchen and then we have the bedroom, with it's nice vanity unit, and finally the bathroom, complete with low level toilet and shower cubicle. As you can see, it's nice and self-contained and, for the money, I think it's a good deal."

"Yeah, it's nice," mumbled Dave, trying to look down the little gap in her white blouse, giving just a hint of cleavage. "And how much did you say this was?"

"Now, let's see," she looked at the clipboard in her hand. "Yes, it's £385.00 per calendar month, to include all services except gas, water and electricity. There's one month's rent in advance, held as a deposit and refunded at the end of the let, which runs for a minimum of six months."

"Jesus Christ, prices have gone up in the past few years." Dave thought, as he frantically tried to work out if he could afford the place.

"It is fully furnished to quite a nice standard and I think you'd be hard pushed to find somewhere as good as this for the same sort of money."

"Yeah, I can see that, and you say it's the only one you have to show me?"

"Well, I could show you a lot more, but they would all be

dearer. Perhaps you'd like to think about it?"

"If I could. Can I give you an answer on Monday?"

"Of course. However, you must appreciate that if another firm offer were to be received, we could not hold it for you."

"The only thing I'd like you to hold for me darling, is my cock, preferably between your tits," he thought.

The woman had become aware of Dave's attempt to look down her cleavage, and moved away. "So, you'll ring me Monday then?" she continued.

"Yes definitely, one way or another."

They walked out of the room, back on the landing, down the stairs and out onto the side path.

"Excuse me," Dave said politely. "You don't fancy a drink do you? I've got the rest of the day off and we could ..."

"I don't think so," snapped the girl, slamming the door shut and marching off out of the property. "I'll wait to hear from you then?" she shouted and was gone.

"Yeah, OK." murmured Dave as he followed her out, got into his car and drove back to the guest house. He'd bought a paper on the way and had decided to look through the small ads and hopefully find something more financially suitable. Parking right outside the Kimberley, newspaper under his arm, he walked straight into the house, up to the reception area and rang the little brass bell. "Let's have a word with 'Whistler's mother' about dinner," he mused, tapping his fingers in no particular rhythm on the counter.

"Yes?" said Mrs Marshall, as she thrust her head through the little serving-hatch, sucking at her gums.

"Thank God she hasn't got her teeth in," thought Dave. "Yes, I'm sorry to bother you, but would it be possible to stay on a few more nights. I've still got some business to finish."

"Of course, stay there and I'll be right round."

"Please don't put your teeth in."

"Right," said the landlady, "now how many more nights would you like to stay?"

"Just three, over the weekend, should be sorted out by Monday."

The old lady fumbled through some registration cards, as if

she had hundreds of people staying. "Friday, Saturday and Sunday, that's no problem."

"Oh, and could I have an evening meal tonight please?"

"Of course Dear. It's steak and kidney pie, chips and peas. How's that?"

"Fine, what time do you serve it?"

"Well, as you're the only resident, whatever suits you?"

"About seven would be perfick," said Dave, imitating a silly TV character.

"Seven it is. It'll be £2.50 for the meal, but that includes tea or coffee."

"Great, can I pay for it all with one cheque?"

"That's fine, settle up with me on Sunday sometime and I'll have a proper VAT bill ready for you."

"Great. Can I have my room key please?"

"There we are," said the old lady as she handed him his key.

"I'll give you a call just before seven then."

"Thanks."

He went straight up to his room, treading very precariously on the rungs. It seemed every one of them moved under his weight. Inside his room, he opened the paper at the small ads and, after finding the section on house renting, started to scrutinize the properties. Unfortunately, he did not notice the headlines on the front page, with its update on the rapist and request from the police for certain members of the public to come forward and eliminate themselves from the enquiry. He took out a pen from his jacket pocket and made rings around all the ads that looked interesting.

"What the fuck's that smell?" he muttered. "Cat's piss?" He opened the wardrobe to see the offending items. His trousers and underpants, still wet with urine, and crumpled up in the corner. "Gordon fucking Bennett, what a pong." He picked them up and held them at arm's length. "To the John."

Grabbing his overnight bag, he cagily opened the door and, peering around the door frame, checked it was clear. There was no one about, so he swiftly walked to the bathroom and darted inside. Filling the bath about a quarter full, he threw his clothes into the warm water, mixed in some bubble bath from his bag, and gyrated them, creating a mass of pretty pink bubbles. He had a pee in the loo and then emptied the bath water. Laying out one of the guest house' bath towels, he placed his jeans and undies inside, rolled the lot into a cylindrical shape, and carried it back to his room. Unravelling the towel, he put the 'cleanish' clothes back onto the floor of the wardrobe and draped the towel over the chest of drawers. Turning on the television, he flopped onto the bed. BBC1 had an old western on, being shown for the twentieth time and on BBC2 an Australian soap opera. He plumped for the film and fell asleep where he lay.

"Mr Price, Mr Price," Mrs Marshall was banging on the door, "It's nearly seven, your evening meal's ready."

"What, yes, OK. Just coming."

He rolled over onto his side, his eyes having great problems adjusting to the light from the television screen.

"I'll be down in five."

* * *

Janice had got home from her part-time job, tidied up the house a bit and had prepared a meal for herself and Sarah. As she didn't have to wait for Dave to come home from work, she'd decided to have dinner early.

They chatted over their food and Janice felt good, better in fact than she'd felt for a long time. They seemed more like sisters than mother and daughter and were having a joke, when the doorbell rang.

"Oh God," said Janice. "I hope that's not Dave."

"You and me both," added Sarah.

She placed her cutlery down on the table and went to the front door. Turning on the outside light, she slowly opened it and was face to face with Southampton's 'finest'.

"Good evening madam," said the older man. "Sorry to bother you but are you Mrs Price?"

"Yes, who wants to know?"

"I'm Chief Inspector Quinn and this is Sergeant Crouch. Is your husband home please?"

"I'm sorry, he's not."

"Well, would it be possible to have a little chat with you then?"

"Aaa ..." Janice hesitated and the younger man produced his warrant card.

"It is very important, but it won't take long."

"Well, I've just started my evening meal, couldn't you come back a little later?"

"'Fraid not madam. As I've said, it's rather important," said Quinn, placing one foot inside the door.

"What's it about? Dave's not in trouble, is he?"

"Perhaps we could come in and discuss it," Quinn continued authoritatively.

"I suppose so," she held open the door and gestured them into the house.

"Who is it mum?" shouted Sarah from the dining room.

"It's the police love. Could you take our dinners into the kitchen and put them in the oven please," Janice said as she led the two constables into the lounge.

"Yeah, sure. What's wrong?"

"And you are?" said Quinn as he entered the room and came face to face with the lovely Sarah.

"That's my daughter, Sarah, from my first marriage."

"Well, Sarah, if you could do as your mother has requested, we'll have a quick chat with her and be on our way."

Sarah got up from the dining table with the plates, muttered something about 'bloody pigs' and left the room.

Janice sat down on the sofa and Crouch closed the door.

"OK, let's hear it, what's he done now?" said Janice, sighing slightly.

"We don't know that he's done anything but we need to get in touch with him and wondered if you could tell us where he is?"

"Well, to tell you the truth, he no longer lives here. We've recently split up and he's living in a guest house in Shirley.

"Really? And when did this happen?"

"Only yesterday. Things haven't been too good between us lately, and we've decided to have a break for a while."

"I see, may I?" Quinn pointed to the chair which was next to the television, and sat down in it. "We're making enquiries into the attempted rapes, which were perpetrated in the St Mary's Street area, and wish to speak to him. Perhaps you know where he can be contacted?"

"Well, yes, but ..."

"It's purely routine madam, just need a few questions answered, nothing else."

"Hang on," Janice got up and walked over to a little note pad which was by the 'phone. "Here it is, the Kimberley Guest House in Shirley, that's where he told me he was staying."

"Thank you, did you get that Sergeant?"

"Yes sir," answered Mike, speaking for the first time and frantically scribbling in his note pad.

"Just a few questions to ask you, and then we'll go."

Janice walked across the room to the dining area and picked up her cup of coffee. Quinn looked at her and nodded to himself. She was a handsome woman, no doubt about it. She took a sip of her coffee and hesitated. "Um, would you like a drink? Tea or coffee?"

"Yes please," said Crouch.

"No thank you Mrs Price," countered Quinn. "The sooner we put this one to bed, the sooner we get to go home."

"OK," said Janice, tilting her head from one side to another. And Quinn continued: "Can you tell us, if you can remember, where your husband was on the last two Wednesdays, between ten and twelve?"

"Last two Wednesdays," Janice repeated. "Um, yes, he was out playing snooker with some work mates."

Crouch was furiously making notes.

"I see, and do you remember what time he came home?"

"Look, I must admit he's not my flavour of the month at the moment, but I'm sure he didn't have anything to do with those rapes."

"As I said, this is only routine. We've got to eliminate anyone who might have been in the area so that we can get the real villain."

"Well, both evenings, it was very late. I'd gone to bed, so it was well after twelve."

"And the next morning, when you saw his clothes, was there anything unusual about them, were they torn? Dirty? Bloodied? Anything like that?"

"I don't think I should answer that."

"And why?" Quinn leant forward.

"Well, it was one of the reasons we started rowing. His clothes were disgusting, you know, covered in vomit and things."

"Just vomit, or anything else?"

"Hard to tell really. They were so filthy that I even threw one of his sweatshirts out."

"I see. You haven't got any of the soiled items have you?"

"No, I washed what I could and threw out the rest."

"No matter, just one other thing, does your husband ever wear that new aftershave 'Corduroy Vert'?"

"Yes, that's his absolute favourite. He wears it all the time, is that important?"

"Maybe," Quinn stood up. "Anything else to ask Sergeant?"

"No, I don't think so."

"Well, we'll be off then. Sorry to have interrupted your meal, but you've been very helpful."

"I hope I've said the right things. Just because Dave and I have split up, doesn't mean I wish him any harm."

"Of course not, Mrs Price, don't worry. If your husband was playing snooker with some mates, he's got an alibi and therefore no problem."

The two police officers left, and Sarah came back into the room.

"What was that all about?" she asked.

"Nothing, they were just making enquiries, routine they said."

"Well nothing would surprise me about Dave."

Janice stood in the middle of the room with her thoughts and Sarah went back to the kitchen to get out the dried up remains of their dinner.

* * *

Dave had finally got up and gone downstairs for his evening meal. The food was reasonable English fare, and plenty of it. As he finished the meal, Mrs Marshall appeared from the kitchen. "How was that dear?" she asked.

"It was fine, thank you. Can I have a coffee please?"

"Of course, won't be a minute."

Dave sat thinking about the flat he'd seen and decided he could not afford it. He'd spend all of Saturday flat hunting and perhaps go to the pictures in the evening. He lit up a cigarette, just as his coffee arrived. Mrs Marshall cleared the table of dirty crockery and placed the coffee in front of him.

"Cheers," he mumbled, blowing smoke into the room.

He finished his cigarette and coffee almost simultaneously and made for his bedroom.

The old staircase groaned and creaked under his weight and he was sure it moved more each time he used it. Back in his room, he flopped on the bed. A little look at the magazines seemed to be in order and, after finding the envelope, sat almost goggle-eyed looking at the large-breasted women.

Downstairs, the two policemen were ringing the reception bell.

"Yes, can I help you?" asked the landlady, through her little serving hatch.

"Good evening madam, have you a Mr Price staying here?"

Mrs Marshall shut the hatch and walked around into the reception area.

"Can I ask who wants him?" she snapped.

"Sorry madam, Southampton CID" replied Crouch, once again producing his warrant card.

"Oh, yes he's in. He's just had a meal."

"Could we see him then?" said Quinn, in a gruff tone. "Which room number?"

"Um, first floor, room number one, you can't miss it, top of the stairs, and ..."

"We'll find it, thank you."

The two officers climbed the rickety stairs, stopping every other step.

"What a dump," said Crouch, clinging to the bannister as if his life depended on it.

"I've seen worse," muttered Quinn as they reached the landing and walked to the door. Crouch banged on the door with two hefty knocks.

Dave was sitting on the bed, his member in his hand, glancing at the middle spread of 'USA Brabusters'.

"Who is it?" he yelled, jumping almost three feet in the air, desperately trying to ram his enlarged penis, purple head first, back into his trousers. His 'Jap-eye' gaping like a startled fish's mouth.

"Police, Mr Price. Can we have a few words with you?"

"Police," repeated Dave, jumping to his feet in absolute panic, as he tried to stuff the magazines back into their envelope. He was shaking so much, he quickly gave up the idea and threw them under the bed quilt, uncovered.

The police banged again.

"Mr Price, please open the door." Their tone was starting to get decidedly nasty.

"Yeah, alright, keep your hair on, just coming," Dave stuttered breathlessly as he finally did up his trouser zipper. He took three steps needed to reach the door and opened it cautiously.

"Yes?" he gulped, looking red faced and guilty of something.
"Mr Dave Price?" asked Quinn in a sinister tone.

"Um ...yes, what do you want?" Dave croaked in a squeaky voice.

"We'd like to ask you a few questions. May we come in?" said Quinn as he held up his warrant card and flashed it in Dave's face.

"Well, it's a bit inconvenient at the moment, I was just getting ready to go out," he puffed.

"OK, perhaps you'd prefer the station."

"No, no, it's just that you couldn't swing a cat in here, but come in if you must."

"Thank you sir, it won't take long."

Dave walked back into the room, along the side of the bed,

and stood by the wardrobe, the two officers followed. The three men stood facing each other around the bed and Quinn started. "Could you tell us where you were on the nights of the 3rd and 10th of March please?"

"Wait a minute, haven't I seen you before?" Dave asked the younger policeman, as he sat down on the edge of the bed.

"That's right sir," replied Crouch, taking out his notebook. "I spoke to you in the Coach & Horses on the 10th and I believe it's true to say that you were at that establishment on the two nights in question."

Quinn interrupted and seemed annoyed. "Thank you Sergeant," he snapped. "Let's let Mr Price tell us where he was, I'm sure he doesn't need prompting by you."

"Sorry sir."

"Ummm ... yes that's right, I was at the pub on both of those nights and in fact stayed there until closing time."

The claustrophobic atmosphere was stifling, and Dave felt as if the two officers were almost on top of him.

"I believe there was a strip show on?"

"Yeah, so what?"

"You went straight home after the shows?"

"Yeah, after drinking up time."

"I see, well your wife tells us you did not get home each evening until well after midnight, perhaps nearer one."

"Could be, I was drinking all night and time has a way of slipping by."

"That may be so, but if you left the pub at eleven, eleven fifteen and you didn't get home until one, you must have gone somewhere else, surely?"

Dave hesitated, sighed and rubbed his chin. "I know, I went back to my office for a cup of coffee. Yeah, that's right, to sober up a bit, you know, didn't want to get it in the neck from the missus."

"And how did you get home?"

Dave's jaw dropped and his shoulders arched. "Look, what's this all about?"

"Just answer the question, how did you get home? Surely it's not difficult. Did you get a taxi, drive, walk, fucking swim? How?" Quinn was getting angry, a slap in the face would sort this little pervy out.

"OK, OK." Dave flopped onto the edge of the bed. "I know it's stupid, but after I'd had the coffee, I felt sober enough to drive home."

"Someone has told us they saw your car in St Mary's Street at about eleven thirty. Did you drive to your office via St Mary's Street.

"Wait a minute, the rapes, that's what this is about, isn't it?"

"That's correct, your car is that blue Ford Fiesta outside isn't it?"

"Yeah."

"The one with all the marine equipment stickers on?"

"Yeah, so?"

"So you did drive up St Mary's Street then?"

"No, I didn't. I drove from the pub, along Andersons Road, and into Canute Road. I went nowhere near St Mary's."

Quinn decided to try a different tact. "Could I ask why you and your wife have split up. Is there a sexual problem between you two?"

"Is that what the old slag told you. She's got no right to discuss our private business."

"So there is a sexual problem?"

"None of your business, it's not against the law to leave your wife, is it?"

"Look, you little perv..." Quinn nearly lost it, but gripped his hands together, and continued. "No sir, it's not against the law, but to get drunk and make advances to young women is."

"What do you mean? I've never ..."

"What about your receptionist, Miss ..." Quinn looked at Crouch for a name.

"Miss Winton, sir," Crouch interjected.

"Yes, Miss Winton. What about her?"

"Joanne?" Dave looked puzzled and Crouch took over.

"I went to your office today and Miss Winton says you grabbed her. Is that not true?"

"Bloody little prick teaser, she led me on, and then ..."

"And did Miss Wright lead you on as well?"

"Who the fuck's Miss Wright?"

"Oh, you don't know Miss Helen Wright, who works at Bluffers wine bar, then?"

"Oh, that little fat cow, what is this?"

"You don't seem to have a very high opinion of women, do you? Your wife's a slag, your receptionist's a PT and this young barmaid is a fat cow. Charming, I must say."

"Look, I know this ..." Dave started, but Quinn interrupted him " ...doesn't look good. I think you ought to come down to the station and we'll get a statement."

"What! You arresting me?"

"Not yet sir, we just want you to help us with our enquiries, that's all."

"Well, I'm not sure that ..."

"I'm sorry, I'm not asking, I'm telling. Now get your coat and follow us, please." The please was added with venom.

"This is all a big mistake, I've done nothing." Dave stated angrily as he got up.

"Well then, you've got nothing to fear."

"Bloody harassment, you've got no right ..." his words froze in mid-sentence as the three girlie mags slipped, almost in slow motion, from under the quilt and slammed onto the floor.

"Now what have we got here?" said Quinn sarcastically, as Dave's face turned scarlet. The top magazine had landed on its back and opened to reveal an enormous pair of 'bristols'. Quinn bent down and picked up the books, holding them almost at arms length, as if they were dirty. "Like big boobs do we?" he asked.

"Dave froze on the spot, trying stupidly to look surprised. "Um ..."

"You see, the two woman assaulted were big breasted, now that's strange, isn't it Sergeant?"

"Yes sir," said Crouch staring at Dave. "Very strange indeed."

Quinn dropped the magazines on the bed and Crouch leaned over, trying to get a better look.

"Right Mr Price, down to the station I think."

Dave grabbed a coat and started to follow Quinn, who'd already opened the door.

"What about the mags sir?" asked Crouch. "Shall I take them to the station with us?"

"No point Sergeant. I'm sure Mr Price will want them later for a little game of 'pop-out-Peter', yes?"

"Aw," complained Crouch.

Dave grunted and followed the two police officers down the stairs, into the back of their police car and to the Civic Centre police station.

"Detective Quinn," said the desk sergeant as they entered the police station, "We've had another call which I think might be related to the St Mary's Street case."

Quinn stopped in the foyer. "Take him down to one of the interview rooms Mike, I'll be along in a moment."

Crouch punched the security code on the wall lock and led Dave away.

"What have you got for me?"

"Well, about an hour ago, a Mr ..." the desk sergeant referred to some notes on the desk, " ... Clarke 'phoned. He's the warden at the Mayflower Park, to say he'd caught a guy in a blue Ford, having a ... um ... a ..."

"Yes, go on, having a what?"

"Well, to put it bluntly, having a wank."

"What, in the park with his 'Peter' out?"

"No," the sergeant laughed. "Not in the park, sat in his car, chucking himself off."

"Oh God, and don't tell me, the car was registered to a certain Mr Price, yeah?"

"Nearly. Registered to Calvin Marine, but driven by ..."

"Mr Price," they said in unison.

"OK, thanks. The sooner I get this little pervy put away, the better."

Quinn turned and walked across the foyer to the security door. "Do us a favour will you? Get one of the uniform lads to get a statement from the park warden tomorrow."

"Certainly, I'll put young Harris on it, it'll do her good." Quinn chuckled to himself at the thought of the rookie WPC Harris getting a statement about masturbation in a parked car, and went into the back office, laughing.

Dave had been seated at a formica topped table set in the middle of the interview room. The table had two chairs each side, with a large black 'Neal 6221' dual deck tape recorder, on one end, and a pile of photo-statted single page leaflets, scattered over the recorder's top. Dave stretched to read the leaflets. "Tape Recording Procedures" were the only words he could make out. The room had bare walls, painted in standard beige emulsion, with little pieces of Blu-tak in no particular order, scattered across the wall that was facing him. Quinn walked in, solemn faced, and sat down in the chair opposite Dave. Crouch moved away from the table, and stood by the door, his arms folded in front of his chest.

"Right Dave, you don't mind if I call you Dave, do you? Good" Quinn said, almost parrot fashion.

"We're going to tape the interview on two tapes. One will be sealed and used as an exhibit for the purpose of any criminal proceedings, and the other as a working copy. Is that clear"

Dave sat silently, his eyes glazed over, as if in shock.

"I said, is that clear?" demanded Quinn.

"Yes," mumbled Dave in a very faint and squeaky voice, screwing up his nose like some small rodent.

"Now the next thing, you have the right to your solicitor being present. Do you wish to have one?"

"I don't know. I've never been in a police station before."
"You pathetic little turd, two minutes in a cell with a dirty great convict's knob stuffed in your mouth, will sort you out," Quinn thought. He hated men like Dave, so big when it comes to pushing women around, but just worms in reality. He tried to push his thoughts to the back of his mind. "Well, do you want your solicitor present, or not?"

"The only solicitor I know did my house buying a few years ago. I don't suppose he'd be much good at this."

"I see, and his name is?"

"Christopher Brown of Brown, Vincent and Maclean. Their office is in Hedge End."

Quinn sighed loudly and cleared his throat. "Do you want him present? Surely it's not that difficult, is it?"

Dave looked around the room, as if in search of some sort of divine guidance. "Suppose not," he muttered.

"OK then, let's proceed."

Quinn took two brand new cassette tapes from the little drawer in the table; unwrapped them and slotted them into the tape recorder. Pressing the red record button, he continued: "I am Detective Inspector Quinn starting an interview with Mr David Price, timed at ..." he glanced at his watch. "20.35 hours on Friday 12th March 1993. The other police officer present is Sergeant Crouch. I am interviewing ..." he stopped again, and looked at Dave. "Full name please."

"David Malcolm Price."

"Date of birth please?"

"Twentieth of February 1954."

"And your present address?"

"Well, I used to live in Hedge End, but ..."

"I said your present address, PLEASE."

Dave took a large intake of air and rubbed his eyes: "Kimberley Guest House, Languard Road, Shirley."

"You have been offered, but have waived, your right to have a solicitor present, is that correct?"

"Yes."

"No other officer is present and this interview is being conducted at Southampton Civic Centre police station." Quinn stopped, consulted the leaflet, and continued. "Before we go any further, I must caution you, that anything you say could be used in evidence against you. Please tell us of your whereabouts on the evening of Wednesday the third of March."

"Um. I went to the Coach & Horses pub at about seven and left at about eleven."

"And then?"

"Um. I left the pub and went to my office for a cup of coffee, just to sober up, you see, and then drove home."

"And where is your office?"

"In Canute Road, about two minutes walk from the pub.

"Two minutes walk? I thought you said you drove to your office."

"Yeah, yeah. I drove to the office, but it's only a short distance from the pub."

"And after coffee at your office, you drove straight home?"

"Yes, I got home just after twelve. You can ask my wife, she'll tell you. I was living in Hedge End then."

"When you left the pub, did you drive to the office via St Mary's Street?"

"Of course not, I've told you, I went straight to my office."

"So you went nowhere near St Mary's Churchyard?"

"For Christ's sake, how many more times. I went straight to my office."

"And when you left the pub, what state were you in, Drunk?"

"Not legless, not so drunk I didn't know what I was doing, if that's what you mean."

"So fairly drunk?"

"Yeah, fairly drunk. I think I might have thrown up in a lorry park, you know, the one in Andersons Road."

"So you didn't go straight to your office, you stopped at a lorry park?"

"Yeah, I think so, it's all hazy."

"I see, so you might have driven round to St Mary's in your drunken haze and not remembered. True?"

"No, I didn't go anywhere near St Mary's."

"OK, let's jump a week. What about the evening of Wednesday the 10th March?"

"Exactly the same, to the pub, back to the office for a coffee and then home."

"I see, and does that include throwing up in the lorry park?"

"No, I wasn't so drunk last Wednesday. There was a fight in the pub and the show finished early."

"A fight? We weren't informed of a fight. Did you get involved?"

"No, of course not, just a few locals got a bit carried away with a stripper. I stayed in the loo until it was over."

"So after this 'fight' you went back into the bar and finished the evening there, did you?"

"Yeah, no, um ...hang on, no I left the pub and went to Oxford Street for a couple of beers. Yeah, that's right. I remember now."

"So, it wasn't exactly the same as the previous Wednesday?"

"No, I'm sorry, I got a bit confused."

"And what time did you leave the Coach & Horses?"

"About nine-nine thirty."

"And then?"

"Um ...I drove to Victor's wine bar and had a drink there."

"What? Until closing time?"

"No, I only stayed for half an hour, it was so dead. I left by ten."

"And then where?" Quinn sighed, this was getting tedious.

"Walked across the road to the Grosvenor Arms."

"And you stayed there until closing time?"

"Yes, that's right, then I drove to the office and had a coffee."

"Let's see if I've got this right. You started drinking at about seven in the Coach & Horses, had a few in Victor's and then finished the evening at the Grosvenor?"

"Yeah, that's right."

"And after this little pub crawl, you still drove home?"

"Yeah, but I sobered up first. I told you, with some coffees at the office."

"Jesus Christ, man. How many coffees did you have? What sort of prat are you? Don't you have any regard for other road users? Haven't you heard of 'Don't drink and drive'?"

"Of course, and I'm sorry, but that's what happened, I'm not proud of it."

"And on this second evening, you didn't go anywhere near the subway at the top end of St Mary's Street?"

"No, that's in the complete opposite direction."

"On both evenings, you say you drove home. Was that to the house in Hedge End that you shared with your wife?"

"Yes."

"But you no longer reside there?"

"No, I moved out yesterday."

"And would it be true to say that you were asked to leave by your wife?"

"No, not at all," Dave seemed to get a little indignant, and Quinn felt he might have hit on a nerve. "She didn't kick me out, no matter what she says, it was a mutual agreement."

"So, it had nothing to do with the fact that, on both these evenings, you told your wife you were at snooker with workmates, when in reality you were at a cheap strip joint?"

"Look, what I told my wife has nothing to do with you."

"Only to prove that you are a liar."

"Oh come on, surely everyone's told a little fib to their wife. It helps make the marriage work."

"Well, it didn't help your marriage much, did it?"

"Fuc..." the words died away and Dave dropped his head.

"I'm sorry. What did you say?" snapped Quinn.

"Nothing."

"Well, did your leaving have anything to do with those porno mags we found in your possession?"

"No," Dave stood up, "I can see what you're trying to do, to make me look like some kind of pervert, but it's not like that."

"Please sit down Mr Price, you're not helping yourself. Let's talk about ..." Quinn opened his notebook. "Miss Joanne Winton, the receptionist at your place of employment."

"What about her?"

"When she was interviewed by Sergeant Crouch, she claims that one afternoon, whilst under the influence, you grabbed hold of her and tried to kiss her. Care to explain that?"

"I've told you before," Dave paused, "that was a complete misunderstanding. I though she was up for it, but she wasn't. No big deal."

"No big deal? You grabbed hold of a young girl in your office and think it's no big deal."

"She's a little prick teaser, I ..." Dave sat quiet again.

"OK then, what about Miss Helen Wright. She came in to see us and was not happy about your approach to her. It seems you tried to grab her in the High Street. Is that true?"

"What is this? I've never heard of Helen what's-her-name, I don't even know her."

"Really, well she knows you. She says you met her in a wine bar in Hedge End, does that jog your memory?"

"Oh, her? I didn't grab her. Christ, I only asked her for a drink, that's all. Grab her? I didn't touch her."

"So you do know her then?"

"Yes, but I didn't know her full name, it was nothing, really, you've got to believe me."

"Another misunderstanding was it? She led you on as well, did she?"

"Yes, I ..."

"It's funny isn't it, that every woman you come into contact with seems to fancy you. Perhaps it's the aftershave you use."

"What? I've told you, I didn't touch them."

"But you would have liked to, wouldn't you? That Helen, nice bit of stuff, is she?"

"Not at all, she's fat. I only asked her for a drink because I felt sorry for her."

"Oh, very magnanimous, I get it, you felt sorry for her, so you tried to assault her, is that it?"

"No way! You just don't understand."

"You say she's fat, but really you mean she's got a big breast, just like the girls in your magazines, you like 'em big breasted, don't you?"

"I don't think I should say any more, perhaps I should have a solicitor present."

"Well, just one more question. Were you in Mayflower Park today, around lunchtime?"

"Yes," Dave said timidly, looking worried. "Why?"

"We've had a report of a person exposing himself in a Ford car, which happened to have your registration. Any comments on that?"

"As I said, I think I should have a solicitor present, you're twisting all my words."

"OK, fair enough. That's all for now. Do you have anything more to add?"

Dave folded his arms sulkily and shook his head. "No," he mumbled.

"Do you wish to clarify anything you have said?"

"Nope."

"I am handing you a notice number TR3 which explains in detail the tape recording procedure. The time is 21.14 and I am turning the recorder off."

Quinn switched off the machine and ejected both tapes.

"You will note from the notice that a copy of the recording we have just made can be obtained from the Crown Prosecution Service in Basingstoke. Quinn placed one tape on the table, and held the other one up to Crouch. "Could you seal this tape please and get Mr Price to sign across it."

Crouch took the tape and sealed it with a large sticky label and placed it in front of Dave. "If you could sign over his label please."

As Dave signed, Quinn started again.

"Now, let's get a few things straight. We can place you at the scene of both assaults, you have the mentality to do it, and you're going through some sort of emotional sexual crisis, so why don't you admit it. We'll see what we can do for you, maybe get some help, you know, psychiatric, and it'll all be OK. What d'ya say. Surely it's what you want to do?"

Dave looked across the table, his haggard face slightly unshaven and deeply lined, was tinged with sadness.

"I know you don't like me, you think I'm guilty, but I'm not, and there's no way I'll admit to it."

Tears were starting to well up in his eyes, but Quinn felt no pity, just anger, just rage, the bad side of his nature was starting to rear its head. He got up from the table, and walked around to Dave and, leaning over, whispered: "When you were born, and they threw away the placenta, they dumped the wrong part. 'Nuff said."

Dave moved sideways, trying to avoid listening to anything else.

"Right Sergeant, take this 'gentleman' to the front desk, get him a car back to his guest house, and get him out of my sight."

"Yes sir, this way please," snapped Crouch, as he opened the door and gestured for Dave to follow.

Dave left the room, head down, and Quinn sat back in his chair. He rubbed the stubble on his chin, trying to think of the best way to handle the case. Crouch returned fairly quickly.

"Well sir, our man I think."

"He's got to be Mike. Can you go and see the young girl from the wine bar tomorrow and pop into the Coach & Horses and see if you can get anything else, anything at all. I'm sure someone must have seen something, it might be easier for you, as the landlord and I don't see eye to eye."

"Yes sir," said Mike sarcastically, feeling slightly aggrieved at having to work Saturday. "Is that all?"

"Yes Sergeant, that is all, and may I remind you that sarcasm is the lowest form of wit, and people who use it are the lowest form of shit."

"Sorry! If that's all, then I'll be off."

"Yes, goodnight," said Quinn, with a wry smile on his face. "Oh, and don't work too hard."

He listened to his Sergeant walk down the corridor and sat looking at the wall, with only his thoughts as company. "Keep the pressure on, that's all I have to do, and this guy will crack like a bloody walnut."

Chapter 6

As he sat in his room,
with nought but his thoughts,
and feeling so low and depressed,
he just couldn't figure,
or make any sense,
of how his life was in such a bad mess.

After the police had left Janice, she and Sarah had finished their meal, (the small part that was edible, after its second time in the oven), and were sitting in the lounge.

"So what are you gonna do tonight mum?" asked Sarah.

"Well, I think I'll pop over to see your grandad and ask if I can borrow his car this evening and then go round to Doreen's and see if she fancies having a drink. You know what she's like, any excuse."

"If you like, I'll come with you. We could have a girls' night out. Eh?"

"Don't be daft, I'm fine, you go out with your friends, you don't want to spend the evening with us old fogies, surely?"

Sarah didn't need much convincing, she had a heavy date, and didn't really want to cancel it.

"Well, if you're sure, but I don't mind, honestly."

"No, I haven't really seen Doreen since her divorce and we can have a good old natter."

"Come on then, I'll race you to the bathroom," laughed Sarah and they ran out of the lounge and chased up the stairs, giggling like schoolgirls.

* * *

Dave was dropped back at the guesthouse at about 9.30 and was shaking as he entered the reception area. On hearing the front door open, Mrs Marshall came from her back-room and stopped by the stairs.

"Are you OK, Mr Price, no problems I hope?" she asked sympathetically.

"No, I'm fine thanks, just some routine questions. I was a witness to a minor road accident and they just needed a statement."

"Well, if..."

"Just my key please, I think I'll have a wash before I go out," Dave said rather curtly.

Mrs Marshall handed Dave the key and said "Goodnight."

Dave opened the door to his room, walked in and sat on the bed, next to the magazines. He quickly put them in their envelope and hid them in a drawer. They somehow seemed dirty and soiled now that the police had seen them and he couldn't bring himself to look at them. Lighting up a cigarette, he drew very hard on it and blew the smoke out of his nose. "Fucking needed that," he murmured, through the blue haze. He felt like crying. His whole life seemed in ruins. His marriage was on the rocks, his job was on the line, he was living out of a suitcase in a room the size of a toilet and, to cap it all, he was now chief suspect in a rape case. Could it get any worse? He had to pull himself out of it, but how? He'd have to go for a few beers, think it all through and, hopefully, it would all seem a lot better in the morning.

After finishing his cigarette and throwing the butt out of the window, he took his little overnight bag to the bathroom down the hallway, had a wash, shave and covered himself in his favourite after-shave. He suddenly felt decidedly human again and, after changing (into his last set of clean clothes) he left the guest house and made for Shirley High Street. He walked past the Duke of Cornwall knowing that it would be a mistake to go in there again. Only a few hundred yards further, he came upon the Painted Wagon. It could be loosely described as a youth theme pub, with its brightly painted frontage, strategically placed spotlights and blaring music. On the bar windows it advertised a games room with 4 pool tables, fruit machines and pin ball tables. It was hardly Dave's type of drinking house, but he was desperate for a beer and walked in. Inside, it was even gaudier. Pink painted woodwork, with pale blue carpets. It had obviously just been refurbished. Surprisingly, it was fairly empty, with only half a dozen males, scattered in various corners of the room. Dave went straight to the bar.

"Have you got any real ales?" he asked the svelte barmaid.

"What's that?" she questioned, above Jimi Hendrix' rendition of Dylan's 'All along the watchtower' blasting from six sets of speakers, all seemingly aimed at Dave.

"I said, have you got any real ales?"

"Oh yeah, Webster's bitter."

"Pint of that please darling," screamed Dave, just as the record ended, letting everyone in the pub hear the last two words.

As the barmaid poured the pint, Dave looked at her. She certainly was thin, but not unattractive, and Dave noticed the little line of her panties showing through her skin-tight jeans. She turned and walked back towards him. She had four earrings in each ear, a stud through her nose and a little tattoo of a spider on her neck.

"One pound eighty please," she said, just as the opening chords of 'Purple Haze' came vibrating across the bar.

Dave handed over the right money and headed for a table as far away from the speakers as possible. This was difficult, as the whole pub was wired for sound and not one area escaped the relentless beat emitting from the jukebox. Dave sat down, lit up a cigarette and glanced around the bar. Every person was playing one machine or another.

"God, the youth of today. Can't they go out and have a quiet drink?" Dave mused, as he sipped his beer. If he'd thought that Hendrix was loud, the next track proved him wrong. The speakers on the wall actually shook, as Black Sabbath hammered out some well tried guitar riff. Dave couldn't stand any more. He finished his pint in one gulp, stubbed out his cigarette and left. As he stood on the pavement, his ears were still ringing.

"What a fucking row," he muttered and started to walk further along the road. It was starting to get chilly and he wished he'd worn his old brown anorak, but he'd left it in the car. He quickened his pace and, after a few minutes, came upon another pub, the cleverly named Shirley Tavern. This was an old Victorian drinking house which had long since past its sell by date. The window frames were only just covered in flaking white gloss paint and the door seemed to be hanging off its hinges. Dave walked in. It was empty except for an old couple sitting at a table in the corner, and a middle-aged man at the bar.

"Good evening," said a very plump barman. "What'll it be?"

Dave smiled: this was better, a nice quiet pub. He glanced at the two hand-pumps and made his choice.

"A pint of 'Strong Country' please."

"I'm terribly sorry, that's off, got the 'Flowers' though," said the barman, in a heavy Dorset accent.

"OK, a pint of 'Flowers' then."

"Right-ho, straight glass or 'andle?"

"Straight please."

The man collected the correct vessel from underneath the bar and gave one of the hand-pumps a full pull. He stopped and held the glass up to the light and smiled, as if pleased with himself, and proceeded to fill the glass to the top. The whoosh of the beer hitting the glass was a most pleasing sound.

"There we are, one pint of wallop, just as you likes it."

"Thanks."

"One pound fifty please."

Dave paid, took a sip of the beer and walked over to a table, precariously positioned under a dart-board. Dave tried the beer again, it was nectar and although the pub was in dire need of an overhaul, the booze could not be faulted. Around the room were nostalgic photographs of Southampton in the twenties, each one with a little hand written title and date. Two more gulps and the beer was gone and Dave returned to the bar for a refill.

"Same again Squire?" asked the large barman, grinning and revealing that his two front teeth were missing.

"Yes please, that's the best pint I've had in years."

"All down to the pipes, me dear. Gotta clean 'em regularly. Dirty pipes, dirty beer, that's what I always says."

Dave went back to his table, lit up a fag, trying to make some sense of his current predicament. He tried to recall his movements, from leaving the Coach & Horses and waking up in the office, but it was no good. It was a total blank. He picked his ear and then his nose and thought hard, but there was no way he could remember his movements that fateful Wednesday evening, or indeed the Wednesday before. He'd somehow lost two or three hours of his life and he was going crazy trying to piece the whole thing together. While he was mulling over his beer, another couple entered the bar.

"Evenin' Jack, evenin' Nellie, you're late tonight," said the cheery barman. "How ya been?"

"Fine thanks, Colin, how's the missus?"

"Oh, a bit better. This damp weather don't help, plays murder wiv her joints."

"Know the feeling," replied the man, rubbing his elbow. "Give us a pint and a sherry for Nellie."

"Quick as you like."

Dave listened to the polite conversation for a while and then descended back into his own thoughts. He'd finished his beer and returned to the bar for a refill, this time with a large gin and tonic chaser.

"Is there an off-licence around here?" he asked the barman, after he'd received his change.

"Yes, Squire, just a ways up the main street, but you'll have t' hurry, I believe it closes at harf-ten."

Dave glanced at his watch, it was 10.20.

"Crikes, is that the time, can I leave the drinks here. I shan't be long."

"As you likes," nodded the barman, still grinning.

Dave left the pub at speed and ran up Shirley High Street. As the man had said, the off-licence was not far and Dave rushed in. He bought a bottle of gin, a large tonic water and twenty cigarettes. The shop assistant placed them in a carrier bag and Dave returned to the tavern, in under five minutes. His drinks were still on the bar.

"Got there OK?"

"Yes thanks, I'm down here on business and fancy a little nightcap when I get back to my digs," he added, almost as if he felt that he had to justify himself.

"I see," continued the barman. "Where you staying then?"

"Just down the road, at the Kimberley, d'you know it?"

"I'll say. Is it still run by old Irene Marshall?"

"Yes, she's still there," said Dave laughing. "She looks older than the building itself."

"You could be right, she used to be a regular here. Oh, I'm going back now, must be twenty years. Used to come in here a lot, don't think she gets out much now, mind you."

"Really?" questioned Dave, trying to look interested.

"Oh yeah. She still got those dreadful teeth? I remembers when she got 'em, never did fit her."

Dave nodded as he laughed and picking up his drinks returned to his table. The warmth of the atmosphere and the quality of the ale made it a most conducive place to drink and Dave felt strangely warm and almost happy, just sitting there. Dave surveyed his surroundings again and noticed over the bar lots of mementos of a life at sea. It was obvious the old boy behind the bar had, at one time or another, spent many years as a sailor. Dave drank two more pints and another large gin when the unthinkable happened.

"You're very last orders at the bar please," went out the cry. It was obvious that this was not a pub where you had a lock-in. Dave leapt from his seat, almost stumbling into the table, and ran to the bar.

"Keep your hair on Squire, there's still a bit more time," laughed the jolly jack-tar. "Twenty minutes drinking up time."

Dave played it down and ordered another pint and large G & T. A large ship's bell was rung to the call of "Time," and Dave knew there was no point even asking for any more. He finished his drinks, went to the toilet, which was even more run down than the pub, and after slurring "Goodnight," walked out into the street. By now, it was freezing, and even in his inebriated state, Dave stood mortified by the cold. He stumbled and staggered down Shirley High Street like a destitute, his co-ordination completely gone. He tried to quicken his pace and almost fell over. He was seeing double but still nearly got run over as he crossed the street and walked into Languard Road. He saw his car and, for reasons best known to himself, decided to get out his anorak, even though it was parked outside the guest house. Struggling to find his keys, he opened the passenger door, stretched over into the back and fell in, banging his head on the driver's door.

* * *

At 12.11 Christine Hill walked from Shirley High Street into Church Road, on her way home from the evening shift at the Shirley 'Spud-U-like'. She was a pretty girl of nineteen but walked with a terrible limp, the legacy of a near fatal car accident she'd had when eleven years old. Because of this, she was painfully shy and kept herself to herself. She lived with her parents on the second floor of a block of flats, just at the back of Shirley, and walked this route every Friday and Saturday night. It was only a five minute walk and, although a chilly March night, she was in no particular hurry. She hadn't noticed she was being followed.

A man of average build and height, wearing a brown car coat, jeans and Nike trainers was keeping an even distance behind her. He had a pom-pom hat pulled down over his ears, which for the time of the year did not look out of place. Church Road was not very well lit, and only ran some six or seven hundred yards before it reached a row of council houses and flats, built in the mid-sixties and now unfashionably dated.

He quickened his pace and caught up with the girl just as she reached the slightly wooded area in front of the first block of flats. As she walked across the grass and between the two trees, ceremoniously planted in 1982 by a young Princess Anne, she slowed slightly and looked around. It was then that he pounced. Grabbing her roughly by her hair, he easily threw her onto the grass, her injured leg crumpling under her. She yelled out in pain as her teeth dug into her top lip, causing blood to spurt from her mouth. The man stopped for a moment, giving Christine enough time to roll over onto her back. She glanced up in absolute fear, but in the half light could not make out any features. She noticed the man was wearing gloves and was taking them off. In blind terror, she kicked out with her good leg, but missed her target. She screamed at the top of her voice and her attacker, who had seemed strangely subdued, ran off, cutting between the trees and round the back of the flats.

Suddenly, the area was alive. Several people came running from a ground floor flat, a man out walking his dog seemed to appear from nowhere and four or five youths, obviously on their way home from the pub, all arrived at the scene at once.

"You OK Pet?" said the man with the dog.

"Yes, I think so," said Christine, as several people helped her to her feet.

She spat out some blood and rubbed her mouth.

"Where d'you live?"

"Just in there," she replied, pointing at the flats behind. "I'm OK, honestly, I've just cut my lip a bit."

"Someone had better call the police."

"I'll do it, I only live there." Christine's father had heard the commotion and was pushing his way through the throng. "Chris, Chris, you OK? What happened?"

"Oh, daddy, thank God." She grabbed her father tightly around the waist and started to cry. "It was horrible, a man tried to rape me, he pulled my hair and threw me onto ..."

"Alright love, you're safe now," reassured her father and, turning to the crowd asked, "Anyone see the bastard?"

"No, he was long gone when I got here, he ran round the back, I think."

"Right lads," said one of the youths, "let's go see if we can catch him."

And with great bravado, the five lads ran off into the night.

"Is this your glove sweetheart?" said a kindly old lady, bending over and picking a glove up from the ground. Christine froze when she saw it, her pupils dilated and her jaw dropped. "No!" she snapped, snuggling back into her father's chest, "it's his, the man's."

"Give that here," demanded her father. "The police will want to see that. Has anyone called them?"

"Yes, the guy who lives in that flat has just gone to do it."

By this time, another twelve or so people had arrived and questions were being asked by everyone to everyone.

"Come on darling, let's take you home," said her father. "When the police arrive can you tell them we live at number 26?"

"Sure."

"Of course."

"You bet."

All the people there seemed to answer together and Mr Hill took his daughter home.

The police finally arrived at 12.56 (Friday being a busy night in Southampton) and all the necessary statements were taken. At about two o'clock, Dave Price opened his eyes and wondered where the fuck he was. When he realised he was in his car, he then wondered what the hell he was doing in it. He struggled to sit up and eventually managed to open the door. "Christ, it's fucking freezing," he yelled as he slammed the car door and ran over to the guest house. He felt in every pocket but could not find the key. Walking back to his car, he opened the door again and saw the guest house key, together with his own car keys, on the seat.

"Oh, what a prat." he sighed and proceeded to snatch them from the seat and slam the car door again.

As he arrived once more at the guest house door, it flung open. Mrs Marshall was standing in her winceyette dressing-gown and was obviously not amused.

"Was that you banging the car door?" she demanded.

"No, I didn't take the car tonight," he slurred incredulously.

"Well, I think it's disgusting, people banging doors like that and waking up the neighbourhood ..."

"Yeah, yeah, quite agree. Now if you don't mind, I'm going to bed."

"Well, as it so happens, I do mind. Look at the state of you. This is a respectable establishment, we don't care to ..."

"Shut up you old bag, I'm going to bed."

He pushed past her and started up the stairs. Glancing down at the front of his trousers, he noticed what the old lady had been talking about. He'd obviously urinated while asleep and a huge wet patch was clearly visible around his flies.

"Well I never. I think you'd better leave in the morning, you're nothing but trouble ..."

Dave had reached the top of the stairs, but he could still hear her rabbiting away. As he fumbled to unlock his door, he turned and shouted:

"FUCK OFF and good night."

"I heard that, you disgusting pervert, never heard language like it before. I don't know what the world's coming ..."

Dave missed the end of her sermon and fell face down onto the bed and, within seconds, was asleep.

* * *

D.I. Quinn had been informed by telephone of the latest incident and had arranged to meet Sergeant Crouch in the Civic Centre police station at 08.30

"Didn't think I'd see you here this morning Sir," said Crouch as Quinn walked into the back office. "What's the score?"

"The score, young man," Quinn snapped, obviously not amused at having to work, because he'd promised to take his wife shopping and she had given him a lot of hassle when he told her that he'd have to go in on Saturday morning, "is that the bastard's struck again, this time in Shirley."

"I see and you think it's the same person as the St Mary's villain?"

"Gotta be. It has all his usual trademarks but this time he dropped a glove."

"Really?"

"Yes, and I wouldn't mind betting our friend David Price was drinking in Shirley last night, got pissed and can't remember where he was."

"And forensic should give us something on the glove?"

"Obviously. Now make us a cup of tea and then we'll pay the little prick a visit."

Crouch made the tea and at 08.53 they put on their coats and walked through the back exit to the police car. Quinn opened the door and was almost knocked back by the smell of greasy bacon.

"What the bloody hell ..."

"Sorry Sir, got in early and popped out for a quick buttie before you arrived," apologised Crouch sheepishly.

"You must have worms," mumbled Quinn, shaking his head, whilst holding his nose.

"Only in my garden, Sir."

* * *

It was pitch black, and people were shouting, some even screaming, when suddenly a blinding beam of light hit Dave's face. It was possibly a spotlight and it caused him to squint and place his hands over his face.

"Who's there?" he murmured, "I've done nothing."

He opened his eyes and jumped, it was a dream, but not like any other dream he'd had, it seemed almost like a premonition. He was shaking and felt ill. Looking around his tiny room, his eyes started to focus and he remembered where he was. A chink of light was shining through the gap in the curtains, highlighting the tiny pieces of mote hanging in the air, it was early morning and obviously a sunny day. He scratched his privates and felt the warm, damp urine, still not dry from the previous evening. Rolling over, he let his legs dangle over the edge of the bed.

"What the fuck did I get up to last night?" he queried, and got up, walked over to the little basin in his room, and spat. Watching the huge yellowy-green blob slowly disappear down the plughole, he turned on the tap. He looked at his watch and it flashed 07.31 at him.

"Fuck it, I'm not getting up yet," he thought to himself and took off his soiled clothes and climbed back into bed, this time under the covers. As he slipped once more into a troubled slumber, the darkness and strange sounds came back. He'd always had nice and erotic dreams, but now there was something nasty, evil, disturbing, trying to get at him. He jumped, his pulse racing, his whole body sweating as he sat bolt-upright. The problems of the last few days and the excess of alcohol he'd consumed were obviously getting to him.

The two police officers had driven the short distance from the Civic Centre to Shirley and had been shown into the guest house by Mrs Marshall. They stood in the small reception area and Quinn spoke.

"We're here to see Mr Price again, can we go right up please?"

"Of course. I'm glad you've come actually, I had a bit of trouble with him last night."

"Really? How?"

"Well he arrived back here very late, drunk as a lord and cursing and swearing like nobody's business. He was very rude to me, you know."

"I see, and did you notice anything else about him? Anything different?"

"Well, if you'll excuse my French, he'd pissed himself. His trousers were soaking and he didn't seem completely with it."

"What time did he get back, exactly?"

"Must have been quarter past two. Yeah, I heard the car door slam, TWICE, and came down to see what all the noise was."

"He'd gone out in his car, had he?"

"Well, he said he hadn't, but I'm sure it was his car door that was slammed. If you look outside, you'll see there's only a few cars in the whole street."

"You don't remember if he was wearing a brown coat and had a glove on I suppose?"

"No, just a sweatshirt I think, definitely didn't have any gloves, I remember thinking he must be freezing."

"OK, thanks, can we go up now?"

"Of course, you know which room it is?"

"Yes, I'm sure we can find it. And thanks."

The two officers climbed the rickety old stairs and Crouch turned to his boss and asked, "Do you think there's any significance in the car Sir?"

"Yes Mike, I think he wore his coat and gloves out and put them back in his car, before coming in here."

"Mmm," Mike pondered his superior's words, "Yeah, that's probably right."

They arrived at the door and Crouch banged on it twice. Dave was still in bed but troubled by his thoughts and dreams.

"Yes? What? I don't want any breakfast," he shouted, thinking it was Mrs Marshall.

"Mr Price? It's the police, could you open up please? We've some more questions for you."

"Now fucking what?" Dave growled, getting out of bed and looking for something to wear. He'd urinated in both pairs of trousers and couldn't even find a clean pair of underpants. The police knocked again.

"Alright, alright, I'm coming, just putting some clothes on."

He rummaged through the clothes on the wardrobe floor, they were smelly but dry. He put on the pair of jeans and the sweatshirt he'd worn two evenings previously. Walking to the door, he pulled it open in one jerk.

"Oh! You two again."

Both of the officers pulled back momentarily as a strong smell or urine, BO and stale cigarette smoke leapt from the open doorway.

Quinn screwed up his nose and said: "Mr Price, we'd like you to accompany us to the station. We've some more questions for you."

"What about?"

"Not here, at the station please. If you'd finish getting dressed, we'll wait here."

Dave closed the door slightly and struggled with his socks and shoes but was ready in a few moments. He walked out of the room and stood on the landing next to the two policemen. "Can I at least brush my teeth and have a quick wash please?"

"If you must," said Quinn, realising that it was a good idea, "but please be as quick as you can."

Dave re-entered his room, picked up his little overnight bag and walked down the hall to the bathroom.

"Christ, I'm glad he asked to do that," said Crouch, "what a bloody whiff."

Dave stood in the bathroom and looked at himself in the mirror over the sink. His bloodshot eyes barely focusing on the mess reflected in the glass. He brushed his teeth, splashed a little water on his face and decided to forego a shave, it was too much trouble. He walked back onto the landing.

"Have you got a coat?" asked Quinn probingly, "it's pretty cold out there this morning."

"Yes, in the car," Dave answered, wondering why the sudden interest in his welfare.

"And gloves?"

"Yes, I've got gloves, but I very rarely wear them."

"Good, perhaps we can collect them on the way."

"As you wish." Dave shook his head as they followed him downstairs. With three grown men all walking down together, the stairs seemed as if they would collapse under the weight. Mrs Marshall appeared as they left the building.

"Good riddance to bad rubbish," she yelled as they walked across the road.

"What's the matter with that old bag?" Dave asked, but neither of the officers answered.

They stopped at his car and Dave looked puzzled.

"The coat and gloves Sir," Quinn prompted.

Dave shrugged his shoulders and fumbled for his keys. His old car coat was on the back seat and he reached for that first.

"The Sergeant will take that," said Quinn abruptly.

"I thought you wanted me to wear it?"

"No, we want to look at it, and your gloves?"

"Gloves? Yes, they're in the glove compartment, good place to keep them. Eh?" joked Dave. "Hey, that's weird, there's only one here. Hang on, perhaps the other one's fallen down the back." Quinn watched and prayed that he wouldn't find it.

"No luck Sir? Perhaps you dropped it somewhere last night?"

"Not possible, I didn't wear them last night. I haven't worn them for ages."

"Really?"

"Nope, not there, don't know where it is."

"We might be able to help you with that problem."

"What?" Dave looked surprised and puzzled.

"Just give the glove to the Sergeant and let's go to the station."

They walked over to the police car and Crouch opened the back door and gestured for Dave to get in. Quinn followed him into the back and Crouch got into the driver's seat. They travelled the mile or so in silence and Dave was led into the station and taken straight to the same interview room he'd been in the previous evening.

"Sergeant Crouch could you take Mr Price's glove and jacket to be labelled and then get them off to the lab.?"

Crouch left the room immediately.

"What's this all about?" Dave asked looking bemused and somewhat bewildered.

"You'll soon find out, once we start the interview."

Quinn opened two tapes and placed them on the table in front of Dave.

"Um, sorry to be a pain, but can I go to the loo before we start please?"

Quinn tutted, "You'll have to wait until the sergeant gets back which hopefully won't be long."

True to his word, Crouch returned in a few minutes.

"Take this gentleman to the toilet please Sergeant."

"Yes Sir."

Dave stood at the urinal, desperately trying to pee. He was feeling particularly vulnerable and squeezed his hands tightly together, making the knuckles go white. He once again couldn't remember exactly what he'd done the previous evening, other than having had a few drinks at the pub in Shirley. No matter how hard he tried, he couldn't produce a drop, even though his bladder was full. He broke wind loudly and decided to give it up as a bad job.

Crouch made him jump as he poked his head around the door. "Nearly done?" he questioned, screwing up his nose at the disgusting smell in the room.

"Yeah, suppose so."

Dave was led back to the interview room and placed in a chair opposite Quinn.

"Do you think we can start now?" said Quinn irritably.

"Any chance of a cup of tea or coffee? I'm parched."

"What do you think this is? A bloody cafe, you don't ..." Quinn stopped mid-sentence knowing he shouldn't get rattled. "OK. Could you please make us three teas Sergeant and be as quick as you can."

Crouch left the room.

"If you try to rile me, I promise you trouble. If this is some little game of yours, I swear I'll ..."

"Sorry, I only asked for a drink, surely you can't begrudge me that?"

Quinn leant over and whispered softly, "I wouldn't give you the snot off my nose or the drips off my dick, you little spunk-bubble."

Dave moved back in his seat, every time Quinn whispered something, it was always offensive. He remembered the last time and the comment about the placenta. They sat in silence until the sergeant returned with a tray of teas.

"If Mr Price is quite ready, perhaps we can start, or would he like a cushion?" said Quinn, playing to the gallery.

Dave frowned and picked up his tea. He wanted a cigarette but didn't dare ask for one, not yet anyway.

Quinn placed the tapes into the tape machine and pressed the record button.

"I am Detective Inspector Quinn starting a second interview with Mr David Price, currently resident at the Kimberley Guest House, Languard Road, Shirley, timed at nine-thirty on Saturday 13th March. I must first caution you and warn that anything you say may be used in evidence against you. The other police officer present is Sergeant Crouch and I am interviewing ...please state your full name."

"David Malcom Price."

"Date of birth?"

"Twentieth of February 1954."

"No other person is present and this interview is being conducted at Southampton Civic Centre police station." Quinn stopped and checked the recording level and then continued. "Do you wish to have a solicitor present or are you waiving this right?"

"I dunno, what's this all about? I told you everything I know yesterday."

"Another attempted assault took place last night in the Shirley area of Southampton and new and important evidence has come to light. I ask again, do you wish to have a solicitor present, or are you waiving this right."

"Look, I've had a dreadful night, hardly slept a wink, you've dragged me here basically from my bed and you start throwing all these questions at me. For Christ's sake ..."

"Surely it's a very simple question. Do you want a solicitor present? Or can we continue without one?"

"I need to go to the loo again."

Quinn slammed his finger on the stop button. "Look, I've already warned you, any pissing about and I can get very nasty. If you want to play it that way, then fine."

"I'm sorry. I couldn't go just now, but now I ..."

"OK, OK, last time, go to the loo, have a slash and then get your ass back in here."

Dave thought he was going to be punched in the face and cowered back.

"Get him out of my sight."

Dave followed the sergeant again to the Gents and at least managed a small stream. This time, Crouch stood next to him, half tempted to look down into the urinal.

"I've got to warn you Mr Price," he said in a very kind manner, "if Quinn gets nasty, I fear for the worst."

"Look, don't try the old 'one hard-one soft' copper routine with me, I've seen all this on the telly."

"As you wish, if that's how you see it, you can't say I didn't warn you."

Dave shook his member and pulled the foreskin back and forth a few times, he was very surprised he'd had the nerve to say what he'd just said, and was shaking badly.

They walked back to the interview room and it was obvious that Quinn had momentarily calmed down a little.

"Before I start the tape again," he said softly, "and strictly off the record, we've got you bang to rights on this and it's going to look a lot better for you if you confess to the three assaults, and with no previous form, I'm sure we can get you a reduced sentence, possibly in one of those open prisons, and surely that's best, isn't it?"

"You must be joking, I'm not confessing to anything, I'm innocent, d'you understand, bloody innocent."

"Dave, think about it, with a good brief, a bit of psychiatric help, well, obviously it was the booze, no doubt about it, you just give us a break and we'll see what we can do."

Dave sat quietly listening, whilst shaking his head.

"No, no, no, this ain't right. I think I'd better have a solicitor present, this is getting out of hand."

"OK Mr Price, as you wish." Quinn turned to Crouch, "Isn't it strange Sergeant, suddenly Mr Price feels he needs a solicitor, did we touch on a sore point, you think?"

Dave's mind was in overdrive. Did he need a solicitor? Did he have a solicitor? Surely if he was innocent calling for one now made him look guilty. The thoughts flooded his mind, the booze from the previous evening making everything seem hazy, as if he was not really there. Like a dream. Perhaps it was.

"Look, I haven't got a solicitor. Well, not really, so I suppose I don't need one. Yet."

"Well, the choice is yours, when I restart the tape, I want you to make it quite clear that you were offered one. OK?"

"OK. Can I have a cigarette please? I'm gasping."

Quinn could quite easily have punched him there and then. First a pee, then a coffee, then another pee, now a fag. He coughed, and nodded to Crouch, who left the room and returned almost instantly with an ashtray. Quinn calmed himself as he spoke.

"OK have your fag and let's try to get this over as quickly as possible."

Crouch admired the way Quinn had turned the whole solicitor issue into an admission of guilt. He was a good detective, no doubt about that.

"Dave, think about this, when you're drunk you can't remember even where you were, so how can you be so damned sure you didn't commit these crimes. How can you be sure? Honestly."

"I know it looks bad, and I'll agree, I can't remember exact details, but surely ..."

"Dave, Dave," Quinn reached his arm across the table and

touched Dave's hand, "you were drunk, the bitches were asking for it, these things happen, we're both men of the world, I understand, I really do."

"I know that. Yes I was drunk, yes I like the women, but I couldn't, really, I couldn't ..."

"We found one of your gloves at the scene of last night's assault. How could that have got there. Tell me that?"

"I dunno, I never wear the things, they were a Christmas present, you know, an unwanted ..."

"I'm sorry Dave, that's just not good enough. The girl last night has told us her assailant wore a brown car coat and was wearing gloves. The lab will tell us if it's your glove or not. Come on, level with yourself, you did it and now you must pay. That's only fair, isn't it?"

"I can't remember, I honestly can't remember."

"Well, we've got enough for a conviction, so let's just piece it all together, tie up the loose ends, you'll feel much better if you talk about it, get it off your chest."

"Hang on, you haven't heard a word I've said, have you? I'm innocent, I don't know how my glove got there or who put it there, but ..."

"Dave, your gloves were in your car, your car was not broken into, was it? You must have worn them out. True?"

Dave put his head in his hands and felt warm tears welling up in his eyes.

"I've had enough of this pussy-footing about. You've got two choices, we can do it the civilised nice way, or we can do it the hard way. You decide."

Self-pity was starting to swell up inside him and Dave looked up at Quinn, but saw no hope in the dark cold eyes facing him across the table.

The mood was changed by a knock on the door and a uniformed officer leant into the room and whispered something to Crouch. Crouch smiled.

"Jackpot, the gloves are a perfect match."

"Well, that's it Dave," Quinn sighed and took out his note

pad, "I arrest you for the assault and attempted rape of Miss Gladys Umbala on Wednesday 3rd of March, Diane Michells on Wednesday 10th of March, and Christine Hill on Friday the 12th of March. I must warn you that you are not obliged to say anything, but anything you do say may be used in evidence against you."

Dave nearly fainted. When was he going to wake up, this dream had lasted far too long already.

"Do you wish to have a solicitor present, if you do not have one, we can get the Court to provide you with one, or do you wish to waive this right?"

This was now serious, the gloves, how did they get out of his car? Had he really fallen asleep? Or was that part of a dream too? He wiped his eyes and looked around the room.

"I haven't really got one, so could you get one for me." He said timidly.

Quinn frowned. "OK Sergeant. Will you please find out who the solicitor on call is and ask him to present himself here, as soon as possible."

"Yes Sir."

"Oh, but before that, could you take Mr Price to the Desk Sergeant, get him booked and taken to a cell please."

Crouch held the door open. "This way please."

Dave got up slowly and followed Crouch from the room, back into the main office and up to a small counter.

"Morning Mike," said the policeman behind the counter, "what we got here?"

"Mr David Price. We've started a taped interview, but have subsequently charged him with the attempted rapes, the details are all here." Crouch handed over a large brown folder. "Could you do the necessary, and take him to the cells please?"

"Nice one," mumbled the Desk Sergeant under his breath. He was obviously pleased with the outcome.

Dave was duly booked, read his rights again, this time under the Police and Criminal Evidence Act (PACE) and asked to empty his pockets.

"Can I keep my fags?" he asked, almost pleadingly.

"Sorry Sir, not just yet. Get you settled in then see where we go from there."

"Well, can I have one now then?"

"'Fraid not, no smoking area," said the Sergeant, pointing to a large sign. "Plenty of time for a ciggy later."

Dave was taken down a long off-white corridor and placed in a holding-cell. He sat down on the bed, which ran the length of the room, and wriggled his behind to get comfortable. The springs were obviously shot as they groaned under his weight. It was a small square room, only marginally larger than the one at the guest house, with a tiny commode and hand basin in one corner. The window was set high above him and surrounded in bars and cobwebs.

Crouch returned to Quinn, who was still meditating in the interview room. Quinn looked up, his thoughts shattered as the door opened.

"Classic case Mike," Quinn started without prompting. "Man falls out with his missus, and she stops his nookie, gets pissed, and takes out his sexual fantasies on some poor girl, who just happens to be passing. I hate bastards like him. He had it all, nice house, good job, lovely family and it's still not enough. Makes you want to throw up. They convince themselves they're innocent and sometimes, like this prat, can't even see what they've done. They're worse than hardened criminals, at least when they're caught, they usually put up their hands and say 'fair cop', not this type of prick though. I hope he gets ten years."

"Maybe," said Crouch, not quite convinced, "Psychiatrists say it sometimes goes a little deeper than ..."

"Fucking psychiatrists, what do they know? They always take the side of the villain, always some goody-goody who thinks we should treat this sort of vermin with kid gloves, I tell you Mike, if I had my way, I'd ..."

"OK, point taken Guv."

"And don't call me Guv. Ah, bloody youngsters, not a clue, not a pissing clue."

Crouch rubbed his hands down the sides of his trousers, he'd heard the rumours about Quinn, but had always found him to be a good straight copper. They'd all said he was mellowing in his old age, but the look in his eyes at that moment made Mike Crouch pleased he was on Quinn's side. His hard upbringing in Manchester was still very much in evidence, and it was blatantly obvious, he could still turn nasty when the mood took him.

"I've 'phoned the solicitor on call, it's your favourite, Baden-Smith. The poor sod's always on call."

"Oh God, heaven help us, that bloody idiot. The reason he's always on call is that he's a crap lawyer, and it's the only work he ever gets," Quinn sighed and looked into the air. "That's all we need, a sodding prat like him. Still, they'll make a good pair together."

"Oh, he's not that bad."

"Not that bad? He's a balding, four-eyed walking disaster, with bad breath, chronic acne, who could quite easily double for a horror movie, and as for personal hygiene, well, it's two words he's never come across."

"You don't like him then?" laughed Crouch.

"Oh, forget it, they deserve each other. They can sit and have cosy little chats about skin disorders and halitosis."

"I think you're being a bit harsh, but ..."

"Now Mike," Quinn switched back into his official Inspector mode, "can you go and get a full statement from the Helen Whatshername girl, but don't bother with the Coach & Horses mob? I think we've got enough without any more crap from that little prick, Phil Smith."

"Right-ho sir, and then home?"

"Yeah, s'pose so, I'll get one of the other lads to sit in on this one with me."

"Are you sure, I don't mind coming back if ..."

"No, you get home to your wife, I'll finish up here."

Crouch left the room at speed, obviously anxious to get home. Quinn was not in such a hurry. He loved his wife dearly and had no problems at all with the marriage. It was just that he loved police work, it was his life, and the wrapping up of a case like this was almost a drug to him.

"I think I'd better ring Mrs Price, not that she's much interested in her prick of a husband, and let her know what's going on, and then a statement to the local rag," he mumbled to himself as he left the room. "Not a bad day's work after all."

Dave had paced his cell, and after about ten minutes, lay upon the bed. He lay on his side facing the wall, and noticed several pieces of graffiti, crudely carved into the brickwork. 'All coppers are bastards," seemed to be a popular one, but 'Fuck the pigs' was by far and away the most common. Dave closed his eyes, he was so tired, he had to have some sleep. He lay dozing for what seemed like hours, when the door flew open and a uniformed policeman entered with a very strange scruffy-looking man. Dave woke up instantly, rolled around on the dilapidated bed and swung his legs over the side.

"Mr Price?" said the man, who had the worst skin affliction on his cheeks that Dave had ever seen. "I'm Laurence Baden-Smith, and I've been assigned your case, if you want me that is."

Dave took a deep breath and rubbed his eyes: "You a solicitor then?" he questioned.

"Yes, I'm supplied by the state and can work with you through the legal aid system, if you have insufficient means."

"Really. Well, I think you've got your work cut out then."

"Come now, Mr Price, I'm sure it's not that bad. I've only just got your dossier, so I'm not au fait with it yet, but ..." he paused and turned to the policeman. "Could you leave us now please?" he said, and the copper left the cell.

Baden-Smith sat down on the other end of the bed and opened the large brown file that he'd obviously been given by the police. "Right, give me a few minutes to familiarise myself and then we'll see about getting a proper room organised."

Dave watched the man and felt slightly nauseous. It might be the booze, of course, but more likely it was the look of his solicitor. He wasn't quite sure.

Baden-Smith wore an old raincoat, which made Columbo look like a fashion victim. The front was crumpled and stained and the sleeves had a shiny, almost slimy look to them. His face was covered in blotches and spots, the biggest one, on the side of his nose, looked ready to burst at any moment. He was almost completely bald, but had grown the left hand side long, and had it swept across the crown of his head. It was impossible to guess his age, but it had to be forty plus. Surely this man dressed more smartly when he appeared in court? If he didn't, then Dave knew his case was sunk.

As he turned the pages in the file, he muttered, and made little whimpering noises, and after a while, this started to get Dave agitated.

"You ain't got any fags on you, have you?"

"What? Cigarettes, um, no, I don't smoke."

"Well, they took a packet off me when I was charged, no chance of getting them back, is there?"

"Please Mr Price, I need to read this and then we'll go to another room to talk through it, I'll try to get your cigarettes then. Now if you don't mind."

"Ugly bastard," Dave thought as he nibbled at his fingernails.

Baden-Smith finished reading and closed the file. "Yes," he sighed, "you were right, it doesn't look too good. I suggest we go to a proper room, and set about working out your defence, but from now on, do not, I repeat do not, say anything to Detective Quinn unless I am present. OK?"

"Yeah, sure, he doesn't like me anyway."

"Look Mr Price, Detective Quinn does not like anyone outside of the police force. He's a very difficult man to get on with, and you may find this hard to believe, but he doesn't like me either."

"Not surprised, I've only met you for ten minutes, and I think you're a prick," Dave thought, but answered: "Really?"

"Right, let's go," Baden-Smith jumped to his feet and banged on the door. It was opened, and the solicitor left.

"Don't forget me fags," Dave shouted after him, "and is there any chance of a cup of coffee?"

Walking back to the main police office, Baden-Smith explained to the young officer his need for an interview room.

"You'll have to see Inspector Quinn sir," he said curtly.

"And where is he, pray tell?"

"I'm right here Mr. Baggy-Smith," said Quinn, who'd heard them talking as they walked into the office.

"The name is Baden-Smith, as you are well aware. Any more of this churlish behaviour and I'll report you to your superiors."

"Well you do that," said Quinn, as he walked over to his desk, put on his coat, and made for the door, pretending he was leaving.

"Excuse me, I said EXCUSE ME, I trust you are not going out, only I need to talk to you about my client."

Quinn stopped in his tracks, put his hand on his hip, and turned to face his adversary.

"Well, well, well, you want something from me, do you?"

"I want no favours, just a proper room to interview my client, surely it's his right, or have you found him guilty already?"

"Mr Badger-Smith," he loved twisting the solicitor's name around, and over the years had used Buggy-Smith, Budgie-Smith, Bagpuss-Smith and even Blaster-Smith' all of which seemed to rile him no end, "if it's a cosy little cell you want, then who am I to deprive you." "SERGEANT," he yelled, causing the solicitor to jump, "find this gentleman a nice cell for his interview, will you? I'll be back in half an hour, and we can all have a little chat then."

Baden-Smith frowned. If there was ever a policeman he'd met, who was ruder, nastier or more vile, he couldn't remember when. He'd led a traumatic life, ever since childhood, what with his chronic acne, thinning hair (he'd started to go bald at fifteen), and bad breath, life had always been an uphill struggle for him. He'd been shunned by everyone, even his parents, but had become a solicitor through sheer hard work and single-mindedness, and some stupid kids calling him 'Bloody spotty-Smithy' had just made him more determined to succeed. His thoughts were shattered by the policeman.

"If you follow me."

They walked down the corridor to a door marked 'I.V.R. 1B'. "Your room Sir, I'll go and get your client, if you'd like to wait inside."

"Thank you, oh, and can my client have his cigarettes, please? I believe the Desk Sergeant has them."

The policeman nodded and Baden-Smith walked into the room. Dave arrived soon and sat down opposite his brief.

"D'you remember the ciggies?" he asked.

"Yes, I think the Sergeant has gone to get them now."

"Thanks, um, what do I call you?"

"You can call me Mr Baden-Smith, if you don't mind. Now let's get on with it. Inspector Quinn will be back soon and will want you to answer some questions. Therefore, I think it would be prudent to know what we will say, and what we will not."

"Yeah. OK."

"First Mr Price," said Baden-Smith, in an accent Dave could not really recognise, "I've got to ask you, did you do it?"

"Of course not, just because I have a bad memory, it ..."

"Yes, yes, quite, so we shall plead not guilty to all charges, even the latest one, correct?"

"Bloody right," Dave frowned. "Look, I don't mean to be rude or anything, but you are a solicitor, aren't you?"

"I am your brief, appointed by the Crown. However, as I stated before, you are free to choose another, if you feel I cannot be of service to you," Baden-Smith stated, quite indignantly. Dave sighed, he felt it was a case of the blind leading the blind.

"No, it's not that, only your clothes and everything. I dunno, just ..."

"I am on call. It's the weekend. I will of course be properly dressed and wearing suitable attire when we come before the Magistrate, hoping for bail."

The constable tapped on the door and entered with the cigarettes, matches and an ashtray.

"Will there be anything else?" he asked sarcastically, adding "Sir," most distastefully.

"No thank you," said the solicitor politely, "that's fine."

The policeman left and Dave almost ripped open the packet, "How long will they keep me in here?"

"Well, I will get you before the Magistrate as soon as possible, which should be Monday, so I think it's safe to say that D.I. Quinn will keep you in here until then."

"But I've got no clothes to change into, these are filthy and my razor and things, what ...?"

"I'll arrange for some clean clothes for you, I assume they're with your wife."

"Yeah, Christ wait till she finds out, she'll love all this."

"Surely not?"

"Well, we've just split up, she threw me out really, so I don't expect any sympathy there."

"We'll see, now I think we ought to get down to business. First of all, the gloves, they really are the spanner in the works, you have no idea how one of them was found at the scene of the last assault?"

"None, I never wear them, I just can't see how it happened."

"Really? Well most of the other evidence is circumstantial, but added together, it makes quite a case."

"Whose side you on?" Dave asked, puffing hard on his cigarettes, sending pale blue smoke across the room.

"Really Mr Price, that sort of attitude is hardly productive, is it?"

"Well," Dave said, rolling his head.

"OK, what about the um, adult magazines the police found in your room, were they hard core?"

"No, just big boob mags, no bonking in them."

"Where did you get them, from a newsagents?"

"Ah, that's a bit of a problem," Dave hesitated. "I bought them from a sex-shop in St Mary's."

"Oh, that's good, in a sex-shop, right in the middle of the area where all the assaults took place. Although they're mentioned in the report, it looks like they won't be in the prosecution's evidence. Where are they now?"

"Still in the guest house."

"Pity, Quinn's bound to get a warrant and no doubt produce them."

"So what, it's not a crime to have a few boob books."

"Very true, but when presented to a jury, they certainly won't help. Unfortunately, people who buy goods from sex-shops are frowned upon by society in general."

Dave sighed, stubbed out his cigarette and immediately lit another one.

"No, it's the glove that's the problem," the solicitor continued, "we've got to find a way around it."

"But I told you, I haven't worn those gloves for months, maybe someone stole them and dropped them at the scene."

"Ah, but they didn't steal them, only one glove was dropped, remember, and it is very unlikely that someone would take one glove, keep it for months, and then leave it in Shirley."

"Well, I don't know."

"If both gloves were dropped, then maybe ..."

Baden-Smith and Dave continued their question and answer routine for another hour, but it seemed they were getting nowhere. Finally, the solicitor placed all the papers back into the folder.

"I'll be honest with you, if we go to court with this, I think there is every likelihood we'd lose. Our best hope is that the rapist strikes again and that would put you in the clear, providing of course you had an alibi."

"What sort of lawyer are you, my best chance is for the bloke to strike again, what if he doesn't, what if he feels he's had enough, or moved, what then? Eh?"

"Yes, I know, but I can only advise you as I see it, and if they start bringing in character witnesses, well."

"Witnesses? What bloody witnesses?"

"For a start, there's the girl in your office, claims you grabbed her one afternoon."

"Bloody prick teaser."

"Really, and the young barmaid?"

"Some stupid little fat girl, I felt sorry for her, that's all, didn't do anything."

"Yes, I know, but it's all in the police file ..."

Dave got up, and walked across the room, "Can't you do anything?"

"I'll go and see about bail, and we'll continue this a little later."

Baden-Smith picked up his folder and walked over to Dave and held out his hand. "Later, OK?"

The constable returned to the room and escorted Dave back to his cell.

"What do you think of this Baden-Smith guy?" Dave asked, hoping for some assurance.

"Not for me to say Sir," was all he heard, as the door closed, leaving him alone.

* * *

The solicitor had been told that the hearing would be on Monday morning, as the police still required a full statement from the defendant. Quinn and Baden-Smith agreed to have a further meeting with Dave Price at 15.30 that afternoon. Dave had been brought some lunch and some fresh clothes, (presumably obtained from his wife) and was sitting, staring at the graffiti on the cell wall. It was 14.55, when the cell door opened and in walked Quinn and a uniformed policeman, who took up a position by the door, while Quinn sat on the other end of the bed.

"Well, Dave, this doesn't look too good does it? Why don't we cut all the crap, and see how best we can rectify the very dodgy position you find yourself in?"

"My brief said not to talk to you unless he was present."

"Wise advice, however I might be the best ally you've got, so how about hearing me out."

Dave was confused, his heart was beating so loudly, he was surprised that Quinn couldn't hear it.

"I don't know, its ..."

"You see the trouble is, this Baden-Smith character, he gets all the cases no one else wants, he's got no reputation to lose, so why should he worry what happens?"

Dave shook his head and bit on his bottom lip like a little schoolboy in trouble with his teacher.

"OK, fair enough, you can't say I didn't try to help."

Quinn got up and moved towards the door. Dave turned away and looked up at the little window. Quinn was annoyed and walked back over to Dave, leant down and whispered: "Some big convict is going to stick his cock so far down your throat, it'll whitewash your tonsils. Chew on that Sonny."

Dave sat upright, looking shocked and indignant: "You can't say that, it's police harassment, I'll tell my ..." he nearly said

'Mummy' but stuttered 'brief'.

"Did you hear me say anything Sergeant?" snapped Quinn.

"No Sir, nothing at all."

The two officers left almost immediately and Dave thought he heard them laughing, as they walked up the corridor.

"I hate that Quinn, dirty bastard, always whispering obscenities, and things," he mumbled to himself, wishing he was anywhere but in that grotty little cell.

Baden-Smith arrived just before three thirty and at least looked half-decent. He'd obviously gone home and changed. However, even in a suit, he still looked scruffy. A young constable took Dave and the solicitor to the interview room, and left.

"Mr Smith, Quinn came to ..." started Dave.

"Baden-Smith if you don't mind," interrupted the brief.

"Sorry, Quinn came to see me and tried to get me to talk to him. I told him what you said, and he got abusive."

"That's typical of the man, he's nothing more than a ..." He stopped mid-sentence as Quinn and another officer walked into the room.

"Well, well, well, if it isn't the gargoyle twins," joked Quinn, as he looked at the two men sitting at the table.

"Really Detective Inspector Quinn, this is getting beyond a joke. Any more outbreaks like that and I will report you to your superiors. This is a serious matter and your childish, nay churlish, remarks are bordering on the obscene."

Unfortunately, Quinn knew Baden-Smith was right, it was a most unprofessional thing to say, but he couldn't resist it.

"I'm sorry, you are quite right. I was wrong and I apologise profusely."

"I should think so, now if you've quite finished, let's get down to the business in hand."

Baden-Smith felt elated, it was the first time he'd managed to get one over Quinn, and even Dave was quite impressed at his solicitor's venomous tone.

Unfortunately for Dave, the interview didn't go quite as well. Quinn went through the taped evidence routine and although Baden-

Smith did his best, by interjecting several times, the end result was not good. Quinn turned off the tape.

"OK, let's get down to brass tacks, we've got you on all counts, isn't there some sort of deal we can work out that will help both parties, save some of the court's time?"

"And what did you have in mind?" said Baden-Smith. "What sort of deal are you looking for?"

"If your client pleads guilty, confesses to all three assaults, we'll see what we can do to get him a fairly small sentence, I mean, he didn't actually rape anyone, we might even be prepared to drop the attempted rape case, and with good behaviour, he'd be out in no time. How's that?"

Baden-Smith looked at Dave. "Well Mr Price, it's down to you."

"But I'm innocent, why should I plead guilty to something I didn't do?"

"Please could you leave us D.I. Quinn, we'll give you an answer in a while."

"OK. Oh and by the way, that girl in hospital, the one with hepatitis, it looks as if she's going to be alright, so ..."

The two officers left and Dave looked at his brief. "Have you heard from my wife?" he asked timidly.

"I know she's been told, and brought some of your clothes in, but I don't think she's keen on seeing you."

"Bloody charming, after all I've done for ..." Dave stopped and thought about what he was saying. He'd done nothing for her, she was probably glad he was inside, out of her way, now she'd be able to start her life again.

"I'm sorry Mr Price, it looks like it's you and me against the world."

Was that a joke? Who the hell was this guy anyway? Quinn was right when he said the gargoyle brothers. If this was Dave's only chance, then he obviously had none.

"Let me think about this," said Dave shaking his head and sending dandruff in a ring around his head, like a grotesque floating halo. "I'll sleep on it and let you know tomorrow."

"Fair enough, would you like me to contact your wife and see if she'll come and visit you?"

"No point, leave the old witch alone, I'd rather not see her, not yet anyway."

"OK, Mr Price, I'll ..."

"Just a minute, tell me honestly, what should I do?"

"I won't lie to you. In my opinion, most juries would find you guilty on the evidence the police have assembled. Maybe, and I mean maybe, a plea bargain is your best chance, however it's risky."

"Risky? Why?"

"Well, it will all depend on the judge, sometimes they go easy, but ..."

"I realise that, but Quinn said ..."

"Quinn?" Baden-Smith laughed. "I wouldn't believe anything he tells you."

Dave got up and noticed that the massive spot on his brief's nose was indeed very near bursting. He screwed up his face, not wanting to see the eruption.

"OK, see you later then."

"Goodbye Mr Price, I'll be in again tomorrow, and remember, don't say anything to Quinn, right?"

"Yeah. What if I need to talk to you before then?"

"Oh yes, here's my card, my home number is the lower one of the two."

"Thanks."

Dave was taken back to a cell and Baden-Smith walked into the main office. Quinn was talking on the 'phone, but hung up as the solicitor reached his desk.

"I would prefer it if you did not talk to my client unless I'm present, and that you keep your comments, *apro pos* my professional standing to yourself."

"Fair enough," said Quinn, rather smugly.

Baden-Smith just tutted and walked over to the door. Quinn jumped up and ran over to the brief. "Oh by the way," he whispered into the startled solicitor's ear, "rearrange this well known phrase or saying, 'off fuck'."

"You think you're it, don't you? Well, someone will bring you down one day, and I only hope I'm there to see it."

Baden-smith tucked his brown folder under his arm, opened the door and left.

"Like a cup of tea, Sir?" asked a young copper, lifting up the electric kettle.

"Don't mind if I do," said Quinn "and then it's home to the missus."

* * *

Over the weekend, Dave's life was hell. Although allowed several recreational breaks when he could smoke, he spent most of his time locked up. Saturday night was particularly harassing, the continual comings and goings of assorted villains, drunks, dropouts and the like kept him awake 'til almost dawn. In the cell next to his was placed a very nasty sounding individual, whose entire vocabulary consisted of three words: "Fuck off bastards," which he screamed, mumbled, shouted and whispered in various strange sounding accents and dialects. Then after two hours, he took to shouting the three words, whilst banging (possibly his head) against Dave's cell wall.

"Fuck" BANG, "off" BANG, "Bastards" BANG.

Finally, at about four-thirty, an officer arrived, presumably to shut him up. Dave lay on his bed in the dark and listened.

"It's no good Williams," said an official sounding voice, "you're not going anywhere until morning, so just shut up that row, and let the other cons have some peace."

"Fuck" BANG, "off" BANG, "Bastards" BANG came the reply, followed by a quick, "Fuckoffbastards."

"Right, Williams, that's your last chance."

Dave heard a key being turned in the cell door next to his.

"Oh, you disgusting moron, you can put that thing away."

"You come any closer and I'll piss all over you, you fucking bastard."

"Alright, if that's how you want it."

There was a scuffle and Dave heard more officers arrive.

Suddenly the noise stopped, except for a little sobbing sound. Dave closed his eyes, trying to dream his way out of this reality nightmare, but sleep would not come. Slowly it started again, quietly at first, but slowly increasing in volume, almost chant-like. "Fuck off bastards," just three words, repeated over and over. Dave didn't know the exact time he eventually got to sleep, but he was awakened by his cell door opening.

"Time to get showered," was all the policeman said.

After he'd washed, shaved and sat for ten minutes on the lavatory, he had breakfast and was told that Quinn was coming in to see him.

"Can I make a 'phone call?"

"Of course, when D.I. Quinn gets here, he'll sort you out."

"That's what I'm worried about," mumbled Dave, as he was taken back to his cell. For some strange reason, his mind began to think of the Bob Dylan song 'The Mighty Quinn', the chorus ran through his brain. 'Come on without, come on within, you'll not see nothing like the Mighty Quinn." He'd never liked the song, but now he hated it. He tried to get the tune out of his head, but it wouldn't leave. He started to hum 'Dancing Queen' by Abba, but the two songs somehow mingled into one. He was not happy.

The 'not so' mighty Quinn had arrived at the station, and was carefully studying the case file.

"There's got to be something in here, I just know it," he mused to himself. "The last piece to nail this bastard."

Williams was being escorted from the building by two officers, and was still mumbling obscenities.

"Oh give it a rest Williams," said Quinn, as the entourage passed his desk, "or I'll give you something to really moan about."

Williams went strangely quiet, even he knew of Quinn's reputation, and the two coppers pushed him out, into the cold March morning, knowing they'd see him again soon, once he'd stolen or begged enough money to get so drunk that he'd be deemed a menace to the public.

"I'm popping down to see Price, can one of you lads come with me?" ordered Quinn as he walked down the corridor to the cells.

"Good morning Dave, how are we this morning?"

Dave froze, he knew the voice only too well. "I'm sorry, but my brief says I should only talk to you with him present, can I make a 'phone call please?"

"Of course you can, just wondered if you'd had a change of heart, that's all. Time to reflect a little?"

"If you mean am I going to plead guilty, then I'm not."

"Shame," said Quinn as he scratched his head, and moved closer until he was almost touching. Dave backed away, like a timid mouse, cowering from a cat.

"I've got nothing more to say to you."

"Fair enough, but let me just ask you this,"

Dave frowned, "Oh no not the whispering treatment."

"How do you push shit up a hill without a wheel-barrow? Eh? Just think about it and let me know when you've figured it out."

"You're disgusting, you're worse than most of the ..."

"Careful Dave, we wouldn't like you to have an accident, would we?"

"I'm telling my solicitor," he whimpered, as he shook in the corner of his cell.

"OK, only trying to help, if you think you're going to walk free from this one, then you are very much mistaken. I'll say no more, no one can say I didn't try to help."

Quinn and the other policeman left the cell, slamming the door behind them.

"How about my 'phone call?" shouted Dave, but his words fell short of their intended target. He sat on the edge of his bed, head in hands, and tried to collect his thoughts.

Baden-Smith arrived a little later and had reverted to his oily raincoat and scruffy clothes. The spot on his face had obviously burst in the night and was replaced with a nasty looking open sore that gently weeped an off-white liquid.

"Good morning Mr Baker-Smythe," grinned Quinn, "and how are you this morning? Well, I trust?"

"I will not rise to your bait, just allow me to see my client please."

"Umm ... a little tetchy today, aren't we?"

Baden-Smith said nothing, but tapped his fingers on the top of Quinn's desk.

"John, arrange for Mr Price to be taken to an interview room please, and then take this GENTLEMAN to him."

"Yes sir," said the officer, and left the room.

"Look Quinn, why has it got to be like this, surely we're on the same side, why are you always so rude?"

"Rude? Me? What rubbish! Just because I can't remember your silly double-barrelled name ..."

"It's not just that. Your whole approach to police work leaves a lot to be desired."

Quinn couldn't be bothered to carry on with the conversation, he felt like punching the man, or even kicking him a couple of times in the crutch, but decided against either action. "Whatever you say."

Baden-Smith left the room with the officer and met up with his client in the same interview room they'd been in the day before. "Good morning Mr Price, how is everything?"

"Are you kidding, it's a fucking nightmare. I'm locked in a cell no bigger than a khasi, the food's shit, the next door neighbour's a fucking nutcase, screaming all night and head butting anything that moves, Quinn's got it in for me, I'm prime suspect in a rape case and you ask me how everything is? It's fucking horrendous. That's how it is."

"OK, calm down, you should try and kerb your language, it will not help your case one bit."

"My case, that's a laugh, I haven't got a case, I'll be lucky to get out of here by the time I'm fifty, got any fags?"

"Actually, I did purchase some for you, hang on." He fumbled in his brief case and pulled out twenty Silk Cut.

"Oh not those mild ones, fuck me one puff and they're gone."

"I'm sorry Mr Price, not being a smoker, I thought they were all the same, the tobacconist assured me ..."

"Yes, yes, just give 'em here." Dave grabbed the packet, ripped off the cellophane and took one out. "Got a light?"

"Yes, I also bought some matches."

"Thanks, look, I'm sorry, but I don't think you know what it's like in here, Quinn started again, talking about shit and a wheelbarrow."

"What?"

"Doesn't matter," Dave drew on the cigarette, trying to get some nicotine into his lungs. "What's new then?"

"Well, nothing, I wondered if you'd considered a plea bargain, or whether you wanted to fight it all the way with a not guilty plea."

"You're the lawyer, what do you think?"

"I don't think it would hurt to ask Quinn what deal they have in mind, as much as I dislike the man, it might be prudent."
Dave looked down his cigarette, straight at his brief's weeping sore and cringed. "OK, if you think we should, then why not? What have I got to lose?"

"I'll ask to see him then, do you wish to be present?"

"Bloody right, it's my neck, isn't it?"

"Fair enough."

Baden-Smith left the room and returned very quickly, with a very smug looking Quinn.

Although Quinn couldn't and wouldn't give any promises, he assured Dave that a guilty plea would be looked on with leniency and, in view of all the other evidence, it was the only real option open to him.

Dave still maintained it was impossible to plead guilty when he could not, in fact, remember where he was on any of the occasions that the assaults took place. A plea of guilty with diminished responsibility, due to alcohol abuse, was agreed on as the best solution for all concerned, and Dave finally and reluctantly made his statement.

Quinn left the two men together.

"I hope I've done the right thing," said Dave, puffing on his eighth straight cigarette. "I feel so weird and mixed up."

"I cannot say Mr Price, as we said before, none of the girls was actually raped. You've got a clean record and all these things should be in your favour."

Dave noticed a thin white strand of saliva, sticking between his brief's lips in the corner of his mouth. Every time he spoke it stretched like elastic and Dave wondered why Baden-Smith could not feel it. He remembered back to his childhood and recalled how an English teacher he'd had in the junior school always suffered with the same problem. He smiled as he thought back to those carefree days, his parents to look after him and his whole life in front of him. How different it could and should have been.

"Well, I'll take my leave now, and see about getting bail."

"Oh right," Dave came back to reality with a bump. "Um, will I see you at the trial, I mean, now I've pleaded guilty, is there any need for ..."

"Of course, we've still got to offer a defence, I'd normally recommend some character witnesses, but I don't think somehow we could find too many who would help our cause."

"Surely my wife could ..."

"I don't think it would be in our interest to call your wife, she's ... um, how can I say this? ..."

"OK point taken. I'll wait to hear from you about the bail then."

"Yes, and don't worry, I'll put forward a first class defence, and we'll get the best possible verdict for you."

Somehow, Dave felt awfully lost when his brief said the words. Laurence Baden-Smith stood up, stretched out his hand and left. Dave was returned to his cell immediately. If he'd thought Saturday night was bad, then Sunday turned into the worst night he could ever remember spending. They let him have a fair amount of recreational time during the day, and the couple of meals he'd eaten were, in fact, not too bad. But a strange feeling of dread came over him when he was taken back to his cell later that evening. He'd been given a Sunday paper and told it was a further hour before lights out. He fidgeted on the bed, not able to get comfortable, not able to find a place without a broken spring. He put down the newspaper and made a concerted effort to go over the events of the previous two weeks or so. He was in desperate need of a stiff drink and had the shakes. The problem was he could not exactly piece his fragmented memory in any order. It was one huge blur, almost like a surrealistic painting. Everything disjointed and unnatural. Suddenly it struck him, it was obvious. He had done those things, he had tried to grab that black girl, he had punched the girl in the subway, he could see it all, every detail. It was so vivid, he could almost taste and smell it. He was drunk, yes, but not that drunk. Not so drunk that he didn't plan it, just to get back at Janice, prove to her he was a man. He sighed loudly and sucked in a large intake of stale prison air. He was all the things Quinn said he was. He lay on the bed and put his hands over his eyes.

"Why? Oh why? You bloody idiot, you bloody stupid idiot."

He was talking loudly to himself, rocking back and forth, tears of anger and pity filling his eyes. The lights went out and he fell into a restless, light sleep, with all the images coming at him, leaping from his subconscious, from the corners of his mind. Everyone was there, his wife, his step-daughter, Joanne from the office, the girl from the wine bar, the big black girl he'd often dreamed of. All naked, all dancing around him in a slowly decreasing circle. It was a harem, and he was the Sultan. Of course he'd done it, they'd wanted him to. He rolled on the bed, half in ecstasy, half in disgust. It was almost as if good and evil were battling for his very soul.

Good against bad.

Right against wrong.

Love against lust.

There wasn't one Dave Price, but two. Each calling to him, each offering advice, pleading with him to join them. He was singing and crying simultaneously, it was an all-time high and low in one moment. Ejaculating and urinating in tandem. For some unknown reason, he opened one eye and froze. There hiding in the darkest corner of the cell stood Quinn, a smug grin breaking out on his face. He knew, he'd known all the time. He could read Dave like a book.

"You know, don't you?" Dave asked quietly.

"Of course Dave, I've always known."

"Will you help me?"

"Oh no, you're beyond help, no more whispering, you're going to get what you deserve."

"What's that?"

"You'll have your tag-nuts parted by a nice big dick."

"Tag-nuts? What are they?"

"They're the little bits of shit that hang from the hairs on your ass. Some nice prisoner is going to part them with his penis. That's what your reward is."

"Won't it hurt?"

"Oh yes, but after a while, you'll come to enjoy it, maybe take it in your mouth without gagging."

"No, I don't want to, you can't ..."

"Yes we can. In fact, we've got Williams outside, you remember, he was in the cell next to you last night. He's dying to see your little tag-nuts and he's got a huge dick, so big it will probably make your botty bleed. What we call a 'porridge ring-sting', you'll like that, won't you?"

"No, No, No ..."

The cell door flew open and a police officer ran into the room.

"Price, Price, you alright?"

"What? Yes, thank God you're here. Quinn's been here. He's been threatening me again."

"Come on, D.I. Quinn is at home with his wife, you prat, it's just a dream, that's all, and I've got enough to do without having to molly-coddle you."

The door slammed shut and Dave was left alone again.

* * *

The hearing to decide bail was held on Monday morning and, although Baden-Smith tried to argue the case, the public prosecutor had all the answers. Price had pleaded guilty to three assaults, was not living at home and the police felt that it would be better to remand him, without bail, pending the trial. The magistrate agreed and the whole thing was decided in less than twenty minutes. It was also decreed that Price should be seen by a psychiatrist for a full report, prior to the trial.

Back at the police station, while Dave waited to be transported to Winchester prison, Baden-Smith tried to reassure his client.

"Look, it might be that the psychiatric report can work in our favour, if it can be established that due to emotional distress you acted out of character. We may have ..."

"Hang on a second, surely being found mad, as well as everything else, can only make things worse?"

"Not mad, diminished responsibility. You've been under tremendous pressure, your job's not working out, the split with your wife. This could be just what we need."

"I'm not so sure," moaned Dave. "I can see me ending up in a mental institution and them throwing away the key."

"Nonsense, just answer honestly, and it'll be fine, you'll see it can work to our advantage."

Dave shook his head as he was taken in handcuffs to a waiting police van and driven to Winchester prison.

Marcus Billingsley was the psychiatrist assigned Dave's case and, in fact, seemed quite a nice bloke. He listened to Dave's revelations about sex and fixation with oral stimulation, with sympathy and total understanding. He used words like "anamorphous" and "exsusciatate licentiously" which Dave did not understand but they sounded good and, after a couple of sessions, Dave felt, for the first time in months, relaxed. Unfortunately, although the words sounded good, they in fact indicated an abnormal development towards lust in a base, perverted and unnatural way.

The next few weeks were truly hell for Dave. Fortunately, due to the nature of his crimes, he was kept away from the other prisoners, but this made him feel completely alone. When his case finally came to trial, having no family or friends meant the courtroom was virtually empty. A few local pressmen, a couple of law students and a few members of the public were the only people in court, apart from the families of the three victims.

Dave was led into court, head down, and positioned in the dock. He glanced around the room but could only see angry faces. His wife was not there, but then she had not visited him once, in all the time he'd been held, so it was hardly surprising.

The clerk to the court read out the charges and Dave was asked how he pleaded.

"Ummm ..."

"Mr Price, would you please make a plea?" snapped the old

judge, obviously running out of patience and already primed on the answer.

Dave hesitated and looked around the courtroom again. The sight of Baden-Smith in a wig, that balanced like a pea on a pyramid, almost made him laugh.

"Not guilty your honour," he spurted, after what seemed an eon.

Baden-Smith's mouth dropped, causing a particularly nasty looking cold sore scab on his bottom lip to crack, and the court erupted.

"I'm sorry Mr Price, could you repeat that?" queried Judge Edwards, glancing menacingly around the court, causing the hubbub to subside slightly.

Dave gulped and spluttered, "Not Guilt."

"Mr Baden-Smith could you approach the bench please, and you Mr Weintroub," ordered the Judge, obviously unamused.

The two opposing counsellors moved to the front of the court and stood in front of the Judge.

"Mr Baden-Smith, I was briefed that your client would be pleading guilty and that was the sole reason why an early appearance in court was granted."

"Um, well your honour, so did I," mumbled the bemused brief.

"I see, so you cannot explain the plea then?"

"No your honour," puffed Baden-Smith, licking his cold sore and grimacing in pain.

"If I may interject here your honour," said Weintroub, the crown prosecutor, "we have a signed confession and if this is some attempt, by the defence, to waste precious ..."

"Yes, yes, I'm fully aware of the implications. We haven't time to start this case now, so I'm calling a recess, but you can tell your client I'm not happy, not happy at all."

"Sorry, your honour, but I had no idea ..."

The case was deferred and Dave led away.

The next few weeks were hell for Dave. Baden-Smith saw his client on several occasions, but was unable to make Dave change his mind on the plea.

Eventually, the heavy court schedule allowed for the case to be reheard and Dave was duly taken back to court. Baden-Smith did his best, stating that his client had always been a model citizen, with no previous convictions whatsoever. He argued that the police's case was based purely on circumstantial evidence and that Dave had only signed the confession because he was under duress.

Unfortunately, the prosecution had a field day. Witness after witness was called, from Joanne to Helen Winton, and even Diane Michells, who was still convalescing from the Hepatitis virus she had contracted when assaulted, made a 'bedside' statement which was solemnly read to the court. A picture was painted of a man who was totally unable to handle his drink, life, sexual urges, or any other problem that may come his way. Someone who masturbated in his automobile in public places, who frequented sex shops and strip shows, and read dubious 'adult' magazines. The glove that was found at the scene of the last assault was positively identified as the defendant's and he also fitted the description given to the police by all three victims. He had no alibi and could be placed in the area on each occasion. To say that he was up a creek without a paddle was the all-time gross understatement. Even Marcus Billingsley, the psychiatrist, gave damning evidence, suggesting a very abnormal sexual fantasy with women who were well endowed. D.I. Quinn and his confession and tapes all made sway with the jury.

On the second day, both counsellors started their summing up, but even here, Dave's case proved wanting.

Stephen Weintroub, the sharp prosecutor for the crown, was a natural, and made every statement from every witness sound like the gospel truth. He wasted no words, speaking with eloquence and panache and a wry Jewish sense of humour. Baden-Smith on the other hand, simply struggled. He was a hick lawyer, more suited to handling motoring offences than cases like this, and was clearly out of his depth.

The jury were dispatched, and returned almost immediately. Obviously it had been an easy case to deliberate upon. Although the media interest locally had died away, two national tabloids had representatives at the trial. Dave stood motionless as the foreman read the verdict.

"Guilty your honour, on all six counts."

"And is this the verdict of you all?"

"Yes, your honour."

None of this was happening, it was just a nightmare from which Dave would soon awake. He thought back to his childhood, those happy halcyon days, when he was growing up in the sixties, with his mum and dad.

But were they really happy? Or was it just his memory playing games with him? His parents had always lived their lives as though they were single. He had no real friends at school, because he had no interests. He was useless at sport, below average academically and totally nonplussed about hobbies. He'd grown up a loner. Even though he liked the company of other people, they obviously did not like him. He was one of life's tragic casualties and feeling very sorry for himself. He had no dreams (other than perverted sexual ones) no ambition to help lift him above the norm. It was true, wanker is as wanker does. 'Pop up Peter' was all he'd ever been good at.

Quinn was going to be right, the only Pearl Necklace he could look forward to was from a male prisoner, straddled across his chest and giving him the whitewash treatment.

His daydream (or daymare!) was shattered, the Judge was about to deliberate.

"Before I pass sentence, have you anything to say to this court?" asked Justice Edwards, looking down at Dave over bifocal spectacles, with a face like thunder.

Dave's goose was not only cooked but served up in a little cherry sauce.

"Um, yes, a-your honour."

"What? Please speak up man. If you've something to say, then spit it out."

Dave cleared his throat, he felt weak on his legs, and sick in his stomach, but somehow continued: "Yes, your honour," he said, this time much louder. "I am very sorry for everything, I was drunk, and can't explain my actions at all. It's just like my brief said, when I drink I seem to do things, um, you know, things that are nasty, I can't help it, I can't even remember doing them."

"I see, is that all?"

"Yes, I'm just very sorry."

"You seem to think that because you were drunk at the time, this in some way excuses your behaviour, in some way makes it acceptable for you to do as you wish. Well, it does not, we have a duty to protect the people of this country, we can't have a person like you committing heinous crimes of this nature and saying sorry, but I was drunk. You're a menace to society, who doesn't deserve to be walking free."

The judge stopped and made some notes.

"You have been found guilty on three cases of actual assault, and three cases of attempted rape." He paused again and scratched his nose. "This court sentences you to seven years."

At this there was pandemonium, obviously all of the friends of the victims were pleased with the verdict and started clapping and cheering.

"All rise," said a voice from the front of the courtroom, and the judge was gone.

The words didn't sink in at first, and Dave looked up, to see Quinn smiling.

"No, wait, it's not right, you bastard Quinn, you did this, you ..." Dave's words faded as he was dragged from the dock, through a tight corridor, and back to his cell.

Sgt Crouch was the first to congratulate Quinn and the smiling policemen left court, on their way to a few drinks at the local hostelry.

The papers had their story, and several reporters left the court, hot foot for the Price's residence in Hedge End, hoping for a statement from Janice Price. This story might have possibilities yet. The word 'Exclusive' was obviously being muted.

However, they were all to be out of luck. Janice and her daughter had gone away for a few weeks and could not be contacted. She had foreseen this and guessed it would all be forgotten within a matter of days, when they could return and settle down to normal lives.

Chapter 7

A chill wind 'cross the Solent blew,
and rubbish, into corners thrust,
while in his cell, Dave sat and knew,
there was no one, that he could trust.

The March wind could not touch him now,
nor sun, nor rain, nor thunder,
no ray of hope, could ease the pain,
or lift the cloud he's under.

As the m.v. *Bergen Tide* sailed up the Tagus river, past the Belem Tower and into Lisbon harbour, Able Bodied Seaman, Jorgen Knutsson, had just finished his night-watch. The 11,000 tonne, conventional cargo vessel had sailed straight from the dry dock at Southampton, after a major refit, to commence a freight carrying service between Lisbon and Gothenburg, Sweden. The eleven days spent in Southampton had been very boring for Jorgen, and besides a few days on watch, he'd had a lot of time on his hands. Most of this, he'd spent in pubs and bars, and the Derby Road red light district.

He flopped onto the bunk bed in his cabin, and lit up a 'Marlborough' cigarette. He wasn't a typical looking Scandinavian, being small of frame, with brown hair, and a fairly pale complexion. Through the porthole, he could see the mild spring Portuguese sun glinting on the blue water.

"Surely Lisbon would be better than Southampton," he surmised to himself. "What a dreadful port and town."

He stretched out on his bunk, tired from his night on watch, and thought of the young prostitute he'd slept with a few times. She was quite nice, but all the mucking about with poxy condoms, was no pleasure to him at all. He remembered walking down St Mary's Street, well intoxicated, and ducking into the churchyard for a desperately needed slash. The strong smelling steam from his urine, causing a cloud, that was whisked away on the chill night air. Drinking all day, and then roaming the streets all night, was a recipe for disaster. He saw the big black girl, walking along the pathway, and although she was nothing to look at, he could recall that she had massive knockers. He only wanted a bit of fun, maybe a blow job or the like, but she started screaming, and he had to hit her, no big deal. The girl in the subway, however, was rather tasty, and Jorgen had not really wanted to punch her. But she too, had to scream and shout, when all he wanted was a shag.

"Bloody stupid English girls," he chuckled to himself, as he stubbed out his cigarette and thought of the better times that would definitely lie ahead in Lisbon.

* * *

Janice and Sarah had gone to South Wales for a few weeks, and were staying in a rather nice hotel in Tenby. Janice had heard the outcome of the court case from her mother, and was sitting in her room reading the newspaper. There was a small piece about it in the middle of her 'Express' and she read the column several times with a smile on her face.

How easy it had all been.

Well, the thought of Dave raping anyone was pathetic. He was a prick, of course, and the police were so sure, so convinced that he was the one, that she had to help, didn't she?

When Sarah first told her about Dave masturbating in the bathroom, she wanted to kill him. No, not kill, but maim. Cut off his stupid little penis and poke it up his ass, or sellotape it in his mouth. And the night she borrowed her father's car, to have it out with him, that was what she was going to do. She was the person who had telephoned the police with Dave's car description, but that was just for starters. Arriving at his guest house, just before eleven, she parked by his car and waited. She knew he'd be in some pub and would soon come crawling along the pavement, like a bloated slug, and she'd be ready for him.

Finally, she saw him in her mirror, even drunker than expected, but instead of going into the guesthouse, he opened his car, and fell inside, collapsing in a drunken stupor. She went over, fully determined to deal with him, in the way, previously described, she had brought the kitchen knife with her, and was ready. But much to her surprise, he was out cold, perhaps even dead. Unfortunately (for her) he grunted, broke wind violently and started to dribble down his chin.

"You disgusting little pervert," she said, so angry, she was unable to decide what to do first. Wake him up, give him a piece of her mind, then cut off his dick, or just castrate him while he slept? It was a very cold night and the wind caused the hairs on the back of her neck to stand up. She shivered, and clenching her hands, blew into them. She suddenly noticed his old car coat on the back seat and stretched over to retrieve it. Quickly pulling it on, she stood in the car doorway, still undecided as to her next course of action.

Then it came to her. Why, how, or where from, she could not say, but a plan popped into her head. She remembered he kept an old pair of driving gloves in the glove-compartment, and reaching over him, she took them out. Quietly closing his car door, she returned to her own, opened the boot and put on a black bobble-hat, that her mother sometimes wore for gardening, or the long walks she enjoyed taking in late autumn. "Easy, easy, easy," she said to herself as she walked up Shirley High Street, "just find a girl, push her over, drop one glove, and then be off, no one need get hurt, I'll send the girl some flowers the next day, and the Police will have their man."

It was a cracking plan.

Although it all sounded easy, as she strolled up the road, she soon realised that as it was late, the only people about were drunken males. Throngs of them, wobbling and weaving along the pavement. She pulled her hat down, making sure that none of her hair was visible. It was so strange, if she had been recognisable as a woman, walking alone at that time of night, in that part of Southampton, she would surely have been subjected to streams of sexual abuse. But in her guise as a man, no one noticed or spoke to her. She walked what seemed miles, and reached the top of the High Street. Turning around, she realised she could not just walk up and down aimlessly, that in itself would be suspicious.

"Damn, and double blast it," she muttered. "What now?"

As luck would have it, she spied a young girl crossing the road, who although limping terribly, was still moving at a fairly brisk pace.

Janice watched her turn into Church Street, and followed discreetly on the opposite side, gaining all the time. As the girl reached the grass verge in front of the council houses, Janice took a deep breath, she was getting a little uncertain as to the validity of her plan, and started to hesitate slightly.

"No, you've come this far, do it," a voice screamed inside her head, and she grabbed wildly at the girl, pulling at her hair, and causing her to fall to the ground.

"Enough, enough," demanded her conscience, and she obeyed.

The young girl kicked out, but missed, and Janice carefully dropped a glove as she ran across the grass verge and to safety, behind the council houses. Her heart was beating so loudly, and her breathing was so heavy, that she thought she might collapse. Gaining her composure, and confidence, she slowed down slightly, and started to relax. She heard some voices behind, but did not dare look.

As she made her way back, she quickly pulled off her bobblehat, took off Dave's old brown car coat, and carried them both across her arm. By this time, the streets were deserted. Getting back to the cars, there was no one about, and Dave was still oblivious.

She opened his car, threw in his coat, placed his glove back in the compartment, and once more quietly closed the car door. Driving back to her house, she was concerned for the young girl's safety, but not sorry for what she had done. It had all gone exactly to plan, and now that bastard husband of hers would be 'banged up' for years.

After a few more minutes of gloating, she looked out of her hotel window, and across the gorgeous bay of Tenby. It was a lovely evening, the sun glinting on the seagulls' wings as they searched for food, squawking and squealing, as only scavengers do.

Her daughter had been right, there was no shortage of men wishing to take her out, but she'd decided to play the field a little, before making another long-term commitment. Sarah arrived back from taking a swim in the hotel's indoor swimming pool.

"Come on mum," she laughed, "haven't you started to get ready yet?"

"No, but after the last few years, I figure I'm ready for anything."

And she was.

* * *

Dave had been transferred to a medium security prison, and kept apart from the other prisoners, for his own safety. He spent his time trying to recall his movements on those fateful nights, but to no avail. Baden-Smith had promised to make an appeal, but Dave knew it would not help. The only thing he couldn't work out was how his glove had been found in Shirley. He never wore them, and even if drunk, wouldn't put them on to go to the pub. So how had it got there? There must be an answer, and he'd probably spend the next seven years trying to figure it out.

Chapter 8

*Retribution, revenge, murder and hate,
was the only way to clean the slate.*

The next few years passed fairly uneventfully. Dave had changed his solicitor and lodged an appeal with the High Court. Although he was still found guilty, the sentence was reduced to four years which, with good behaviour, and a favourable response from the parole board, would mean him serving only about two.

Obviously his conduct was exemplary. He spent most of his time in a type of solitary confinement, due to the nature of his crimes.

Generally, the prison officers had been fair, particularly Harrison, who was older, and much more understanding than most. With little else to do, Dave had enrolled in a couple of Open University courses, Home Economics and Mathematics. He didn't care if he passed them, and only took them to occupy the time. The sexual dreams had disappeared completely, and he no longer masturbated.

The prison was run, as most are, with several unscrupulous 'Barons' battling endlessly for supremacy, but Dave had almost no dealings with them at all.

It was July 1995, when he received great news from the Parole Board. Providing he kept his nose clean, he would be released back into the community in two months. For the previous two years, he'd thought of nothing else but freedom, but now the time was approaching, he was less than enthusiastic. Janice's lawyers had obtained a 'quickie' divorce, and he obviously knew his job at Calvin Marine would no longer be there. Prison offered a strange security, three meals a day, his own cell, with a few comforts allowed. He wasn't sure he could cope in the real world.

In the past, he'd always taken his recreational periods alone, but with four weeks of his sentence left, it was decided he should be allowed to mix more with the other prisoners, in order to help him start adjusting to his new life.

Although totally frowned upon, homosexuality is not as

widespread in prisons as is commonly believed. There were of course a few cases, but it was not rife.

Unfortunately, in the attempt to rehabilitate Dave, (or perhaps to teach him a lesson), he was put in a cell with Tony Anderson, car thief, petty arsonist and raving sex pervert. A stocky man, with receding hairline, plastered back with hair gel, downy goatee beard and strange green eyes. It was often said that 'Anderson would fuck a frog, if it didn't hop', although he'd never been convicted of a sexual crime. Anderson had the top bunk in their cell, and masturbated violently every night. Dave would lie awake, listening to the grunts and slapping, in great fear. Whenever he had his back to his cellmate, Anderson would grab him between the legs and shout obscenities at him.

With only two weeks of his sentence to go, Anderson, somewhat predictably made his move.

In the corner of the cell was a small commode, which Dave had to slop out each morning. He always tried desperately, only to use it for urine, preferring the toilets in the main block. Anderson was the opposite, he'd shit in the commode twice a day, straining and farting, as if marking out his territory, happy in the knowledge that Dave had to empty it.

Dave had been assigned to kitchen duties, which was considered a perk in prison, and only saw Anderson at meal times and in the cell at night.

It was September, and the evenings were starting to draw in. When 'lights out' was called, the cell was left in almost total darkness, the small barred window affording what little illumination there was.

Dave was lying on his bunk bed reading, while Anderson was sitting at the little table writing a letter, when the lights went out. Besides the odd obscenity, his cellmate had hardly spoken two words to him in the couple of weeks they'd shared confinement, when: "Oi, you," he said, "how about giving me a blow job?"

Dave gulped. "What?" he muttered, somewhat stunned.

"You heard."

"Um, no thanks."

"Why not, you cunt? I've heard you like it."

Dave was speechless, he wanted to scream for a warden.

"I've heard you like your chutney locker fucked and I've got just the tool for the job."

Dave squinted in the half light, he could see Anderson sitting with his erect penis in his hand.

"You must be joking, who told you that? I've only got a couple of weeks to do and want no trouble."

"Exactly, so the last thing you want is a reprimand from the governor for fightin', ain't it?"

Dave squirmed, and felt sick, although he'd built up the upper part of his body, quite considerably while he'd been in prison, thanks to sessions in the gym, he felt sure he was no match for the surly Anderson.

"Just bend over the table, and there'll be no trouble."

"Fuck off, I'd rather do extra bird than let you touch me."

"That's fine by me."

Anderson got up, walked over to the beds, and stood in front of Dave with his penis in his hand, shaking it gently.

"Get away from me, you perve," he stuttered, and tried to crawl along his bunk and away from his assailant. He was only dressed in a T-shirt and underpants, and Anderson grabbed him around the neck, and pulled him onto the floor. Quickly he secured an arm-lock, and pushed Dave's arm high up his back.

"Get off, you prick," yelled Dave, then screamed in pain, as his arm was pushed even higher. He was face down on the cold cell floor, and Anderson sat astride him, just over his legs, ripping his underpants down with his free hand.

Dave wriggled, and tried desperately to get up, but Anderson was too heavy for him. He could feel the probing penis, rubbing between the cheeks of his behind, hoping for a way in.

"Please don't, I ..."

Anderson lay flat on his victim, still pushing the arm-lock even higher, and Dave was in excruciating pain.

"Alright, alright, stop now, you're breaking my arm," he breathlessly begged.

Anderson just giggled, and put his tongue in Dave's ear, talking in a gruff voice, he murmured, "All I want is that sweet virgin asshole of yours, if you struggle any more, I'll break your fucking arm, and that's a promise."

"Please ..." the word died away in agony.

"No one's gonna help you, the screws put you in with me 'cause they hate perverts like you, now just relax, and we'll both enjoy it."

Dave made one last superhuman effort to shift the deadweight on his back, arching slightly, trying to get his knees under his body. This elevated his torso slightly, and allowed Anderson to penetrate almost completely. He let go of Dave's arm, slipped backwards a little, and grabbed Dave around the waist, ramming his penis up and down Dave's back passage.

"Ahhh ..." Dave screamed, the pain so great that he almost passed out.

Anderson started pumping backwards and forwards, and as he pulled back, Dave jumped forward onto his feet, stepped over his bewildered attacker, and ran to the cell door. Shouting at the top of his voice for help, he banged frantically with his fists. Anderson was quickly to his feet, and grabbing Dave by the hair, rammed his face full force into the metal door. When the officers on duty arrived, they found Anderson sitting on his bunk-bed, with Dave unconscious, in a pool of blood on the floor.

"Alright Anderson, what happened here?" snapped Keough, a rather nasty skinheaded screw, reputedly more violent than most of the inmates.

"Well Mr Keough, I think he was sleepwalking or somethin' and ran into the door, can't really say, I was dozing off meself."

"Oh really? Well when Price comes round, he'd better have the same story, or your bollocks are mine. Clear?"

"Crystal, Mr Keough," said Anderson, smiling, as the two officers picked up Dave and dragged him from the cell and to the prison hospital.

Dave opened his eyes slowly, and wiped some blood from his nose.

"You alright?" said a very soft spoken voice, and Dave glanced around to find himself in a hospital bed, being comforted by a tubby man with bleached blond hair. "You seem to have taken quite a knock, right on your nose," said the man.

"Brilliant deduction," Dave thought as he gently touched his throbbing forehead. He looked again, allowing his eyes time to adjust to the dimly lit ward. The eight beds were empty, all but the one next to his. The blond man had gone, but the person in the next bed spoke.

"If you want the orderly, you have to push the bell, just on the side, there."

Laying next to him was a young man, who looked dreadful. He was painfully thin, and obviously seriously ill.

"Jesus Christ, what the fuck's wrong with him?" he thought, as he pushed the bell.

"OK my sweet, just coming," said an effeminate voice from the end of the ward.

Dave's nose was obviously broken, because it was impossible to breath through it, and with his fingers, he ran the length of the bridge, feeling several bumps and turns. His head was pounding and his bottom felt like a red hot poker had been rammed lengthwise up it.

The blond haired man came bouncing up the ward.

"Hello, I'm Justin, your orderly, how you feeling, not so good I think?"

"What are you? King of the understatement?"

"Just take it easy."

"God, what happened?" asked Dave, still a little bemused.

"Well, when they brought you in, they said you'd been sleepwalking, and crashed into the cell door."

"What? And you believe that?"

"Well, my friend, you've got a problem if that's not what happened. If you were fighting, there will have to be an enquiry, and that could affect your parole."

"You know about my parole?" asked Dave, amazed at the man's knowledge.

"Of course, I know everything that goes on here. Oh, and I could tell you some stories, believe me."

"Bloody brilliant, that bastard Anderson tried to rape me. He gets away with it, does he?"

"It's not for me to say, but I reckon you'll be in here for a week or so, so it may be as well for you to bite your tongue."

Dave sighed, "Could I have a drink please?"

"'Course pet, nice coffee, how about you Malcolm?" he turned to the other bed, "fancy a nice coffee?"

"Yeah, why not? With all this excitement, need something to steady me nerves," replied the young man quietly.

Justine skipped from the room, whistling, 'Gonna wash that man right out of my hair'.

"Christ, where did they get him from?" said Dave.

"Oh, he's not so bad, just a little too camp for most people's taste."

"Really," said Dave, hoping never to meet another gay in his life.

"By the way, I'm Malcolm Evitts."

Dave looked over at the pitiful person next to him, he'd never seen anyone who looked so ill.

"Hi, I'm Dave Price, pleased to meet you."

The two men exchanged niceties, and Justin returned with the coffee.

Dave watched the young man struggle to lift the cup to his lips, Justin tried to help, but was waved away.

"I'm OK." said Malcolm, trying to be independent.

"Oh, nearly forgot, the Doctor will be in to see you in the morning, and then you'll have to give a statement," added Justin, leaving almost as quickly as he'd arrived.

The two men chatted for a while, but Dave was in no mood for conversation. He knew he'd have to agree to Anderson's ludicrous story, and fell into a troubled sleep.

The ever jolly Justin burst into the ward at seven, "Morning boys, this is your early morning call, tea or coffee?"

They then had breakfast in bed, which for Dave was an absolute luxury. The Doctor arrived just after eight, and after a five minute check-up, pronounced a broken nose, facial bruising, and gave Dave a bottle of mild painkillers. Dave had declined to mention his sore lower regions, feeling it would take some explaining.

The two inmates were again left alone, and Dave turned to his ailing companion. "What you in here for?" he asked sympathetically.

"What the hospital or the prison?"

"Well, the prison?"

"I used to do drugs. Stupid I know, but that's how it is."

"I see," said Dave, somewhat disapprovingly. "What heroin and things?"

"Yeah, and things," laughed Malcom. "And you?"

"Um, I ..."

"It's alright, you don't have to say, Justin told me last night before you came round."

Dave felt embarrassed, and dropped his head. "I'm innocent though, honestly."

"I'm sure you are," said Malcolm, sounding as if he was being patronising, which he wasn't.

"Really I am, but no one believes me."

Dave then relayed his story, and explained the whole scenario prior to his arrest.

Malcolm listened intently, he really seemed interested.

"And so you see, although it's possible I did the crimes, I know I didn't."

They discussed the case further, and Malcolm relaxed onto his pillow, then said, "Well, if the dropped glove was your nail in the coffin, so to speak, who else could have put it there?"

"That, my friend, is the million dollar question. I had a company car, and the only other keys were in the office, and with my wife."

"OK, and who else knew where the gloves were kept?"

"Well, no one really, except.., wait a minute, no it's not possible, my wife couldn't have committed the assaults, no way."

"Maybe not, but she might have taken the glove, just a thought. Had you done anything to upset her?"

"No, not at all, I ..." Dave stopped, why was he lying to himself, of course he'd upset her, she'd kicked him out for Christ's sake, she was obviously a little peeved.

"Hit a nerve have I?"

"I, um, sort of did something to her daughter, nothing much, but if she found out, she'd have probably killed me."

"And this little thing you did to her daughter, could she have found out about it?"

"Nah, no way."

Dave's mind was in overdrive, but if she dropped the glove, what about the actual assaults, it made no sense at all. "Unless," he thought, "she had an accomplice, someone to set me up. No it's too way out."

Just then his thoughts were disturbed.

"Good morning Dave, goodness you look dreadful."

Prison officer Harrison, who was the only screw Dave liked, was standing at the foot of the bed.

"Hello Mr Harrison, yeah, I'm not too good."

"Well, they've asked me to take your statement, the Governor wants a full report."

Dave said he'd been sleepwalking, and walked into the door, and although Harrison didn't believe a word of what was said, he wrote out the report accordingly. He was due to retire soon, and didn't really want any hassle this late in his career.

"And you are sure this is what happened? I know of Anderson's reputation and this looks like his work to me."

"Honestly, Mr Harrison, that's what happened, but you could do me a favour."

"Well, Dave, I'm not sure ..."

"It's not much, just that I've only got two more weeks to do, and then I get out of here. I wondered if I could have my old solitary cell back, just till I leave."

"No promises, but I'll see what I can do."

"Oh thanks, I just want to do my time, and get out of here in one piece."

Harrison got up from the seat he was sitting on by Dave's bed, patted him on the shoulder, and left.

"He's magic," said Dave to Malcolm. "Only reason I've managed to stay sane."

"Yes, I've heard he's fair."

Justin returned, wanting to hear the latest. "Well, what did you say?"

"Sleepwalking, what else? That bastard Anderson's got away with it."

"Umm," Justin scratched his head, "maybe not, hang on a minute and I'll be back, you know what they say, 'faint heart never fucked a brown hatter'."

Dave watched the orderly walk to his little office, just to the right of the ward.

"Justin will sort something out, you'll see," said Malcolm, clenching his fist in obvious pain. "Look, tell me it's none of my business, but what's wrong with you anyway?"

"Wrong with me?" sighed Malcolm, "that's a laugh, you name it, I've got it, had it, or will probably get it soon."

"Eh?"

"I've got full blown AIDS, and every extra day of life for me is a bonus, or punishment, depending on your point of view."

"God, I'm sorry, you a ...then?"

"Am I gay you mean?"

"Yeah."

"Yes I'm gay, but the irony is I was always so careful, and contracted this from drug abuse. Just desserts you might say."

"Bloody hell, I'm sorry, truly I am."

"Don't be, my friend, I'm past help."

"What, your ..."

"Well, they've given me a few months yet, and called me a special compassionate case, great eh? They're letting me out to die."

"When?"

"Hopefully some time next week."

"And then?"

"My mother died a few years ago and left me a nice house. I've decided to die there."

"What, on your own?"

"Well, it's the one thing you can do on your own, isn't it?"

"Suppose."

"Come on, a gay with AIDS hasn't got that many friends, they'll send a social worker around I guess, but I want to die with some dignity, at least that's the theory."

"Fuck me, here's me feeling sorry for myself, when you ..."

Malcolm smiled, and rolled onto his side. "Oh, by the way," he added, "don't worry it's not easily caught this AIDS thing, you know, contact with blood or semen, you're quite safe."

"Yeah, I knew that, I wasn't worried for myself."

"It's OK, there's so many strange myths going around, I just wanted you to know the facts, that's all."

"You OK, d'you want to rest?"

"No, I'm fine."

"Well, where's this house of yours?"

"In Woolston, just the other side of the Itchen Bridge. Know it?"

"Yeah, where in Woolston?"

"In Obelisk Road, a rather proud old four bedroomed, right at the top end, where it joins St Anne's Road."

"I know Obelisk Road, what number is it? Perhaps I could come and see you, you know, when I get out, before you ..."

"Die?" laughed Malcolm, causing him to spasm violently.

"You OK? Shall I call Justin?"

"No," he coughed, "I'm alright, honestly. It's number 142, and you're more than welcome, at any time."

They lay quiet for a while, and Dave again thought of his ex wife. "I'll get even with you," he decided, "if it's the last thing I do."

Justin returned, still whistling a little tune, this time 'Dancing Queen' by ABBA. "Right, if you say I gave you this, I'll deny it, and say you stole it from the infirmary."

"What is it?" asked Dave, as he was handed a small vial of white powder.

"Now look, you're on kitchen duties, right?"

"Yeah ..."

"Let's just say that this will inflict a terrible curse to the botty department."

"Eh?"

"Frequent evacuation of the intestines, chronic diarrhoea, to you, so chronic, whoever takes this, will piss through their ass for a week."

"Right." said Dave, still puzzled.

"Love a dove, have I got to spell it out for you. When you serve Anderson, sprinkle it onto his dinner, and score even, yes?"

"Oh brilliant, thanks Justin."

"My pleasure, but remember."

"Yeah, understood. I didn't get it from you."

Dave lay back on his bed, and let his mind go walkabout. "This would partially settle the score with Anderson, next would be that slug in clothing, Baden-Smith, then the bastard Quinn, and the final piece of my holy trinity, that whore of a wife of mine."

Revenge was his God now, and it had given him a reason to look forward to getting out.

He was released from the prison hospital after 4 days, and the goodly Harrison had managed to arrange for Dave to go back to a single cell for the few remaining days of his sentence. He had easily laced Anderson's food, the day before he was due out, and had heard through the prison grapevine that his victim had been taken ill during the night, and was under medication at the hospital. He'd also heard from Justin that Malcolm had been released, but was now very close to his call from God.

Dave had spent those few remaining days, working on his plan for revenge. The plot thickened, which was more than Anderson's shit did.

* * *

Dave was released from prison, and assigned a parole officer in Southampton. The conditions were quite clear. He had to report once a fortnight, on Thursday afternoon, and also attend a weekly therapy/rehabilitation class, run by one of the departments in the DHSS.

He travelled back to Southampton by train and, walking to the city centre, checked his bank account, at a cash point, being pleasantly surprised to find that it was still in credit by £196. He withdrew one hundred pounds, and went into a pub near the bank. A trendy fizz palace, it sold no real ales, but was handy, being just off the High Street.

He didn't really feel like drinking, but it seemed to be what he should do. After just two pints, and a couple of cigarettes, Dave left the public house, and got a bus to Woolston, which is a suburb on the western bank of the River Itchen. As the bus trundled across the dreaded toll bridge, Dave looked across Southampton's skyline. He could see the Civic Centre with its neo-classical clock tower, built in 1933, thrusting magnificently 156 feet into the air. Its fine white Portland stone frontage, offset by the green stains from its brass roof. The grain-silos in the old docks, grey container cranes in the Eastern docks, and the spire of St Mary's Church, surrounded by the fine oak trees that grew in its churchyard. All the older structures lived side by side with a lot of new building work, that had been completed while Dave was away.

In fact, there were many towers and buildings he did not recognise. The bus stopped and he alighted in the centre of Victoria Road, the main shopping area of Woolston. After over two years in prison, it was a strange feeling to be able to control one's own movements, and Dave walked up and down the street several times, just because he could. He would obviously need somewhere to sleep, and plan his next moves, and this was where he was hoping that Malcolm would oblige. Joining Obelisk Road at the Victoria Road end, he walked its whole length, eventually arriving at number 142. He stood outside and surveyed the house. It was a gorgeous looking, double-fronted Victorian building, with a small front garden, and parking space at the rear.

Dave took a large intake of air, opened the gate, and walked up the path to the front door. There was a hand written message pinned over the bell push.

'If I don't answer within 2 minutes, I'm DEAD. Love Malcolm'.

Dave smiled, then panicked. "Oh God, what if he's ..."

He pushed the button three times and waited, listening intently, ear pressed against the glass panel of the door. "Phew! there's some movement." Through the frosted glass, he could just make out a shape, moving rather precariously, on its way to the door. Obviously with some effort, the door opened, and Malcolm stood before him, looking more like an Oxfam advert than a man in his prime.

"Hello Malcolm, how are you?" he beamed, somewhat relieved to see his young friend still alive.

Malcolm squinted, allowing his bloodshot eyes time to adjust to the late autumn sunshine.

"Yes?" he croaked.

"It's me, Dave, Dave Price, you know, we met in nick. I said I'd look you up."

"Oh, I'm sorry, my eyesight's so bad in daylight. I keep the curtains drawn all the time, please come in."

Dave followed the frail young man down a passageway, past two closed doors, and into a small kitchen-diner at the back of the house. They sat at opposite sides of a cottage dining suite. Dave broke the silence, he felt he had to.

"Well, how's it been?" he asked, rather awkwardly.

"Not so good mate, bloody legs playing me up."

It had to be said. "I'm sorry to ask, but how can you live like this?"

"I'm OK, it's how I want it. A social worker calls once a day, and does the washing and cleaning, and I get 'meals on wheels' delivered, not that I eat much."

"Look, the last week or so, I've been thinking, I'm at a loose end, so to speak, and nowhere to stay, except the dreadful hostel in town. So how about I move in, and look after you? I'd be no trouble, just a bit of company. What d'you say, perhaps give it a trial, if it don't work, you only gotta say, and I'm off."

"Well," Malcolm was embarrassed, not because he wanted Dave to leave, he'd love him to stay, but felt it might be too much of a burden.

"Please, I'll do the cooking and washing, and look after you proper," he paused, "it would really help me out, just until I got sorted, then ..."

Malcolm put up his arm, and smiled. "Of course you can stay.

My house is your house, I just wouldn't want to become too much of a task, and jeopardise our friendship."

Dave shook his head. "You let me stay here, I'll be the housewife. How's that?"

Malcolm laughed and coughed, almost in unison.

"Alright, alright, you can stay."

"Brilliant. You won't regret it, I'll do the shopping, cooking, anything you want, you've only to ask."

"Fine, I've got plenty of money, Mother left me it, and ..."

"Hang on," Dave interrupted indignantly, "I don't want your friggin' money, this is a chance for me to be useful, and get myself sorted out, I'm no mercenary."

"I'm sorry, I didn't mean it like that, it's just that, well, you know ..."

"Great."

"Oh, there is one thing though."

"Yeah."

"I'm not very good at getting to the lav on time, I wear incontinent pants most of the time, and it's not very pleasant when they need changing. The home-help they send usually does it for me."

"Listen, after two years in prison, I can handle anything, if I'm going to look after you, that will include the nasty jobs as well as the better ones."

Dave sounded so sincere, he was starting to believe himself.

"OK, I'm in your hands as they say, though not in the Biblical sense I trust."

Dave frowned slightly, he missed the gag.

"Well, I feel a little sleepy, and think I'll take a nap, but do help yourself to anything you want, most of the jars and canisters have labels on them. Usual stuff, coffee, tea, etcetera, all in the top cupboard."

"Let me help you up the stairs," Dave said caringly.

"Oh, I don't sleep upstairs, my room's at the front of the house."

"OK, let's get you there then."

Dave gently helped Malcolm along the passageway, and into the room on the left. The curtains were drawn, and the room was dark, save for a red Mickey Mouse night-light on the bedside cabinet. Malcolm was so light, Dave had no trouble getting him onto the bed.

"Do you want to take your clothes off?"

"Best offer I've had in years, but no thanks, I'll kip on top of the covers, it's too much effort to keep taking them off."

Dave stood back and watched the frail young man struggle to get comfortable. "Anything else you want? Drink?"

"No thanks, I'm fine. Oh by the way, when you do handle any of my undergarments, you know pants and things, you should always wear gloves. There's no real problem, but it's better to be safe than ..., you know."

"Sorry?"

"Yeah. There's a large box of disposable surgical gloves on the dressing table, and another in the kitchen."

"OK."

"The house has three bedrooms upstairs, pick any one and get yourself settled in. You look like you're travelling pretty light, so help yourself to any of my old clothes that fit you."

Dave looked down at himself, he'd left prison with only the clothes he stood up in, and had no idea what his wife had done with the rest of his clothing. Dumped them presumably. But now, with this latest stroke of luck, he had no need to find out.

Dave thanked his host again, and left the room, deciding to have a look around, before he did anything else.

The door on the right of the corridor, opposite Malcolm's room, opened into a rather pleasant sitting room. Trapped in a time warp, it was decorated in seventies brown check wallpaper, complete with the obligatory (for nineteen seventy three) beige valour suite, and strange art-deco table lamp. The only other door off the passageway, just before the kitchen, opened onto a descending staircase. Dave found a light switch, just inside the doorway, and carefully walked down the bare wooden stairs and into a cellar. At some time, it was obviously going to be turned into a wine cellar, as there was a rack along one of the walls. The others being left to plain brick.

Unfortunately, although the rack was in place, an absence of wine was painfully noticeable.

Dave left the cellar, and entered the kitchen. It was well fitted, and had all the latest features. A small utility room fed off to the left, which in turn lead to the back door. He peered through the glass, and saw an old Volvo motorcar, parked under a corrugated lean-to.

"All this and wheels too," he said to himself as he went upstairs, finding three large bedrooms, one with a shower room en-suite.

"Ah, the master bedroom, this has to be it."

Opening the fitted double wardrobe, he found it full of men's clothing. Obviously they were Malcolm's. He rummaged around, pulling first one item, then another out, and laying them on the bed. There were about a dozen smart shirts, three suits, several pairs of casual trousers, a couple of polo shirts, at least ten T-shirts, two pairs of denim jeans, and several more outrageous pieces of clothing that Dave would not be wearing. Unfortunately Dave's shirt collar size was 16½, and all the dress shirts were only fifteens. However, all the more casual items of clothing did fit him, including the almost brand new pairs of Levi jeans, which somehow Dave felt might not belong to Malcolm.

He walked to the window, and drew back the curtains fully, letting the late autumn sunshine bath the room with a glorious amber glow. He sat on the bed, slowly took out a cigarette, and lit it. Its blue smoke illuminated and highlighted the mote swirling in the atmosphere. He was happier than a pervert in a sex shop; it was difficult to believe that at last the luck had turned his way. He was secretly dreading looking after Malcolm, the whole thing repulsed him, but if he was to put his masterplan into action, he needed a base to work from, and from what he'd seen, he knew this to be the place.

Chapter 9

Made to live a life of hell,
two years served in a prison cell,
and happy thoughts could not dispel,
REVENGE was all that he could smell.

During the two years of Dave's internment, Janice's life had improved immeasurably. After her 'quickie' divorce came through, she led the life of a latter day 'Merry Widow'. She had plenty of relationships but kept them all on a purely platonic basis. Men of all ages seemed to throw themselves at her. She'd dated several forty year olds, even more in the thirty-something bracket and one 'toy-boy' of twenty-three. Her first husband, perhaps because of his Greek upbringing and insistence on moral family values, had been very prudent in his choice of insurance policies and had left her very well provided for. A second policy had matured and her income was easily sufficient to allow her to indulge herself.

After a short holiday in Tenby, while the trial was taking place, she'd taken several longer breaks abroad, including a stay with her in-laws in Limossal, Cyprus.

Sarah had married her 'yuppy' boyfriend and lived in absolute luxury in Chichester, West Sussex. Janice saw her daughter regularly and often stayed over at week-ends in their palatial five bedroomed house.

She'd almost completely forgotten about Dave, putting the whole episode behind her. She didn't even know he'd been released from prison, and didn't want to know.

Although Sarah's husband, Rupert, had offered to buy Janice a little house somewhere in Sussex, so that she could be nearer her daughter, she always insisted on staying in Hedge End. She liked her house, it was close to her parents and friends, and with the new M27 motorway, bypassing Portsmouth and going direct to Chichester, she was only forty minutes drive-time away from her daughter.

She bought herself a two year old MG metro automobile, and

spent a lot of her time driving between her home and West Sussex. All she wanted now was a grandchild, and her life would be truly complete. Fortunately, Sarah and Rupert were trying for the same thing.

***

Dave had settled in his new surroundings, like a diabetic takes to saccharin. He'd convinced the social worker that she was no longer needed, and cancelled the 'meals on wheels' delivery. He kept most of his dealings with the DHSS on a very impersonal level, which seemed to be the only way to get things done. He made sure Malcolm was not involved at all, telling him that there were financial cutbacks in all local government departments.

Whilst looking through one of the drawers in the kitchen, Dave had found a fairly up to date bank statement confirming that Malcolm's account was in credit by more than ten thousand pounds. It was obvious that he'd been left a small fortune by his mother.
Dave did all the shopping, using Malcolm's cash-card to obtain money from the bank's cashpoint, and used the old Volvo car to get him around. It was strange to Dave, but his host had been very trusting, and possibly, because he didn't have long to live, seemed to have no regard for money. Dave found he could basically come and go as he pleased, only having to prepare a few meals a day, do some washing, and get Malcolm in and out of bed. Clearing up his incontinent pants was, as expected, the foulest job of all, although over the past few weeks, Malcolm had been eating so little, that his excrement resembled that of a hamster. Little black pellets the size of peas, thankfully with little or no smell. Even though he quite liked the man, he secretly hoped the end was near. Playing nursemaid was starting to become tiresome.

He hadn't been to see his parole officer once since he'd been released, and with his new found home and wealth, had decided to keep it that way. He was untraceable, or so he thought, and that was how he wanted it.

In the evenings, after he'd put Malcolm to bed, Dave would

sit watching television, planning his next move. Baden-Smith was to be the first. He was easy to find, and hopefully even easier to deal with.

Dave had found, whilst going through Malcolm's private papers and possessions, an old syringe, presumably a throwback from his host's drug taking days. And this, he was going to use as his weapon of revenge. An injection of Malcolm's infected blood should give his ex-lawyer the necessary reward he deserved, a legacy to remember until he died.

On several occasions, whilst shopping in Southampton City centre, Dave had waited in his car, outside Baden-Smith's office, and soon discovered that the solicitor, being a creature of habit, generally left his place of employment at five thirty and walked to his yellow Nissen car, which he parked in the Grosvenor Street multistory car park, just two minutes walk away.

One morning, after Dave had been resident for three weeks, a letter arrived for Malcolm, marked 'Private and Confidential' and although he was tempted to vet it, as he did with most incoming mail, he decided it might be best to let his host open this one himself.

"Oh, it's a letter from Justin," said Malcolm, rather excitedly. Dave frowned and thought 'poofter'. "You remember, the orderly from the prison hospital."

"Oh, that little que..." his voice died away, there was no point in upsetting Malcolm.

Malcolm quickly read the three pages, stopping and laughing at various intervals. He held the letter up. "Here you are, wanna read, you're mentioned in dispatches."

"What? Justin knows I'm here?"

"Yes, I wrote to him."

Dave was angry, he didn't want anyone to know of his whereabouts, and wondered how the letter had been posted, without his knowledge. "I don't remember posting a letter for you to the prison."

"No you wouldn't, the postbox is just across the road, I posted it myself one afternoon while you were shopping."

"I'd rather you hadn't," Dave said, rather menacingly, "I didn't want anyone knowing where I was."

"Don't worry my friend," Malcolm laughed, "I didn't say you were staying here, just that I'd seen you, keep your hair on, what little of it's left."

Dave decided that all mail from that moment on, out or in, would be censored. He couldn't risk a slip up, it was imperative that his 'hideout' remained a secret.

Over the previous few weeks, Malcolm had received quite a few letters, mostly from friends, and Dave would have to work out a way of stopping all further correspondence. He'd already mastered Malcolm's signature, paying some bills by cheque was far easier than going to the cashpoint everyday, and figured it would be fairly simple to scribble a note, in Malcolm's shaky handwriting, stating he was going away, possibly abroad, and that would be that. The only real problem was going to be the doctor, and he might not be that easy to fob off.

"Well? Do you want to read this or not?" Malcolm asked, breaking into Dave's train of thought.

"What? Oh yes, sorry, I was miles away."

Dave fumbled in his shirt pocket for his horn-rimmed National Health prison-issued spectacles. Another legacy of his stay in prison, reading in poor light had badly impaired his sight. He put them on his nose, and started to read:

Dear Malc,

It seems I was a trifle hasty, when I told you that Jimmy and I were an item. He says I'm not his type, and he wants someone more macho! (is that possible???). Well, bugger him I say, (no pun intended), and it looks like it's all off. Anyway, enough about me and my love life (or lack of it). How are you? Well, I hope. I'm so pleased that Dave made contact with you, and have I got news for him, (pass me a pillow, I feel quite faint). As expected, Anderson was admitted with chronic diarrhoea, so bad in fact, he developed piles (shame!), and needed medication for them. I accidentally doubled the medicine the Doctor prescribed for diarrhoea, and he became so constipated, that he started shitting house-bricks, which made his haemorrhoids look like grapes from hell. I'm sure Stephen King could write a horror story about them. Tell Dave that should make the score even.

There was some trouble in D wing last week, the Jocks and the Greeks up to their usual pranks, and six of them ended up in here. Unfortunately, I didn't fancy any of them!!

I really hope you're not suffering too much, and if there is anything I can do, just ask. I'm hoping to get over to see you one afternoon next week, but will ring before I come (that's the problem with having a bell on your willy, it always rings before you come!).

Well must go, things to do, shirts to iron (or lift?) etc. See you soon,

Lots of love,
Justin.

Dave laughed out loud, "Brilliant, tell him I owe him one."

"Really," said Malcolm jokingly in a very effeminate voice, keeping the gay theme going.

"Not that, you know what I mean."

"Yeah sure, I'll write to him later. Perhaps you could post it for me?"

"Of course, but don't mention I'm living here please, I think that's best left as our little secret."

"Vot ever you say, Mein Kapitan," Malcolm answered in a German accent, finger over his top lip, and arm stretched in a Nazi salute. Unfortunately, the excitement had been too much for him, and he fell back onto the bed, coughing and holding his chest.

"Hey, careful, you know what the doctor said, you should take it easy."

Malcolm sighed, his eyes wet and bloodshot. "I think I'll have a little rest now."

"Of course mate, you just relax, can I get you anything?"

"No thanks, I'm fine."

Dave left the room, and went into the kitchen. All of the mail that Malcolm had received over the past few weeks, was neatly arranged, and packed into an old 'Cadbury's' chocolate box. Dave took it from the Welsh dresser and opened it, looking at the addresses.

"Once I get his letter to Justin," he said to himself, "I'll copy the handwriting, and write to all of his friends, telling them he's off to France, for a long holiday, and hopefully, that should be an end to it."

The dreaded Doctor, strangely named Jonathan Dicks, called fairly regularly to check on Malcolm, always insisting that he should be hospitalised, in order to receive proper care and attention. Fortunately, Malcolm would not hear of it, and demanded to be left in his own home. Every time, Doctor Dicks reluctantly agreed, but was obviously far from happy with the situation. Dave knew that if Malcolm became so ill that he could not continue to argue his case, the Doctor would immediately have him placed in a hospital. This was the one problem Dave could see no answer to.

In the time he'd been out, his lifestyle had changed fairly dramatically, he still smoked like a trooper, but very rarely drank, preferring to keep his mind on the job in hand. The broken nose he'd received at the hands of Anderson, and dark droopy moustache he'd grown, had definitely given him a harder, almost Neanderthal look, and he would not have looked out of place on a National Front demonstration. His dreams had slowly started returning, but with Malcolm in the house, he felt slightly awkward about masturbating, and very rarely relieved himself.

Malcom's skinny body had become a mass of weeping bed-sores, and on the Doctor's orders, Dave kept them medicated and clean, as best he could, this being another job he loathed.

On Tuesday, September the 26th, after helping Malcolm to eat his evening meal, Dave waited quietly by the bed, while his benefactor fell asleep. Putting on some gloves, he carefully placed the syringe he'd earlier found, against a particularly large and septic looking scab. Drawing back the plunger, he attempted to draw up some of the pus from the inflamed wound, being careful not to disturb his colleague. He was no nurse, and took several stabs at it, until satisfied that, at least some of the infected matter was present in the syringe. He laid the instrument in a tiny plastic case, and left the house. Fortunately, Malcolm seemed to be retiring earlier each day, and he checked his watch as he crossed the Itchen Bridge. It was 5.15.

He drove to the car park he knew Baden-Smith used, and after sighting the yellow Nissen, parked one floor below, on level C. Climbing the stairs, he walked across the concrete floor, and stood behind a pillar. His plan was simplicity itself. As Baden-Smith went to open his car, Dave would jump him from behind, stick him with the syringe in the neck, and bingo, one very sick solicitor. He had to be very careful, he couldn't afford to be recognised, that would ruin everything, he still had two more scores to settle.

It was almost six o'clock, and Dave was starting to panic. "Where the fuck is the prick, he's never been this late before, he'd better turn up or ..."

The car park was empty, save for two or three other cars, and Dave caught sight of his reflection in the window of a brand new Ford Escort. He liked his new look, it suited him, and he held his stomach in, flexing his muscles as if he was in a strong-man pageant.

It was nearly 6.15, and Dave was getting very impatient, undecided, as to whether calling it a day or not. "Five more minutes, and I'll have to try again tomorrow," he mumbled to himself, tapping his fingers on the cold concrete pillar, that stood between him and Baden-Smith's car. Suddenly, he heard the door to the stairwell open, and peering around the pillar, he saw his intended victim waddle across the car park. He quickly put on a pair of his disposable gloves, carefully took out the syringe, and held it shoulder high like a dagger. Baden-Smith reached his car, and opening the back door, threw his old brief case onto the seat. Dave leapt like a madman from behind his cement hiding place, and ran the couple of steps to the yellow car. Grabbing the solicitor across the face, with his left arm, he rammed the syringe into the large jugular vein on the side of his throat. Baden-Smith screamed, and fell to his knees, hitting his head on the car door handle as he went down. Dave withdrew his weapon, and ran to the stairs, throwing open the door, making it crash against the wall. As he descended the steps, he could hear horrendous screams and cries for help, echoing around the almost deserted car park. Jumping quickly into his trusty Volvo, he started the engine, and was driving down the ramps on his way out.

For the first time in years, he somehow felt satisfied, as if he'd actually achieved something worthwhile. "This definitely deserves a drink or two," he thought, as he drove back towards Woolston. "Can't be too long, just in case Malcolm wakes up, if the worse comes to the worse, he's my alibi."

After two very swift pints in a pub in Victoria Road, he returned to the house. Parking in the car-port, he entered by the back door, and flopped onto a chair in the kitchen. Finding some gin, he made himself a large G and T, and turned on the little portable television set on the Welsh dresser.

"Phew," he sighed like a comic book hero, and settled back for a quiet evening, getting slowly pissed.

For some unknown reason, he decided to check on Malcolm, which was something he rarely did. Walking along the passageway, he opened the bedroom door, and immediately realised something was seriously wrong.

Malcolm was lying face down, his head deep in his pillow, and he never slept like that. Dave raced across the room, "Malc, it's me," he uttered, as he gently turned his friend over onto his back. Even to someone of Dave's limited medical knowledge, it was painfully obvious the man was close to, if not already dead.

"Oh God, not yet," he said rather callously, apparently more concerned with his own situation, than that of Malcolm. He pulled at his chin, trying desperately to think of what to do next. On the floor, by the bed, was a half finished note to Justin, the handwriting so shaky, it was almost illegible. Dave picked up the letter, and returned to the kitchen.

Taking the chocolate box from a drawer in the dresser, he carefully arranged all of the contemporary correspondence in neat, little piles. There was basically four friends who seemed to write regularly, as well as the current letter to Justin.

"Right, a short note to these five," he muttered to himself, as he found a writing-pad and some envelopes. "Where shall we disappear to? That's the next thing."

He remembered seeing some books in one of the smaller bedrooms, and went upstairs. "Aha," he said, as he found a world atlas. Turning to the map of France, he looked South for an obscure town or village. "Aix-en-Provence, yeah, perfect, Gawd knows how you pronounce it, but that's the place for me."

He spent the next hour, scribbling notes, some weren't right and ended up in the bin, but eventually, he'd written five almost perfect, but curt letters. Addressing the envelopes, he took them to the car, and placed them on the passenger's seat. "Post them in the morning, now the wretched Doctor." He telephoned the number, but unfortunately all he got was his answering service.

"Is it urgent sir?" said an officious female voice.

"Of course it's bloody urgent, the man's dying, or even dead, is that urgent enough?"

"Being rude will not help, I'll contact the Doctor immediately and he should be with you within an hour."

"An hour? Christ woman, this is life and death."

"Blaspheming will do no better," she replied, her tone turning obtrusive. "I suggest you ring the hospital and request an ambulance."

Dave was seething, and slammed down the 'phone. Perhaps he should call the hospital. He walked to the cupboard, and poured himself another gin and tonic. He'd never had to handle a situation like this one, his parents had died while he was very young, and it had all been arranged by others. He did know that if he got the Death Certificate, he could probably arrange a speedy, and quiet funeral, and hopefully, stay exactly where he was. Sure, he'd be able to stay in the house, who would stop him? The only room in the house he hadn't searched was Malcolm's, and although it seemed somehow irreverent to rifle through the belongings of a dead man, Dave felt strangely compelled to do it.

Malcolm's sad and sightless eyes stared to the ceiling, like the eyes of a dead fox, Dave had once seen lying by a roadside. It was no good, he couldn't do it, he pulled the sheet up, and covered the body completely. He obviously knocked the bed, causing an arm to flop out, fingers pointing to the ground, like a corpse from a horror movie.

"Jesus Christ Almighty!" he yelled, shaking and wiping his brow. "Don't do that."

He roughly rammed the arm back under the bed-linen, and sighed loudly, beads of sweat appearing on his brow.

The room was sparsely furnished, but had a huge antique chest-of-drawers in the corner by the bay window. Dave opened the top drawer, which was full of underwear, the second had T-shirts and socks, but the third was literally crammed to the brim with papers and documents.

"OK, let's ..."

The door-bell sounded, causing him to leap about a foot in the air, banging his knee on the opened drawer. "Oh, fuck," he shouted, as he pushed the drawer shut, and went to the front door. He yanked it open, still rubbing his shinbone. It was the not too happy Doctor Dicks.

"Good evening, I believe Malcolm's taken a turn for the worst."

"Yes, please come in."

The doctor frowned, and followed Dave into the bedroom, somewhat surprised to find the body already covered with a sheet.

"Um, couldn't stand the sight of his eyes," Dave mumbled awkwardly.

"Exactly what was your relationship with Malcolm?" asked the Doctor, in a very suggestive tone.

"Not what you think, I'm his cousin, David Evitts."

"I see," Dicks continued, whilst examining the body, "and did you sleep together?"

"What? Look I don't like your tone, I'm as straight as ..." he couldn't readily name a famous heterosexual, "as the next man, I was here to look after him, and that was all."

"OK, keep your hair on." Malcolm had used that phrase earlier, and it put Dave on edge, "only if you were, I'd strongly suggest you had a HIV test immediately, and if you weren't, then it might also be in your interest to do so."

Dave mumbled some obscenity, and went into the kitchen. After a few minutes, the doctor followed him.

"I did warn this might happen, he should have had proper care ..."

"Yes, I know, you've said it all before," Dave interrupted rather rudely, "but it's what he wanted."

"Did you call an ambulance?"

"No, there didn't seem any point."

"Well, I'll be in touch, and someone will call to collect the body in the morning, when I'll arrange for the autopsy to be done."

"Autopsy? Why?"

"When someone dies, it's the law to have the cause of ..."

"But it's obvious, he died of AIDS, what else do you need to know?"

"Mr Evitts, he didn't die of AIDS, as you so eloquently put it. He died of some other cause, true most likely induced by the virus, and that is what has to go on the death certificate."

Dave tutted, he didn't want to make too much fuss, just get the thing over with quickly.

"I'm pleased to see you're so compassionate, after your cousin's death," the Doctor said, as he picked up his bag, and headed for the door.

"It's alright, I'll see myself out," he shouted, and was gone.

"Fuck it." Dave yelled, "I really handled that well, didn't I?"

As the Doctor got into his car, he wondered why he'd never heard of a cousin before, he'd been their family GP for years, and had always assumed there were no other close relatives alive. It always seemed perfectly logical that Dave and Malcolm were lovers, but maybe not.

"None of my business," he mumbled, as he started his car, and drove to his next appointment.

Dave waited ten minutes to make sure that the Doctor didn't return and went back into Malcolm's room. Pulling the large drawer, containing the personal papers, Dave struggled to get it into the kitchen. It was just nine o'clock, and the television set was still on.

He tipped the entire contents onto the kitchen table, and started rooting through it, most of it was rubbish, mementos of passed liaisons, old birthday cards, bank statements, the birth certificates of Malcolm, and his parents, letters from solicitors and accountants, insurance policies, love letters, and a signed photograph of Elton John. It gave Dave a fairly accurate insight of the Evitts family, the substantial amount of money paid, when Mrs Evitts died, which was used to pay off the mortgage, together with a letter from the bank, offering to help Malcolm invest his money wisely.

"Christ, this is thirsty work," Dave said. Finding that he'd finished off the gin, he walked over to a cupboard, and took out a bottle of Vodka, he'd noticed earlier. "Beggars can't be choosers," he muttered, as he opened the alcohol, and poured a half-pint measure into a tumbler. "Right, where was I?"

He carried on sifting through the mountain of important, and not so important documents, when he came across a Yorkshire Building Society paying-in book, neatly contained in a little plastic wallet. 'Platinum Account' was printed in large letters on its cover. Dave slowly opened the book, glanced at the figure shown at the end of the column, and slapped it shut.

"Fucking hell," he yelled, as he opened it again, "Over thirty grand, and it's all mine."

He placed the little green booklet back into its holder and threw all the other papers back into the drawer, before returning it to Malcolm's room. Almost racing back to the kitchen, he drank the vodka in one, and refilled his glass. "Tell me it's real," he said as he opened the book again. The actual balance shown was £30,124.52, and it had not been updated for three years, which meant there was even more in the account, once the interest was added. It also meant that he could easily go to the Building Society and withdraw the money, being so adept at Malcolm's signature, he could confidently use the account, as if it were his own. He sat back with his thoughts, how could it get any better?

On the television set, the main ITN 'News at Ten' was just finishing, and Dave thumbed through a newspaper, to see what was on next. "Ah, after the local news an old Clint Eastwood film, that will just about round off the evening nicely."

He placed the Building Society book in his shirt pocket and went to the toilet, he was feeling hungry, and decided to have a fry-up. Pulling the frying pan from the cupboard, he took some eggs and bacon from the fridge and started to prepare his evening feast.

"And now the late news from the 'Meridian' area," said a very pompous looking newsreader. "Police are tonight treating as suspicious the body of a man found dead in a Southampton car park, and are asking for anyone who was in the Grosvenor Street area of the city to come forward. The man, a local solicitor, was apparently about to get into his car when attacked, and anyone with any information should contact the Police at the Civic Centre Police Station. Another horse has been attacked in North Hampshire, and police think this is part of a ..."

Dave's jaw dropped, and he broke his egg in the frying pan, causing the yolk to run into his bacon.

"Dead? Baden-Smith dead, how?" he pushed the frying pan to one side, and sat at the table, taking another large swig of vodka. "He must have banged his head on the concrete floor, or perhaps had a heart attack. Oh, this day gets better and better, only that cunt Quinn and my whoring wife to deal with, and I can live my life in total luxury. Cheers Mate." he shouted, raising his glass to the ceiling.

* * *

D.I. Quinn was sitting at his desk in the Civic Centre police station, reading some notes, when Sgt Crouch arrived. It was eight thirty two.

"Good morning sir," he said as he reached his boss's desk, "have you heard about Baden-Smith?"

Quinn looked puzzled, he'd only just arrived, and very rarely listened to the local news broadcasts.

"No what? He hasn't won a case at last?" he joked.

"Oh, you haven't, well, that man killed in the car park last night, it was him."

"What? I've only just got in, where's the file? It should be on my desk."

"Just being prepared sir," interjected an officer from across the room, "you should have it shortly."

"Shortly, what's happening around here, a man is dead, and I've got to wait for the file."

"It's the government's fault sir, we've had cutbacks on the secretarial staff."

"Sod the cutbacks, and fuck the secretarial staff, get across there Mike, and get them to get their asses into gear, I should have been informed immediately."

"OK," said Mike, wondering if there would be time to grab a quick sandwich from the canteen on his way. He was starving.

"What happened Jeff?" Quinn asked his colleague, as Crouch hurriedly left the room.

"Don't know much, I think old Baden-Smith was attacked as he got into his car last night. Word is it's a mugging."

"A mugging?" shouted Quinn, never in a good mood in the mornings. "What person in his right mind would mug a scruffy looking turd like Baden-Smith? The only thing you'd get from him is a nasty skin rash."

Jeff smiled awkwardly; he knew the two of them never really got on, but surely now the man was dead, Quinn could show a little compassion.

"Well, stranger things happen, maybe it was a druggie."

Mike went to the typing office, sandwich in hand, and inquired about the file.

"Just doing it now," said Michelle, a large old woman, with grey hair, and a bright red face. "You're keen, aren't you?"

"Yeah," Mike stopped and finished his mouthful of cheese and tomato, "it's Quinn, and you know what he's like."

"Well, our friendly Mr Quinn will have to wait, I've only got one pair of hands, and after all these cutbacks ..."

"Yes, I know, when you're ready."

"Well, there's not much in it yet, we're still waiting for the pathologist's report."

"Fair enough, I'll take what you've got, I'm sure old Quinn will want to see Doctor Sherwood himself anyway."

The woman handed Crouch the file, and quickly stuffing the remainder of his food in his mouth, he went straight back to his superior.

"Christ Mike, where you been? To the scene of the crime itself?"

Mike stood silently as Quinn opened the file.

"Not much in here is there?"

"No sir, Michelle said she's still waiting for the cause of death from the pathologist."

"Right, that's as good as any place to start, come let's go see him now."

Mike tutted under his breath, and screwed his face up behind Quinn's back.

In the couple of years since the David Price trial, Mike Crouch had taken several police exams, passed them all, and was waiting for a position to take up his promotion. Quinn, on the other hand, was stuck exactly where he was. The Force, or his superiors to be precise, believed he was too volatile to handle a more senior position, and they were happy for him to stay at Southampton as a Detective Inspector. He was a very good policeman, everyone knew, and accepted that, but he broke too many rules, (and limbs) to ever aspire to anything higher. Since the Price case, (for which he got a commendation), he'd never really got the opportunity to shine quite so brightly.

The two officers arrived at the Path. Lab., and Quinn tapped twice on the frosted glass door, then entered. Crouch as usual was in tow. Sherwood was leaning over a microscope, at the back of the room, and looked up. He was a very tall (well over six foot), rugged looking man, with masses of facial hair, particularly around his eyebrows, and a thick tangled head of hair, which resembled a giant 'brillo' pad.

"Hello, Quinn," he said, glancing with one eye over the microscope, "here about Baden-whats-his-name no doubt?"

"Right first time, Toby," answered Quinn.

Nearly all the policemen, even the most senior called him Mr Sherwood, or Doctor, but not Quinn, he seemed to delight in calling people by their first names.

"Well, it's interesting, I'll say that."

"How so?"

"It's obvious that Baden-Thingey was jumped from behind, he's got mild abrasions to his face, and around the eyes, and was stabbed in the neck by a needle, probably a syringe. But now it gets interesting, he was stabbed in the jugular vein, and injected with some kind of liquid, presumably poison. But our friend had no knowledge of needles, because he bypassed the jugular and hit the carotid artery, and injected air. Bingo, one dead solicitor."

Quinn frowned: "So what are you saying?"

"What I'm saying, and at this moment it's only conjecture, is that our friend tried to inject Baden-whatsit with something nasty, didn't fill the syringe correctly, hit the artery by mistake, and well ..."

"And this something 'nasty' what is it?"

"Oh come on man, it only happened last night, I haven't finished my findings yet, should know definitely in a couple of days."

"But why do you think that the person accidentally injected the air? Maybe he wants us to think he knows nothing about these things, when in fact he was aiming for the carrot-whatsit artery."

"Two reasons Quinn, first, if he was just going to kill, in the way you've suggested, why bother to have any other substance in the syringe, and secondly, the way the needle was inserted. Anyone with the slightest knowledge of simple inoculations would never ram the syringe in at such an acute angle. Christ, he was lucky the needle didn't snap off. No, this was an accidental killing, he hit the carotid by mistake.

"So, any thoughts on motive, apparently nothing was stolen."

"Quinn, you're the policeman, I'm just a poor MO giving you the facts."

"Well ..."

"As I've already stated, I honestly believe our villain meant to wound his victim, rather than kill him, but once I've analysed the substance that I've found, you'll have my full report."

"OK thanks Toby," Quinn scratched his head, "I look forward in anticipation to reading your report. Soon as you can, eh?"

Quinn and Crouch left the lab and returned to their office.

"Mike, go round to Baden-Smith's office, and see if you can get all the cases he was currently working on, and any of the more serious ones over the past couple of years. I have a hunch this could be a revenge crime."

Crouch looked at his watch, surely tea and biscuits were the first order of the day.

"Now, Mike."

"Yes sir, it shouldn't take long, he hasn't taken on any legal aid work for a while, not since that rape case he lost a couple of years back."

"That's true, Price wasn't it? Get me that file as well, and see where that prick Price is now. I've a feeling he may be out."

Crouch left, and Quinn sat at his desk, stroking his chin. "Strange," he thought, "very strange indeed."

* * *

Dave Price had spent a few weeks sorting out Malcolm's affairs, the post mortem was over, and he'd had the body cremated. It was a very strange funeral, because he was the only person in attendance. Obviously, all the friends had bought the 'going to France' trip, and he'd not heard from any of them.

He'd gone to the Yorkshire Building Society in Southampton, just to make sure he would have no trouble drawing money from the account. A very attractive oriental girl had served him, and when asked for a signature, he scribbled Malcolm's effortlessly. He actually liked the signature, thinking it was rather clever. A capital M & E followed by small v-i-t-t, was finished by the letter 's' written back across the double 't' making a dollar sign.

With the hundred pounds he withdrew, he returned to Woolston shopping centre, and bought two nylon straps, each with self-locking ratchets on their ends. These were generally used for securing suitcases to roof-racks, but Dave had other ideas for their usage. In the house, he'd moved Malcolm's bed down into the cellar, and covered it with an old rubber tarpaulin. He'd found some worn items of underclothing, which would otherwise have been washed, if not for Malcolm's demise, and threw them onto the floor. He was always careful to wear gloves whenever he touched anything that had belonged to Malcolm.

"Right, everyone needs a break," he chuckled, as he left the cellar and went to the bathroom for a shower. He still had sixty pounds left, and decided to go out in search of some 'rumpy-pumpy'.

Since Malcolm's death, his sexual appetite had returned, and so had the dreams.

After showering, he dressed in jeans, T-shirt and denim jacket, and splashed half a bottle of 'Corduroy Vert' on his face and neck. It was nearly seven thirty when he got into his car and drove into Southampton.

A Thursday night, in early October, in a town like Southampton was not going to be too lively. But he had money in his pocket, and a feeling that his luck was about to change. He'd made a conscious decision to avoid any of his old haunts, and drove around the inner ring-road, looking for a hostelry. Spotting the 'Maypole' a small Whitbread public house near the old fruit and vegetable market, he pulled up and stopped just yards from its door. Entering the bar, he was relieved to see that they sold real ale, even though it was only Strong Country, one of his least favourites.

"Evening," he said to the barmaid, who was standing with her back to him, apparently slicing lemons. She turned and smiled, and Dave lit up like a firework. She had glorious auburn hair, cut in a bob, a thin elfin face, with perhaps a little too much eye make-up, and the sweetest little figure Dave had seen in a very long time.

"Sorry, I didn't hear you come in."

"I'd like to come in," Dave thought, "come into your mouth."

"What can I get you?"

"Um," Dave stammered, totally disorientated at finding such a peach, in a pub like this.

"What would you like to drink?" she politely asked again.

"Oh yeah, pint of Strong Country please darling."

The word 'darling' sounded totally out of place from a Neanderthal looking National Front skinhead type. The girl looked slightly troubled as she poured him his beer.

"Live around here?" he asked in his best macho voice, lighting up a cigarette in Clint Eastwood fashion.

"Wanker!" the girl thought as she struggled for an answer.

"Um, no, I live in Totton, with my boyfriend."

"Lucky old boyfriend I'd say," grinned Dave, flashing his yellowed teeth.

How she didn't throw-up was a mystery. She placed his drink on the bar in front of him. "One pound seventy please."

Dave nonchalantly handed her a twenty pound note, nodding his head as if he were loaded.

"Haven't you anything smaller?" she asked, "Only it's been quiet tonight, and I've not much change."

"No probs, here's a fiver," he swaggered.

She took the note, walked to the electronic till, pressed the button marked bitter, and returned with his change.

"Thanks lover," he said, stretching his neck, to look over the bar at her legs. She returned to her duties. Dave tried to start a conversation, but the girl would have none of it.

"It's quiet, how about some music?" he said, rolling up the sleeves of his denim jacket.

"Sure," she replied without turning round.

"What type of music d'ya like?"

The girl banged the knife down, sighed and turned, "Mainly House, Acid, Hip-hop, little bit of Grunge, and some twentieth century Soviet composers, Shostakovich, Prokofiev and a little Rachmaninov."

Dave had not heard of any of them.

"But you wont find them on that jukebox, it's mainly pop and country."

She had decided he was obviously one allegro short of a Brahm's symphony, and hoped he would get the hint from her rather abrasive tone.

Dave did and shut up.

After three pints, he decided that, if he was to get laid, then he was going to have to pay for it. He finished his beer, stubbed out his sixth cigarette, slipped from the bar-stool and said "Goodnight."

"Bye," shouted the barmaid, sighing as if she had just lived through a life threatening drama.

As he opened the car door, he glanced at his watch, 09.38 it illuminated digitally. He followed the Ring Road southwards, around the City, passing the Civic Centre, and into the top of Portswood, turning into Nichols Town and Derby Road, the red light district. He remembered back to his last visit to the street and smiled. How naive he was then, his years in prison had certainly toughened him up. He wanted a shag, and wasn't afraid who knew. He parked discreetly in a side road, and climbed from the car, walking around the corner and into Derby Road. It was a cold night even for October, and Dave unrolled his sleeves, and buttoned up his coat to the collar. The place was unbelievably quiet, and still. Several of the houses had reddish lights shining through partially curtained windows, a few had lights hanging in their porches, with signs, mainly 'Model, please ring' on prominent view.

Suddenly, out of nowhere, a Rastafarian appeared, his ginger dyed dreadlocks hanging from a multi-coloured 'benie' hat.

"I is called 'Brother Man', what you after then?"

Dave jumped back. "Jesus shit," he yelled, his heart pounding in his chest.

"Name your pleasure, Brother Man get it for ya, at a price." The black man grinned, showing a huge white flash of teeth.
Dave hesitated, still trying to get his breath. "Um, ever heard of a pearl necklace?"

"Course man, loves 'em meself. Little problem though, all de girls insists on Johnnys, know what I'm saying, man?"

"Well, it's impossible, how can you have a pearl necklace, if you gotta wear one? Surely you got someone, eh?"

"Maybe I has, maybe I ain't," he shrugged his shoulders, "but it'll cost ya."

"Of course, how much?"

"Gotta be a ton man, gotta be dat."

"A hundred quid? Bloody hell, I don't want real pearls."

"Best I can do, you knows this AIDS ting, them all scared."

"Fuck me, I'd rather have a wank," Dave stormed, and turned back towards his car. Brother Man followed.

"Hey wai' ta minute, how much you got to spend, Brother Man sort someting out."

Dave stopped. "Yeah?" he puffed.

"Well, I warns you man, she ain't much to look at, but I tink for, say, fifty, it can be sorted."

"Look, I'm not paying fifty quid, to poke some old fat boiler, it ain't worth it."

"She ain't fat, but she's pretty old, you come see, it'll be good."

"No it's OK, I've just gone off the idea."

He walked to his car, looked around and the black man was gone. Driving back to Woolston he was somewhat annoyed. Was he ever going to get his lay?

Since Malcolm's death, Dave had taken the newspaper, 'The Daily Sport', cutting out all the big breasted women that were featured each day, and keeping them in a little box-file he'd found. Back at the house, he took a new bottle of gin, and his file straight to his bedroom and retired for the evening.

Friday morning broke damp, cold and cloudy. Dave could see the sky through a tiny gap in his bedroom curtains. He looked at his clock.

"Christ, 9.17, no point getting up yet," he moaned, and rolled over, his back to the window.

He had obviously been having one of his favourite dreams, because he had an enormous erection. He tickled the end of his member, and fell back to sleep. In seconds, he was with the gorgeous mature woman he'd seen in one of the pages of the newspaper. A forty five year old, with a breast size much bigger than her age. Dave was laid on his back, pulling at his penis, waving it at her suggestively. She'd oiled up her tanned, and massive moulds with baby lotion, and was about to ... Dave opened his eyes, the door-bell was ringing.

"Who the fucking hell is this?" he complained. It rang again. He rolled from the bed, and peeked through the drawn curtains. A smartly dressed man of about thirty, was standing back from the door, looking up at the house.

"Bloody Social Services no doubt," he said, jumping back from the window, his penis still erect. "Well, I've told them he's dead, cancelled all his benefits, what the hell do they want now?"

He put on an old dressing gown of Malcolm's (which he had washed several times, just to be on the safe side) and went downstairs to the front door.

"Yes?" he snapped rudely.

"Hello, sorry to bother you, but I'm looking for Malcolm."

"Eh?"

"I'm an old friend of his, Kelvin Barber, I was passing so I thought I'd ..."

"He said he'd written to all his friends before he left," Dave interrupted in a gruff voice. He recognised the name, and knew a letter had been sent. "He's somewhere in France, Axes de Provence, or something'."

"Oh, he's left then?"

"Of course, why wouldn't he?"

"Well, it's just that the letter was so ..." the man struggled awkwardly, looking for the right words.

"Was so what?" Dave demanded, pulling the dressing gown tight around his middle, to keep out the chill air.

"Well, I know France very well, lived there for six years in the eighties, and Aix-en-Provence hasn't got a clinic for HIV sufferers. I checked with a French friend of mine, who lives in Lyon, and he'd heard of no such place."

"Well you fucking would, wouldn't you, you cock-sucking sausage jockey," Dave thought, and almost uttered.

"Only, I knew Malc very well, and it seems strange he would go off like that, considering how ill he was. It was not his style at all."

"Malcolm's style? Don't make me puke. His style was having a Frankfurter shoved up his ass-hole, you shirt-lifting prick."

Dave was by now burning up inside but remained quiet.

"Can I ask who you are?" said the man calmly.

Dave wanted to slam the door in his feminine face, but resisted the temptation, realising one stupid move now, could ruin the whole plan.

"I'm sorry, how rude of me, please come in, I'll make some coffee, and explain all."

The man followed him into the kitchen. Dave thought about killing him, and putting his body in the cellar, but assumed that others would follow. He switched on the electric kettle, and they sat opposite each other, around the kitchen table. "My name is David Evitts, I'm

Malcolm's cousin, and only surviving relative. I've been looking after him for the past few months, and when he became very ill, it was obvious that no more could be done. I washed, cooked, and saw to his every need, but in the end ..." Dave left a pregnant pause, wiping his eyes.

"I'm sorry," said Kelvin, "I didn't think."

"That's OK, I begged Malcolm to go into a hospice over here, pleaded with him not to leave all his friends in England, but he wanted to have his last few days in the sun. I'm not exactly sure where he went." His voice was low and compassionate, "but he had a lot of money, left from his poor mother's untimely death, and bought an ambulance to take him across the Channel to France. It was fully equipped, with a qualified nurse, and everything." Dave glanced up at the man, "And that's all I know. He hasn't written, but when he does, I'll let all his friends know. He's left me a book with all the addresses in."

The kettle clicked off, and Dave slowly got up, wiped his eyes again. "How do (cough) you take your coffee?"

"Black, without sugar please," said Kelvin, choking inside.

Dave made the coffee, and they chatted for a while.

"When I first saw you, I thought you were one of Malcolm's... you know ..."

Dave did know, and nearly lost control, perhaps he should kill him after all.

"Well, I'm sorry to have bothered you," Kelvin said, getting to his feet, "you've got my address?"

"Of course, and I promise you, you'll be the first to hear, if or when, anything happens."

"Thanks Dave, and thanks for all the kindness you've obviously shown to Malcolm, you're a true friend indeed." They shook hands, and the man left. Closing the door, Dave flopped against the wall.

"Phew, that was close," he mumbled, as he returned upstairs, hoping to finish his business with a certain large breasted lady. With a little bit of luck, she'd be getting a pearl necklace for breakfast.

* * *

Quinn was troubled. Something didn't fit. He'd learnt from the forensic lab that the mystery substance injected into the neck of Baden-Smith was contaminated blood, and was totally convinced that this was not the work of some smashed junkie, after money to fund his habit. All of the cases that the solicitor had handled in the past few years were either domestic disputes or motoring offences, and surely no one would kill their solicitor over six penalty points on their driving licence. He kept going back to the Dave Price case. He didn't know why, maybe it was just a hunch, but that was the only serious case the man had handled in years. Quinn felt obliged to explore the avenue more fully.

Sgt Crouch walked into the office, wiping his mouth, and stood in front of his boss's desk.

"Ah Mike, good, glad you're here, I think we need to visit Winchester nick."

"Really?" said Mike, somewhat puzzled, "Why?"

"Just a hunch, but I'll bet my pension, this is something to do with that Price cretin."

Quinn had already done some digging. He'd discovered that Price had been released from prison, several months earlier, and that he'd not been in contact with his probation officer since he'd been out. The mere fact that he was breaking his parole was in strict violation of the Probation Act, and Price was already on the wanted list. He also found out that Dave Price had made no claims for social security, and Quinn wondered what he was living on. Whenever he had run his thoughts through Crouch, the younger officer offered any number of reasons for the anomalies, but Quinn did not care for, or agree with, any of them.

"It's only ten, let's go before lunch."

"Yes sir," moaned Crouch, quickly realising the reason for the visit to the prison, and not happy with the motive behind it. They drove out of Southampton towards Winchester, taking the recently finished M3 Motorway, turning off towards St Cross, and then Oliver's Battery, before arriving at their destination, just after ten thirty. They showed their warrant cards, and were taken straight to the Governor's office.

Paul Bartlett, the Governor, was a massively fat man, perspiring like a Sumo wrestler on a marathon, even in mid-October. Quinn immediately disliked him. The two officers were offered a seat, while the fat man went in search of the file on Price. Returning, out of breath, Bartlett flopped into his large leather reclining seat, and opened the file.

"Right, what's this about?" Bartlett politely asked.

"Just inquiries, he's skipped a few probation meetings."

Bartlett was not convinced, this was too high level for something as trivial as that. He put on his reading glasses, and glanced into the file.

"Ah yes, Price, two years in solitary, a few weeks sharing a cell, then released. No real problems, you could say a model prisoner really."

"Model? The man was a convicted rapist," snapped Quinn, as he listened to the supercilious chatter of the huge man.

"I'm well aware of his form, Detective Quinn, I can only speak as I find, and within these walls we had no trouble from him, except the incident with the sleep walking."

"It's Detective Inspector Quinn actually, what trouble?"

The Governor explained the details, possibly too flippantly for Quinn's liking.

"Well, Mr Bartlett, can we see Anderson and the hospital orderly?"

"What for a parole violation?"

Quinn glanced daggers, and said nothing.

"Of course, my dear friend, I'll arrange it immediately, would you like a drink while I organise an interview room?"

"Yes please," beamed Crouch.

"No thank you," snapped Quinn almost simultaneously, giving his young colleague a very scathing look.

"Um, perhaps not," added Crouch, sheepishly.

The Governor shrugged his large shoulders, causing four or five additional chins to appear around his neck, and left the two men in his office.

"My God," Quinn said, almost before the man had left the

room, "no bloody wonder the prison service is in such a state, with a fat prick like that in charge."

"Oh, be fair sir, surely size is no criterion for ..."

"Yes, yes, just shut it Mike."

After ten minutes, Bartlett reappeared. "Right, I've arranged for Harrison to show you to the interview room, Anderson's there already, and after you've finished, Harrison'll escort you to the hospital. Oh, by the way, I think you'll find that Harrison knew Price, so he might also be able to help with your um ...inquiry?"

Quinn and Crouch left the office with the elderly prison officer and were taken along two corridors, before arriving at a room with a large iron door.

"How long have you worked here?" Quinn asked Harrison.

"Too long sir," smiled the old man, "hope to retire later this year."

"Perhaps we can talk later?"

Harrison nodded, and opened the door, holding it open for the two policemen.

"Well, well, well," said Quinn sarcastically, "if it's not old 'Pee-Wee' Anderson, up to your old tricks again, I see."

Anderson snarled, showing a slash of broken and cracked green teeth.

Quinn and Crouch sat opposite the convict, at a graffiti covered formica topped table, as Harrison closed the door, and took up position outside.

"What ever it is, I didn't do, don't know about it, so fuck off."

"Charming, I must say, it's nice to see you again, you scabby sausage-sucking slime-ball. We're here on other business."

"Yeah, what?"

"I believe you shared a cell for a few nights with a certain Dave Price, and he's gone AWOL, know anything about it?"

"Fuck all. But I remember him, and he's a fucking pervert, shouldn't be allowed to share a cell with no one."

"Really? And pray enlighten us why?"

"Hadn't been in the cell more than a couple of nights and the bastard's after sucking me cock."

"Oh, what a shame, and you'd hate that wouldn't you?"

"Fuck off, I don't have to talk to you."

"Fine. No problem. Could you leave us alone for a minute Sgt Crouch, I just want a private word with our friend."

Mike Crouch got up to leave, and Anderson was obviously filled with panic. He knew of Quinn, they'd met on several previous occasions, and he knew being left alone with him was a very precarious, and potentially dangerous, situation to be put into.

"Hang on, sit down, maybe I can help you. What is it you want to know?"

"That's better, you slug. Now, just tell us about Price."

"Nothin' to tell, he tried it on one night, hit his head on the cell door, and claimed he'd been sleepwalking. I didn't want no trouble, so I went along with the story."

"Very magnanimous of you, I didn't realise he was a brown hatter, his preference always seemed to be big breasted women."

"You can swing both ways, you know. After a couple of years without nookie, even an asshole becomes attractive."

Quinn screwed up his nose at the thought of Anderson's lower passage. "OK, but did he have any friends in here, anyone he liked or talked to a lot?"

"Nope. He was years in solitary, I don't think he knew anyone else. Oh, although he was fairly friendly with old Harrison, the screw, but then everyone is."

"So he said nothing to you about any plans he had when he got released."

"Nothin', the only thin' he said to me was, 'let's suck your cock'."

"Well, thank you Anderson, I'll just say that, no matter how long I was locked in here, you are one asshole I'd never find attractive."

Crouch sniggered and the two officers got to their feet.

"Thanks again," said Quinn, leaning across the table, and whispering into the convict's ear. "If, or when you get out, and I pick you up for anything, I'll bang your scrotum so far up your asshole, you'll need to gargle with mouthwash to soothe it. Comprende?"

Anderson pulled back, with an incredulous look upon his face, wanting to reply, but deciding against it.

"Come on Mike, there's an awful smell of shit in here, and I think it's on his breath."

Quinn tapped the door, and Harrison opened it, let the officers out, and carefully turned a huge key in the lock until it clicked.

"Hospital please Harrison. What do you know about Dave Price?" said Quinn as they followed the guard back down the corridor.

"Not a lot really sir, he kept himself to himself ..."

"Well, he would in solitary," interjected Quinn humorously

"Very true sir," smiled the old man, "but you shouldn't believe a word that Anderson says, I'd have ten Prices any day. He's real bad news."

"I know my friend, I know."

They arrived at the infirmary, and were greeted by the ever bouncy Justin. Harrison did the introductions and left.

"How can I help you gentlemen?"

"Oh God," thought Quinn, "not another chutney-locker bandit."

"We're trying to trace the whereabouts," said Crouch, thankful to be able to get a word in, "of Dave Price. We believe he spent a few days in the hospital before his release."

"Well," said Justin, thinking that Crouch was rather cute, "he was only in here for a short time, after having his nose re-arranged by Anderson, and I'm not sure that I can really help you."

"Did he have any friends that you know of?"

"Can't say, although he became quite chatty with young Malcolm while he was here, and Malcolm wrote to say that Dave had been in touch on the outside."

"You wouldn't still have the letter I suppose?"

"Sorry, no."

"But you're sure they met up, are you?"

"Don't know about met up, Malcolm just said Dave had been to see him. He was very ill you see, and was let out for compassionate reasons."

"How ill?"

"Dying, the poor lamb, he had the dreaded AIDS, and not long to live, by all accounts."

Any sympathy that Quinn might have had, disappeared when the nature of his illness was mentioned.

"Where'd this Malcolm live In Southampton?"

"Yes, in Woolston, can't remember the address."

"That's OK, we can get it from the Governor."

"Mind you, you're too late, got a note last week, saying he was going to France."

"Really? Do you think he might have taken Price with him?"

"Highly unlikely, they hardly knew each other."

"OK thanks, what was his name again?"

"Malcolm Evitts."

They returned to the Governor's office, got the address, and left.

Once in the car, Quinn ordered Crouch to drive straight to Woolston. Crouch looked at his watch, another late lunch, and his stomach was already rumbling.

"What a way to run a prison, fat sweaty governor, old senile guards, gay hospital orderlies. More like a bloody holiday camp," moaned Quinn, as they drove back towards Southampton. As they left the M3, and headed across the city towards their destination, Crouch felt obliged to say something. "Is there any point going to the house sir?" he asked, "I mean, if this guy's gone to France, it's pretty obvious he's taken Price with him, and that's why he's vanished."

"Maybe Mike, but I don't think so. Price is still in town, I can smell him."

Crouch silently tutted, and slightly shook his head.

They pulled up outside the house in Obelisk Road, and walked through the overgrown garden, up to the front door. Dave was upstairs, sitting on the bed, picking his toenails, and eating them, when the bell rang.

"Who the fuck now?" he mumbled, as he walked over to the window, and peered down into the garden below. "Oh fucking hell, not Quinn," he yelled, his heart pounding like a bass-drum in a marching-band. The bell rang again, followed by three heavy bangs on the door knocker. Dave ducked down terrified, so scared that his bowels moved, causing him to break wind violently.

"Let's look 'round the back," ordered Quinn, and they walked along the side of the house, and into the carport.

"Now that's strange," observed Quinn, peering through the kitchen window, "if they've gone to France, why is there a couple of dirty coffee cups on the draining board. Eh?"

"Perhaps they just up and went," suggested Crouch, his hunger so severe, he felt faint.

"Something smells Mike, and it's not the Woolston sewage farm."

They walked back to their car, and Quinn glanced up at the bedroom windows, and pondered.

"How's this, the Evitts character goes to France, and leaves old Pricey boy to look after the house."

"Possible, I suppose, but he'd still need money to live on, and where's he getting it from?"

"Maybe Evitts left him some, who knows?"

They returned to the station in silence, with Quinn's mind working overtime.

Dave kept a very low profile for the next week or so, only going out when it was necessary, and even then only at night. Breaking his parole was enough to see him back inside, and it was imperative to play it cool. He'd bought a couple of big boob girlie magazines, and spent most of his time, drinking and wanking. He had everything prepared for his wife Janice, and felt it was now right to put plan 'B' into action.

Chapter 10

Help me Lord, for I have sinned,
but there's still two more to be syringed.

Janice had been keeping herself very busy. With the forthcoming birth of her grandchild, she spent every weekend with her daughter Sarah and her husband, returning on Mondays to her house in Hedge End.

She didn't know that Dave had also been busy, parking his car just outside Lambourne Gardens, at weekends, and keeping a note of all her movements. It was Monday the 23rd October when he made his move. It had been raining for three days, and with heavy cloud cover, it was still dark at seven o'clock in the morning. Dave parked the car, just a few hundred yards from the house, and casually strolled down the drive, along the side path, and up to the back door. He still had keys to the house, and although he knew that Janice had changed the front door locks, chanced that she had not altered the rear one.

Selecting the key from his fob, he sighed, as it turned, unlocking the door. He'd made provisions to smash the window, but was grateful that it had not been necessary, as this was a much safer option. He pushed open the door, and walked into the kitchen. Nothing much had changed, except for a couple of paintings of fruit, hanging over the draining board. If, as he hoped, Janice was a creature of habit, she should arrive home at about eleven. He had plenty of time.

Taking off his rucksack, he went upstairs, into the master bedroom, and unloaded its contents on the bed. Two rolls of strong adhesive tape, three lengths of nylon twine, and a small foam rubber ball, he'd bought from Woolworths. He sat on the bed, and thought back to the times he'd spent there. Mostly they were fond memories, and he felt a small tinge of sadness that it had now come to this. The mood did not last long, as his thoughts focused on what he'd gone through in the past two years. He pushed the rucksack and its contents under the bed, carefully readjusting the quilt, so that nothing was visible. He walked across the hall, into Sarah's old bedroom, and opened one of the drawers of her dressing table. Not surprisingly, it still contained a few items of her underwear. He pulled out a pair of extremely brief lacy panties, and gently sniffed them.

"Um, I can still smell that sweet little fanny," he said, even though he couldn't, she hadn't worn them for two years. Opening a second drawer, he found an old brassiere, and held it up, marvelling at the size of the cups.

"Fucking hell," he moaned in ecstasy, shaking at the thought of her gorgeous brown breasts. Taking out his penis, he rubbed the bra and pants along its shaft. The feel of satin and lace quickly giving him an erection. He placed the brassiere on the carpet, and continue to rub his member with the pants. Almost immediately he reached the vinegar stroke, and ejaculated into one of the upturned double 'D' cups. He was still panting, as he roughly wiped the purple end of his manhood in the briefs, before throwing them back into the drawer. How he wished it had been the real thing. Struggling to get his meat back into his trousers, he went into the guest bedroom, shut the door, and flopped out onto the bed. Now the wait.

Janice had left her daughter in West Sussex, at about ten, and had stopped at the large Marks and Spencer store in Hedge End, to buy a ready-meal for her lunch. It was twenty to twelve, when she finally arrived home, and Dave jumped, when he heard the front door open. He slipped quietly from the bed, and stood at the door listening intently. He heard her high heels, click-clack on the hard tiled kitchen floor, and rightly assumed she was making herself a cup of coffee. After twenty minutes, he started to get impatient, his hands were clammy and itchy, as he rubbed them up and down the front of his jeans. Without warning, he heard her leave the kitchen and climb the stairs. His heart pumped madly, and he held his breath, as she passed by the closed door he was hiding behind. Janice entered the master bedroom, and started to get undressed, she was obviously going to take a shower. She broke wind loudly several times, causing Dave to suppress a giggle.

"It's true then," he thought, "even the Queen farts."

Janice walked into the bathroom, and Dave heard her turn on the shower tap. He'd have to time it right, to catch her at her most vulnerable. Janice showered quickly, she was hungry, and looking forward to her chicken lunch. She towel-dried herself in the bathroom, and returned to the bedroom.

"Do it now," a voice shouted in Dave's head, and he quietly opened the door, and ran into the adjoining room. Janice was standing naked by her dressing table, and turned as she saw a reflection in the mirror. Her face and jaw dropped.

"Dave?" she uttered in fear and disbelief, "what do ..."

Dave lunged forward, and punched her on the side of her face, causing her to fall backwards, hitting her head on the edge of the bed. She landed motionless in an untidy heap. For one brief moment, Dave thought he'd killed her, but she coughed gently, and regaining his composure, he roughly threw her onto the bed. He quickly pulled out the items he'd hidden earlier, and rolling her onto her stomach, crudely tied her hands, and then her legs, until he was reasonably satisfied she was secure. She started to come round, and was muttering deliriously. Pulling back her head, he thrust open her mouth, and inserted the foam-rubber ball. Carefully peeling back some adhesive tape, he ripped off a four inch strip, and gagged her with it.

"Well, ex-wife, how's that then?" he whispered into her ear, "I bet you didn't think you'd be lucky enough to see me again, did you?"

Janice had almost regained full consciousness, her pupils wide and dark with fear. She tried to scream, but could make no sound.

"You see my love, I figured out it was you who set me up, and now, it's your turn to pay."

She shook her head violently, trying to explain, trying to reason with him.

"I've landed on my feet, no thanks to you, and I'll tell you what we're going to do," he paused, lit up a cigarette, and walked around the bed. "I've got a super house, with a special room just for you, and you're going to be a prisoner there for twenty six months, exactly the time I spent in jail, and if you're good, I'll let you go. How's that? Fair or what?"

Janice again tried to scream, but nearly choked on the foam ball. She was absolutely petrified, and wet the bed.

"Oh, having a little pee-pee are we? Well don't worry, Dave's gonna look after you."

He glanced out of the window, it was still raining. "You just stay there, like a good girl, and I'm going down for some lunch, but don't worry, I'll be back."

He bent over and roughly stroked her pubic mound. "Um, nice, but plenty of time for that later."

He left the room, and Janice pulled at the twine holding her wrists, but it just cut into her skin. She wriggled on the bed, and managed to get her legs hanging off the side. With a gentle rocking movement, she tried to propel herself onto the floor, but froze, as she saw Dave standing in the doorway, grinning at her pitiful attempt at freedom.

"Sorry my love, did you want to get up? Let me help you."

She lay still, pleading with her eyes, a trickle of blood ran from her nose. Dave lifted her onto his shoulder in one movement, the weight-training sessions paying off, and carried her in a fireman's lift, into the spare room. Dumping her into the wardrobe, he closed the door and locked it. She heard him go downstairs, and started to cry in sheer desperation.

Dave found the Chicken Supreme that Janice had bought from the supermarket, and decided to have it for lunch. He heard the 'phone ringing in the other room, and walked into the lounge. After five rings, the Ansa-phone sprang into action.

"Hello, this is Janice, I'm sorry I'm not here to take your call personally, but please leave your name and number after the long tone. Thank you." Beep ...

"Hello mum, it's Sarah, just making sure you got home alright, can you ring me when you get in. Bye."

"Fuck it," muttered Dave, "have to move a little bit quicker than I'd wanted, and if she gets worried, she's bound to ring her grandparents, and ask them to pop round."

The microwave oven bell rang, indicating his food was ready, and Dave duly ate the meal.

"I'll have to move her this afternoon," he surmised as he climbed the stairs, "too risky to wait until dark."

Opening the wardrobe, he roughly dragged Janice out, "Now my lovely, there's two ways we can do this. I'm going to roll you in the hearth-rug, and after bringing the car up to the door, load you into the boot. If you stay quiet, and don't struggle, then fine, but if you can't do it that way, I'll punch you hard in the face, and carry you down in a fucking coma. What's it to be, easy or hard?"

Janice nodded, as if accepting the easy option.

"The easy way. Good. I'll put you back in the wardrobe again, get the car, and we'll go home. OK?"

Janice tried to speak. If only she could talk to him, explain what happened, she was sure he would see reason. She desperately tried to communicate with a series of nods and winks, but to no avail.

He did what he'd said he'd do, and went for the car. It was raining very hard, and the sky was dark and overcast, which suited Dave perfectly. He reversed his Volvo up to the front door, so that the boot was practically under the porch. Before getting out, he checked that there was no one about. Leaping along the side of the car, he unlocked and opened the hatchback door, and went back into the house. He collected the 6 x 4 Chinese rug (made in Belgium) from its place in front of the lounge fireplace, took it to the bedroom, and unrolled it on the bed. It all went like clockwork. Rolling Janice effortlessly into the mat, he carried her downstairs, and threw the package into the open boot of his car. Slamming the door shut. Returning to the house, he collected up his belongings, had a last check around, and left for Woolston.

* * *

By six o'clock, Sarah was becoming very worried. Her mother was a creature of habit, and it was most unlike her not to be home. The infernal answering machine gave her no comfort at all. As Dave had predicted, she 'phoned her grandparents, and asked them to check. The grandfather drove around to Lambourne Gardens, and was somewhat surprised to discover his daughter's car in the drive, alongside the house. Using his spare key, he went into the house, fully expecting to find Janice asleep on the settee. When he didn't, he too became worried. He scratched his grey head of hair, and tried to figure out an acceptable solution. He noticed the dirty plate in the kitchen, and thought she might be with one of the neighbours. A quick call at the Mellor's house next door soon proved this theory unfounded. He drove home, and after consultation with Sarah, called the police.

* * *

D.I. Quinn had also been busy. Through Dave's old employers, Calvin Marine, he'd obtained the man's banking details, and discovered that, since he'd been released, the account had only been touched twice. A cash withdrawal on the day of his release, and one a few weeks later from the Woolston branch.

"Mike, this Woolston connection is too much of a coincidence. I want you to go over to Obelisk Road again, and if you can't get a reply, see if any of the neighbours have seen or heard anything lately."

"OK sir," said Mike, less than interested, he still believed that Baden-Smith was an accidental killing by a junkie, and was starting to get a bit fed up at Quinn's insistence on the possibility of a link with Price. It was almost six o'clock, and he'd already decided that he would call at the address in Woolston, on his way to work the next morning.

"Goodnight Guv," he shouted as he left the office, knowing it would wind Quinn up, and it did.

* * *

Dave drove slowly, and carefully, back to his house, the windscreen wipers, slashing through the pouring rain. Pulling into the carport at the back, he unloaded his ex-wife like a sack of potatoes, and carried the bundle straight down into the cellar. Throwing her onto the bed, he unrolled the rug.

"Well, darling, this is your new home, how do you like it?"

It took several seconds for Janice's eyes to get adjusted to the light. The single bare lightbulb, gently swinging on its cable, making an almost Hitchcockesque scene. She glanced around the damp room, three bare-brick walls covered in cobwebs and dust, with the wall to her left, racked from floor to ceiling. She craned her head, and noticed a pile of old clothing laying in a heap in the corner. Although Dave was given explicit instructions by the Doctor to destroy all of Malcolm's old clothing and bed linen, he'd kept a few pieces for the next part of his plan. He noticed her looking, and lighting up a cigarette, spoke:

"I've kept some of my old roommate's things," he gloated. "Oh I forgot you didn't know Malcolm did you? Well he died of AIDS recently, you see," he leant over her, his foul smoke-smelling breath making her feel nauseous, "I want you to have the threat of AIDS hanging over you, just like it was for me in prison."

She struggled to speak.

"You want to say something dear? OK, I'll take the gag off, but if you shout, it'll go back on for a week. Understand?"

Janice nodded frantically.

Dave ripped the adhesive tape off with one sharp pull, causing her eyes to water.

"Now let's take the ball out, there we are, what would you like to say?"

Janice coughed and cleared her throat, she was gasping for a drink, and had difficulty in making the words come out.

"Dave," she mumbled quietly, gulping for air, "why are you doing this? What have I done to you?"

"Ha! now that's a good one." He looked at her naked body, she'd put on a little weight in the past few years, and it suited her. "You set me up with the glove, didn't you?"

"No, I didn't," she coughed, and lowered her voice to a whisper, "can I have a drink please? I can hardly speak."

"Well, if you didn't put the glove there," he said, sitting on the edge of the bed, gazing at her very tempting vagina, "how did it get there? Walk?"

"I don't know, honestly, perhaps you dropped it, how would I know?"

"You see my love, you'd have got away with it, except you were the only person with another key to the car. I admit I can't work it all out, for all I know you had an accomplice, but the fact remains, the glove was dropped by you, or by someone helping you. I never wore the damn things, I'd even forgotten they were there."

"But Dave ..." she pleaded.

"Enough, I have no wish to discuss it further. Are you hungry?"

She wasn't, but quickly decided that, if he went for food, she might be able to escape. "Yes, I'm," she coughed, "famished, and thirsty, I haven't eaten since breakfast this morning."

"Of course you haven't, what a dreadful host I am."

He stood up and unzipped his flies. "How about a nice plump purple sausage, for starters?" He pulled his member out, it was half erect. She turned her head away, burying it into the rug, she desperately wanted to scream, but somehow couldn't. He crouched down, and started kissing her mound, trying to push his tongue into her most private part. The exotic smell was making his penis grow visibly. What could she do, she was trussed up like a Christmas turkey, but she certainly didn't want a gobble.

"Don't Dave, please ..."

He jumped up, his face red in rage. "Look, you fucking whore, either give me a blow job, or no food for a week."

She gulped, and whimpered. "No food."

"What?" he screamed, "OK, have it your way, I'll just wank into your face anyway."

He pulled his foreskin back and forth, but something about the pathetic sight of the woman on the bed, totally turned him off. The moment was lost.

He walked around the bed, trying to decide what to do next. "Please, can I have a drink at least, and I'm freezing, surely you're going to let me wear something, even in prison you had clothes to wear."

"Alright, alright, I'll bring you a drink a bit later, and sort out an old dressing-gown for you."

"I also need to go to the loo."

"Now, there I can help you. I've got quite a dab hand at looking after bedridden people, there's a nice china pot under the bed."

He bent down, and pulled out a rather pretty Victorian chamber pot, the outside covered in roses.

"I can't go like this."

"No, of course not, I'll untie your legs, but any trouble, and you're in the shit. Get it? You want to go, and if you make ..." He could see she was not amused, "Oh suit yourself." He untied her legs slightly, and lifted her onto the potty. She struggled to keep her balance, the potty was freezing on her bare skin.

"Can I at least have some ..."

"Privacy?" he interrupted. "No, this is what it's like in prison, you can't even crap, without some bastard watching you or wanting to shove his prick up your ass. Hey, that's an idea, never had the old anal treat, maybe ..."

He moved away from her, rubbing his chin, and grinning sickly. Tears were welling up in her eyes, as she looked at the man she'd once shared her life with. What had he become? Cropped, skinhead haircut, ridiculous moustache, and the nose, it was certainly different than she remembered. She was convinced he meant to kill her.

"Dave," she said softly, "can't we talk about this? I realise you had a torrid time in prison, but how can this help?" She stopped and sniffed, sending several tears rolling down her cheek, and into the corner of her mouth. "How will this solve anything?" she continued. "I've got money now, if you need some, I'll ..."

"Just have a piss or a shit, will you? I get turned on by the sound of the turd hitting china."

It was no good, she couldn't go. Dave was pacing around the room, thinking of the best way to tie her to the bed, so that she could sleep, but not escape.

She tried to stand, but fell face first onto the dirty floor. Dave moved over to her, and picked her up, fondling her breasts, as he threw her back onto the bed.

"Why?" she whispered, tears now flooding from her eyes.

"Look, I've had enough of this self-pity crap, it's your punishment, now shut the fuck up, or you'll get another slap. I'm going upstairs in a minute, so I'd better get you ready for bed," he snarled, lifting a large carrier-bag from one of the wine-racks.

"What about the drink you promised?"

"Later. I'm going to tie you with some nylon straps, they won't cut so much as twine, and you should be able to sleep."

"Sleep?" she questioned. "I'll die from the cold first."

Dave walked to the pile of clothes, and selected an old towelling dressing gown. "This'll do. I'll put it on you, after I've secured your legs, one thing at a time."

He opened his bag, and placed several items on the end of the bed. "Lie on your stomach please," he commanded, and she duly obeyed. He climbed onto the bed, and sat astride her, just below her bottom.

"You sure you don't fancy a cucumber up your chutney locker?" he suggested gleefully. "We might both enjoy it."

He ran his finger up the crack of her buttocks.

She shook at the thought of anal sex with him, surely even Dave would not rape her in that way. He smelt his finger, then scratched his head, this was proving more difficult than he'd imagined, how the hell did they do it in the TV programmes? "Untie her hands, and put on the dressing gown, and then ..." he shook his head, "too risky," he thought. Standing up, he surveyed the position again.

"Look, I'm going to untie the twine, let you put on the gown, and then secure you in the bed. As I've said before, any attempt at escape, and I'll punch you so hard, you'll be out for a fucking week. OK?"

She nodded, but realised, if she was ever going to escape, it was going to be now or never.

Rolling her onto her back, he slowly untied the rope from her legs, and then her hands. She wiggled her fingers, like a concert pianist, trying to bring back the circulation.

"Right, put this on."

She swung her legs over the edge of the bed, and tried to stand up. "Oww ..." she yelled, as her muscles objected to this sudden movement. "Hang on a sec, let me get the feeling back."

Dave moved back, as she did a strange series of exercises,

obviously trying to loosen up her leg and back muscles.

"That's enough, just put on the gown, and lay back on the bed," he snapped.

Picking up the dirty item, she pulled it across her shoulders, and Dave moved towards her. Without warning, she brought her knee up, full force into his groin. He screamed and fell to the floor and she leapt over the bed, and started up the stairs. Unfortunately, Dave was up in a flash, and managed to grab the flaying end of the dressing gown, before she had reached the top. With one tug, he pulled her back down the stairs, and crashing onto the cellar floor. They landed in an untidy heap together.

He screamed again, as he broke her fall. "You fucking cocksucker," he yelled, "you've broke me fucking leg."

She jumped up again, and tried once more to ascend the rickety old staircase. But it was all in vain, he managed to grab her around the neck, and stop her in her tracks.

"Right, you fucking cunt," he yelled, as he pulled her into the cellar, and threw her onto the bed, "now you've fucking 'ad it."

She scratched wildly at his face, trying to claw his eyes. His cheeks turned crimson, as she thrashed out time and time again. With some sort of super-human strength, he did not budge, but managed to throw one punch, connecting flush on her nose, and knocking her unconscious. Her arms flopped lifeless by her sides, as a gush of blood, ran from both nostrils across her face. He got up, wiping his wounds, carefully with the tips of his fingers. The weals and scratches, already so painful he could hardly touch them. One particularly deep wound, just under his eye, was bleeding quite badly, and several of the others were weeping. He punched the air, in anger, and cursed loudly, unsure as to what his next move would be. "Kill the bitch," said a little voice, but he ignored it. Collecting all his articles of restraint, he set about securing Janice to the bed. He pulled the strops that he'd placed around her arms very tight, and tied each one to the corners of the steel, ornate head-board. He used a third one to secure her legs, and wrapped it under the bed, pulling at the ratchet-lock, until he was satisfied she could not escape. His face was stinging so badly, it made concentration very difficult.

"OK, bitch, you wanted it this way, so be it."

He took a rather soiled pair of mini-briefs, from the pile of clothes on the floor, and rolling them into a smallish ball, inserted it into her mouth. She gagged slightly, obviously starting to regain consciousness. He ripped off a length of adhesive tape, which he stuck across her lips. Her nose was bleeding very badly, and the tape would not stick properly.

"Damn and double fuck," he yelled, ripping the first piece of tape away, and crudely wiping her mouth with an old rag he'd found. Lifting her head, he wound the tape right around her entire face and head, finally stopping after three turns. He threw the remainder of the tape on the floor, and left the cellar, switching off the light at the top of the stairs. In the bathroom, he surveyed what was left of his face. He was ugly enough before, but now looked like an extra from the film 'The Living Dead'. He carefully, and very gently bathed the wounds with some antiseptic washing lotion.

"Oh, bloody hell," he muttered as he cleaned each scratch mark. He would be scarred for life, of that there was no doubt. He returned to the kitchen, poured a ridiculously large gin and tonic, and drank it down in one. He found his cigarettes, and lit one up.

"Let her stew until tomorrow," he mumbled to himself, hoping that the pain would subside, at least enough to let him get to sleep. He turned on the television and set about finishing off the whole bottle of gin. At twenty past ten, he checked that the doors were all locked, and taking the last dregs of his drink, went to bed.

Just after twelve, he was awakened by a noise outside his bedroom door. Someone, or something was moving about. He lay still, his heart pounding, as the door slowly opened. In the half light, he could see it was Janice. Jumping from the bed, he moved menacingly towards her.

"Dave, Dave, it's alright, let's not fight any more, I could of escaped, but didn't."

Dave stopped, he didn't trust her, why was she being nice, perhaps she had a knife or something.

"Stay there. What's the catch?"

"No catch, look, it's just me."

She held her arms up, and turned around. It was true, she was concealing nothing. "You didn't tie those ropes very well, and I easily got out of them."

Dave was stunned, he didn't know whether to grab her, and take her back to the cellar, punch her again, or hear her out. "Um ..." he struggled to find something to say.

"Look," she moved into the room, and Dave got a better look at her naked body, "when you said about taking me from behind, I got so excited, my whole body almost had an orgasm, I'd never thought about it before, but it sounds risky and daring, you know, sort of forbidden, and illegal."

"What? You want me to give you it up the ass?"

"Yes, but you'll need to be gentle, it's my first time." She smiled, and moved closer, until they were standing face to face.

"Where's the trick? What have you got up your sleeve?"

"Nothing, come on, I'm getting horny just thinking about it."

Dave had read that some women did like to have anal sex, but this was totally out of character for Janice. He wasn't sure, but was also getting aroused at the thought of it.

"OK, kneel on the bed, with your ass out," he commanded, and she duly obeyed. He wasn't sure exactly what to do, but pulled her cheeks apart, and standing on tiptoe, pushed his erect member down the dark passage. It seemed surprisingly easy, and he was inside her immediately. She squealed a little, and then started to make cooing noises. Dave was ecstatic, grabbing her around the waist, he pumped backwards and forwards.

"When you've finished, it'll be my turn," said a very deep and gruff voice, causing Dave to stop mid-stroke. He could feel a hairy chest, and jumped back.

"What the fu..." he yelled, as he looked again, and saw Tony Anderson, kneeling on the bed, his ugly face grinning in the dimly lit room.

"What's the matter, want your turn now?"

Dave went to scream, but suddenly woke up, finding himself face down on his bed, holding his pillow in a precarious position. He shook violently as he came out of his slumber.

"What a fucking dream," he sighed, as reality slowly returned. He crept downstairs, to check on Janice, but there was no movement, or noise, so he figured it was all OK.

"God, if I ever see that bastard Anderson again, I swear I'll kill him," he said quietly to himself, and returning to his bedroom, attempted to go back to sleep. He tried to clear his mind of the nightmare he'd had, and have one of his more traditional dreams.

"Come on Olive Orbs, Dave's got your necklace waiting."

* * *

Sgt Mike Crouch had driven across Southampton at eight-thirty, and arrived at the house in Obelisk Road, just before nine o'clock. Getting out of his car, he walked to the front door, and rang the bell.

Dave stirred slightly, and grunted.

Crouch rang the bell again, and also banged on the door, with the inside of his fist.

Dave stayed in bed, his left eye so swollen, he could hardly see out of it. "Whoever it is can fuck off," he moaned, carefully examining his wounds with the tips of his fingers.

Crouch eventually gave up, and walked around to the house next door. Ringing the bell, the door opened immediately, on a chain-lock and a lady in her sixties peered through the gap.

"Yes?" she croaked.

"Good morning, Madam. I'm Sgt Crouch from the Southampton constabulary and wonder if I could ask you a few questions please?" he said, in a booming police voice, thrusting his warrant card between the door.

"What about?" she asked, squinting at the young officer.

"About your neighbour, Mr Evitts, can I come in?"

"What?"

"Oh God, not deaf as well."

"I said," he shouted, "can I come in, it's about your neighbour, Mr Evitts."

"Who?"

"Your next door neighbour, Mr Evitts," he shouted, causing two passing schoolgirls to snigger.

"He's dead."

"Who is?"

"Young Malcolm, he died last month, the Doctor told me."

"Doctor, what Doctor?"

"I have the same Doctor, you see, he told me."

"Look, Madam, can I come in, please!"

The old lady struggled for several minutes, before finally opening the door.

Crouch entered, and after a cup of tea, eventually got the full story. He now wondered if Quinn's theory was right. He drove to the police station, stopping only for his obligatory Macdonalds breakfast.

Quinn had been trying, without much success, to find out about Evitts' finances, with no living relatives, it was proving very difficult.

Crouch arrived, with tomato ketchup still wet in the corners of his mouth. "Sir, I think you may be onto something," he said chirpily.

"Really? What did you find out?"

"Well," he sat on the edge of Quinn's desk, "the old gal who lives next door says her Doctor told her that Evitts died, about a month ago."

"That should be easy to corroborate, all deaths are registered, and get off my desk."

Crouch looked a little upset, but stood up.

"Who's the Doctor then?"

"A Doctor Dicks."

"What?" Quinn laughed, "Doctor Dicks treats gay guys for AIDS, how strangely appropriate."

Crouch was not amused.

"I'll bet his nickname is Dirty."

Crouch frowned again.

"So what is Dirty Dick's telephone number?"

"Very droll," mumbled Crouch, as he handed over his note pad, "the top number, beginning double four."

Quinn made a call and arranged a meeting for 11.30 at the end of the Doctor's morning surgery.

The surgery was in Portsmouth Road, Woolston which being the main road across the Itchen Bridge, made the practice an easy one to find. It was a beautiful imposing Georgian building, set a few hundred yards from the road, behind a row of trees. The police car turned into the drive, and the two officers walked straight into the building, meeting the Doctor, in the large entrance hall.

Dicks was an archetypal G.P., red bulbous face, grey receding hairline, and an adequate beer-gut, from too much ale. For once, Quinn liked the man instantly, his obvious jovial disposition and hearty attitude to life seemed to fit his position and station perfectly.

"Good morning gentlemen, I take it you're the police?"

"Yes, and thank you for seeing us at such short notice," Quinn said politely.

"No problem. I believe it's about young Malcolm?"

"Yes, what can you tell us about him?"

"Come into my office." They followed him into his consulting room. "Please, sit down."

"Thanks."

"Well, he was a tragic case. Mother and father died, leaving him lots of money, which he could never really handle, then he contracted the dreaded AIDS virus, did some time in prison, and died last month. Apparently a practising homosexual, but a pleasant lad for all that."

"And when exactly did he die?"

"Um, let me see," the Doctor consulted some notes on his desk. "Here we are, September the nineteenth, got a call from his cousin, but when I arrived, the poor chap was already dead."

"His cousin?"

"Yes, that's what the character said, nasty looking individual. God knows where he came from, turned up like a bad penny. He was living at the house with Malcolm for a few weeks prior to his death."

"Are you sure he was his cousin. Did Malcolm confirm that?"

"No."

"And did you get his name?"

"He said he was Dave Evitts."

Quinn smiled, and gave Crouch a very satisfied and nonchalant look. "Really, and what did this Dave Evitts look like?"

"Nasty piece of work, short cropped skin-head haircut, darkish hair, medium build, possibly done some weight-training as his upper torso was fairly well developed, and a ridiculous droopy moustache. Oh and a broken nose."

"Well, I think that's our man, and where did he go after the death? D'you know?"

"Not a clue. Still at the house for all I know."

"Thanks Doc, you've been a great help. We may need to see you again, but we'll let you know."

"No problem."

The two officers left, and although Quinn was tempted to drive the short distance from the surgery to the house in Obelisk Road, he told Mike to head back to the station.

"Right Mike, this has got to be done by the book. I want no slip-ups, get a search warrant organised, and remember, gloves to be worn at all times. It could be that our friend Anderson was right and old Pricey has turned shirt-lifter. In which case he might have AIDS too."

As they arrived at the station, the desk Sergeant called out to Quinn. "Sir, we've had a report of a missing person which Patterson is handling, but when I booked it in, I recognised the name and address, and thought you might be interested."

Quinn sighed, he was really too busy for all of this. "Really? Why?"

"It's Janice Price, the one who was married to ..."

"Oh God, Mike, get that bloody warrant, and get it now. I think the bastard's kidnapped his wife."

* * *

Dave eventually crawled out of bed, at eleven o'clock, and dragged himself into the bathroom. He was genuinely surprised, and angry, when he saw his face. No wonder it was killing him. He had three huge grazes across his forehead, and two very deep scratches down the left hand side of his face, one which had missed his eyes by a fraction. Those which weren't bleeding, were weeping, and the skin around his eye was grotesquely swollen. He gulped loudly.

"Fucking bitch, she'll pay for this."

He stormed down into the cellar, throwing the light switch on his way down. Janice was still securely tied, spread-eagle fashion, with her face covered in dried blood. She blinked at the brightness of the light, as he walked to the foot of the bed.

"Look what you've done, you slag."

She gazed up at him in anger, not fear, she loathed him as much as he hated her. He ripped the tape from her face, with a sadistic pleasure, and pulled the pair of tiny briefs from between her teeth. She gagged for air.

"Know what these are?" he gloated, "know what you've had in your fucking mouth all night?"

She turned her head away.

"I'll tell ya, Malcolm's filthy underpants, like the taste, did you? AIDS on a plate."

She refused to let him see she'd been rattled, her mouth was so dry it was difficult to speak. "You're mad," she said quietly, "and need help."

"That's what you think is it? Well, until I get some sort of respect from you, you'll get no food, no drink, and I won't change the bed. You can lie in your own shit, until it chokes you. How's that for mad?"

Her nose was throbbing, but she'd rather die than show him, anything other than her venom. "Kill me, I don't care. There's nothing you can do that would make me hate you more than I do at this moment."

"Kill you, oh no, that's too good. I've told you, you have to serve your sentence, just like I did. But, don't worry, I'm sure to be able to think of a few more 'choice' things to do to you yet.'

This wasn't what he wanted, or expected. He wanted her to beg for forgiveness, and plead for help. "Well, suit yourself, I'm off out, but I'm sure by tonight, we'll hear a different tune."

She raised her lower body, and urinated, in an act of total defiance.

"Good, you can lay in that all day." He re-rolled the briefs, and after a slight struggle, got them back into her mouth, and re-taped her lips.

"Goodbye darling, see you tonight."

He stamped up the stairs, and slammed the cellar door so hard that some of the plaster around the frame fell to the floor. He kicked the little pieces of plaster into a corner.

"You're a fucking mother's minge piece," he yelled, before walking into the kitchen, and flopping into a chair. Although he didn't really want to go out in the day, his face was so excruciatingly sore, he'd have to get to a pharmacy, and obtain some medication for the pain. He hadn't washed, shaved, or even changed, and was still dressed in the clothes he'd worn the previous day. Starting the car, he drove to the main shopping area of Woolston. He remembered seeing a chemist shop opposite Woolworths, and managed to park outside it.

Almost over his head, three police vehicles hurtled across the Itchen Bridge. Quinn and Crouch in the first, with back up from another car and van. Seven officers were involved. Screeching to a halt outside the house, Quinn directed four officers around the back and led the others across the front garden, and up to the front door. Banging several times, Quinn bent down, and shouted through the letterbox.

"Police!"

Janice jumped, she could hear noises, but was unsure as to their origin. She lay in fear, thinking it could be Dave returning.

Quinn stepped back. "Right, the door," he ordered, and Crouch put his full weight behind a shoulder barge, and the door flew open. The officers at the back had also gained entry, and the policemen faced each other down the passageway.

"No one here, Sir," shouted one.

"Right, you two search the downstairs, Mike, Jeff, follow me upstairs."

A routine, but thorough search was instigated, and as Quinn came out of the last bedroom, he heard a call from downstairs.

"Sir, we've found her."

He charged down the stairs, almost tripping on the last step, and came face to face with one of the policemen, standing in the cellar doorway, pointing down into the gloom. Quinn leapt down the steps, and stopped as he reached the bottom, visibly shaken.

"Oh God, Mike, Mike!" he yelled, "Get the blanket from the van." He walked over to the wretched woman who lay before him, and gently removed the tape from her mouth.

"Don't worry love, you're safe now."

Janice spat up the cloth, and burst into tears. At last she could release her pent-up emotions.

Quinn undid the straps that held her, and cradled her face into his chest. "Where's the bastard gone?" he said calmly.

She coughed, and tried to speak, but could make no sound.

"Someone get a glass of water, and where's that bloody blanket?" he shouted.

Mike arrived with a blanket, and Quinn placed it around the woman. Jeff brought some water, and she drank it in one gulp. "It's alright, take your time, Jeff, another glass please, where is he? D'you know?"

She coughed again, her throat was so dry. "He tied (cough) me up, and put dirty clothes in my mouth, he said ..." she stopped, and wiped her eyes, "he said they were AIDS infected, and I'd get the ...oh God help me."

"OK, OK, take it easy. Mike have you called an ambulance?"

"Yes sir, it's on it's way."

"Try and get on your feet, let's get you out of here, some fresher air will help."

She cleared her throat, wanting to spit, but couldn't.

Quinn and Crouch got her to the kitchen, and she drank two more glasses of water.

"I scratched his face, and it looked bad, so I think he's gone out for some ointment. Can I have a bath please?"

"It's alright, love, honestly, we'll get you straight to hospital; they'll sort you out. Don't worry. Um, how long ago did he leave, do you know?"

"No more than fifteen minutes."

Quinn left her for a moment, and she could hear him shouting. "Mike, get straight down to Woolston, he shouldn't be too hard to track down, even for you."

"Yes Sir," said Crouch sulkily. It wasn't his fault they'd just missed him.

"And find out where that bloody ambulance is. Jesus Christ, it would be quicker to walk."

Quinn re-entered the house. "What the hell are you lot hanging around for, get searching, I want this place turned upside down. Understand?"

Dave had gone into the pharmacy, and startled the young female assistant.

"What have you got for scratches?" he snapped.

"You'd better see the pharmacist," she replied, trying desperately not to stare.

A scruffy bearded man, in his early twenties, came to the counter. He too was shocked at the severity of the injuries.

"I had a bit of trouble last night, what can you give me?"

The man just stared.

"You deaf? What cream can I buy? It's killing me."

"I'm sure it is, they are some of the worst scratches I've ever seen, how did you get them?"

"What difference does that make?"

"Well, I think you need a tetanus injection, and really ought to go to casualty to have them properly dressed."

"Look bollock-chops, I ain't got time for that, just give me something to take out the sting."

"There's no need to be rude, I'm only trying to help."

"Yeah, yeah, I'll go to my own Doctor later, can't you just let me have something quick now?"

The pharmacist was far from happy, but didn't want any trouble. He took a large tube of antiseptic cream from a shelf behind, and handed it to Dave. "Three pounds, ninety please."

"Oh, fuck it, I've come out without any bloody money," Dave thought, as he went through his pockets. As luck would have it, a five pound note was screwed up in the corner of his back pocket. He sighed, and handed the crumpled money to the man. Dave left, and the pharmacist pondered on whether or not to call the police. The marks were obviously inflicted by a human, and it ought to be reported. As he turned to make the call, Mike Crouch walked in.

"Good morning. I'm Sgt Crouch of the Southampton constabulary, I wonder if you've seen a man with ..."

"Scratches on his face?" said the chemist, stopping Mike in mid-flow. "Two minutes ago, you just missed him."

"Did you see which way he went, when he left?"

"Sorry, no, I was about to call the police, and in you came. Amazing."

Crouch ran from the shop, and stood on the pavement. "Crouch to D.I. Quinn, please come in," he shouted down his walkie-talkie.

Quinn was helping the para-medics get Janice into the ambulance, when a colleague called him into the house. "Sir, it's Mike for you," he shouted, pointing at the black transceiver in his hand.

"Now, take it easy, I'll be into the hospital to see you later, and don't worry, everything will be alright," Quinn assured the sad and sobbing woman on the stretcher, and ran down the path. "Yeah?" he puffed, "Quinn here."

"Our suspect has just left Boots and I think he's probably headed back to you. Over."

"Oh shit, if he sees the ambulance and police van, he's bound to leg it."

It was too late. Dave was driving along St Anne's Road, which joins Obelisk Road at the top end, when he saw the melee. Vehicles parked on the pavement, the ambulance with its blue lights flashing, and people leaning over garden fences, pointing at the house. He drove straight past, and turned down Archery Grove, which conveniently brought him back onto Portsmouth Road. He carried on heading out of Southampton, driving towards Netley, without any real idea of where he was going. It was controlled panic.

"Oh fucking hell," he shouted, banging the steering wheel,

"my money's in there, the cheque book, building society book, all my clothes, in fact, everything I fucking own. I should have realised that cunt Quinn would be back. The bastard."

He drove past Netley, and turned to join the M27 motorway at Junction 8. As he reached the intersection, he saw a sign, Hedge End – two miles. Of course, he could go to Janice's house, he had a key, she must have some clothes, and probably even some money. Speed was of the essence.

Quinn was standing outside the house when Mike pulled up.

"OK, was he driving, walking, or what?" he snapped.

"Don't know, the chemist didn't see him, and nor did I," said Crouch, still wondering why he was getting the blame, for Price's apparent escape.

"Wait a minute, wasn't there an old car out the back?"

"Yes Sir, a Volvo."

"OK, it's not there now, so we have to assume he's driving that. Get inside, and find the log-book, if we have the registration number, we might get lucky."

Dave arrived at Lambourne Gardens, and parked right outside, in the driveway. It didn't matter if anyone saw him now. Running down the side path, he let himself into the house. "Right, calm down and think. Clothes first." He went to the bedroom, and rummaged through the wardrobes. He was in luck, he found a couple of men's shirts, a pair of jeans and several pairs of underpants and socks, presumably belonging to Sarah's new husband. He threw them all into an old hold-all he'd found, together with a single continental quilt, from the bed in the spare room, and went down to the lounge. He emptied the pot on the mantle-piece of its loose change, and found a brand new cheque book in the unit drawer.

He ran into the kitchen, and found her handbag on the work-top, exactly where she'd left it the previous day. Finding her purse, he emptied its contents out, and carefully pulled out three ten pound notes, and placed them in his back pocket, together with a few credit cards, and a little change. "Right, that will have to do," he said, slightly disappointed at the lack of funds he had taken. He left the house, and driving back to the M27, headed for Portsmouth.

Mrs Mellor, the next door neighbour, full time nosey parker, and professional gossip monger, had watched Dave leave from behind her curtains. She'd seen Janice's father, and knew about the disappearance, and telephoned the old man, who immediately notified the police.

Quinn and the gang were still at the house in Obelisk Road, and had found the car's log-book.

"Right Mike, get this number to Central, and let's see if we can't catch the little shit, before he gets too far."

Crouch gave the information to H.Q. and was told of the sighting.

"Sir, it seems our friend has gone round to his old house in Hedge End, and left with a case."

"Shit. He's probably got hold of some clothes, I'll finish up here, you and Jeff go to the hospital, and see if Mrs Price can tell you what he's likely to have taken. And go easy with her, she's one frightened lady."

"Right."

"Oh, and by the way, we've found an old plastic box, with a syringe in it. So this could well be a murder case now."

* * *

Dave was petrified. He had little money, and knew with the marks on his face, he'd be easily recognisable. Quinn would get a full description in the press, and TV news bulletins, so it was imperative for him to lie low. He'd decided he'd have to live in the car for a while, and park up somewhere quiet. He'd need some provisions, and pulled off the motorway just before the Portsmouth junction, and drove into a Tesco supermarket, conveniently situated a few hundred yards from the motorway. As he parked, and left the car, his mind was working overtime.

Why hadn't he taken some cutlery, just a knife and fork, together with a plate, would have sufficed. And food, how did he forget to take food, and toilet rolls, the list was endless. Trudging around the supermarket, he decided on his priorities, booze, fags, and some food he could eat with his fingers. He counted his money, thirty eight pounds, twelve pence, was the sum total of his wealth. How ironic it seemed, only yesterday, he had thousands to play with, and today, pennies.

He put two bottles of the supermarket's own label gin, a four litre pack of tonic waters, a large piece of Irish cheddar cheese and two French baguettes into his trolley, and went to the check-out.

The young teenage girl stared anxiously at the scarred face. "Ooo, that looks painful," she said caringly.

"Yeah, sure," snapped Dave, he had no need to be reminded of the obvious.

The girl shrugged her shoulders, and rang up the few items. "Twenty four pounds, thirty two pence, please," she said, then added, in a local accent, "How d' it happen then?"

"Got into a fight with a bloody nosey check-out girl."

She said no more, handed him his change, and watched him walk to the tobacconist's kiosk.

He counted the remainder of his money, and glanced at the cigarettes on display. He had just enough for five packets of Royals, which were on special offer. He returned to his car. "Right, if I'm careful, the food should last two days, but then what? Perhaps I can go back to Janice's, maybe get some more food from there." It wasn't much of a plan, but the best he could think of.

He drove from the car park, out towards Corhampton, through the Forest of Beer, passing West Meon, and into the lovely Hampshire hamlet of Prior's Dean. Turning off the main road, he drove a short distance, and pulled into a little lay-by, very secluded, and well off the beaten track. He switched off the engine, and glanced into the thick forest glen, that was to be his home for the next few days at least. It had been one of the warmest Octobers on record, so at least he'd have no problem with the cold. He reached into the back of the car, and took the antiseptic cream from the little Boots' carrier bag, and carefully applied it to his face.

"Fuck you, Janice, it's not over yet, not by a long chalk."

* * *

As Dave had rightly supposed, Quinn had distributed a full description, together with a very poor photo-fit picture to all the usual media. The young girl from the supermarket had telephoned and given a full account of her encounter with the fugitive. It was now two days since he'd been seen and Quinn was getting noticeably agitated.

"OK, so where's the bastard gone?"

"Well," said Mike, trying in some way to appease his governor, "we know he bought a few items from Tesco's, which presumably means he's got no money, other than the money he took from his ex's purse. He didn't have time to plan anything, so he must be 'holed up' somewhere."

"Oh, brilliant Mike, thank God you're on our side. He's holed up in Hampshire somewhere. Well, thank you Mr Sherlock Bloody Holmes, tell me something I don't know."

"If he had a full tank of petrol, he could have driven anywhere, remember, we don't know if he had a credit card."

"True, but my guess is, he's got no money, little petrol, and no means of getting any." Quinn's rich Mancunian accent had returned, a sure sign of his anger. "So he's still in the area. Yeah?"

"Have we still got someone watching the house in Hedge End?"

"Yes Mike, and the one in Woolston, I don't think he'll be stupid enough to return, but you never know."

"What did we get from the Portsmouth police?"

"What do you think? Sod all."

Mike's stomach was rumbling, it was nearly two hours since he'd eaten.

"Oh, go and have some lunch, I'll see you later." Quinn banged his fist on the desk. "I want this bastard so bad, it hurts."

* * *

Although it was extremely mild for the time of year, it had been raining for two days. Dave had finished the bread and cheese the previous day, and with precious else to do, had almost finished the gin as well. It was only nine thirty in the evening, but with no other option open to him, Dave climbed into the back of his car, and fell into a very troubled sleep. Tomorrow was going to be 'D' day, he knew that, but how was he going to get some money? He seemed to have several avenues open. He could sell the car, possibly, or he could commit a robbery. There were a few small shops in West Meon, which might be suitable. Although his face had considerably healed, the deep scars and scratches, around his eyes, would make identity very easy. But, should he care? He was already wanted for kidnapping, and probably murder, another small misdemeanour, would surely make no difference.

George Duegard, a farmer, born and bred in Prior's Dean, lived a fairly frugal life. His farm had no television, only a radio, and as he had no interest in current affairs, he did not read the newspapers. Every morning, just before five, he drove his tractor to his only arable field, passing the Volvo in the lay-by. He kept himself very much to himself, but on the third morning, stopped and looked inside the vehicle. He'd heard of the new-age travellers, who park and live on farmers' land, and adjudged Dave to be one.

"What's he doin' here?" he asked himself, as he climbed back onto his tractor, "got no right to be here, bloody bums, the lot of 'em."

He finished his work, at about ten, and decided to stop at the local pub for 'something to keep out the cold'. Inside the bar, the local bobby, P.C. Skinner, was also having a medicinal drink.

"Here," he said in best Hampshire Hog tongue, "what you gonna do about that skinhead parked outside my field? Wants no trouble mind."

"What skinhead's that, George?" laughed the young policeman.

"Parked just by the turnin' into my field, been there three nights though, right ugly-looking bugger."

"I'll look into it, what type of car is it?"

"Buggered if I knows, old Volvo, I thinks."

P.C. Skinner vaguely remembered a fax from HQ about a Volvo, and suddenly started to act interested.

"Three days you say, and where is it parked?"

"In the lay-by, right by Nightingale Wood, opposite side to my field. Don't want no trouble though."

"No, OK, you've seen someone inside have you?"

"Yeah, told you, ugly bugger, new age whatsit, if I's not mistaken."

Skinner drank his beer, and left. Driving past the parked car, he made a note of the registration without stopping, and telephoned his superiors in Portsmouth as soon as he arrived at his house, which doubled as a little rural police station.

"Yes Skinner, message understood, do not, repeat do not, approach the vehicle, this man is dangerous."

"Where?" shouted Quinn, "hang on, hang on," he put his hand over the 'phone mouthpiece, "get me a map of the Petersfield area, it's the Pompey police, they think they've found Price." An Ordnance Survey map of the South Downs, was placed on the desk. "OK, give it to me again. Yeah, up the A32 from Wickham to West Meon, through West Meon, past Privett, and the A272, then the first left towards West Tisted. Yeah got it. It looks like a small lane, can you seal both ends until we get there? You can, great, we're leaving now, and will patch into you on the way. OK, thanks, see you."

"Right lads, we've located him, he's been living in his car, in a lay-by near Privett, wherever that is. They will seal the road, and let us have the blag, but remember, if he sees us coming, and runs across into the woods, it'll be the devil's own job to flush him out. No sirens. OK? I want Mike and Jeff with me, and we'll enter from the Meon end, David, Colin and Stuart, you come in from the Alresford side, but only as back up. Mike, organise two prison vans to follow, and Colin get onto the helicopter crew, we may need them if he does a runner."

Quinn studied the map, and ran his finger up and down the tiny track. "Right you bastard, time to pay up."

The squad assembled, dressed in protective gear, and were all issued gloves.

"Right, let's go, and remember, no cock-ups."

The two police cars left the station, one travelling northwards towards Winchester, while Quinn's car drove across the Itchen Bridge, and south towards Portsmouth.

Dave woke up, and was surprised to see it was well gone ten o'clock. Sitting around all day made him strangely tired. He'd found a tree with a low branch, and did pull-ups each day, just to keep in some sort of shape, but that was all, by way of exercise, he'd managed to do. He got out of the car, and stretched. God he was hungry, he'd have to find something to eat, and decided to make that his first priority. He walked a few yards into the undergrowth, and urinated against an old English oak. The toilet arrangements left a lot to be desired, and he'd been forced to use moss as toilet paper. He smelt his hands, and frowned.

"Fucking hell, think I need a bloody good wash as well as food," he mumbled to himself, as he returned to the car. He sat in the driver's seat, turned on the radio, and lit up a cigarette. It was his last pack.

* * *

Janice had been let out of hospital, and was back at her house, with Sarah. She seemed to be coping well, but still had to wait for the results of tests she'd had, to determine whether she had contracted any diseases or not. Sarah kept reassuring her mother, but deep down they were both very worried.

"Why don't we go for a holiday, just you and me, what d'you think mum?" asked Sarah.

"Maybe, but not just yet. Give me a little time, eh?"

* * *

Quinn was on the radio. "Bravo-alpha one to all following vehicles, remember this guy may be infected with AIDS, please exercise extreme caution at all times, don't let him bite you, scratch you, or even spit at you. If he tries, either lay him out, or leg it. Understood? I want no heroes, OK?" He turned to his two colleagues. "Look, we can't be sure if Price was sleeping with Evitts, so you let me challenge him first, you two are just back up. Got it?"

They both nodded, and carried on in silence. Arriving at the junction of the A32, having driven along the beautiful Meon Valley, they stopped, and Quinn got out and spoke to the policemen standing in the middle of the road by their car. Crouch could hear them talking, but could not quite make out what was being said. Quinn returned to the car.

"OK, find out if the others are in place."

Mike picked up the radio, and asked the question.

"Not quite, Sir, they're about five minutes away."

"Tell them to get a bloody move on, as soon as they are at the other end of the road, they are to stay there, while we go in. Has everyone got that? Good."

Mike relayed the orders, and was given an affirmative reply. Quinn tapped his fingers angrily on the roof of the car. "Come on, come on." After four minutes, the radio informed them, that all was in place.

"Right, let's get the bastard."

The police car sped up the tiny lane, and screeched to a halt, just yards behind the parked Volvo.

Dave was sitting listening to 'Annie's Song' by John Denver, and glanced around as he heard the noise behind him.

"Oh fucking hell," he shouted, as he jumped from the car, and ran into the woodland. Quinn was like a man possessed, and did a magnificent rugby tackle, sending Dave crunching to the ground, into a pile of wet fallen leaves.

"Right you bastard, you're well and truly nicked. Now, come on Mr Macho-man, throw a punch, give me an excuse to break your fucking neck."

Dave lay still, grinning to himself, his yellow teeth protruding over his bottom lip.

"David Price, I'm arresting you for the murder of Lawrence Baden-Smith, and the kidnapping and assault of your ex-wife Janice Price. Anything you say will be taken down, and may be used in evidence against you."

Mike and Jeff arrived and helped pull Price to his feet.

"Smell your wife," Dave said, holding up his filthy middle

finger, and pushing it under Quinn's nose.

"You disgusting pervert," Quinn yelled, but was held back by Crouch.

"Not here Sir," he said quietly, "plenty of time for that, back at the nick."

Quinn was shaking with rage, as the other police vehicles arrived. "Get him out of my sight."

Dave was handcuffed, and led to one of the vans. He stopped, and, turning to the detective, said venomously: "I'll tell you this Quinn, don't matter how long they lock me away for, no matter what they do to me, when I get out, and you know I will, you and your fucking family are ..."

He was dragged into the police van, the end of his sentence dying in the damp country air.

As the van pulled away, Price was smiling, and trying to peer out of the barred back window, still holding up his middle finger.

Quinn watched in silence as the vehicle drove away.

"Don't worry Sir," Mike reassured his governor, "we won't see him again, not for at least thirty years. It was just talk, nothing more."

Quinn said nothing, until the van had disappeared around a bend in the road. Pensively, he walked back to the police car, "I hope you're right Mike," he said quietly, "I bloody well hope you're right."

Epilogue

Was justice done? who can tell?
who has the right to say?
is life itself a sentence, pray?
or just our time in hell?

Fortunately, all the tests carried out on Janice were found to be negative, and after three years in Hedge End, she finally moved to Chichester, to be closer to her daughter and two grand-children. She never re-married, and never really got over the treatment she endured during her traumatic internment.

Calvin Marine was taken over by a large chandlery group and John Calvin received a substantial pay-off. He used the money to set up a yacht chartering company in the Greek Isles, and moved with his family to Kos, making it the headquarters for his thriving leisure business. Joanne continued working for him, running the booking agency side, in the UK.

Tony Quinn did not achieve further promotions, and took early retirement, somewhat disillusioned with the Police Force, and its 'gently-gently' approach, and modern policing tactics. He remained in the Southampton area with his wife, where they both joined a local amateur operatic group, and were enthusiastically involved in all productions. He never visited his home town of Manchester again.

Michael Crouch, however, rapidly rose through the ranks, and became the youngest ever Chief Constable of Hampshire. He was always indebted to Quinn, and they remained friends for many years. He genuinely believed the force had lost an excellent policeman, through its inability to accept anyone who was not always in the main stream of Police thinking. When any problems arose, he would always solicit, and act on, the advice given by his older colleague.

David Malcolm Price was sentenced to life, but only served nine years, dying from an AIDS related illness in a top security prison hospital. Ironically, he did not contract the virus from Evitts, but from his only homosexual encounter with Anderson, who was later diagnosed as a carrier.

When he was cremated at Southampton Crematorium, ex Detective Inspector Quinn was the only person present. He smiled as the cheap state-supplied coffin moved slowly into the furnace. The only possible threat to his future happiness had, at last, been laid to rest.

THE END